MW00582627

FLAT EARTH

BY
BRENT GOLEMBIEWSKI

Edited by: JLMG
Cover Design: Crystal Fiss
Ailerons Font Design: Adilson Gonzales
ISBN: 978-1-7348875-1-8 (eBook)
ISBN: 978-1-7348875-0-1 (Paperback)

1st Edition

For more information, e-mail: babajagapublishing@gmail.com

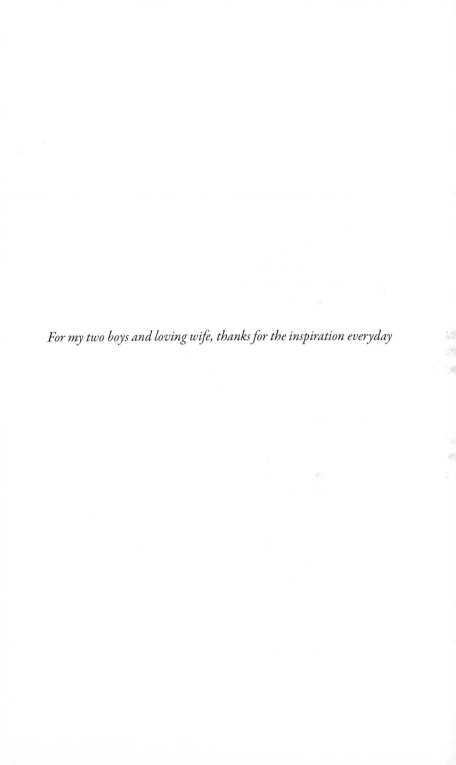

For my two boys and loving wife, thanks for the inspiration everyday

"A long time ago, people believed that the world is flat and the moon is made of green cheese. Some still do, to this day. The man on the moon is looking down and laughing."

—Vera Nazarian.

CHAPTER ONE

In a clear blue sky, the moon watched over a baseball game in small town America. James gripped the bat between his hands, twisting and squeezing his fingers. His weight shifted from one foot to the other; his hips wiggled back and forth. The pitcher eyed the signs behind home plate and shook off the first two before nodding at the third, then slid his fingers along the seams of the ball in his leather mitt. Beads of sweat rolled down James' face from his soaked baseball cap as he readied himself for the pitch. He rocked back and forth at a slow, even pace, jaw clenched, waiting for the ball to be delivered.

The pitcher began his wind up, his left foot kicking up into the air as his body twisted to the right. James squinted, searching for the first sign of the ball. The pitcher's hand came down sharply over the top, releasing the ball with an intense spin. James' eyes picked it up immediately and watched it rocket toward him. Down the center the ball came, it was his last chance. His eyes fixated on the tiny ball as it rapidly approached, he swung.

Solid contact. His eyes never left the ball, continuing to follow it. The pitcher, now on the left side of the mound, ducked as it whizzed by his head. James continued his follow-through, then dropped the bat and began his run to first base. It was short-lived. The second baseman didn't even have to move and caught the line drive with ease. James slowed his run as he heard the umpire yell, "Game over!"

James turned, dejected. He shuffled to the bench and was greeted by his catcher, Paul.

"Good start to the season I would say."

James kicked the dirt as he entered the dugout, his shoulders sagging, arms hanging limp. He took a seat next to Paul and aggressively flipped his bat to the ground then reached down for his cleats. His hands dug hard into the laces as he untied them.

"Would have been better if we won," James responded.

"Yes, but these guys won the championship last year. Only losing by three isn't too shabby," Paul replied.

James didn't want to hear any of it. The game was over and they lost. Not only that, there were two men on base; he could have tied up the game! James struggled with his competitive nature and this was one of those times. He continued packing his bat and glove and heard a sweet voice call his name. He glanced up to see a pretty brunette running toward him from the stands.

"James, James!" she called. "You did so well, 3 for 4, I believe, your hit in the fourth inning tied the game!"

It was his girlfriend, Carol. They'd grown up together, but were never really friends. Once girls stopped having cooties though, he felt much differently about her and they'd been dating for a few years now.

"Still lost," James responded, putting his head back down to concentrate on what he was doing.

"I know what will cheer you up, what say we go into

town and grab a milkshake?"

James couldn't stop himself from smiling back at Carol's glowing face. He rested his forearms on his knees as he answered, "Sure, I could go for some ice cream."

He finished removing his cleats and slipped on his hardy, brown leather boots.

"See you tomorrow at school," Paul said as he waved goodbye.

"See you at school," James replied, climbing out of the dugout and taking Carol's arm.

The two walked away from the field toward James' pickup truck.

"Strawberry, I think I'll get strawberry today, I've decided that's my favorite," Carol started. "What are you going to have James?"

"I don't know," he replied, still thinking of the outcome of the game.

He had a tendency to dwell on such things. His eyes stared, unseeing, at the ground as they approached his old beat-up 1940s pickup truck. He escorted Carol around the back of the truck where his tailgate lay open from the recent work on the farm. A few wheat stalks still remained and multiple well-used tools lay on top of them. They continued around to the passenger door. James opened it and the door made a squeal as the metal hinges rubbed on each other.

"Thank you, James," Carol stated, arm still inter-locked with his.

She pulled him closer, then ran her finger up his chest

to his chin and slightly lifted it. Their eyes met, and James forgot what he had been thinking about. *Wow was she beautiful, with her pretty green eyes, soft tan skin, and light brown hair.* He felt lucky she would put up with him, especially when he was acting like a child.

"You played well, I enjoyed the game today, now let's forget about it and go get one of Sam's yummy shakes."

She leaned up and kissed him on the cheek. She was a bit shorter than him, most people were. At 6'2", he was the tallest kid in school. He gently helped her into the truck as the seats were hard and worn from years on the farm.

"Chocolate, I think today is a chocolate day."

"That's better," Carol beamed. "I like seeing you happy."

James shut the door then walked around the front of the pickup.

He really needed to fix up this old rig. A pretty girl like Carol shouldn't have to ride in such a jalopy. James opened the driver's door, which also squeaked, then hopped in.

"Anyone else going to Sam's?" he asked.

"Yes, I believe Missy, Margo and Barbara said they were going."

"Barbara, huh? That means Rich will be there."

Rich was the typical popular high school kid. His father was the mayor and Rich felt that his father's power trickled down to him. He wasn't necessarily mean or rude to James in particular, but his attitude was difficult to be around. James had been raised by two hard-working wheat farmers and understood what it took to run an operation their size, long grueling hours of work. But Rich had everything handed to him and expected everyone to pander to him. They were both on the baseball team and James felt that he spent more than enough time dealing with Rich's ego on the ball field, let alone outside of the park.

James started the truck. As usual, it took a few attempts, but soon they were headed into town. The high school was on the west side of town and Sam's Diner was clear across on the east. It wasn't that far though. It was a small town, but James liked the size. He felt too many more people would make everything seem overly crowded. He was most content in small groups; crowds really made him feel uncomfortable. Carol, on the other hand, was the type of girl who loved everything and everyone. That was one of the things that attracted him to her. She always lit up the room and knew how to make sure everyone had a good time.

They proceeded through town, past the grocery store, the leather shop and the newly built Sears. The town had about twenty large buildings, but nothing taller than the Grand Hotel which towered five stories over Main Street. The streets were all cobblestone with small sidewalks on each side. As a kid, James loved going into town and riding over the bumps of the cobblestones. His father's truck didn't have a great suspension and would bounce like crazy.

Today that feeling came back to him. His father

had given him the truck to make the trips to school and handling the farm easier. James was starting to take over the farm as his father's health had taken a turn and their operation was one of the top producers for the town. Not only the town, but the whole county. Each year, more than three quarters of their wheat would ship out of town. No one wanted to find out what would happen if their farm struggled.

James continued down the road, past the local theater where he and Carol had gone on their first date. After months of getting up the courage, he had finally asked her out. It was your typical dinner and a movie. They ate at Giovanni's, a local Italian restaurant, and then went to see a horror flick that he couldn't have cared less about, but it got him closer to Carol.

"I guess we are the last ones here," Carol said as she noticed their friends' cars at the diner.

Sam's Diner. It was a neat little place that started its life as a railroad car. The current owner, Sam, bought it dirt cheap and converted it when the rail lines stopped. It was the local hangout for many of the high school kids, a great place for a burger and fries on the weekend. James pulled his truck into an empty spot next to a bright yellow Chrysler Windsor Highlander. James' eyebrows tightened as he saw it. He knew exactly who drove that car. He half thought of hitting it, but knew that no good would come of it.

"Oooh, its Rich's car, isn't it so pretty?" Carol chirped. "I really like yellow, it's my favorite color."

James' eyes tightened even more, then Carol grabbed his hand.

"We should get in there, I'm really craving that strawberry milkshake," Carol smiled up at James.

He quickly snapped out of his thoughts. "Sure let me get your door," he offered, jumping out of the truck. He made his way around the back, gallantly opened the door and gave a bow.

"You're so silly James, that's why I like you," Carol tittered at his overly embellished act.

He took her by the arm and they walked toward the door.

"Great game today. You almost had 'em." Will, one of the locals who loved baseball and watched every game, was standing in his usual spot outside the diner. Nobody really knew what he did for work, but you were sure to find him in one of two places, the ball field or the diner. He slipped a cigarette between his lips, pulled out a metal lighter, lit up the cigarette and offered one to James.

"No thank you, Mr. Will," James replied. That was another thing, no one knew Will's last name. Or at least, none of James' friends did.

They walked inside to a big "hello" from the man behind the counter sporting a soda jerk hat. Sam always worked Saturday nights and took pride in welcoming each customer. James glanced to his left and spotted their friends all sitting between a couple of booths. The girls wore twin set sweaters and below the knee length skirts. Margo's was smooth with a small black and white checkered pattern while the other girls' were solid and pleated. Their saddle shoes kicked in time to "At the Hop" on the juke-box.

"James!" one of the boys called out. "Good to see that you finally made it. You played really well today."

James clenched his jaw. Carol had helped him put it out of his head momentarily, but now it was back.

Jason, their left-fielder, was very quick and batted above average, but he knew baseball as a career wasn't in the cards, he was more of a middle-of-the-road kind of guy. He was about 5' 9" with dark brown hair and a slim build. He sported a light blue button down shirt and pleated trousers with a brown leather belt hugging his hips. James and Carol approached the table.

"You know I don't like to relive our losses," he stated. "I had just put it out of my mind."

"Sorry boss," Jason replied.

He could get away with slips like that. Jason had been his best friend since they were ten and they'd been through a lot together.

"Yeah, too bad you couldn't get on base. I would have driven in the winning run."

It was Rich, and James had known there would be a comment of some sort coming from him. He shrugged it off and just shook his head, acting like it didn't bother him. He executed it poorly and everyone could tell. Just then, Sam walked up.

"Can I get you ladies and gents anything?"

The orders came flying in; a few burgers, fries, a

couple of milkshakes and they were all set.

"How's the crop looking this year?" asked Tommy. He was very stout, short and stocky and, as the only lefty on the team, he naturally played first.

"It seems to have been a wet spring," Barbara piped in.

"Why do you care?" sneered Rich.

He had been dating Barbara for a couple years now, but never treated her very nicely. James suspected she was trying to endure it for the prestige of dating Rich.

"Yes, it's been wet which means—"

The door of the diner swung open and they heard Sam belt out his friendly "hello". In walked three teenagers that James and his friends would rather not have seen anytime soon. The newcomers scanned the room, saw James and his friends and started heading that way. They were dressed in jeans and varsity jackets with a large "C" on the left side. They were part of the Colton Baseball team, the team they had just played. The reigning champions. They continued to walk toward the booths.

"Seems like you guys got a little better over the off season," stated the tallest one, who stood slightly off to the side.

Rich stood up and faced them. "You bet we did. Wait until next game; we are going to clobber you."

The big one, who quite frankly gave the impression that he spent all day lifting train cars and not a lot of time reading, gave a slight chuckle and pointed at his chest with his thumb, "We were only playing at half speed. There is no way any wheat farm boys from Eggerton are gonna beat us."

While none of them wanted to admit it, he did have a point. In the last five years, they had never beaten Colton, not once.

"Just you wait. This will be the year," Rich retorted, starting to get a little heated. "You guys are so famous I don't even know your names," he continued.

The three stopped short of Rich, eyeing him from about a foot away.

"Are you going to let your girls play?" scoffed the third Colton player, a smarmy little pretty boy. "They could probably play better than you."

Rich's anger intensified, he was known to be a hothead. His hands formed into fists.

"She could hit a home run off of me," he winked at Barbara.

Margo gasped. Rich cocked his fist back and began to swing, but James was too quick for him. He'd guessed what was about to happen and had the wits to make a move. He found himself behind Rich and quickly grabbed his arm.

"No need to get switched off over him," he reassured Rich.

Rich rounded on him, eyes bulging, lips pressed so tightly together they'd paled. He shook off James' grip, but knew that James was right and tried to calm himself down.

"You had your fun, you beat us on the field. Why don't you head on out before something bad happens?"

James suggested to the three.

The pretty boy just snickered and turned to walk out, "Let's go boys; let them cry in their shakes. There's better food in Colton."

The three left the diner without another word, though the tall boy looked like he genuinely wanted to stay and talk about baseball.

"What were you thinking? Someday that anger of yours is going to get you in trouble," Jason admonished.

"What were they doing here in the first place?" Carol asked. "They knew you would be here, why would they come by and try to start trouble?"

"You know how the corn farmers are; think they're better than the rest of us," Rich answered. "They are just looking for trouble, and one day, I'll give it to them."

"Sit down," said James, fed up with Rich's shenanigans. "You would just get yourself switched off. You almost got yourself switched off today."

"Yes, you should be more careful," Barbara began.

"Oh give me a break, Barbara. Nothing would have happened to me. I've seen people switched off, it's only temporary."

With that, the food arrived. Sam brought it all out on a large silver platter and began setting each item on the table.

"Who had the strawberry shake? I believe it was you, Miss." He slid the large, clear, Y-shaped glass across the table to Carol.

"Oh, it's perfect, I love the cherry on top," she

brightened and immediately forgot about the altercation.

After the food arrived, the boys did very little talking. They were beat from the game and just thinking about getting their energy back. The girls on the other hand, started talking to each other about school, dresses and other trivial things. The boys did their best to ignore them and paid more attention to their food. Then Carol changed the conversation.

"My science teacher says there is a meteor shower tonight, should be fun, anyone want to watch it?"

"No, I'm too tired from the game," Jason replied.

"We are catching the new monster flick at the theater tonight," Rich announced, expecting a reaction as it was opening night and tickets were hard to come by. Reactions were faked or nonexistent because everyone knew he acquired them with his father's help.

"Rich got Margo and I tickets as well," stated Tom, their shy short stop, who hadn't said a word through the entire ordeal.

"Looks like it's just you and me kid," James said to Carol.

He was beat from the game, but knew she was really looking forward to seeing the stars; it was all she'd talked about on the drive to diner. As the meal wrapped up, everyone went their separate ways. James escorted Carol to the truck and helped her inside. He knew exactly where he was going to take her, far away from the town lights and the sky glow, where the stars shone much brighter.

He started the truck and they headed down the road. Carol leaned over and put her head on his shoulder while they drove down the bumpy street. He smiled down at her and enjoyed her arm around his. No words were exchanged, they just drove.

CHAPTER TWO

James pulled the truck into his family's southernmost wheat field. It was the beginning of the season and the stalks were a mere 6" tall, about average height for an early season grow. He followed a dirt trail between two fields all the way to a large flat rock. He knew the spot well as he'd spent many summer nights watching the same stars as a boy.

"Here, grab a blanket." He pushed the pickup truck's seat forward to reveal a couple of plaid blankets rolled up behind it. "They'll cushion the hard ground and keep you from getting your skirt dirty."

Carol grabbed two blankets and James took her hand. He had never taken her to this spot before. As a matter of fact, he hadn't taken anyone to this particular spot before.

"Follow me," he guided her along the spring wheat field to his rock.

He climbed up and asked for the blankets. After spreading them out, he took her hand and helped her up. She had little trouble since she was pretty nimble herself. Once on the rock, they sat down facing west. Carol's eyes widened.

"Is that the wall?" she asked, her voice shaking slightly.

"Yes, but you don't have to worry. I've been much closer while harvesting our fields and never had any issues," James reassured, clasping her hand.

She took a deep, shaking breath. "Are you certain?"

James could see she was very anxious. He gently

placed his hand on her face and turned her toward him. Their eyes met, his voice as soft as his caress, "Trust me."

She nodded in agreement, but James, still sensing her fear, cajoled, "So, what did that old kook of a science teacher tell you about the meteor shower?"

"He is not a kook you silly, he's a very smart man, and I enjoy his classes, the stars are amazing all the way up there."

"So what's this shower all about?"

"It one happens once a year over a span of two days, lots of meteors to watch, but he said tonight would be the best night to see it."

"I wonder why that is?"

"Something about the way the Earth is tilted today, and where the meteors are coming from, and some other stuff, makes it the best."

"Huh."

Just then, the brightest shooting star they had ever seen gleamed through the sky.

"Wow, did you see that? He was right," James perked up.

"The tail on that one was so long, it was like a line of fire, trailing behind it!"

That was just the beginning. Soon another appeared, then another and in no time the sky was littered with them. They'd begun counting after the first couple, but realized it was futile to continue. Streak after streak continued to fill the sky. They lay still, hands clenched in disbelief. *Why hadn't they seen or heard of this before?* It was quite the awe-inspiring sight, so close that they felt as though they could reach out and touch them. The show continued for over an hour and they watched as if it was the July 4th fireworks display. Then, as quickly as they multiplied, the meteor numbers started to fade until they were completely gone.

"That was quite the show," murmured James, who had said very little over the past hour except the occasional "Look at that one!"

"Mr. Johnston was right about the show," he continued, still staring at the sky. "You said it was supposed to happen for a couple of days?"

"That's what he said."

James, deep in thought, spun toward to her, "Why did it stop then? Wouldn't it continue for both days?"

"I'm not sure, he just said it would happen for two days, I'll ask him Monday at class."

"Well, it's getting late and I don't want your mother to worry about you, let alone your father. Wouldn't want him switching off the electricity on us. That would be really bad for our watering system."

"He wouldn't do that, probably just give you a stern talking to," she giggled.

"I don't want that, either. In fact, that might be worse."

Carol's father worked for the electric company. He was a hulk of a man who always seemed to be concentrating very hard on whatever he was doing, that's how James saw it. He grabbed the blankets then jumped off the rock. After placing them on the ground, he twisted to catch her as she slid down. They walked to the truck, still searching the sky for more lights and dazzling comet tails, none came.

Settled in the truck, they headed to Carol's house. She lived on the north side of town, conveniently about a half of a mile from the power plant. Convenient for her father anyway. For James, it was quite the hike to get out there, but he didn't mind the time alone in the truck. His mind wandered from the night's events to his truck and he started wishing he had the funds to fix it up properly. He was pretty practical and knew that if he put a little money into it, the payback would be multiplied. He planned on keeping it as long as he could find parts for it and hoped it would run for a long time. His mind drifted off to another place, but he was brought back to reality when Carol gently placed her hand on his thigh.

"Thank you for the lovely evening, I really enjoyed it, and the spot you picked out was perfect, I'm sorry I was a bit nervous at first."

"I'm glad you liked it," James beamed. "I've never taken anyone there before; it's my favorite place to go relax and just think."

About this time, they arrived at Carol's home. It was late, but the lights were still on and they could see a shadow behind the window curtains. The house was a cute little three bedroom cottage with a wraparound porch, Victorian style decorations on the columns, and a turret on the left corner. There were only two other houses within a mile and it bordered the Rangel wheat field.

"Mom must be waiting for me," Carol mused. "Dad is probably in bed, he tends to work early on weekends, and there have been more than a few power outages lately."

"Can I walk you to the door?"

"Sure, I'd like that."

They headed up to the house and stopped on the porch, still holding hands.

"How 'bout I pick you up for church tomorrow?" James asked.

"Sure, I'll be ready to go by eight, can you stop by then?"

"I most definitely can and look forward to it," he was always excited to spend time with her.

He had a great time with Carol and was glad he'd be able to take her to church in the morning. Just then, the door swung open, Carol's mother stood there with a look of panic on her face.

"There you are, my baby," she squealed as she jumped through the doorway to hug her daughter.

"Everything alright, Mom?" Carol's face transformed from amused to concerned; she'd never seen her mother so jumpy and distraught. "We're home at a decent hour."

"I know hon, but your father's been getting multiple calls tonight about power outages, and a few fires, some in town, so I was worried."

"I'm fine, Mom, James takes good care of me, I watched him play baseball then we went and watched the meteor shower after dinner."

"Oh, I saw some of that, never seen anything like it before," her mother loosened her hold just enough to look at both of them.

"Really?" James inquired.

"My science teacher, who is very smart, said it happens every year at this time, so it must be true."

"I don't know about that, I've seen a few shooting stars over the years, but never that many at once."

James looked at Carol, puzzled. *If this had occurred every year, how had she not seen it?* Carol's house was on the outskirts of town and the sky was fairly open. The only light pollution came from the power plant which sat with nearly all of its lights extinguished.

"I'm just glad you're home, let's get you inside for the night, thank you James for taking care of her."

"You're welcome Mrs. Grambling. My pleasure."

Carol left her mother's embrace, reached over and grabbed James and pulled him toward her. She pressed her lips against his cheek.

"Goodnight, James, see you tomorrow."

James blushed as he opened his eyes to see Mrs. Grambling smiling at the romantic sight. He was very shy about affection in public and was a little embarrassed at what Mrs. Grambling had just witnessed.

"See you in the morning," he managed, then turned and headed down the porch steps.

Carol waved to him as he pulled away from the house then shut the door behind her. Alone with his thoughts, James sped away to his house. He kept thinking about what Carol's mother had said, that she had never seen so many shooting stars in one night. *Maybe she just didn't pay much attention to the skies or had typically gone to bed before they arrived. It was strange that they came and went so fast. If it's supposed to happen over two days was there more to come? Or was that it?* His mind continued to mull over things and eventually he found himself at home.

His house stood between two rows of trees planted by his father to reduce the wind that came over the fields in the fall. It would blow as hard as 50 mph, but only for a few days. The wind had caused plenty of issues with the house before the trees grew tall enough to protect it. James parked the truck and headed in the front door. It was a modest house, ranch style, with four bedrooms, an average sized kitchen and one bathroom. The lights were out. It was going to be an early morning on the farm. James quietly made his way to his bedroom and crawled under the covers, his mind still thinking about the night's events.

The next morning, James awoke to his father's quietly authoritative voice. "Good morning, James. Late night?"

James, still groggy from sleep, managed to spit out a grumbling, "Sort of."

"Well, we need you to gather the eggs for breakfast and then take a look at the machinery on #6 and run some tests on it."

"Sure thing, Father," he said as his limp arm slid off the bed.

On a normal day, he would have already been up fetching eggs, milking the cows, and watering the animals, but because of last night's events, he forgot to set his alarm. His father was a good man and seemed to understand that James was a high school boy, so he usually cut him some slack on the weekends. James dragged himself out of bed, threw on his overalls, then headed out to the barn to milk the cows and accomplish his other chores. Afterward, he walked into the kitchen to the smell of frying eggs and freshly cooked bacon.

"Morning, Mom," he greeted, seeing her working at the stove.

"Oh, good morning, honey. Did you have a late night?"

"Yeah," James yawned. "Carol and I watched the meteor shower after dinner at Sam's Diner."

"Meteor shower, was it nice? Haven't seen one of those in years."

James' nose and forehead scrunched, his lips pursed, "Did you see one last year at this time, Mom?"

"No, can't say I did. Matter of fact, I was probably your age the last time I saw a meteor shower. Not something that's very typical around here."

James went back to thinking about the evening as his mother served him scrambled eggs. *Strange. Neither Carol's mother nor his had seen a shower like that before, but Carol's teacher said it happened every year.* The gears continued to turn in his head, then a beam of sunlight flickered through the window causing James to squint.

"What time is it?" he blurted.

"It's about 7:30. Why?"

"Gosh, I'm going to be late!"

James shoved in a mouthful of eggs then ran out grabbing some bacon on the way. "Thanks for breakfast Mom!"

He quickly headed to his closet and grabbed his best church clothes. They were his best because they were his only ones. Soon dressed, he headed out to the truck, hopped in and took off, kicking up dust along the way. He didn't want to be late to pick up Carol, that wouldn't go over very well. He sped down the roads with ease since it was still early on a Sunday morning. James arrived at her house about 5 minutes after eight, hopped out and jogged up the front steps. Before he even made the porch, Carol opened the door.

"Pushing it kind of close?" Carol teased. Her eyes were stern, but her lips were quirked.

"Sorry. I slept in. Had trouble falling asleep last night. You?"

"A little, my dad didn't get home until very late, seems there were seven power outages in various parts of town."

"Any word on the fires your mom mentioned last night?"

"Yes, my dad said that there was only one on the east side of town, something knocked out the power lines, the downed lines caught part of the Connor's wheat fields on fire."

James approached Carol, "Did they put it out?"

"Yes, my dad said it only burned about half an acre before the fire department was able to extinguish it."

"That's good," said James as he reached for Carol's hand. "Don't want to be late for church. Let's get going."

They arrived at the church a few minutes before service began and headed inside. It was the only church in town and nearly everyone attended. A few people might miss due to work or sickness, but you could usually find everyone there. Carol and James had discussed their plan on the drive over, they were on a mission. Mr. Johnston would surely be at church and they had some questions for him. The service went as usual, singing, communion, and a fire and brimstone sermon, then finished with a prayer. Both Carol and James were distracted during the service and really picked up none of it. They were intent on finding Carol's science teacher. Near the end of the sermon James spotted him four rows up and eight seats to the left. Upon the conclusion of the final prayer, they made a beeline for Mr. Johnston.

"That was a great game yesterday. You boys are showing promise."

James was intercepted by Pete, one of the elders. He was an older gentleman with a balding pate of slick black hair. Also a farmer, he owned the property to the south of town.

"You going to play in college?" he asked, rocking heal to toe.

"I'm not sure yet," James responded looking past him, eyes fixed on Carol's science teacher.

Carol glanced back at James and saw him waving to keep following the teacher.

"Your father going to sell the farm if you do?" Pete continued.

His operation had the second largest producing farm behind James' family and he had been trying to purchase it for a few years now.

"I don't know." James fidgeted, trying to be polite but wanting to get out of the conversation quickly. "You'll have to ask him. It was nice talking to you, sir, but I have a few things I need to attend to."

James broke away from the conversation only to be stopped by Rich. His eyes almost rolled. He knew this was not going to be a fun conversation.

"You guys should have joined us at the movie last night, it was spectacular, and so scary Barbara couldn't stop holding me all night."

James feigned interest, "That's great." He had played the game long enough to know things always ended badly if you were too short with Rich. "What are your plans for the day?" James quickly added, working on getting the conversation over with as soon as he could. His eyes shifted around watching everyone pack up and leave. He began rubbing his fingers together.

"Oh, not much. I think we might just cruise around town, maybe go check out old man Connor's field. Heard he had a fire last night. You should come."

"Sounds fun," James said with a forced smile. "But I think Carol and I are just going to have lunch, then I need to get back to my chores."

"Sucks working on a farm. You should take that college scholarship to play ball and dump this place."

"You know I can't do that," James' eyebrows dropped into a scowl. "I hope you have fun cruising today. I need to go catch up to Carol."

James headed toward the large double doors that led to the parking lot. Outside, he saw Mr. Johnston climbing into his car. Carol was standing beside the passenger door and it appeared as if they were finishing their conversation. James wasted no time and hurried over. He arrived as Mr. Johnston pulled away. Carol turned to him and smiled as if she had some news.

"What did he say? What did you ask him? Why hasn't anyone seen this before?" he spat out question after question, his eyes intense, hands slightly raised leaning toward her.

"Slow down James," Carol responded, giggling a little. "Just wait and I'll tell you."

"Ok, so what did he have to say?" he eased back a little.

"I'll tell you on the drive, I'd like to go get lunch if that's ok?"

"Sure," James answered, pressing his lips together, his eyebrows slanted. He grabbed her hand and they headed to his pickup.

"Let's go to Sam's, they're having a Sunday special today and I want to see what it is, plus our friends will probably be there and I want to show the girls my new dress," Carol suggested as she gazed at the scenery out the window of the truck.

"Sure, now what did he say?" James insisted. He didn't hear a word she said after Sam's. That was enough to get them started and to change the conversation to the matter at hand.

"Well, he told me that this happens every year, but this year is special because of the tilt of the Earth, that and the position of the sun makes the meteors appear to be closer than usual, he said this tilt hasn't happened in fifty years and that's why it seemed so spectacular." Carol paused to take a breath. "But here's the best part, tonight it will be even more brilliant than last night, that's what he told me, although last night was supposed to be the best, but can we go to your rock and watch them again tonight?"

James glanced over at Carol and saw her pleading like a child with her hands clenched together, puppy dog eyes, the works. He knew she was playing around and that there was no way he would say no.

"Nope," he tilted his chin up and looked away, his face stern. He watched Carol out of the side of his eye. "We have school tomorrow and I need my rest for classes."

Carol pouted and just sat there with her mouth slightly open. James did his best to hold back a grin, but gave in quickly. "Just kidding, of course we can," he answered, only to be punched multiple times in the shoulder by Carol's petite hands.

"You big tease," she said, playfully punching him

again. He was good at getting responses from her. Maybe he should have taken up acting class.

CHAPTER THREE

They arrived as the night before. As the sun set, they grabbed two blankets and headed for the rock.

"The wall still gives me the creeps," Carol shivered while James helped her up onto the rock.

"Don't worry about it. Once the show starts, you'll forget all about it."

They laid down to enjoy the last of the setting sun behind the colossal wall a couple thousand yards away from them. The orange ball descended, illuminating the sky in a beautiful assortment of pinks, reds and oranges. Carol fidgeted with her hands, trying to ignore the wall.

"This is the furthest west I've been," Carol admitted, turning her head to look at James.

"Well you can't go much further. I've only gone maybe another thousand yards." He pointed off into the distance. "Our field ends there, so for obvious reasons, I've never traveled any further." Keeping his voice even, he rambled a bit more, watching Carol's reactions, in an attempt to soothe her.

Then it began. The meteors cascaded to Earth, just as they had the night before. One fell, then another, and another and soon the sky was filled with them. James and Carol gazed in amazement. They could almost feel the meteors zipping by; they appeared even closer than the night before. A thunderous roar came from overhead and the ground shook. Carol grasped for James and pulled him close. They watched as a meteor barely cleared the wall.

"Did you see that?" Carol gasped as the roar continued above them. Just then, another meteor came hurtling over them. Carol held on tight to James. He tried to be brave, but inside he was scared too. *What was going on?* The meteors kept coming, amazingly missing the wall each time.

"Maybe we should go." Carol's voice was quick and James could see her breathing heavily.

"Where to? They're all around us!" James exclaimed above the noise, holding his hands over his ears.

They had never heard anything like that before, the rumble was low and rattled everything around them. James looked at his pickup truck. The whole thing was shaking and it looked like the bumper was about to pop off. He glanced around to see if it made more sense to stay or go.

"I think you're right. Let's get out of here."

James slid off the rock, spun around and waited for Carol to jump down to him. He caught her with ease and hurriedly set her down.

"Come on," he shouted as he grabbed her hand and dragged her to the truck.

They climbed into the truck in a rush. James attempted to start it, but no luck. Carol watched him, her face pale, lips quivering, eyes welling up.

"Come on, baby," he pleaded with the truck, frantically turning the key in the ignition, it failed to start.

The rumbling seemed to be getting louder as more meteors passed overhead. Carol hysterically looked around; this was not the beautiful night she had expected.

"Third time's a charm," James let slip under his breath, this time pumping the gas.

The truck came alive. He threw it into reverse and began driving backward. After a couple dozen feet, he whipped it around to the right. Carol slid over and was now pressed into his side. She grasped him tightly as the truck spun around 180 degrees. In drive now, James stepped on the gas to accelerate. The little truck gave all it had, kicking dirt all over the place. His tools bounced around the bed then flew out in a trail behind them. He flicked his eyes up to the rearview mirror to see what he only could describe as an explosion. Dirt flew everywhere. It was in the distance and not an immediate threat, but he wasn't taking any chances. He kept on the accelerator. The sky began to grow dim, but they weren't sure if the rumbling was still going or if it was just his truck. He slowed down a bit. The sky continued to darken, but the rumbling was almost gone. He stopped the truck to regain his composure. Carol, who had been closing her eyes since the truck accelerated slowly opened them.

Shaking, Carol whispered, "Are you ok?"

"Yeah, I wasn't expecting anything like that. You?"

James' hands slipped off the wheel, partly due to sweat and partly because of the withdrawal of adrenaline. He had been working overtime to get them away from the threat and was now depleted.

"I love you, James," Carol said grabbing him tightly.

He didn't know how to respond, she had never said such a thing to him before. He thought that he loved her, but was concerned that it was the near death experience talking.

"I love you, too," he gently responded, knowing that saying anything else would have crushed her. They sat in the pickup for a few minutes in silence, decompressing. In the distance, they could see the lights of town. James wondered how it had looked from there. *Had they seen the meteors and felt the ground rumbling?* James felt Carol give a slight shudder and saw that she had fallen asleep. The whole event must have completely taken it out of her.

"I'll take you home," he said more to himself than to Carol, knowing she couldn't hear him.

He shifted the truck into gear and inched forward. His mind was racing. *Did Mr. Johnston know this was going to happen? Was he just guessing? Where did he get his information?* Question after question popped into his head.

In no time he pulled up to Carol's house. He caressed her head and whispered, "Wake up sleepy head."

Carol came to very slowly.

"Where am I?" she asked almost instinctively and not quite awake.

"We're at your house. Let me help you up."

He gently pushed her upright then eased out his door. He ran around quickly and opened the passenger door with a loud squeak.

"Here, take my hand," he said offering it to her. She

stumbled along as he led her up to the porch. "Are you going to be alright?"

"Sure, goodnight James, thanks for saving me."

She gave him a kiss on the cheek then headed inside.

The next morning, James awoke to his alarm clock clanging. He rolled over and shut it off. He had fallen asleep almost precisely when his head hit the pillow. He'd never had excitement like that before, if that's what you wanted to call it. Football had some adrenaline packed play, and baseball was such a mental game he always slept well, but never like that. He peeled himself off of the sheets, stretched, then headed to do his chores.

After finishing, he arrived in the kitchen to the smell of fresh pancakes and hot syrup.

"Morning, James," his mother said, still working at the stove. She didn't even look behind her, somehow she always sensed when he was there. He sometimes felt freaked out by how good she was at it.

He took a seat at the table, "Morning, Mom."

"Morning, son," said his father as he sat reading the newspaper at the table, seemingly in his own world.

Trying to act like nothing much had happened, James replied, "Morning, Father. Anything good in the paper today?"

"Nah, just the typical Mayor election scandals and the farmer's guild complaining about funding."

"How's that going by the way?" James queried, attempting to keep any questions off of him. "Pete asked me at church if you were planning on selling."

James' father forced a laugh, "Selling? To that shyster? I'd rather burn my fields than sell to him. Did he ask if you were going to take that scholarship to college?"

"What are you talking about, Father?" James rebutted as if he had no clue what his father was talking about.

His father folded the paper down to peer over it at James, "This is a small town. Word travels."

James' chin dipped slightly. Slumping in his chair, rubbing the back of his neck, "I didn't want you to worry. I know you need me and can't handle the farm on your own."

"I can hire help if need be. Production's been good the past few years, provided the machines hold up. Don't you worry about us, we'll get by. Make the best decision for you. The farm will always be here, it's a necessity for life, and those things don't just disappear."

James' mom placed a stack of pancakes in front of him.

"Eat up, you need that fuel for your mind," she turned back to the stove. "How many pieces of sausage would you like?"

"Four please," James replied. He felt guilty for not telling them, but also blessed to have parents who seemed to understand his mind. "I'm sorry. I'm sorry for not telling you."

"Don't fret over it, sometimes we hurt the ones we love by trying to protect them. Just remember that in the future. Your mom and I knew that this would be a possibility when we saw how gifted you were in sports. I thought it would be football, but of course your mother called it. Longer career in baseball too, so that's a good thing."

"I don't know if I'm going to take it," James spoke up. "I haven't accepted it yet."

"Well, you should," his father grabbed his cane and used it to stand up.

"Your youth will depart and, as I said before, this farm will remain. You only get one chance at an opportunity like that. It's the choices we make that guide us along our path. This one's a big one. Don't choose a path for the wrong reasons."

His father walked over to his mom, kissed her on the cheek then headed to the door.

"I'll be messing with those machines if you need me," he said as he walked over the threshold.

James sat there staring at his pancakes. *Why was life so difficult? And to add into the mix, what on Earth happened last night?*

"Eat up, you don't want to be late for school," James' mom insisted.

He finished up and headed to school.

James walked up the steps, still thinking about his decision. It was a fairly large school made of brick and sandstone; it always reminded him of a cathedral, the kind he had read about in books. It was the only school for miles and housed every grade from K through 12. The school was divided into four parts. Every three grades, students moved to a different section. This was his senior year, then it was full time on the farm or off to college. College for most of the kids was a dream, only one out of every twenty would be selected to attend, and less than that ever got a scholarship. Prior to James, only one other kid in the past 10 years had been offered a scholarship, and he'd turned it down to stay on the farm. Farming was their life. Most of the classes they took revolved around growing crops, changing over the soils, re-fertilizing the ground, and not over-using it. Almost a quarter of the girls would work farms, too. Sometimes more if the boys were graduating in smaller numbers. But right now, James' mind was anywhere but on farming.

"James! What a weekend, how did the rest of Sunday go?"

"Hey, Jason." James was actually glad to see him. He could almost always help when James was struggling. "It was good, kind of weird, but good."

"Nice, that's good. Wait, what? Weird, what do you mean?" Jason's body straightened, realizing what he heard.

"Did you hear or see anything strange last night?" James' eyes darted around at the students passing by as they reached the top.

"There was some rumbling, but it just sounded like thunder."

"Did you see any clouds around?" James asked, one eyebrow raised, awaiting the response.

"No, well I don't think so. It was dark, hard to tell,

especially with the sky glow."

Jason lived above the Rusty Nail Tavern in the middle of the town. His mother had owned the bar for as long as he could remember. James found it odd that the meteor shower wasn't noticed in town.

"Has anyone mentioned lights in the sky or any noise other than thunder?"

They opened the doors and headed inside.

"No, can't say that I've heard anyone talking. Why, did you see something?" Jason tilted his head slightly.

James wanted to tell him, but thought it better to keep it to himself. "Not really, I heard the growling of the thunder, but that was about it."

"Oh, okay. I'll see you at practice after school," Jason said as he turned to go to class.

This was their last semester and they had split off into specialties based on aptitude tests they had taken as freshmen. James scored high in mechanics while Jason's scores favored fertilizer research, so the last couple of months they only saw each other in the morning and after school. James felt they'd been growing apart because of it, but tried his best to keep up the appearance that nothing was wrong.

He grabbed his books then headed down the long corridor to his classroom. He passed through the doors and saw two large automated bailer machines.

"Ready to start the practical application?" his instructor brightened when he saw James enter the room.

Professor MacDunna really pushed James through

the course. Of the three students in the class, James was the best. Tim Connor and Rex Lutz were the other two. James always found it funny that only the direct descendants of the farmers made it into the mechanics course. He nodded back at Professor MacDunna. "Sure."

But he knew he would only be going through the motions that day; his mind was somewhere else. The day passed slowly. "James, did you hear what I just said?" was heard from the professor more than once as he noticed James wasn't paying attention. Soon enough, the bell rang.

"Don't forget to tell your fathers about the new update coming out next month," the professor insisted as the three packed up their books to leave class.

James just nodded and headed out the door. He made his way back down the hallway and, in the distance, could see Carol smiling, arms crossed against the books over her chest. She appeared to be no worse for wear and was sporting cute pig tails.

James spun one of the curls around his finger, "I like your hair."

"Thanks," she beamed.

"You seem to be doing well in light of last night's events."

"Events?" she frowned.

James cocked his head slightly, stopping with raised eyebrows.

"What do you remember about last night?"

"It was great, you sure know how to show a girl a good

time."

"Be more specific."

"What's wrong, you don't remember, you took me to your wheat field, we headed out to the large rock and watched the meteor shower."

"And?"

"And it was amazing."

Shaking his head from side to side, he insisted, "What happened next?"

"You took me home, James it was a lovely time, I really enjoyed it." She took his hand in hers. "Everybody's going to the diner, we should get going."

"But, I have baseball practice," he retorted.

"Didn't Jason tell you, your coach gave you the day off, he had some things he needed to attend to."

James was confused, but it wasn't the first time they had a day off and frankly his mind wouldn't have been on the game anyway.

"Sure, let's go."

They began walking toward the front of the school.

"So, nothing scared you last night?" he continued.

"Aside from you saying you loved me, no it was fun, I'm hoping there will be a meteor shower like that again someday soon."

James felt the opposite. *He scared her by saying he loved her? She had said it first. Plus, being chased by meteors! How could she forget that? He hoped to never be in a crazy situation with meteor explosions ever again. What was going on?*

CHAPTER FOUR

They arrived at the diner and James helped Carol out of the truck. She tucked her hand around the crook of his elbow as they headed for the door. Will stood in his usual spot outside. He tossed a used butt on the ground then reached for another out of the small box he held.

He held one out toward James, "Cigarette?"

"No thanks Mr. Will," James replied, holding his hand up to wave off the offer as he continued toward the diner.

"Look in your field," Will whispered as James walked by.

He turned to see Will give him a wink, but James kept walking.

"There they are. What took you guys so long?" they heard come from their typical booths. Rich was being his loudmouth self.

"James' class let out late," Carol replied as they walked toward their seats.

"Sure it did," Rich jabbed. He seemed even more vocal than usual.

James was bursting inside to ask countless questions, but retained his composure.

"What did you guys do this weekend?" he asked.

"You know most of it. You were with us, except in the evenings," Rich shot back, sliding his arm around Barbara.

"So how was last night?" he rephrased.

Rich continued talking as if there wasn't anyone else

in the room, "Good. Didn't do much, actually came back here and got late night burgers. How about you guys? Did you enjoy the lights in the sky?"

"You saw them?" James perked up.

"No. Carol said you guys went out to some field and watched some balls of light flying around."

"They were meteors and they weren't just flying around, they were streaking across the sky, it was beautiful," Carol retorted.

"Whatever, I'm sure it was quite amazing, but the burgers were, too." Rich began laughing at himself, and the others did, too. Though they were mainly laughing at him, not with him, but he didn't see the difference.

"Did you guys hear any loud noises?" asked James.

"Just the sirens on Saturday night I think, when the fire broke out and the power outages started," Jason chimed in.

James, who was leaning forward this whole time as if in a secret conversation, slumped back into his seat. *Had he dreamed the whole thing? He had never done drugs, so he didn't think that was an option.*

Rich snickered, "What's the matter, were you expecting a Wild West story?"

James decided to play it cool even though he wanted to tell them what actually happened, or what he thought had happened.

"No. I just heard a bunch of thunder last night and was wondering if you guys heard it, too."

They all nodded their heads in agreement. James

wanted to say more, but left it at that. The waitress walked over and took their orders and the conversation turned to normal things; how hard the math test had been and what they were doing the next weekend. All the while, James couldn't get the scenario out of his head; it was such a crazy experience. *How could Carol have forgotten about the life threatening episode they had endured together?*

After a couple of hours of small talk, they trickled out of the diner. Carol and James were the last ones left.

"What's on your mind?" she asked, knowing his guard was down. She always did that to him.

He stared down at the table mentally connecting the scars in the Formica to create shapes.

"Lots of things," he muttered, slipping his hands into his pockets, trying to figure out how to respond.

"Like what?"

He tried to deflect. "Like taking the scholarship. My parents somehow found out about it."

"It's a small town, you know how people talk, there's always some bit of gossip going around."

"Thanks," he said flatly, looking over to see her smirking as if she knew what his father had said. "I know that it's a small town, but I only told a couple of my closest friends."

"You mean Jason, who gossips more than any girl I know."

"You've got a point, but I didn't think it would get back to them." He turned to stare out the window. "I just owed them more."

"You have given them everything, you work so hard fixing those machines, your father couldn't run the farm without you."

"I know that, and that's why I don't think I can take the scholarship."

"James," Carol began. "You know they would do anything for you, and want to see you happy, that's what all parents want for their children."

"You sound like a wise monk," he responded. "You're an old soul, and that's part of what makes you so amazing."

"I don't know about old, well I just read a lot, and I did learn a thing or two in my psychology classes, you should take the scholarship, it's what's best for you, you know how scarce college is, let alone a scholarship."

"I know. Sometimes I wish the decision could be made for me."

"Let's stay for a milkshake, that will cheer you up, chocolate?"

"Sure. Chocolate," James said with a half-smile.

The next morning was the same. James woke up, did his chores then headed in for breakfast. His mind was still bouncing all over the place when suddenly, "look in your field" popped into his head. *What was Mr. Will talking about?* He scouted the fields almost every day. But the image of the wink burned in his mind. He normally ran a sweep of the fields on Saturday morning, but he couldn't wait until then, so he decided to skip school and check them today. He headed over to his truck and then remembered the race to escape the meteors. His tools had bounced out of the truck. He hadn't thought of searching yesterday as his head was spinning. He approached the truck and peeked into the rusty bed, empty. His tools were indeed missing.

If his scouting trip did nothing more than find his tools it would be a win. He needed those tools for repairing the machines and prepping them for the harvest. They were custom made, not easily replaced and not cheap. He headed out, taking his time. He wanted it to take all day; it would give him time to think as he had plenty going through his mind. James began on the northern side of their land, and worked his way in a zigzag pattern south, along paths they had cut for that purpose. Everything appeared as it should. He continued his pattern and reached the western edge of the field.

There it was. The wall. It had been some time since he had gone past the edge of their fields to the west. He forgot how imposing it was. It rose straight up from the ground and he guessed it was about 400 feet tall. It seemed to be made of a dark gray, almost black, metal with a matte texture on it. From this distance, the wall appeared smooth, but he had seen it through binoculars when he was younger and noticed it had grooves carved in a multitude of square and rectangular patterns. He shut off his truck and just stared at it, mesmerized.

The wall had been there longer than anyone who was alive knew, but then again, he imagined that if a person lived past 70 they were lucky. The history books said it was built two hundred years ago. He had learned about it as a child, the time when most people are very inquisitive. Enough details were given to satisfy most children's curiosity, but they all eventually learned that it didn't help to question anything about the wall. As they grew, there were better things to do. His recent experiences made him begin to question things again. *What was on the other side of the wall?*

Sure, he knew the book answers. Amongst other things, it was said to have a defensive system should anyone ever get too close. He had never seen or heard of anyone attempting it, they were all too busy living their lives, but he remembered the fear in Carol's eyes when she realized how close they were to it that night on the rock. He came back to himself and realized he needed to continue his scouting.

James started the truck again and headed down the path. The trek continued. On the horizon, he could see the rock where they watched the meteor shower the past weekend. He initially wanted to head straight there, but composed himself and continued the pattern he had set up. In no time, he found himself at the rock. The blankets lay strewn on the ground. He stopped the truck and got out to pick them up. After placing them back behind the seats, he continued on foot toward the area where he thought he had parked the truck that night. His head swiveled from side to side, searching for any indication he'd made a hasty retreat.

Then he found it. Two large gouges in the ground where his tires would have dug in during their frenzied exit. He gazed east toward town and saw the path he took to exit the field and began to follow it. He started walking at first, then jogging and eventually running. Soon enough, he came upon his tools. They were all over the place and some of them would be too heavy to carry back to the truck. He piled them up and headed back to the truck. His mind raced. He was relieved that his memories of the event were correct, but in the same moment confused as to why Carol didn't remember. *Maybe her mind blocked it out due to the intensity of the chaos?*

He made it back to the truck quickly and headed for the tools. As he followed the path, he instinctively looked in his rear view mirror.

"The explosion," he said out loud without even realizing it.

He hurried to the tools, tossed them into the pickup then turned the truck in the direction of his best guess toward the impact area. He didn't see any of the meteors actually hit the ground, but they sure were coming close. He passed the rock and continued west toward the wall. His heart worked overtime as his anticipation grew. James continued on, but then slowed down; he was getting close to the edge of their field and still hadn't found anything yet. The truck slowed to a roll. The wall seemed larger than he remembered it. He came to a stop at the edge of their field. He looked northwest, past the fields, toward the wall and saw nothing but wild grass standing about four inches tall. He then focused his attention to the southwest and finally spotted it; a small mound of disturbed earth showed above the grass. He wished he had those binoculars he'd had as a kid, but he'd given them away for some forgotten reason.

He hopped out of his truck and climbed into the bed. The view was better, but not quite good enough. He jumped up on the top of the cab then cupped his hand over his eyes and squinted. Sure enough, there was fresh dirt sitting on top of the grass probably a hundred yards past the field's edge. He really wished he had those binoculars. James sat down on the cab and just stared off into the distance at the wall. *Were the stories true? Would you be switched off if you approached it, or worse, killed?* His mind spun. He was wild with curiosity, but also trying to be cautious. *Curiosity killed the cat.* But the draw to see what was implanted in the ground was growing stronger inside him. Finally, he hopped off the truck.

I'll just take it slow. Our field technically goes another 50 yards on the map. It was true. His great, great, granddad had planted the fields 50 yards away from the actual plot line for fear of the wall. He hoped the map was correct. The impact zone looked to be another 25 yards or so. Still, he could get a closer look, hopefully come away fulfilled and then head back home. He began walking toward the fresh dirt, staring up at the ever more imposing wall. At this point, even with the naked eye he began to notice the grooves he remembered as a child.

He continued, warily, until he reached the boundary of his fields. He had guessed about right, the fresh dirt was now a mere 25 yards outside of the plot line.

James stood there, searching for any indication of what might resemble a meteor. He glanced back at his truck. *Maybe I can drive it over here and get a bird's eye view.* He quickly squashed that idea, deciding the risk was too great. He gazed up at the wall. *Wow, was it big from this vantage point.* James stared for a moment as he rubbed his chin, thinking. His eyes then shifted to the ground, his interest peaked. He had to see if there was really something there. He inched one foot forward past the line then carefully brought the other foot in front of it. *Two steps in. He wasn't switched off, so far so good.* He continued three steps, then four. His confidence grew as he moved forward. Ten steps and he was almost there. He could see a small crater about the size of half a basketball court. The earth had been pushed out on both sides, but the majority of it was to the west. The shower they had watched came from the east so this must have been the impact of one of the meteors. Initially, he thought maybe something had exploded, a power line perhaps. No one knew what was beyond the field. He looked into the hole and did a double-take. His head inched closer as he squinted and saw metal. Shiny metal, like chrome.

CHAPTER FIVE

James knelt down to examine the crater. The trench was short but deep, about eight feet he guessed; the kind a high angle impact would create. The dirt had sprayed around the impact site like water hitting a flat surface. As he moved to peer closer, a sparkle caught his eye. There seemed to be an object embedded in the dirt, part of it reflecting the sunlight. What he saw looked almost like chrome metal, like Rich's car's bumper. He jumped down into the crater and reached out to feel it. The texture was smooth and shiny like glass. James raked his eyes over the ground inside the crater and saw more metal sticking out of the dirt in front of him. He began unearthing the extraterrestrial object with his hands. He continued to dig around the metal until he had uncovered an area the size of a basketball. He concentrated on one side of the object to see if he could dig around it and dislodge it.

"Ouch," James screamed, pulling his hand back in pain.

He examined it. Something had thinly sliced his forefinger, almost like that time he ran his finger the wrong way along his father's razor. He reached into his pocket and pulled a rag out to cover his injured finger. Still curious and not about to let a little cut deter him, he continued. The metal that had been so smooth above the dirt was a jagged, tangled mess of bent, sharp edges below it. His digging had almost dislodged it, but he needed to work on the other side. Scraping more dirt with calloused hands used to working the soil, he quickly found the same on the other side, and leaning into it, freed it from its earthly bonds. Clang. The object fell into the deepest part of the crater. James was quick enough to get out of the way and now stared down at a pile of twisted chrome metal.

The object was curved on one side, but mutilated on the other. It looked as if it belonged to a larger piece and had been ripped apart.

"Clang?" James said to himself.

He had dropped plenty of large metal tools into the dirt working on their farm machinery; they never made that sound. His mind continued to think. *The bed of his truck made that sound.* He carefully reached down to pick up the metal scrap and caught a glint of sunlight down by his feet. Not thinking anything of it, he studied the piece. It was light, much lighter than anticipated. As a matter of fact, he could lift it with one hand. It didn't look like any piece of metal or machinery he had ever seen before, it just looked like twisted metal.

He decided to take it home with him to examine it further and placed it up on the edge of the dirt mound to allow him to climb out. He picked up his left leg to begin the very short ascent, but his second step wasn't as well placed and his right leg slipped. Unable to stop his momentum, he face planted into the dirt in front of him. He was stunned. *What had just happened? It felt as if he were standing on ice.* James shook it off, leaned back and brushed as much of the dirt off of himself as he could.

He looked down, saw his own face staring back at him and reeled in surprise.

In the bottom of the crater there was about a square foot of more metal showing, so shiny it had a mirror finish. James forgot all about the other piece he'd dug up, fell down on his knees and began to dig again. He worked at it for a few minutes and continued to unearth more and more. By this point, he had uncovered about five square feet. No edges in sight, no seams. Nothing to break up the glistening mirror finish.

Afternoon had come and gone, it was approaching evening. James realized time was slipping away and it was time to head back home. He climbed out of the crater, this time making sure he had a good foothold. He picked up the hunk of metal and headed back to the truck. The whole discovery had kept his mind elsewhere and he never once thought of the wall behind him. He headed straight to the truck and placed his find in the bed then proceeded home.

"What happened to your hand?" his mom asked as he entered the living room.

"Nothing much, just cut it on the equipment I was working on." He hated lying to his mom, but didn't think he should explain what he had been up to that day until he figured out what it all meant.

"Come into the kitchen and I'll get you fixed up."

He followed her into the kitchen where she opened a cupboard and grabbed bandages and ointment.

"Mom, do you know anyone who's gone out to the

wall?"

She turned and looked over her shoulder at him. He could tell she was uneasy at the question. "No, why do you ask?"

"I was out tending to my chores and, while driving the fields, I took in its size and began to wonder."

"Wonder what dear?" she waived him over to the sink and began washing his hand. "You cut it pretty good, but I think you'll be fine."

"I was wondering what was beyond the wall. I know we're taught what's beyond, but has anyone ever seen it?"

"Somebody had to build the wall. It's for our safety. I never really gave it too much thought. I think what the books say is the truth, and if it keeps us safe, I'm okay without seeing the other side."

James winced as the hot water ran through his cut. It was pretty deep, but didn't do any serious damage. He looked at his mom and she smiled back at him.

"Thanks, Mom," he said, returning the smile.

She finished up, dried her hands and turned to grab her apron. "I'm going to start dinner shortly."

"I'll skip it tonight; I have some work to do on the machines."

"At least take a couple apples," she admonished as she tossed him two enormous Honeycrisp apples, his favorite.

"Thanks, Mom," he turned to head out.

"Don't work too hard, you still have school tomorrow!" she shouted as he left the house.

James headed to his truck, which he'd left near the

barn. He stopped to assess his find. As he examined it, he thought something seemed oddly familiar about it. He picked it up, very carefully this time as he didn't need any more cuts, the one he had was burning enough as it was, then walked into the barn and considered the two giant harvester machines inside. His father had been prepping them for the coming harvest and multiple panels lay open.

James set the scrap on the workbench and proceeded over to harvester #4. He crawled into one of the compartments; it was large enough to stand in but had multiple tubes, wires and other mechanical parts that made it difficult to move around. He maneuvered himself into the heart of the machine where he found the power supply panel. It had only been opened once to his knowledge, during a summer when he was ten. It was essentially maintenance free and merely required monitoring through steam dials on the exterior of the machine. His father had replaced it that summer. The replacement came from out of town, but he was young and didn't really ask any more about it.

James pulled a Phillips head screwdriver from his back pocket and began unscrewing the panel that hid the heart. After some time, and almost 20 screws, he had the last one loose and pulled off the cover. There it was, the power supply. It was a chrome box with a mass of wires and pipes that were attached to the steam gauges protruding from it, but it was the chrome he wanted to find. Even in the dimly lit bowels of the machine, he saw his image staring back at him again. It looked like the same metal as the piece he found in the field. He touched it; it was smooth as ice and cold. *Could it be made of the same material? But the object had fallen from the sky. The power supply was extraterrestrial.*

"How are things going in there?" he heard his father ask out of nowhere.

"Just tidying up a few things in here," he responded, placing the plate back and tightening the screws.

"Good. Mom just wanted to make sure you still didn't want any supper."

"I'm good, thanks. I'd like to get ahead of some of these tasks before the season hits."

"Okay. If that's the case, can you clean out the bailing bay on #3 and figure out where the twine is binding?"

"Sure," James answered, still sliding the screws into place and tightening them as fast as he could.

"Thanks, James. You're a pretty good kid," he heard his father reply. Then silence.

James finished the last screw and crawled out from inside the machine. His first thought was on the workbench. *He had left the piece out, had his father seen it? How was he going to explain it if he did?* James walked over to the piece he'd found and tried to think of answers to all of the questions he may be asked. He studied the object, the metal looked the same. He ran his hand over it and it felt the same. He picked it up, being careful not to touch the jagged edges, and examined all sides of it. He tapped on it and it sounded hollow.

"The torch," he snapped his fingers and ran over to grab the cart which held his acetylene torch. In no time, he had it fired up and ready to melt metal. James took the torch and began to place it near the object in hopes of cutting into it to see what was inside. He held the torch an inch from the surface, then cranked it up as hot as he could manage it. The blue flame, steady in a tight V, touched the surface but seemed to do nothing. The metal stayed shiny, it didn't discolor as all of the other metal he had worked with before had done. He pulled the torch away to take a closer look. Nothing. It was like nothing had even touched it.

James placed his hand near the object, no heat radiated. He put it closer, nothing. Finally, he touched it. It was cold. *How could this be?* He had held the torch to it for several minutes. Realizing that using the torch wasn't going to work, he twisted the valves to shut it off. He took a step back and just stared, puzzled. *What was this thing?*

Through the barn door he saw the sun setting. It had been a long day and his body was feeling fatigued. *Better find a place to stash this.* He had a tool cabinet that would do nicely.

That night he had trouble sleeping. No adrenaline drains to help him get to sleep. His mind searched for answers. The wall, the object, Carol's memory loss, he felt they were all connected somehow.

The next thing he knew, his alarm was going off. James shot up in bed. He must have finally fallen asleep.

He grabbed his clothes and headed to the barn. He opened the cabinet and the object was still there shining back at him.

"Gotta think, gotta think," James said under his breath. "Can't miss another day of school. Think, think. Mr. MacDunna. He'll have the answers."

James finished up his chores in record time then headed into school. He was the first one there; most of the teachers hadn't even arrived yet. He waited in his truck thinking of yesterday's discovery.

James woke up to a tapping on his window; he must have fallen asleep waiting.

"You going to sleep all day or are you going to class?" It was Carol, smiling through his dingy window. Behind her stood Jason, Rich and Barbara.

"We were worried about you. Where were you yesterday?"

James squinted his eyes as they readjusted to the sunlight.

"I had a lot of farm work to catch up on."

"Likely story," Jason said. "You just were playing hooky. Where did you go, anywhere fun?"

Jason was teasing, of course. He knew James was as straight-laced as they came. James opened up the door.

"How'd ball practice go yesterday?" asked James.

"Good. I think we're getting better. Since you weren't there, coach had Tommy pitch. He has a new knuckleball, might come in handy when we play those jerks again."

"Glad to hear it."

Fully adjusted to the light, he stepped out of the truck. Rich, Jason and Barbara headed to class. Carol stayed behind.

"You okay, you look like you haven't slept in a few days," she asked with concern.

"Yeah, I'm good. Had trouble falling asleep last night," his voice trailed off.

"Something bothering you, you know you can tell me anything, is it the scholarship?"

He stared off into the distance then breathed a deep sigh.

"You remember the history of the wall and why it was built?"

"Sure, I mean it was a long time ago, I think we were in first grade or so when we had that class."

A whole class. It didn't actually seem like they learned that much from it looking back.

"Do you believe all of it?" he asked Carol, taking her hand as they began to walk toward school.

"Why yes, is there some reason I wouldn't?"

Recent events had filled his head with questions, lots of questions. *Why didn't anyone ever ask questions?* Sure they asked simple questions, but there were larger ones that seemed to be completely ignored or purposely left unvoiced. Like those pertaining to the wall and why it was there. James scowled a bit as they continued to walk. He didn't feel like pushing it too much further and his mind switched back to his goal of speaking with Mr.

MacDunna.

After saying goodbye to Carol and agreeing to take her to the diner after baseball practice, he made his way down the long hallway toward class. He recited in his head the questions he was going to ask Mr. MacDunna. The school bell rang and class started. Mr. MacDunna was drawing the harvester's internal gears on the chalkboard and explaining how they interlocked with each other.

"Now this planetary gear rotates clockwise, spinning around sun gear number 23. It has five speeds based—"

"What powers it?" James interrupted, sitting with his elbows on his desk, hands interlocked as if praying.

"I'm sorry, what was your question, James?" Mr. MacDunna responded.

"I understand how the sun gear works, I've actually fixed that one twice in the past year. I was wondering what powers the machine."

"Well the main drive gear spins the sun gear—"

"No, what powers the whole machine?"

Rex and Tim rolled their eyes at James as if he was asking a stupid question.

"The power supply, is that what you're asking?"

"I understand the power supply drives the machine, but how does it work?"

"How does the power supply work?" his teacher repeated.

James gritted his teeth, took a breath and tried to stay calm. "Yes, how does the power supply work?"

Mr. MacDunna stopped and considered James for a moment, then finally spoke, "That's proprietary information."

James dropped his hands to the desk. "Proprietary, what does that mean? What if I need to fix it?" he asked.

"You can't fix it, just order another one."

"Parts are expensive. I can fix everything else myself much cheaper, why not the power supply?"

"We can discuss it after class if you like, but we need to stay on schedule," the teacher retorted sharply.

He had been shut down. Part of him wanted to start a screaming match, but he composed himself and realized he couldn't win that battle. He slumped back into his chair as the teacher began again, "The planetary gear rotates clockwise..."

The rest of class, James was off in his own world, running things through in his mind. The teacher asked him a few questions and James missed them, asked him to repeat them, then gave him the answer almost verbatim from the book, and let his mind drift again. He had fixed nearly every part of the General Motors Harvester 411, none of it was new to him. Rex and Tim, on the other hand, were not quite as bright and stumbled over most of the answers, but eventually would figure them out. James thought their fathers probably did most of the work on their farms.

The final bell rang. James grabbed his books and headed to his locker. Carol met him there, reminded him of their evening plans, then wandered toward the exit doors. Jason also met him at his locker and the two of them set off to the locker room to change for practice. The drills were typical for a Wednesday, coach liked to keep things regimented, infield and outfield drills, followed by batting practice. Thursdays were a game day so Wednesday practices never lasted long. James went through the motions, but had a little trouble throwing due to his cut finger and asked to sit out. The coach granted his request after checking his hand. He sat mulling over Mr. MacDunna's stance on the power supply. *Why was he so defensive about it?*

The team did their final drill then the coach gathered the team together and went over the procedures for the following day. It was an away game, so they had to leave on the team bus before school let out. James and the team headed back to the lockers to clean up and head home.

"You seemed out of it at practice today, you doing ok?" Jason asked as they began putting on their street clothes.

"Yeah, just have a lot on my mind, not to mention this hand. Not sure how much good I'll be tomorrow."

Jason nodded in understanding. "Still plan on showing up at Sam's tonight?'"

"Yeah, I promised Carol, but I think I'm going to take tomorrow off. Can you cover for me at the game?"

"Sure, I can do that. It's Beltline so we should smoke them. I think it would do you good to heal that finger up. Don't want to mess up that scholarship, right?"

"Right," James responded almost reluctantly.

The scholarship. He had forgotten all about it, but he would have to choose soon.

After picking Carol up from her house, they drove to Sam's. This time, they were the first ones to arrive. They headed inside. *Huh. Will was nowhere to be seen, must be too early for him.* James couldn't remember a time when Will hadn't greeted them outside of the diner. Carol took their usual seat in the booth and James followed.

"Two sodas," she requested as the waitress came over.

"Anything else?" she waited, peering over her note pad expecting something more.

Carol looked at James who was staring out the window. "Not now, thank you," she said in her sweetest voice. She turned to James and leaned into his view. He rapidly blinked his eyes then tightened his eyebrows.

"Pretty quiet on the ride over, you doing okay?"

"A lot on my mind, that's all," he snapped. The lack of sleep was getting to him.

"Is it about what you were asking this morning?" she asked quietly as he gazed into her beautiful green eyes.

The door swung open and Rich, Barbara and Jason stepped in.

"You beat us here? That never happens," Rich said in a condescending voice.

"Not today," James warned, he wasn't in the mood to deal with Rich's arrogance.

"What's wrong, having a bad day?" Rich laughed as he walked toward their booths.

James tried to ignore him.

"Leave him alone, he hasn't slept, he has a big decision to make," Carol chimed in.

"Sorry, big scholarship man. Let's see. Should I get a free ride to college or work my fingers to the bone, breaking my back on the farm? Decisions, decisions."

James, probably out of lack of sleep more than anything else, jumped out of the booth and stalked toward Rich who was still standing there mocking him. James cocked his arm back then clocked him on the chin. He'd had enough of the comments.

Rich rocked back then grabbed his jaw with his hand and screamed bloody murder at James. "Geez! My father's going to hear about this!"

"Or maybe I'll just teach you a lesson." James just stood there staring down Rich, his adrenaline pumping, muscles tensing. He had never been in a fight before, no one had, not since before high school. Rich, wanting to prove how macho he was, began to move forward. He took one step.

"Don't!" Barbara cried. "You know what will happen."

He didn't listen and threw a big right hook at James. James ducked and leaned back out of instinct then watched Rich as he followed through and fell to the floor. Barbara screamed and jumped on top of him.

"He switched off," Jason wondered softly under his breath.

James turned to Carol as tears began to well in her

eyes.

His muscles relaxed, brow knitted, and he focused his attention back on Rich. Barbara had propped him up on her lap and was caressing his head.

Eyes unfocused, Rich came to and shakily asked, "What happened?"

"You switched off," Barbara answered. "You tried to punch James."

The four of them just stared at Rich. They had all heard the stories, and were taught about it in school, but none of them had seen it happen before. If anyone over the age of twelve showed rage or physically threatened someone, their body would shut down. They were taught in school that it was a reflex action, something everyone was born with that took over around puberty. The effects would soon wear off, essentially like passing out, that's what they were taught. No one they knew had ever pushed it that far before. James, realizing what he had done, bent down and offered a hand to Rich.

"I'm sorry, Rich," he apologized. "I'm very tired, it's been a long week."

Humiliated by what happened, Rich gained his composure, slapped James' hand away and hopped back up on his feet. "My father will hear about this," he spat again and stormed out of the diner. Barbara scurried after him.

"Great, there goes my ride," Jason quipped.

James looked over to see him smiling. He groaned, "You live three blocks down."

Jason just laughed, "That was pretty crazy. I've never seen it happen in real life before."

"What if he does tell his father, do you think he's going to pull your scholarship?" Carol asked.

"He can't do that, it comes direct from the college. He only has power here in town," Jason assured.

James sat down, letting his body fall into the seat, and landed with a loud thump.

"You okay?" asked Carol, reaching for his hand.

James put both of his hands on his head, leaned over with his elbows on the table and stared down at it for a minute.

"I don't know what came over me," he lamented.

Jason was still grinning and almost danced as he moved around the table toward James. "Don't worry about it, he deserved it. Wish someone would have stood up to him sooner."

"We should probably get going," James mumbled, dropping his hands and raising his head to look at Carol.

She stroked his forearm with her hand gently. "Yep, probably should, things to do and all that."

The three left the diner, Jason first followed by Carol then James.

"Cigarette?" Will was back outside as they left.

"No thanks," James responded, staring down at the dirt.

"Find anything?"

James glanced up into Will's wondering face, but didn't really register what he'd said, so he kept walking without answering, Carol on his arm. Once in the truck, Carol leaned into him and placed a hand on his thigh.

"You can't be doing too good, I've never seen you like that before, it was a little scary," her brows were raised, her mouth slightly open.

"I know. Just a lot on my mind lately and I'm not sleeping very well." His body showed it too, bags under his slightly bloodshot eyes.

"Well you should get home and rest, you have some big games this weekend."

James put the truck in gear and checked the rearview mirror as he started to reverse. Visions of the meteor impact flashed in his mind. He put the truck in park.

"Remember what I asked you earlier about the wall and what you believe is on the other side?"

Carol placed her hand on his forearm, her gaze intent on his. "Yes," she said slowly.

She was caught off guard, thinking his mind was on the scholarship and how he had just clocked Rich.

"Do you believe what we're taught in school?" he questioned.

"Yes I do, I do believe the Earth is flat."

CHAPTER SIX

James woke up naturally around 6am, he had shut off his alarm clock to try and catch up on his sleep. This morning started similar to yesterday. He'd hurried through his chores, skipped breakfast, grabbed a couple of apples and was in his truck on his way out to the impact site. The sun shone overhead, a few white puffy clouds scattered throughout the sky and the temperature was warm. It would have been a wonderful day for the great game of baseball had the crazy events of the past week not occurred. Still, he tried to enjoy it as he dragged two shovels out of his truck bed. He approached the edge of the field and looked both ways as though he was crossing a street. *What am I doing?*

He stood and gazed up into the sky, then, as he brought his head back down toward earth, the view of the sky was interrupted by the ominous wall.

"Flat," he said to himself, narrowing his eyes. "I guess we would just fall off."

He pictured Rich, full of himself, waving at all the girls, walking along then, oops! Right off the edge. *'Bye Rich.* Coming out of his daydream, he shook his head and started toward the crater. He was less cautious this time and walked straight there. Gazing down into the hole, the mirrored surface reflected back at him. He threw the shovels into the crater. As they hit the floor a metallic echo rang through his ears. James had no idea what he was doing or what he hoped to find, he just jumped in and started digging. He tried to be methodical about it and began clearing the metal toward the wall thinking that closer to the wall he may find something different. This proved fruitless and after a few hours, he was back at the pickup getting water and a snack.

He leaned his back against the truck then slid down to his butt. Sitting on the ground, eating a Honeycrisp, he stared at the crater and the wall beyond.

What's on the other side?

He was never really the inquisitive type in his youth, but the desire for answers erupted in him like a volcano. Finishing his apple, he tossed the core aside and walked back to the crater. He observed his progress, wiping the sweat from his forehead. Then he spotted something. Something he hadn't noticed before. Like the wall in front of him, there looked to be a barely noticeable line in the metal, slightly exposed to the air above. He quickly slid back into the crater and knelt down to examine it. Sure enough, it was a seam, maybe some sort of panel he could use to get access to whatever was underneath.

He began digging with his hands. The seam continued for a foot or so then turned 90 degrees. His hands continued to follow it as he slung dirt everywhere. The more he scraped away, the more excited he became. It turned another 90 degrees. His mind was putting it together, the pattern was emerging. It was definitely a square panel. He finished uncovering it, then stood up and put his hands on his head. There were no screws, no handles, no hinges, no bolts. Just four seams. And they weren't welded. The plate, if you wanted to call it that, fit almost seamlessly into the surrounding metal. He had only noticed it because the dirt that covered the top gave it away. *How was he going to open it?*

James looked up at the sun. It was afternoon by now and he did tell his father he would fix the bailing system in one of the harvesters. He sat down, legs crossed, on the cold metal and stared helplessly at the panel. His excitement from earlier was gone. Picking himself up, he grabbed the shovel and raised it as a lumberjack would an axe to chop wood. With all of his strength and weight, he swung the shovel downward. It ricocheted off the metal and back above his head. The violent impact and repercussion loosened his grip and the shovel went flying out of the hole like a rocket launching off into space. Dazed, he shook his head and climbed up the side of the hole far enough to see the shovel, 20 yards away, sticking straight up out of the ground. He hiked back down, resolute, and pulled a flathead screwdriver out of his side pants pocket, then got on all fours. He tried to place the business end into the seam. No luck, it was too tight. He pulled a pocket knife from another pocket and tried the same thing. The seam fit so perfectly, he couldn't even get the blade into the slot. Defeated, he sat back, head against the dirt behind him with an unfocused stare into the endless blue sky. There he sat for a few moments.

"Think, think," he told himself, as he listed off all of the tools he had back at the barn.

None of them seemed to be able to do much good for

the predicament he was in. He needed to get under that panel. Something was driving him like his life depended on it. Then, like a soft whisper in his ear, a thought came to him.

Will. He must know something. His comments about the field, about finding something. Tired and filthy, he climbed out of the crater and headed to his truck. "I'll try and talk to him tonight, after dinner," he planned. "But first I better fix that harvester."

He headed back to his house for dinner.

"I received a call today from Mr. Crum. Sounds like you and his son had a scuffle yesterday?"

James stirred his mash potatoes with his fork, not looking up at his father. "Yes, well, sort of," his words tripped over themselves.

"Seems like you quite embarrassed him at the diner."

"It was nothing. Just an argument over something stupid."

James' father had his newspaper up, covering his face while asking the questions. "I see," he said, then bent the corner of the newspaper down to look at James. "He said you got him switched off."

James' mom's eyes widened as she looked at him. "Switched off?!" she exclaimed. "Is he ok?"

"Yes, Mom. He's fine. He came to a few seconds later."

Wringing her hands and completely focused on the conversation, she continued, "What caused it?"

"I punched him in the jaw, then he tried to punch

me," James replied, not thinking about the response as he reached for more potatoes.

"You weren't switched off?"

James' father set the newspaper down. "Fix that bailing system, son?"

His mom scowled at his father.

"Yes, just before dinner. I have to go into town to pick up a few things. Is there anything you need while I'm out?" James did his best to remove himself from further questioning.

"No, but I'd like you to check out harvester number 4's drive train when you can. It feels like a gear's slipping."

"Ok, I'll try and take care of that tomorrow," James replied, turning to walk out.

"Don't stay out too late. You look awfully worn," his mother shouted as he left the house

James was on the road heading into town in no time. He passed the usual sights, but as he hit the outskirts of town, saw lights and sirens in front of him. The new Sears was engulfed in flames and he slowed up, following the looky-loos as they passed. Firefighters were doing all they could to put out the blaze. James shook off his momentary distraction. He had someone to meet. His brakes gave a pitiful squeal as he came to a stop in the parking lot.

Outside the diner, Will stood smoking. James sat in his pickup watching him then looked around. He went through the questions he wanted to ask and mustered up the courage to talk to him. No one he knew had been as close to the wall as James had before. *Would he be arrested if somebody found out?* Finally sensing he had to just do it, like ripping off a band-aid, James got out of the truck and marched toward the diner. Hands in his pockets, head on a swivel, he searched left and right for anyone who might be watching. He had never felt more paranoid in his life. He arrived at the diner's entrance.

"Cigarette?" Will queried, his own hanging out of the side of his mouth.

"No thank you, sir," James replied, but stopped next to him.

Will cocked his head back slightly, appraising James with heavy eyes. "You could really use a cigarette."

He seemed to emphasize the word use. James didn't pick up on it at first.

"No thank you, Mr. Will."

James still didn't know his last name, but he was raised to be polite and didn't want to call an older gentle-man he didn't know very well by his first name. Will reached into his pocket and pulled out a small chrome case. He flicked it open to reveal half a dozen cigarettes. James watched intently, trying to figure out what to say next. His mind raced with possibilities. Will's slender fingers slipped a cigarette from the case and, with his arm outstretched, offered it to James. While this occurred, he put away the case and grabbed the cigarette from his mouth with his other hand and dropped it to the ground.

James was about to say no, but Will, stepping on the

cigarette, spoke first, "You need this more than I do kid."

He waved the cigarette at him again. James instinctively took it from his hand.

"Mr. Will..." he began, but before he could continue, Will spun on his heel and walked away with his head down and his hands in his pockets. James stared down at his hand holding the cigarette, perplexed. *What was he going to do with this?* He looked up in time to see Will turn the corner less than a block away. Watching his answers disappear, he took off running to the alleyway. Sliding past, he tried to stop and looked down the alley. He saw no one. Will was nowhere to be seen.

Even more disheveled, James walked back to his truck. He wanted answers and he wasn't going to find any here. He examined the cigarette. It was plain white with a red stripe down one side and near the top, two small letters in black could be read. "TK". He never smoked or even had a desire to try. *Why would Will insist on giving it to him?* He started the truck and headed home.

Sitting on his bed, James held the cigarette up to the light, still questioning what to do with it. He decided he would attempt to smoke it and slipped it between his lips. It tasted terrible.

"How am I going to light this thing?" he questioned aloud.

He remembered his torch in the barn and slid on his boots, quickly running out of the house. Inside the barn, he headed straight to his torch and lit it. Holding the cigarette in his right hand and the torch in the left he placed the cigarette between his lips once again. He then twisted the knob on the torch to the lowest setting.

"This would be much easier with a match," he mumbled as the cigarette bobbed up and down between his lips.

He raised the torch up near the cigarette and inhaled slightly, hoping he was doing it right. Then, before he could react, the whole cigarette caught on fire. "Darn it!" He released it with a panicked shout and dropped it on the barn floor. The cigarette continued to burn. Unnerved, he dropped the torch as well and stomped on the cigarette. After a few twists of his boot, it was out.

"Geez o'Petes," he sighed, looking under his boot. The cigarette lay there in a black twisted mess of paper. But something else was there, too. The ash fell away and a slim metal rod appeared amidst the detritus. He bent down and picked up the charred remains of the cigarette. As he stood up, he lifted it to eye level to examine what was hiding underneath. James wiggled his nose, he smelled something burning and it wasn't the awful cigarette. His eyes grew as large as moons as he realized what he smelled. It was burning wood.

He turned to see the torch lying on the ground and the wood floor of the barn engulfed in flames. Looking left and right, "What do I do, what do I do?!" He quickly grabbed the torch, stepping over the flaming floor, and closed the valve. Surveying the room, he saw a blanket made of canvas and thought to smother the flames. Hurriedly, he grabbed the blanket and threw it on the fire. It lit up the instant it hit. His eyes wild, he searched for something to put out the fire and landed on the open doorway. There was sand outside that he could use. As he ran out of the barn, he passed a large bucket, then turned back to grab it as he realized that water was probably a better option, and tripped over the hose he had forgotten to reel in earlier that week. He grabbed the hose, ran to the spigot, turned on the water then ran the hose in as far as it could reach. It was at around this time that his father showed up. He'd heard the commotion from inside.

"Good heavens, what happened?" he yelled, as he grabbed the bucket.

"I dropped the torch!" James yelled back, franticly trying to keep the water stream on the fire.

His father quickly filled the bucket with sand and ran in to cover the fire. By this time the blaze was about five feet around. The water was having some effect but it wasn't slowing the fire down quickly enough. James' father kept the sand coming in and then his mom showed up and took the hose. James helped his father throw sand on the wooden floor boards as quickly as they could until the fire was out. The crisis had been averted, but the floor was heavily charred.

"I'm so sorry," James started after things calmed down a bit. "I was working on the harvester, making a new plate for #3 and the torch got away from me." Another lie, but he needed to keep the truth a secret until he could figure out more.

"You got to be more careful son," his father looked at him with stern eyes.

"Yes, please be more careful. We could have lost two of the harvesters, not to mention the barn," his mom fretted, wiping sweat from her forehead. "Or worse, you could have been killed!"

"I'm sorry," was all he could get out.

"Let's make sure it's out then get some sleep, it's late."

"Yes, Father," James said solemnly.

They cleaned up while his mom headed inside. James appreciated the help, but he had to find what was left of that cigarette before his father did.

"I'll finish the cleanup," he told his father. "Like Mom said, it's late and this is my doing."

His father nodded then headed to the house. Once out of sight, James started searching like a hound dog on a hunt. He was on all fours, crawling around in the ash, sand and puddles of water, searching in every nook and cranny he could find. Finally, he spotted it amongst the charred remains of the floor boards. It was a long metal cylinder just smaller than a cigarette. James handled it carefully as he scrutinized it. *What was it?*

In his room, cleaned up and lying in bed, he took it out again for a closer examination. There was nothing strange about it. It was just a simple metal rod. *Why would Will have said he needed it?* He placed it on his night stand, exhausted; it would have to wait until morning.

Morning came and James was up at his alarm. He

rolled over and grabbed the rod.

"Why are you important?" he murmured, staring at it. James slipped it into his pocket and accomplished his daily routine then started off to the crater.

He found it as he had left it, metal exposed and the panel lying there, taunting him, as if to say, "Ha, Ha. Beat you, you'll never get in." James slid down into the hole. He was trying to piece the two together. Will had seemed to know about the find, the hole, and gave him the cigarette to complete the puzzle. *Maybe I'm missing something.* He dropped to his knees and worked his way over to the panel, hoping to see something he had missed earlier, then ran his fingers along the seam, nothing. He could barely even feel the seam it was so tight.

Then as his hand brushed one of the corners, a tiny hole became visible. He hadn't noticed it before because the dirt had been hiding it. He moved closer and took a deep breath then blew as hard as he could to clear the sand and dirt away. Sure enough, it was as plain as day now, there was a small hole the size of the rod Will gave him. Excitedly, he reached into his pocket to pull out the rod. He looked at it once more.

"Here's hoping," he said with a triumphant expression on his face, then placed the rod into the hole.

Nothing. James sat there on his knees. The rod had slipped all of the way into the hole until it was flush with the surface, but nothing happened. He didn't really know what to expect, but was anticipating... something. James sat there a few minutes longer, frowning at the panel with pure disappointment. He leaned forward and placed his hands on the panel to push himself up, when suddenly it lit up. The whole panel glowed electric blue. James jumped back startled, stumbling into the dirt wall behind him. He watched as the panel proceeded to depress down an inch or so then slid out of view. A moment later, the dark black hole that stood before him began to radiate a light orange glow.

James hesitated for a second to make sure nothing was coming out of the hole. He had seen enough horror flicks to know not to just thrust his head in there. After what he thought was ample time for a monster to have rushed out and attacked him for setting fire to his windmill, he cautiously approached. As he looked down, he spotted a ladder on one side leading down to a metal floor. The orange glow continued as a light breeze hit his face, blowing from down below. Hesitant, but dying to know what the tunnel was for and where it led, James decided to take a closer look. He knelt down and lowered his head inside. It was a large tunnel about eight feet tall by eight feet wide. The tunnel seemed to go on forever in both directions; orange lights lined each of the four corners of the tube and glowed softly.

James climbed down the ladder. The breeze was stronger now and felt as if it was blowing in the direction of the mystifying wall. He took a harder look down both directions of the tunnel. They appeared identical, but in the distance, he thought he saw a little bit of light radiating in from one end. He decided to head toward the light.

As James walked, he examined the walls around him. They were smooth and had what he thought looked like cables and wires bunched along one side of the tunnel. There was something very familiar about them. *Where had he seen cables and wires bunched together like that before?* He continued to walk, then it dawned on him. The cable and wire bundle resembled what he had seen inside the harvester connecting the power supply. He felt there had to be more answers up ahead and began to jog as his excitement grew. The light became brighter and details started to emerge. There was a grating across the exit, the largest he had ever seen. He slowed to a walk as he approached it, and his eyes focused past it on blue sky. He didn't feel like he'd been in a climb, but couldn't process why he would be seeing sky in what he presumed was an underground tunnel. James put a hand on the grate then noticed the shape of a door to his right. He slowly approached it and saw grooves that looked like a depressed handle. He grabbed it and gave a tug. With a sound like compressed air releasing, the door slid out of sight. Behind it was a small room with a wall full of buttons on his right.

He stepped inside and gazed at the glowing, blue buttons. A word was written next to each button: "B-Air duct", "1-Earth Level", "2-Defensive Engagement Level", "3-Lookout". James stared at the buttons. *Where was he? Where would the buttons take him?* After a few moments he decided to push the "Earth Level" button, thinking he could stop and get his bearings. He reached out and pressed the button.

"Earth Level," a strange, scratchy voice said.

The door closed behind him. He felt the floor move; he had never had that sensation before, and grabbed the wall as he stumbled back.

"Earth Level," the voice cracked again as the floor stopped moving.

A door on a different wall opened. James squinted against the onslaught of light radiating in and cupped a hand over his eyes to shade them.

"Boy, I wish I had my ball cap," he muttered as he proceeded out the door.

He stepped out onto more black colored metal, his eyes beginning to adjust to his surroundings. James' jaw slowly dropped open. All he could see was blue sky and what he thought was dimly lit stars in the sky. Clouds drifted by and there seemed to be no horizon. He felt as if he could walk right into the sky. He heard the hissing sound again and spun around to see the door close.

He realized where he was. His eyes trained up and up and up, following endless metal panels. He was on the outside of the wall, but merely a few feet from it. This was the closest he had ever been and he was on the other side.

He stood there examining it; the grooves, the panels, it all looked like a magnified version of what he remembered seeing through his binoculars all those years ago. Then it hit him.

"Flat Earth," he said out loud. "You'll fall off the

Earth, so they built walls to protect us."

It was almost verbatim out of one of the history books he'd read in school. The books never detailed who "they" were, it was just assumed that it was the people of Earth's ancestors. He spun around and carefully stepped forward, almost shuffling. He continued for about ten yards then stopped. There was something in the distance. It looked faintly like a table top but it was tilted away from him, as if he was underneath the kitchen table peering up. James continued until his feet were on the edge of the steel he stood on. Bit by bit, he leaned forward. The ground completely fell off, straight down. Clouds covered most of what was underneath, and the table top was now covered in clouds. *The Earth is flat!*

CHAPTER SEVEN

The wind rushed over his face and swirled around his feet up toward his head. *The Earth is flat.* He wasn't quite sure what to make of it. Growing up, plenty of his friends questioned it, but they were given compelling evidence for it and eventually just accepted it. James used to wonder how true it was, and to some extent he still nurtured those questions, but for fear of being an outcast, he'd kept it to himself and suppressed the urge to seek answers. *They were right.*

He stood there taking in the view. He did take a few steps back; he never was very fond of heights. James looked around as the clouds continued to glide by, then turned to head back to the wall. As he made his way, something caught his eye. The land around the outside of the wall was smooth and had little to no features or contour to it, but in the distance, something looked out of place. James decided to investigate. It was probably getting close to lunchtime by now and he felt he had plenty of time to get home before dark. He began to walk toward the anomaly, his mind filled with questions about the wall and whether or not his friends and parents would believe him, or if he should even mention it in the first place.

As he approached, the object came into focus. It might have been something out of a space movie he'd seen at the theater with Carol. It was triangular and completely made of chrome. He saw his reflection growing as he stepped closer. His eyes were even with its top and he guessed it to be about ten feet long. Standing a foot away, he began to circle it. It almost looked like a chrome arrowhead ready to be fired out of a large cannon to wreak havoc on anything it opposed. He stopped after one lap and scratched his head. *What was it?*

Tentatively, he reached his hand out to touch it. As his hand came to rest on the top, he heard a strange mechanical voice.

"DNA match." James jumped back as if he'd been shocked with high voltage.

The top depressed then slid forward along the sharp contours of the chrome object. His eyes were as big as dinner plates. *What was DNA? How had he made the top open?* He moved closer. Inside was a seat in the center and a horizontal cup-like object next to the far wall. He moved closer still to peer down into it. On the opposite wall laid another horizontal cup. Near the front of the seat was a dash, like on his truck, but smooth and shaped with sleek curves. The whole object didn't have a sharp bend or corner anywhere to be seen. *Could this be a spaceship? But those were only found in movies and comic books, they didn't exist. Did they?*

Fascinated by the machine, James thought it wouldn't hurt to climb in and take a closer look. He lowered himself down into the seat, his eyes skimming over the extraterrestrial machine. The seat contoured around his body like a pillow; he felt as if he were floating. He ran his fingers around the edges of the two cups; each looked like you could put a hand into it. Intuitively, he slipped his hands into them and felt a vertical bar inside. He cupped his hands around the bar, like he was holding a baseball bat, it was a comforting feeling.

"DNA verified, initiating start sequence," the voice crackled.

James quickly let go of the handles. The hatch door closed over his head and he frantically pushed on it hoping it would open.

"Auto mode initiated," spoke the ship as it seemed to disappear around him. All that he could see were the controls and the seat. James could see the Earth moving away from him.

"Nooo!" he screamed in a panic, jumping out of the seat.

He came back down quickly as his head hit something solid. James rubbed the spot where he hit his head and glanced up. There was nothing there, he couldn't see anything but sky. He reached up and felt the canopy. It was definitely still there, only invisible. James began to search around the seat for anything that may help him reverse course and land back on Earth. He saw nothing but the two cups, the seat, and the ground falling away from him. The wall and the Earth continued to shrink and then he was thrown back into his seat as he felt immense pressure in his chest. Instinctively, he thrust his hands into the cups and grabbed onto the handles inside.

"Manual override denied," the voice crackled.

The blue sky turned dark and stars came into view.

It was one of the most beautiful sights he had ever seen. The craft continued to climb until he was surrounded by blackness, just the twinkling of stars to keep him from feeling caught in a void. The pressure was gone and he couldn't even tell if he was moving. He lost himself in his thoughts and time seemed to stand still as he admired the stars. He had never seen them so brilliant before. Then, a small sphere appeared in front of him snapping him out of his daze. It continued to grow as he tightened his gaze to make out what it was. Something was familiar about it, but he couldn't quite figure it out. Then he recognized it, there was no denying it. The moon.

The sphere grew larger as he approached. He tried to come to grips with the fact that spaceships were real, he was in one and he was headed to the moon. James stared with his mouth hanging open, trying to comprehend what he was seeing. The craft continued its path straight toward the white glow, never changing course or correcting, as if it was on a string. James could now see exactly where he was heading. A crater, the ship seemed to be aiming dead center into a crater, and he wasn't slowing down. In fact, James felt like he was accelerating. The moon got larger and larger, his hands tightened on the grips, the speed increased, in no time he would impact the surface. Unconsciously, he closed his eyes and gritted his teeth; this was surely going to be his end.

The moment passed. He gradually opened his eyes to be met by a familiar electric blue glow. Four lines of lights surrounded him as he traveled through a small corridor. The tunnel was just large enough for the ship, which had finally slowed. He looked up ahead to see a yellow-orange light coming from the end of the tunnel. The ship quickly approached it, and then out it flew into an open space. James gazed in wonder. Metal buildings were all around, thousands of feet high, like pictures he had seen of New York City and the Empire State Building, only these complexes were several hundred feet taller, sleek and chrome, with windows everywhere. He could see people inside the closer ones. Below, what appeared to be a silver snake ran along a track. James determined it must be a train. He looked up, his eyes squinting because the light was so bright. It was coming from what he thought of as the sky. He thought that the light must be coming from the sun in the sky there above the city, but he could see the outward curvature of the surface and realized he was inside the moon, so it couldn't be the sky. Though it appeared almost exactly like that of Earth, without clouds.

The ship continued its path through the sky and between buildings. He saw more people walking around, some stretching in their windows. Most were wearing well-tailored clothing in monochromatic shades of white, grey or very light blue, but some wore jackets in neutral shades as well. James passed an indoor park with trees, flower gardens, and people jogging. Everything appeared clean and organized, but the city had a sterile, almost calculated feel. He saw a large egg-shaped building with the words "Interstellar Bank Badgers, MLB champions"

on the side. *Baseball, they have baseball on the moon?*
The ship continued on its course and James saw more
buildings, trains and flying ships which littered the sky.
He looked ahead and noticed that he was heading straight
for a medium-sized building. The craft continued and as
he neared the building, it began to slow. He approached
a panel in the wall and it slid open to reveal a square
room. The ship entered and came to rest on the floor.
The light disappeared as the panel shut.

James sat there in the dark a moment then soft white
light filled the room. The ship's skin became opaque
again and the canopy slid open. He crawled out as fast as
he could, he had never wanted to stand on solid ground
more in his life than at that moment. On one knee, James
stood up to gain his composure and figure out where he
was and what he was going to do. He was on the moon
for all he knew, thousands of miles from home. *What
was he doing here? How was he going to get back?* So many
thoughts spun through his head. His first instinct was to
climb back into the spacecraft and try to figure out how
to fly it home. This proved fruitless as all he could get
the ship to do was constantly say, "Denied" in that crack-
ling synthetic voice.

It reminded him of those harebrained space horror
movies he had seen. He really wanted to make it
home, he was out of his element and longed for familiar surroundings. James searched the room for an exit,
there seemed to be a door on the opposite end of where
he was standing. He made his way over to it. The walls

were very sterile except for the occasional cable running along it. Standing in front of the door, he couldn't see any handles or latches. He didn't see a way to open it and then he remembered the ship. He had placed his hand on it and it had opened, maybe he would be able to do the same with the door. He raised his hand and took a step forward to touch the door. Before he touched it, the door slid open. He froze as a body came flying at him, drilling him in the chest. He was planted like a running back being hit by a linebacker. They tumbled five feet to the base of the spaceship.

"Get in the Tetriack, now!" he heard a commanding voice yell at him.

"The what?" he looked up to see icy blue eyes staring back at him with a scowl.

"The Tetria...the ship, get in the ship!"

James heard explosions as large flashes of light appeared. He could see more flying through from the open door.

"Get. In. There. Now."

His tackler pushed off of him, spun around and began firing a pistol back at the open door. Light flashed all over the place as James leapt to his feet. He scrambled over to the ship, slipping once. The blasts were going off all around him, some zipping right by his head; he could feel the energy as they passed almost like a static shock. He jumped into the ship and his tackler jumped on top of him. He let out an "Oomph!" He had not been ready for the impact. His tackler grabbed his hand and placed

it on the inside of the canopy just as a blast hit right next
to it and he recoiled. His hand was again forced on the
canopy.

"DNA accepted, start sequence initiated."

"Auggghh, these old relics are so slow!" he heard his
tackler cry out, frustrated.

It was a girl! She swung her head over as she
seemingly touched random parts of the closing canopy.
At each touch, a light tone could be heard. James sat
there in shock for a moment watching her long, wavy red
hair flowing back and forth as she worked the machine.
It wasn't a natural red like he had ever seen before, but
a fake, American flag colored red. She was small but
muscular, which he could feel every time she moved,
and his chest had felt it when she came flying into him
through the door.

"Move," she said, pushing his hands away from the
cups and sliding her hands inside.

The blasts continued outside but were muffled by the
now closed canopy.

"Open hangar bay door," she commanded.

"Hangar bay door opening," the voice replied.

The ship spun 180 degrees, its opaque skin dissolving
away. James looked outside to see two robotic humanoid
things walk through the door, still firing blasts at him and
this tiny girl as they exited the hangar bay.

Silence. James sat there trying to figure out the right
words. He watched the city drift by as they climbed
higher and noticed that the ship now smelled like an odd

combination of burnt air and sunflowers. He wondered if the light flashes from earlier had anything to do with that. The girl touched the air in front of her and letters and numbers filled the front screen. He could read it, but had no clue what any of it meant. "Shield Power Level". "Cannon Reactors". "Starfinder Navigation System". But then he noticed something that he didn't think was good flashing in the lower right corner, the words "Fusion Cell Reactor Core Failing". It was at this moment he could hear a low beeping sound, then saw flashes all around him. He glanced back to see two ships following them, their light blasts skipping off the sides of the craft.

"Come on, hold." The girl tapped on more digitized buttons in front of her.

The beeping sounds began to get louder. "Fusion Core malfunction, power at 20% and falling," the ship's voice announced.

"Bless it!" she shouted. "Hold on."

Instinctively he grabbed around her waist. The ship spun upside down, the girl was pressed into him as they descended downward in a quarter of a loop. Pressure relaxed as the ship now faced the ground below and it was coming at them fast. He looked back. The two ships had almost mirrored the maneuver and were gaining on them. They had ceased their firing, but were still in hot pursuit. He could make out people walking across a bridge as they sped by.

"Fusion cell at 9%," the ship bellowed.

He saw the girl reach up and tap a few parts of the

canopy, then felt the rush of wind enter the cockpit as the canopy opened.

"This is going to suck, hold on as tight as you can." She manipulated the controls, pulling the ship out of the dive, so that they were now speeding along a corridor far below the building tops.

James looked down, the metal floor of the city seemed inches away as they rocketed toward another building. He looked up to see a dead end approaching. As the girl frantically pushed buttons, he tightened his grip. James grimaced as immediate impact arrived. The ship flipped upside down and made a climb toward the building tops. They were thrown out of the craft. James watched it for a moment above them, sailing even faster into the sky. The two trailing ships followed and began firing once again at the renegade ship. He felt as if time and sound had slowed down. His body, now weightless, was being hurled at the building in front of them. He held on tight to the girl and put his body in between hers and the building, he didn't know what else to do, then the pain hit. His back smacked the building and she crushed him from the other side. Pain shot down his legs as they bounced off the building and landed on the metal floor below. James lay there a moment, his arms went lax and he released his grip on the girl. Staring at the sky above, he saw an explosion as their getaway ship burst into flames. The two pursuit ships circled then sped off together. The girl rolled over and looked down at him. His ears were ringing, but he could still faintly hear her voice and feel her weight on his chest.

"Can you get up?" she asked, but his eyes started to become heavy.

He saw the girl with the beautiful blue eyes leaning over him, her hair curtained their faces.

"Stay awake," she lightly slapped his face, which momentarily sparked some life.

"Sunflowers," he mumbled, then closed his eyes.

"James, can we go get a shake?" Carol asked.

"Sure," he replied. He was standing next to his truck in the school parking lot thinking about buying his mom her favorite flowers.

Then it dawned on him. *How did he get there?*

"James, let's go. Our friends are waiting for us at the diner."

James stood there trying to remember his last steps, what he was doing, how he got there.

"One second," he replied to Carol.

He looked at his hands, then down at the ground, then finally at Carol who was now seated in the passenger seat. He opened his truck door and plopped into the driver's seat.

"Wake up," Carol said.

"What?" James replied as his eyebrows rose.

"Wake up," Carol said as she leaned over and slapped him.

Suddenly, he felt a tug on his shirt. His vision, which had gone hazy from the slap, came back to him. He was back on the metal floor and was being dragged down a tight corridor.

"Can you walk?"

He leaned his head back and rolled his eyes up to see her. The red-headed girl was dragging him, not very well; she was much smaller than him. He tried to move his legs, but they wouldn't respond. Fear shot through him. He couldn't move or feel them. He tried to wiggle his toes, nothing. It was like they didn't exist.

"I can't, I can't move my legs," he said in a slight panic.

He felt his shirt released and the girl moved in front of him kneeling on one knee.

"I was afraid of that." She chewed her bottom lip. "You broke your back when we hit the building. I'm sure we lost the trackers though."

James stared at her in disbelief. *Would he walk again? What was she doing? Why had she shown up being chased by those robotic men?* So many questions filled his head then finally he blurted one out. "Where am I?"

"New Atlantis." She reached around his waist to feel his back. "It's definitely broken. I need to get you to Dr. Vesalius."

She stood up. He watched her place her hand on the wall and a door hissed open next to him. It was at this time that he finally got a good look at her. She wore skin tight, light blue pants that left little to the imagination and a slightly baggy cropped coat resembling a varsity jacket, only it was a solid dark tan color. Her shirt was the same color as her pants and around her chest were leather straps and what looked like holsters housing pistols on each side. He looked away as quickly as he could. He had never seen a girl dressed like that before and felt guilty for staring at her initially. As he turned away, two humanoid robots appeared down the corridor and headed straight for them.

"Halt. Identification required to access that section," the robots demanded.

"Crap!" James felt a tug at his back. She hastily dragged him into the room and dropped him on the floor then hopped out into the alley. The door shut and he was left in the dark. He heard blasts and a couple of screams from outside then the door opened and he saw a silhouette of one of the robots. James watched as the humanoid fell through the door. The girl stepped in, looked at something on her wrist, then walked back over to him.

He scanned the room as she approached. It was full of boxes, like a storage facility. He watched her walk past him and up to a wall. She placed her hand about chest high on the wall. Letters appeared and she began typing. As she typed, she kept glancing at her wrist, then after a few more strokes a large ten foot by ten foot door hissed open. She ran back to James, grabbed the back of his collar and began to pull him toward the open door. Suddenly, the outside door opened. James' eyes grew wide as he tried to help get in the door. His arms still worked and he pushed as best he could.

"About time you helped."

She pulled a weapon from her right holster and tossed

it in his lap.

"What's this?" he asked

"Your survival. Shoot them."

She continued to drag him and almost as soon as the weapon hit his lap, another robot appeared.

"Stop what you are doing and give up the boy!" the robot shouted, stepping through the doorway.

"Shoot it!" the girl shouted. "Just like one of the pistols on Earth."

James had no idea what he was doing. He'd learned about pistols, but never fired one in real life. He grabbed it and tried to aim.

"Pull the trigger!" she shouted, still dragging him.

His finger found the trigger and he squeezed. A loud sound went off and a bolt of light fired from the gun. He had no idea how to aim and his first shot nearly hit the ceiling above the robot. It continued to advance. He felt the girl release him then saw four bolts of light fly over his head shortly followed by loud blasting sounds. They hit their target, two into the chest and two into the head of the robot. The robot collapsed.

"We'll work on it." She grabbed the pistol from his hand and holstered it.

She finished pulling him into the room. Inside, the girl placed her hand on the wall near the door and pushed a few buttons. The doors shut and he felt his body pressed to the floor as the room accelerated up.

"Who's Vestibular?" James asked.

The girl laughed. "Vesalius is a surgeon who'll fix

your back. The problem is getting you there."

"Oh," James replied, feeling a bit relieved. "Will I be able to walk again?"

"Yes, don't worry about that. Like I said, the hard part will be getting there, especially having to drag you everywhere." She glowered at him, "Why did you have to be so big?"

He shrugged. He realized he didn't know her name. "I'm sorry I didn't properly introduce myself, my name is James. What's yours?"

"James, huh?" she began. "I thought it was J."

"J like just the letter or Jay like a bird?" he replied very confused.

"J. Just the letter," she stated with one eyebrow quirked. "I'm Ariel, and before you ask, yes, my parents were big Disney fans."

"Disney fans?" James mouthed "Disney" trying to understand.

"Walt Disney," she stated as if everyone should know who he was.

"The cartoon mouse guy?" James didn't quite understand what her name had to do with a cartoon mouse but decided to let it be, she had already picked up on the fact he didn't know much about the subject. Luckily her attention was drawn elsewhere. As the elevator continued to climb, windows appeared and sunlight shone through. James was amazed at how fast they were climbing and the fact that he couldn't feel it. The buildings out the window all had similar shapes with rounded corners and chrome everywhere. He wondered how they were kept so spotless.

"Almost there," Ariel said. "Ten more floors then we're going to have to move quick."

James looked down at his legs and fear crept back into his mind now that the immediate threat was gone. The elevator rattled as it stopped. Ariel grabbed his collar and began pulling.

"A little help would be appreciated," she grunted with the effort of dragging his dead weight.

James tried his best to push his body along with his arms, it seemed to help a little but not much. Once through the doors, he realized they were outside, at least, that's what it felt like. In the back of his mind he began to remember he was actually inside the moon, but he couldn't tell. He looked up to see Ariel punching at her wrist again. He could see it better now; it was a small bracelet projecting a picture on her arm, she was tapping the buttons that appeared.

"We have five minutes," she stated. "Here," she passed him the blast pistol, that's what he was calling it in his head.

"Cover the door, I'll check the roof."

"But how do I aim this thing?" James looked at the pistol skeptically.

It was shaped like an "L". The long section was comprised of three large tubular attachments with a smaller tube in the middle. The handle looked almost like antique wood and seemed to be a bit small for his hand.

"Here," Ariel came over and grabbed his hand.

"Like this," she pointed the blaster at the door. "Look down the barrel and pull the trigger when anything comes through the door, got it?"

"Yes, I think so." The adrenaline from their escape had completely worn off by now and pain was radiating through his upper body.

He watched Ariel walk away with her other gun in hand. For the first few moments, he focused on the door, aiming the blaster as instructed, but his curiosity got the better of him and his eyes began to wander. The roof was flat with a couple of large can-like structures protruding into the sky. The edges were surrounded by two feet of metal wall, presumably for safety. He gazed out over the city and saw that it gradually climbed as if it were built inside a basketball, this was the only giveaway that he was inside a sphere. The sun above his head shined bright, but the temperature was nice, right in the sweet spot, he guessed about 72 degrees.

The elevator door opened and his eyes swung over followed by his head and blaster-filled hand. It was another one of those robots.

"Do not move, you are being taken into custody."

James hesitated. Ariel told him to shoot anything that came out, but he had never shot anything before.

He let two shots fly and watched as the robot twitched and spun as the shots hit its shoulder and chest region. It fell to one knee then picked itself up. James shot another blast and missed over its right shoulder.

"Hostile action taken, deadly action authorized," the robot's voice boomed as it raised its weapon arm.

The arm exploded from the robot's shoulder and came flying at James, narrowly missing him. He closed his eyes as he tried to duck, then opened them in time to see the robot hit again in the chest by another blast. Ariel ran over to check on him.

"One minute, then we'll be out of here," she reassured.

Just then, he noticed something above and behind her. It looked like a small ship, but as it neared it wasn't so small. It had a similar shape to the one he'd arrived in, but was larger and had more jagged contours. The craft slowed as it reached the building top, stopping at a hover above the floor. A door lifted open and he could see two individuals inside. One hopped out and ran over. He was the biggest person James had ever seen. The man had to have been over 6'8" and his body was all muscle. He had short brown hair and his eyes were a strange yellow-orange.

"This him?" he asked Ariel.

"No, he's inside. I just found this guy laying here."

He quirked an eyebrow at Ariel then realized she was messing with him. He reached down and almost effort-lessly flipped James onto his shoulder.

"Crap, I thought you guys were cloaking," Ariel stated.

"We were, but you know we have to uncloak to board," the giant retorted.

James understood the girl's concern. Past the ship, he could see a dozen other craft inbound. Ariel ran and jumped into the ship.

"Hurry, Zane!" she yelled.

James could feel the pace of the large man quicken and within no time, he was onboard the ship being tossed into a chair. He grunted and gritted his teeth as the jarring increased the pain radiating throughout his body. He watched the door shut in front of him as both Zane and Ariel disappeared. With his legs immobile all he could do was sit there as the pain continued to increase. He felt his eyes getting heavy and struggled with all his might to stay awake. Finally, his battered body got the best of him and he passed out.

CHAPTER EIGHT

James opened his heavy eyelids, his mouth felt dry and hung open and he could feel a bit of drool slipping from the corner. He wiped it away with his forearm. His eyes adjusted to the light in the room. He was lying on a table, smooth and pure white, and it seemed to match every contour of his body like the seat in the craft he'd found on Earth. He raised his head and looked around a room that wasn't much larger than his table, maybe four feet on each side. The walls were white, the ceiling was white. The only thing in there that was not white was him. A door opened behind him.

"How are you feeling, J?" a familiar voice asked.

He turned to see Ariel walk up beside him. At the question, he realized the pain was gone. He looked down at his legs and moved them. He could feel them just as before the accident. Excitement and relief swept through his body.

"How's the patient?" another voice said as the door hissed open once again.

A small young brunette walked in; she looked as if she was maybe 12 years old, but had an air of confidence found in a much older woman. In her hand she held a device and began waiving it over his abdomen. It was at this point he realized he was in his underwear and nothing else. He tried to hide his embarrassment, but it still showed all over his face. He quickly tried to spark up a conversation as a distraction.

"So, how long until I'll be fully healthy?"

"I'd say about now," the young girl replied.

"But how and who are you?" James asked with a look of disbelief.

She continued to move the device around then tilted it toward him.

"I'm your surgeon, Dr. Mallow. Your spine was replaced with a titanium alloy. Your discs were also replaced and your nerves repaired. The procedure is really quite simple."

He stared down at a small square box with a picture of a skeleton inside. The picture showed his bones as though none of his flesh even existed, the bone was bright white and the replaced parts gleamed back shiny and new. James had no idea what to say, but then a question popped into his head almost unrelated.

"I thought you were taking me to see a Dr. Vasalis?" He glanced over at Ariel and caught her snickering.

"Did she say that?" Dr. Mallow replied.

He turned again to see Dr. Mallow glaring at Ariel. "First, it's Vesalius, and second, only Ariel calls me that. I think she gets a kick out of my reaction to it."

James looked again at Ariel who was still smiling.

"My friends call me V. It rolls off the tongue better and I'm not big into titles."

At heart she was still a teenage girl, but her mind was leaps and bounds ahead of her years. She was the youngest doctor in the city and her parents had both been doctors, reconstructive surgeons to be precise.

"You need to get moving. I suppressed your DNA results from the surgery, but with the Kontrolery systems in place, you'll eventually show up. When Ariel gets you to Nova, we can download all the data in your head."

"DNA? Download? Data? What are you talking about?" James asked.

"I'll explain on the way. Like she said, we need to get going. Tracking you will be relatively easy for them, even with us suppressing the information. Here're your clothes." Ariel threw a pile of clothes at him, nothing like he was used to.

"Is there a room where I can change?"

"Just throw it on here, nothing we haven't seen before," Ariel said with a mischievous grin.

Sensing his shyness, V called her over and the two began to talk in the corner. He sat up and pulled the first piece out of the pile. It was a pair of canvas colored pants with pockets all over the place and leather straps wrapped around the legs and waist. He slid them on and, as his hands reached his hips, the waist automatically tightened. He gasped like a frightened child glancing over at the two girls. They seemed unfazed. He moved on to the shirt which was long-sleeved, black and skin tight. On each wrist was a 4 inch square mirror. The next piece was a leather jacket, similar to Ariel's, but thankfully this one was larger and covered his waist.

"Are we ready?" Ariel asked, seeming antsy. "Oh, shoes," she said then reached down to pick up a pair from the ground and tossed them to him.

He took a seat and tugged the first one on. It tightened like the pants, but was amazingly comfortable; it felt as though he was wearing nothing. He slipped the second on with the same response then stood up. It felt like he was walking on soft pillows.

"We can't fly, so we have to take an underground route. They'll be actively searching for us, so I need you to put this on." She frisbee'd a baseball cap to him.

"A baseball cap?"

"Yep, here put it on and let me show you." Ariel walked over to him as he put it on. She reached up and placed both hands over his ears and looked into his eyes. He gazed back at the intense blue then felt a shock around his forehead. He recoiled back.

"What was that?" James shouted.

Ariel turned to walk to the door. "Face suppression. It changes the appearance of your face. Always stings like the dickens when you turn it on."

"What about you? You seem to be on the run yourself. Where's your hat?"

"You're new here so we didn't have any DNA to put into the system and manipulate. We have an insider who changes what the mediators see. It will take some time to get that input so we can roll different codes."

James was confused about the whole thing, none of it made sense. He wanted to start asking questions, but Ariel opened the door.

"This way, we have to move quickly."

He followed her out the door and into a long white

hallway. They walked down to the end and, rounding the corner, saw two robots at the end of another long hallway. Ariel slowed her pace and James almost ran into her.

"Slow down, we don't want to draw any attention from the mediators."

James stared at the humanoid robots. "Is that what they're called? Mediators?"

"Yes, think of them as police. They keep the peace in the city when things get out of hand, but lately their numbers have grown and they're everywhere."

Ariel and James veered down a hall, away from the threat, and found their way to an elevator. They rode it down multiple floors until they reached the bottom and what James thought of as street level. There were multiple people walking around, and while his clothes made James feel asinine, he fit right in. He saw similar outfits amongst the passersby. There were no cars, but multiple trains zipped by. They were sleek looking, and seemed to run on tracks every couple of floors. The tracks jutted out of the sides of the buildings and he watched them stopping at various locations as he and Ariel walked.

"What is this place?" James questioned, eagerly wanting answers.

"It's New Atlantis, but most call it Atlantis for short."

"You told me that already, but who are all these people? Are they alien, are you an alien?"

Ariel laughed. "No I'm human, like you. There have been no aliens ever found to my knowledge."

"But, then where did you come from?"

"You're trying to figure out the bigger picture right? In short, Earth, like you, but a very long time ago."

James studied her. "How old are you?"

"You should know better than to ask a woman her age," she replied with a mischievous grin.

"I'm sorry, I..."

Ariel began to laugh. "I'm just kidding, I'm 19. Were you expecting me to be like a hundred?"

"You said you came here a long time ago, so yes, I was assuming—"

She cut him off. "My ancestors came from Earth. I've lived here my whole life."

They continued walking and passed several store fronts which pulled James' attention away momentarily. Some of the stores were familiar, such as markets and clothing stores. But others had all sorts of strange looking devices inside. Then one in particular caught his attention, a diner. It was just like Sam's from back home. His mind went to Carol. *What was she doing right now? She wouldn't believe what happened to him. Not to mention that he was actually on the edge of the Earth and now on the moon.* His stomach growled, he couldn't remember the last time he had eaten.

"Can we get something to eat?"

"Sure," replied Ariel. "Sam's Diner is right here. Let's grab something quick, we want to minimize your exposure."

"Sam's Diner?"

"Yeah, it's a chain restaurant. They're all over the city.

Guess people still like the nostalgia of the 20th century."

His mind started spinning. *She made it sound like he was in the future. Could the ship he travelled on have been a time machine?*

They walked into the diner. It was set up exactly like the one on Earth, with one exception. On the wall behind the counter, there were multiple screens, and on them a baseball game was being played.

"What's that?" he said pointing at a screen.

"That's an MLB game; looks like the Redheads are beating the Badgers 4-1."

"No, the thing you see it on?"

"Oh, I keep forgetting all this is new to you. That's a DS, they used to be called televisions and were invented after radios."

The only moving pictures he had seen were movies at the theater. *How could it be contained on such a small device?*

"Wait, you have baseball on the moon?"

"Yeah, but it's pretty barbaric if you ask me."

"Barbaric? Baseball?" James asked with raised eyebrows.

"The players are all from Earth, on scholarship, but all that means is they're required to play ball. If they struggle, they're discarded."

"Discarded?"

"The general public doesn't know most of this, but they're killed. They can't go back to Earth with what they know, it's too hard to wipe that much memory. And they're not from here, so they have no use other than baseball."

James realized he could have been one of the players on the screen. He sat down in a booth, pondering the turn his life had taken. Relieved. He no longer had to make that decision.

"So, am I in the future?"

Ariel laughed, still getting a kick out of his questions. She thought everyone knew these things, but remembered he had come from Earth and wasn't accustomed to his new surroundings.

"No, we've never mastered time travel, never even got close."

James looked around the diner, "You said this diner was from the past?"

"Yes, but no."

James leaned back as he read her expression, when a shot of pain hit his forehead like a migraine. He grabbed his head with both his hands and let out a groan. Ariel saw a few sparks shoot out from the ball cap and she immediately ripped it off his head.

"Crap, Grant told me this was his best one." She frowned as James raised his head, recovering from the malfunction, then she started looking around.

"We gotta go. Now."

James saw the intensity in her eyes and hopped out of the booth. She grabbed his arm and gave a sharp tug. He followed as she made her way to the door, but he was stopped short. A mediator appeared in the doorway.

106

Wow that was fast. How did they get there so fast? She had only taken the hat off a moment ago. James stumbled back into the bar top. Ariel drew a blaster from under her coat and, without hesitation, shot four blasts at the mediator dropping it instantly.

"Get up, get up. We gotta go!"

He followed her out into the daylight, two mediators were just outside. She spun around one of them, using it as a shield as she blasted the other then shot the first one behind the head. Both fell with a crash. James stood there in the door amazed and a little scared. Ariel ran up and grabbed his hand, with a strong jerk they were off running.

"We need to see Dillon."

"Dillon, who's Dillon?" his breathing was erratic. *How was she not breathing heavy?* He thought he was in good shape. James began to slow, trying to catch his breath.

"Come on. The air's thinner here, keep up." They continued down the street then Ariel stopped at the door to another elevator. She pressed the call button and they waited. Ariel scanned the streets for mediators, but all James noticed was how her hair flowed around her soft tan skin. He was brought back to reality when a blast hit near his head.

"Yikes!" he said in surprise.

He ducked down and leaned back to find the door now open. As he toppled back, falling with a thud, Ariel swung in effortlessly and shut the door. They were heading up, the first four floors flew by then the elevator came to rest at the fifth. Without a word, she grabbed his hand and out they went. They were now in a hallway with one wall made of sturdy, white fabric, the other huge two-story windows. A few yards down he saw people stepping off of a train. They ran, dodging people like a running back heading for the end zone. In they went just as the doors were closing.

The train took off before they could ready themselves and James went tumbling. He stood up to see Ariel reading a board on the side of the train; it seemed to have multiple names and numbers on it. Must be the stops he concluded.

"Four stops then we get off," she instructed as she threw him a pistol.

"Remember how to use it?" she asked tersely. He caught the weapon and aimed it at one of the walls. She nodded and began searching out the windows.

"Where are all the automobiles?"

"Automobiles?...Oh, there are none. Trains are the only transpo in Atlantis. Only TK have personal transpo."

TK. Why did that sound familiar? The train stopped, people loaded and unloaded then the train began moving again.

"Who are the TK?"

"The Kontrolery. They run the city, like feudal lords if you ask me."

"So, they're royalty?"

"Sort of. Everyone here has bloodlines and those determine who you'll be and what you'll do. Take for instance, Vesalius. She's a surgeon because her parents were surgeons and their parents were surgeons and so forth. TK, on the other hand, are born to govern the city. They've been doing so for hundreds of years."

The train stopped once more and then was off again. Both watched the doors intently, but no threat showed.

"What bloodline are you?"

"Military. My parents were both military until TK disbanded it."

He could tell he'd hit a nerve. Her face fell sad and angry at the same time. Suddenly, the train screeched to a stop, the doors opened and mediators began to flood in. Ariel ran past him to the front of the train and blasted the door to the control room. James stood there watching then felt a buzz go by his ear, the blast hit next to Ariel.

"Shoot them!" she yelled angrily, as she fiddled with the control panel and her wrist device.

He swung around and fired a couple of shots, both missed and ricocheted off the ceiling, harmlessly hitting the floor. The mediators continued their approach, firing more and more blasts. James looked back toward Ariel; she glared back then raised her blaster with her free hand and fired two shots. James heard them hit and turned to see a mediator collapse. He fired again and missed again, but the third shot hit one of the oncoming robots in the shoulder, momentarily halting it. The train took off and

James tumbled then slid toward the mediators, they did the same. He stared up at the city through the clear ceiling of the train, which was moving incredibly fast. As the initial thrust of the train dissipated, James made his way to his feet and began running toward Ariel.

"Down!" she shouted, firing multiple shots around him.

She took off running toward him at a full sprint, continuing the volley of fire. As she approached, she jumped over him continuing her assault. James turned to follow her path and saw robot after robot fall to the ground. *She's amazing.* She made it to the end of the car, waving him to her. He quickly regained his composure and ran toward her. The train began to slow, then stopped and the doors opened. Still running toward her, he watched Ariel step out of the car firing shot after shot. When he arrived, he saw multiple mediators in various states of destruction.

"We need to get out of here. Once we get to Dillon, we'll be safe for a bit."

James just nodded. He still had no idea what was really going on, he just knew she was keeping them alive. They made their way down below street level in another elevator. The door opened to a small alleyway, much darker than anything he had seen thus far in the city. They continued for what seemed like a couple hundred yards then stopped near a door. This door seemed different. It wasn't the same shiny metal as the rest of the city. It reminded him of the wall back home, dark black, almost gritty. Ariel placed her hand on a round plate on the wall.

"Ariel, what are you doing here?" a gruff voice sounded from the other side of the wall.

"We need a place to lay low, weapons and training," she narrowed her eyes at James.

"Sure enough. I image you have a bunch of mediators hot on your trail. Come in, quick."

The door swung open and they stepped inside. Dillon stood just inside the door, eyes quizzical and disbelieving.

"This is Arcturus' son?"

CHAPTER NINE

Dillon had the same build as James, but packed a bit more muscle. He wore an orange t-shirt and jeans, and had a thick brown beard with a few braids in it. His steel grey eyes were severe and he had a jagged scar on his forehead above his right eye.

Ariel blew off the first question, unzipping her jacket, "He needs training and we don't have time."

"Has the boy ever shot anything?"

"Tried. Maybe hit something, but not what he needed to."

James stood there watching the exchange, not really taking any of it in, as Ariel slid the jacket off her shoulders and threw it to the ground. Her holster swung under her arms and her back was covered up as her bright red hair fell. She raked her fingers through her hair, gathered it in her hands, then wrapped a tie around it.

"Let's go then," Dillon said as he pivoted to head down a hallway. His movements were regimented and he seemed to glide as he walked, holding his head high.

Ariel turned to see James staring at her. "Follow him," she gestured with her hand.

Snapping out of his daze, he hurried after Dillon, but his mind was on Ariel and how she kept catching him off guard. They rounded a corner and James was greeted by a wall of weapons. He had seen plenty in his history books and in the science-fiction movies he and Carol watched, but these were like nothing he had ever seen before.

Dillon grabbed one off the wall and tossed it at James. Instinctively he caught it.

"You can catch, that's a start."

"Who are you?"

"Ha! Ariel's not very good at introductions. You got my name. I'm an arms dealer, or was."

"Was?"

"Yeah, since they disbanded the military, these weapons are obsolete. Only machines use weapons now. No need for handles," he chuckled as he grabbed a pistol and turned around.

He walked over to another wall and waved his hand in the air. The wall slid down out of sight, exposing a long firing range.

"I see you at least know how to hold it. Let's see you fire it."

James stepped up to where Dillon was and raised the blaster. He let a shot go and it spun into the ceiling about 25 yards away. Dillon started laughing. "Nice shot kid. We have some work to do. Ya eat yet?"

"I actually can't remember when the last time was."

Dillon took the blaster from his hand and set it back on the wall holder.

"I'll make some food then we'll get to it."

James sat down at the table. Ariel was sitting next to him and Dillon across from them. It was a small kitchen and small table with only four seats, but they were comfortable enough. James was famished and ate the "rations," as Dillon called it, as fast as he could. It was rectangular shaped and resembled a granola bar more than actual food.

"I thought you were going to cook something," Ariel groused as she picked up the food and sneered at it.

"Sorry, child. Can't get that fancy stuff you're used to here. You know that."

James listened to the two of them go back and forth. They had an interesting relationship. Hardly a sentence would go by without a joke being said at the other's expense. Most of them he didn't understand, but would laugh simply from watching their reactions. He picked up a few things. Dillon was living in exile and was to be sent out of Atlantis, but had chosen to stay underground instead. There was a small network of people like Dillon, but not many. James sat back, finished with his rations and felt much more comfortable with his belly full. He had barely noticed he was hungry with all the events that transpired, but with the slow pace since meeting Dillon, had realized he was starving.

"Let's get this started, Ariel says you're time-crunched."

Dillon led him back to the range and began to explain how the weapons worked and how to aim them. James caught on pretty quickly as Dillon was a good instructor and able to make his points clear and concise. They went through multiple blasters, rifles and a quad cannon which was ridiculous! James was knocked off his feet on the first shot and thrown back into the rear wall. Ariel came in at this point.

"You boys done playing? We need to get going."

She didn't want to compromise Dillon and knew the mediators were searching for James. Dillon gave her a wink and picked up the cannon from James.

"This will work better for you," he handed him a holster with a good sized blaster in it.

James examined it as he stood up.

"Let's get going," Ariel took the holster and slipped it around his chest.

She was still without her coat and her proximity caused James to lose himself again. Ariel caught him staring, but just smiled and finished putting on his holster. She patted his chest then turned and headed out.

"She's difficult. Try not to fall for her."

James glanced over to see a knowing grin through Dillon's beard then ran to catch up with Ariel. He still had no idea what was going on, but remembered something about data.

"You said you needed to have Nova download data?"

"Yes, that's why everyone is after you. There's important information in that head of yours."

James reached up and felt his head with both hands. *What information could he have that seemed so important?*

"What do I know?"

"Haven't got a clue. I was told to pick you up and bring you to Nova. Figured I'd learn when you did."

"Who's Nova?"

"He was a member of TK, but didn't agree with some of the things they were doing. You could say he resigned, but as a member of TK you can't resign, you know too much. Like the baseball players, you're executed."

"What does he want with the information?"

"Don't know that either, but I was told it was critical. I assume it's something to take down TK."

"How do we get there?"

"That's the trick. Mediators are everywhere, but I have an idea."

James followed Ariel around multiple halls and corridors then popped out once again on the street. She ran quickly across a courtyard, James in tow. He looked around at a lovely garden with park benches and people playing Frisbee, no one paid any attention to them. Once across, they headed into another building, then up an elevator. A few minutes and 210 floors later they stepped out into an open courtyard, the view was amazing. James couldn't help but admire it and walked toward the railing. He felt a tug on his hand and turned to see frustrated blue eyes staring back at him.

"No time for that," she admonished as she led him around a corner to an outdoor bar and headed up to the counter.

"Is Max here today?"

"Nope, haven't seen him since last night," the bartender responded.

"Crap," she bit her lip, thinking, and turned to search the courtyard.

She noticed one person who was more interested in them than was warranted. James watched the man in the white cloak and saw him talking, seemingly to no one.

Suddenly, a ship rose up behind them. The man pointed in their direction, a bay door opened on the side of the craft and mediators came pouring out.

"Time to test those newfound skills." Ariel pulled both blasters from under her jacket and began firing.

After a couple of shots, James drew his pistol and began to fire as well. His aim was much better than before and he dropped a few mediators, but his skill was nowhere close to Ariel's. Out of the corner of his eye he saw her take something out of her pocket then heard her shout, "Catch!"

A baseball sized object flew toward him and he snatched it out of the sky.

"Push the button and throw it."

He looked down at it to see there was a button near his index finger. He tapped on it and a light started flashing.

"Throw it!"

He chucked it at the ship, the ball spun and landed inside the bay. A moment later, it exploded, pieces flew everywhere and a few mediators that hadn't exited yet were tossed in the air. He saw the whole craft tumble out of sight, smoke trailing up into the sky. Ariel took out the final few mediators then shouted at James to follow her. He sprinted to catch her but made up little ground, she was wicked fast. She ran across a second opening, stopped and dropped down near a small knee-high wall. When James arrived she was peering down over the wall.

"What?" he asked, then peeked over. He could see

all the way to the ground floor. There was also another building about 20 feet away with a courtyard about 100 stories down. Blasts began to zip over their heads and Ariel turned to James, holding out her hand.

"Do you trust me?"

Mesmerized by her beautiful eyes he slowly nodded.

She grabbed his hand and tugged him over the side of the building. James' stomach went into his chest, they were in a freefall, a sensation he had never felt before. He gaped down at the world rocketing up toward him and felt the wind whipping around his body. *Was this the end?* Ariel grabbed his jacket and spun him to face her. She slipped her hand down his arm and grabbed his empty hand.

"When I tell you, click your heals together like Dorothy."

"Dorothy?"

"Ugggh, just click your heals together."

James looked down and clicked his heals together, he felt pressure on his feet, and he saw Ariel do the same.

"Not now, click them again."

James did as commanded and his sink rate increased again.

"Now!" she yelled.

Almost out of surprise, he did.

Their descent decreased again and they were less than 50 feet above the ground when she ordered him to click his heals that last time. They sputtered down, then at about 10 feet his boots gave out and his hands slipped from hers as he hit the ground like a sack of potatoes. Lying on the ground, he felt a tug on his jacket. Moaning, he stumbled to his feet, his legs throbbing with pain.

"This way!"

James struggled to run, but was able to maintain a fast jog. He followed her around the corner to see Zane standing there holding a large rifle, behind him the ship that had carried him to safety was resting on the ground.

"I'll cover you kids," Zane stated, swinging the plasma rifle at James.

He jinked to get out of the way then continued past him into the ship. Behind him, he heard repeated blasts and turned to see Zane letting round after round fly from his weapon. Zane began to jog backwards. Past him, James could see something new approaching them that was much larger than the mediators. The machine had four legs and multiple weapons around its torso. Some looked like rockets, others cannons and still more like rifles. Zane put a couple shots into it with no results. James heard the hum of the ship as it began to lift off the ground,

"Wait for Zane!" Ariel cried toward the cockpit.

"He's got two seconds," was the response from the pilot.

Zane sprinted toward the ship but was hit in the shoulder with a blast. He stumbled forward, the ship eked upwards slightly.

"Don't you leave him."

"We gotta go, whatever that thing is will tear us

apart!"

Zane continued his sprint but was hit again in the oblique. Stumbling still, he was almost there. The ship swung over sideways toward Zane.

"Get ready to grab him," the pilot warned.

The ship was right on top of him. Zane jumped onto the loading ramp and James and Ariel grabbed him. He hung there a moment, his size made it difficult to get him in. With his injuries he was almost dead weight. The machine began firing everything it had, rockets came inbound. Suddenly shots fired from the side of the ship, exploding the missiles in midair.

"Defensive systems are online, cloaking system activated," a voice from the ship stated.

As the bay door closed, it provided them with enough leverage to drag Zane in. They dragged him to the wall of the cabin and Ariel ran into a rear compartment. She emerged with a medical kit, a small chrome box with a red cross on it. James expected bandages when she opened it, but instead saw a gun looking device. She touched the top and it came to life with a series of beeps. Zane groaned in pain, he was bleeding all over the place.

"Hang in there, Zane. Don't you dare die on me, you big lug," Ariel said in a panic while hovering the gun above the damaged skin.

She moved it at a slow pace. It seemed to magically make bandaging appear over the wound. She continued to manipulate the device and James glanced outside to see that they were still climbing. Ariel finished up the bandaging. Zane was out cold so she checked his pulse; it was weak but he was still alive. She exhaled, relieved. She pulled out another device from the kit, this one he recognized. It was an IV.

"No fancy futuristic way to do that?"

"Nope, nothing beats an IV." Ariel found a vein and set him up, then sat beside him, watching over him.

James walked to the large window on the side of the ship and peered out. They were high above the city and headed nearly straight at the sun.

"Why are we flying right at the sun?"

"That's just an artificial sun, makes people feel normal I guess. We need to get to Nova, he's on the other side of the city."

"Was this the plan all along? To catch a ride?"

She nodded.

"Why didn't we get on board sooner?" He was getting more comfortable around Ariel and became less reserved.

"We couldn't compromise Dillon. This was the best way."

"Jumping off a building was the best way?" James' voice raised, his emotions all over the place.

"But did you die?" she asked giggling.

"What, is everything a joke to you?

"Look, I was told to pick you up and take you to Nova. It wasn't supposed to be this complicated. You need to chill out." She had jumped up and was in his face at this point, starting to lose her cool. "I don't even know what's so important about you anyway. Just because your family is a bunch of architects, doesn't make you special."

James' eyes started focusing anywhere but on her. He turned his head then said softly, "What do you mean architects?"

"I think Nova should explain it to you. I don't want to get the facts wrong."

She walked away toward the window.

"Tell me what you know...Please."

"You're not from Earth. You're from here," she started.

"We'll be there in 15 minutes."

James looked over toward the cockpit. Standing there, leaning in the opening, was a woman in her early 30s with her lips wrapped around a sucker. Her hair was blue, cut short like a bob, and it looked like it almost glowed. She popped out the sucker.

"Peanuts?" she jokingly asked, but it was lost on him. He had never flown anywhere before jumping into that spaceship next to the wall. "So, you're J," she walked toward him. Her figure was like Ariel's but more mature. Her outfit was similar to his, baggy pants with straps around the waist and thighs, a leather jacket with lamb's wool around the neck. James stood there staring.

"Don't talk much, huh?" she popped the sucker back in her mouth.

James stayed silent, unsure how to react.

"How's Zane doing? Not looking so hot," she mused. They all looked over at him.

"He'll live. The IV should keep him steady until we reach Nova and can get him more in-depth care," Ariel replied, worry showing on her face.

James turned to stare out the window and gather his thoughts. *He wasn't from Earth, but what about his parents, his friends, Carol?*

"Approaching destination, docking sequence initiated," a modulated voice stated.

James watched as they approached a line of tall buildings once again and the ship began to rotate into position for landing. The woman had gone.

"Who was that?"

"Sonya, she's Nova's pilot." Ariel surveyed James. "You'll have your answers soon enough." She checked on Zane again, not quite willing to leave his side while he was in his present state. James fell back into his thoughts.

The ship docked, the ramp opened and a medical team ran in to grab Zane, then were off heading to the medical bay as quickly as they'd come. The ship had landed inside one of the buildings, the hangar was enormous. It felt like you could place four baseball stadiums into it.

James walked over to Ariel. "I'm sorry about earlier. I have a lot on my mind and death doesn't seem like much fun."

She pasted on a smile and huffed out a breath. "Follow me, let's get you your answers."

James followed her past rows of ships, some small some large, and a few that could have been futuristic automobiles.

"I thought you said there were no automobiles?"

"I said trains were the only transpo. TK have vehicles."

Soon they approached a doorway to exit the hangar. As they proceeded closer, James noticed an individual standing beside the door. He was very elegant, business-like in a black coat and pants with a red undershirt.

"Nice to see you, Ariel," he nodded, and she returned it.

"And you must be J."

James nodded in agreement, but he really preferred to be called James. The whole "J" thing kept throwing him off.

"My name is Sedrick. It's a pleasure to meet you."

He extended his hand and James took it in a firm handshake. He was very formal, but something about it put James at ease.

"This way."

Sedrick led them through a maze of grand rooms, one after another with elegant settings, silver accented couches, leather cushions; each room had a different theme. One of them James didn't want to leave, it reminded him of the library at school. Books were displayed in floor to ceiling wooden cases with a ladder on a track that wrapped around the whole room so the reader could access any book he liked in the two-story space. Now that he thought about it, that was the only wood he'd seen since arriving, everything else in the city seemed to be made of plastic or metal.

They walked past that room and through a few more corridors, then into an elevator. James was finally getting used to the sensation it gave him as they shot upward toward the next stop, the top. At the highest floor, they stepped out with Sedrick leading the way.

"In here," he said as a door hissed open. The room was shaped like the point of a pike, the walls closing into a point at the top. They were nearly all transparent, but had small metal ribs in-between. At the far end of the room sat a desk and a tufted nail-head adorned leather chair. The desk itself was a rich mahogany and it sat on a large red hand-woven rug. Near one of the windows stood a man.

"Welcome," he said, walking along the outer perimeter of the room. "You must have many questions."

He wore a well-groomed beard and a robe in an Asian pattern. His arms were crossed and his robe dragged on the ground as he continued to walk closer to James. His entire aura made him appear wise.

"I will answer all of them in due time, but what you carry in your head is more valuable than anything else here on Atlantis. We must extract it first. Please, have a seat."

James looked behind him to see a chair and he moved back to sit down into it. Two people walked up beside him and placed a metallic cylinder over his forehead. He recognized one of them as V.

"This won't hurt."

Smiling at him, she finished attaching the device and immediately James began to feel groggy and his eyes became heavy.

CHAPTER TEN

James opened his eyes to see a planet staring back at him on a large screen. Scrolling underneath were a series of numbers. He watched for a few minutes analyzing the picture.

"Arcturus."

James' head swung to the right. Approaching him was a smaller gentleman with glasses, holding a glass device that was shaped like a book. He handed it to him.

"Those coordinates have been verified four times. I think it's the one."

He observed multiple people smiling and hugging, some jumping for joy.

"Have you notified the Kontrolery, yet?" he heard himself say.

"No, we were going to let you inform them."

"Very well," James looked back at the screen.

Continuing to watch the numbers scrolling on screen, he tried to turn around and realized he couldn't. Suddenly his body rotated and he saw a larger guy with two holstered pistols walk up. *Finally, someone I recognize.* Zane. James' body turned back to the screen and his arm reached up and touched a few floating buttons in the air, then reached down as a small square box popped out from the console. He grabbed it and handed it to Zane.

"This is the only copy. You know what to do with it. I need to see the Kontrolery."

James realized his voice sounded different and he couldn't control anything. His arms, head, legs, voice... nothing. His body began to walk toward the crowd of elated people, many hugging him or shaking his hand as he passed. He made his way to a door where two mediators stood. James tried to turn and run when he first noticed them, but couldn't. *What was going on?* It was like he was stuck in a live action movie. He passed in between the mediators as one shined an orange light into his eyes.

"Dr. Arcturus, you're cleared."

Dr. Arcturus? He'd heard that name before, but couldn't quite place it. The door opened and he stepped into a hallway. The two mediators followed him until he reached an elevator and rode it up to the top. His journey continued as he boarded a craft and flew through the city for about 15 minutes, then approached the biggest building he had ever seen. It towered over all of the others and instead of chrome, it was adorned in gold. Banners hung around it in emerald green displaying the TK logo he had seen before. As the ship closed in, he saw over a dozen people standing outside, waiting for him. They moved back as the craft landed. The doors opened and he stepped out to cheers, people smiling, laughing and hugging each other. *What could they be so happy about?* James figured it had something to do with what was on the screen, but couldn't quite put everything together. After all, he was just a high school kid in a world he knew almost nothing about. Still, he settled in, realizing he didn't have to perform any actions. It was like being at the movies with Carol, but without the popcorn and hand-holding. He continued past the crowd, mediators in tow. A few people came up to him, enthusiastically shouting.

"Is it true, is it true, you found one?"

James just raised a hand to say "relax" and continued past them. He looked at the building in front of him. He was already above the other buildings, but the top was still maybe fifty stories higher. James walked in past two large doors big enough to fit two elephants and they opened without a whisper.

Inside was a large foyer. Two large staircases flowed up opposing sides following the rounded contours of the outer wall to a second story. Underneath was a short hall that led to yet another elevator. He entered along with his escort. The elevator shot up 39 floors before coming to a stop. The glowing letters on the control panel read "TK Round Table". When the doors opened, he saw 20 people in various brightly colored robes standing around a large golden circular table. They all turned as he approached. James looked around at them and noticed there were males and females who all appeared to be in very good health and maybe in their 40s.

"Welcome, Arcturus," one of them said.

He noticed a spot missing at the table as he approached and stood there.

"You have news we hear," another said.

"You found one," yet another spoke up.

CHAPTER TEN

"When can we leave?" still another questioned.

James put his hand up, signaling them to be quiet. He scanned the room, it was silent with anticipation.

"We have found planet 80121579 in the Ecenteeon system and it has all necessary statistics to support life."

The gallery began to mutter to each other with excitement, some were laughing and others crying tears of joy.

"When can we leave?" someone spoke up.

At this, the murmuring became silent, and all turned to look at him.

"The ship is ready for the New Atlanteans, but we have run out of supplies for the Earth ship."

"You know that was a dream Arcturus, we were never going to complete it, it was too large, there are too many of them," a man to his left stated.

"Yes, you know they have served their purpose, they would crowd the new planet," another said.

"We created them. They are drones simply used to uphold our population," yet another added.

"There is a solution," James replied. "In 18 years, the comet Oumuamua will pass by and we—"

He was cut off by a female on the far side of the table.

"We have waited long enough. We are ready now, the journey will be long enough."

There were cheers in agreement.

"You know the Earth is failing. All those people... it won't sustain them even another 20 years," he interrupted.

"More reason for us to go now. If we wait, there will

not be enough food for all of us," a gentleman to James' left responded.

"They are people just like us."

"Not like us," the woman on the far side shouted, thumping the table with a fist, her eyes filled with rage. "You know that Arcturus. We created them, we can destroy them."

James could see and feel his head shake.

"Very well, I will need a month to ready the ship."

"A month?" the woman questioned. "My sources tell me it can be ready in a matter of days."

"We need to verify the systems. Jumping through space will be a surgical process, precision it essential."

"Two days, Arcturus. You have two days," she waived her hand at him, dismissing him.

James turned and headed out the door. He followed the same path back to where he had begun this strange dream.

Zane met him as he arrived back where he began in the control room.

"Is it ready?" James asked.

Zane nodded and walked toward the exit, James followed.

"What did the council say?"

"You know what they said, exactly what we had talked about. They value themselves and nothing else."

"So are we—"

"Not here, Zane. We can talk more once we are below."

"Very well, sir."

Zane opened the elevator door and the two headed in, flanked by the mediators who were still escorting Arcturus. The elevator doors closed and started down then James felt his head nod to Zane. He watched as Zane produced a blaster in each hand. Two shots and the robots fell, immobile. James saw his arms manipulating the buttons of the elevator, punching in multiple codes. The word "Lockbox" showed on the screen, shortly after that the elevator doors opened. Dillon stood there holding a large cannon, he tossed it to Zane.

"Those buggers will be here soon, I'm sure. I'll cover Arcturus, you stay here and guard the elevator."

James followed Dillon.

"Didn't go for the new plan, huh?"

"You know TK well enough by now. They disbanded the military in favor of those walking computers, they only care about their own lives. If they could, they would get rid of the rest of the New Atlanteans."

They continued down the hall to a room that seemed familiar; it resembled the room in which V had operated on him. As he entered the room, a woman walked by him. She looked like V, but older.

"Is the process complete?" he asked.

"Yes," the woman presented him with a sleeping baby.

"You will someday understand this, but I don't have time to explain it now, J my boy."

Wait, J? He turned and headed out the door. Blasts came down the hall, exploding all around him. He looked toward the elevator and saw that Zane was letting loose with the cannon as wave after wave came at him. He watched Dillon toss a ball over his head yelling, "Down!"

Zane ducked and covered his head as the bomb exploded in the elevator. Dillon turned to James.

"More will be here soon. Go quickly."

James started running down the hallway, clutching the still sleeping child in his arms. He heard more blasts behind him, but didn't look. The end was nearing and he could see a small door getting closer. It was half the size of the others. James opened it and slipped in, it seemed like a tunnel. He slid down and shot out into another room. It was a small hangar, he recognized the ships. There were about twenty of them, all like the one he had flown in to Atlantis. James ran toward one. To his right he saw a woman heading his way, she could be Ariel's twin, but all grown up with blond hair. She had a pistol in each hand and was followed by a short, stocky, bearded man toting similar weapons. James heard blasts behind him, but focused on one of the ships, unflinching. The canopy opened and he placed the baby in the ship.

"Love you, J." He punched a couple of buttons and the canopy closed.

"These ships are relics, will they hold up?"

"Yes," James said, turning to the woman. "I've upgraded this one. It'll work as advertised."

Just then, the woman took a round to the chest; she lurched back, falling toward the ground. James caught her, but she was dead before she hit his arms. He laid her on the ground looking up at the bearded man. The man was visibly pained by her death, but he, Dillon and Zane were busy firing round after round at their pursuers.

"Last one," he heard Zane yell to Dillon, dropping the cannon he held to expose a pistol from his side.

Dillon dropped his rifle and started punching on his forearm. James heard a loud beeping sound and then grinding metal. Dillon started running toward him, picking up the rifle as he went by and Zane turned to follow. The other man did the same. James swung around to see large hangar doors opening. Hovering outside sat a ship, poised to engage. The craft he had placed the baby in rose off the ground and, like a lightning bolt, took off under the ship. Blasts followed the tiny ship as it jinked to avoid the incoming fire. It flew out the hangar door and out of sight. James ran over to another one looking over at the three others. Zane and Dillon made it to a set of ships, but the bearded man was cut down midway. James opened the canopy and jumped inside, arms and fingers frantically moving about, touching floating buttons in front of him and on the canopy. The ship's cover closed as light started flashing around him.

"Hull damaged, shield up," the ship's computer sounded.

More buttons, then James slid his arms in the cup-like sleeves on each armrest of the chair.

"Ok, J. Here's your first flying lesson."

If James had been in control, he would have frozen

right then and there. *Is he talking to me?*

He heard himself, or Arcturus rather, continue to monologue everything he was doing as if teaching someone how to do it. He detailed the controls and systems as fast as he could. James paid attention to every minor detail. The ship sped off toward the hangar doors, which were almost completely open. The large ship hovered in and began unloading its' ordinance at the three craft. He glanced over to see Dillon and Zane successfully maneuvering to avoid the incoming rounds. They fired back with no effect; the ship's shield was too strong.

"Shields 90%," the ship cried.

James maneuvered the craft, avoiding most of the blasts, but there were so many he was hit by a few. He accelerated and with a few spins flipped over the large ship. The others followed. Outside, their situation wasn't much better. They were out in the open and a couple dozen ships descended upon them. James saw Dillon's ship dive down between the buildings. Zane followed, disappearing into the city below. James continued his evasive maneuvers then, spiraling into a loop, dove straight down toward a courtyard. On the screen in front of him, he saw little pictures of ships closing around a center red dot which he learned was him. He accelerated, careening toward the people below. They became easy to identify as he approached. He aimed for an opening in a courtyard with a small pond in the middle. James wanted to close his eyes, but he had no control.

His fingers tapped a series of buttons inside the

sleeves and suddenly, the ground under the pond withdrew to reveal a tunnel. He zipped into it, punching more buttons and the door slid shut behind him quicker than it had opened. Through the tunnel he flew. With a few slight turns, he quickly came to the end. More button touches and another door opened. He shot out the door into the dark black void of space. The sense of speed disappeared, he felt immobile. He looked back and watched the moon become smaller then steered the craft toward Earth. This was the first time James had seen it from space, he was mesmerized.

Multiple plates seemed to hover around as floating puzzle pieces to a sphere. He could almost make out a central hub, or ball, with spokes protruding from it attached to the bottom of each piece. The whole system had that electric blue glow around it.

"J, the history you learned is a lie. The Earth was dying. Earthquakes, tsunamis, tornadoes and global warming all led brilliant scientists to engineer this. The plates are all that remain of our old Earth. It was kept alive in this fashion to supply Atlantis with food and other renewable resources."

James continued to talk.

"You need to save the people on Earth. The Kontrolery doesn't care about them. Flat Earth is dying again and, now that we have found a suitable planet, TK has built a ship to take all of Atlantis there."

Blasts hit the craft and it spun out of control.

"Shields 50%."

James was pinned to his seat. The ship was hit again. James flipped it over and headed back toward the moon, into the jaws of the oncoming attackers. He punched buttons on the screen.

"Full frontal shield," James said.

James accelerated, rounds came inbound as he flipped and jinked, avoiding most.

"Shield 80%."

James slipped through the line. He tapped on the screen again.

"Rear shields 80%."

He accelerated even more, the moon grew larger and larger. He aimed for a crater.

"Shields 60%."

He was taking more and more fire, trying to stay straight on the final approach. He blasted into the landing bay, shots following him.

"Shields depleted, shields depleted, shiel—"

He tapped the screen. "That's enough of that."

He made his final approach, ground impact was eminent and the craft started screaming at him, a siren pulsed.

"Impact, Impact."

James hit the ground, the ship bounced and tumbled.

CHAPTER ELEVEN

James opened his eyes and V was standing next to him. He was breathing heavy, sweat covered his body and a quick beep came from a monitor on the wall.

"Is that it?" he blurted out, his eyes flicking about. He sat up and looked over at V.

"Calm down, J. You're fine." She did her best to reassure him in her typical doctor-patient tone.

"I know that, but where's the rest?" James raised his arms and placed his hands on his head.

"The rest? We're done with the extraction, what do you mean?" V asked, squinting and leaning in closer.

"The rest, the rest, what happened to Arcturus?" he shook his hands in front of him, his face intense, eagerly awaiting an answer.

Ariel came into view. "Whatcha talking about? You were out cold."

James turned and faced her, still waiving his hands. "I was in his body, it was like a movie."

V checked his vitals. "This isn't something we typically see. We extracted the data, a series of numbers. What do you mean like a movie?" V intoned, still working on the machine.

"I was staring at a screen with a planet on it—"

V quickly looked up and stopped him, "Planet 80121579, we extracted the coordinates for it. That's what we were searching for."

"Why?" James' hands fell slightly, his eyebrows

tightened.

"Since we extracted it, TK can't get it. It's no longer in your head, not as data anyways."

"But what did I see?"

"I'm not sure. This was old technology my mother worked on years ago. There were lots of bugs back then."

"Bugs?"

"Mistakes, anomalies, etcetera."

Was he the baby in the dream? Was that V's mother? Ariel's mother?

"Jolt prepared your new DNA profile, it's ready. We need to get you into the system, follow me."

"This had better work better than that cap he programmed for Grant. I don't know where his head's at these days," Ariel grumbled.

James hopped off the exam table and followed V to another room. She had him place his hands and feet on different plates. He found himself staring at a screen while it scanned his face and eyes. Ariel stepped in as he was finishing up.

"V says you're in the system. It will be much easier to move around the city."

James was lost in his thoughts. "That's nice," he responded almost out of reflex.

"That's nice? You're darned right it's nice. I won't have to babysit you anymore."

James looked over; Ariel had a big grin on her face. She had an aura of light-heartedness around her, even in such serious circumstances, that just seemed to lift his spirits.

"Go out for a bite?"

"Sure, food sounds good."

He felt exhausted. V had told him he was only out for ten minutes, but it felt like days. He wondered about going out for food, but Ariel was confident nothing would happen to them because James was in the system. He had no idea what that meant, but he was safe; he was with her. They left the building and headed to a small alley filled with maybe a dozen restaurants.

"What type of food do you like?" Ariel asked as they drew closer.

"Just scrambled eggs and bacon sounds good."

"Ever had Chinese?"

"No, I've lived in the same town my whole life."

"Wanna try it?"

James didn't want to let her down, she seemed pretty excited about it. He agreed and she led him to a restaurant with a lit sign that read "Hong Kong Food and Lounge". Though the "Food" was much dimmer than the other words so it just looked like "Hong Kong and Lounge", which for some reason made him laugh. The place was decorated with Asian accents, palace style, the lighting was dim, and red and gold accents covered everything. It was a stark contrast from the pristine city outside. They sat in a booth, which reminded him of the diner back home. His mind wandered. *What were his friends doing at this moment? What would they say when he told them the stories?*

"J." His daydream was cut short. "So, did V tell you what they extracted?"

"Yes, it was coordinates to a planet, number 80121579."

Ariel examined him a moment. "Do you know what that means?"

James started laughing. "No, matter of fact I haven't got a clue what any of this means. This is crazy. I think I'm in a dream, then I'm in a dream's dream. I'm on the moon, I've never even seen a plane in real life, I—"

Ariel reached over and gently grabbed his hand. James stopped mid-sentence.

"I'm just trying to figure this all out."

"I don't have all the answers, but what that planet does is allows the Exodus to launch very soon."

"Exodus?"

"Yes. TK built a ship years ago. Their lead scientist, Dr. Arcturus, was in charge of tracking distant planets to find one suitable to hold life. Once found, they would fly there and set up a new world. The ship's been sitting idle for 17 years."

"I don't understand what that has to do with me? Why would anyone want to stop that?"

"TK will leave the people on Earth behind. They'll take the people from Atlantis and leave Flat Earth to crumble and eventually shut down. Earth was like their pantry, now they have a new one. Well, if they get the coordinates they'll have a new one."

The waiter came over and Ariel ordered for both of

them. She assured him he would love it all.

"You said Dr. Arcturus was their lead scientist?"

"Yep, he had a soft spot for the Earth and didn't want to leave all those people to die. He tried to convince the council to build a second ship larger to take 'em, but they refused. So he and a few others with the same ideals hid the coordinates. I just recently learned they were in you."

"Who am I?"

"You're J. Dr. Arcturus' son. I thought you knew that."

James' head emotionally exploded. *He was the baby in his dream. Was any of this true? What about his parents on Earth?* He went silent, searching for the words. The food arrived and, after quickly saying grace, he began eating. The food was amazing, he had never had anything like it. Back home, the town only housed the diner and two other restaurants. He'd only read about the Asian culture in school. Ariel lifted her wrist above the table.

"What's that?"

"Dillon wants to see us, says there's something urgent. Zane's going to meet us there."

"Ok, but what's that on your wrist? You're always playing with it."

"It's everything. Tracks vitals, tells me where I am, how to get places, talks to people, everything. It's called a Datacle, everyone has one. We need to get going soon."

"Oh, can we finish eating?" James was hoping for more time to digest, and not just his food.

"Sure, let's go in ten."

James quietly ate his food, Ariel did the same. They finished up and headed out then hopped on a train on the first floor, then one on the 10th, then another on the 7th. Then they took the long descent down to the underground to meet Dillon. The location was new to Ariel, she had never been to this part of the city. She continued to follow her directions on the Datacle. After several turns down alleys and tight corridors, they were met by a small steel door.

"You try," she turned to James. "Let's see if your system stats work."

James slipped in front of her and placed his hand on the wall. He heard Ariel laughing behind him. "What?"

"Not there," she pointed to another panel about a foot away.

"How do you tell?" He was embarrassed and didn't want it to happen again.

"This line right here." She pointed out a small horizontal line about 12 inches wide, just below eye level.

"All door panels have that indication."

James adjusted his hand. The door hissed open. Ariel nodded and they headed inside. Ariel went first, down a hall that opened up to a large room. There was a set of stairs centrally located in the room and they climbed up two floors. The next door opened and they found themselves in a large hangar. Ariel scanned the area, something didn't seem right. They continued walking down a row of ships, they were laid out everywhere. She checked the meet location, they were going in the right direction.

"These are TK ships, where is everybody?"

James could feel the tension and he became uneasy as well. Denying their gut feelings, they continued.

"So those are TK vehicles?" James asked.

"Yes, what are they doing here?"

James shrugged his shoulders as they continued down the path. Reaching the far side, a door opened. Dillon was leaning on the wall.

"There they are. What took you guys so long?"

"What's so urgent it couldn't wait?"

"Chill, Princess. Trust me, it'll be worth it."

Dillon escorted them into a smaller room. It seemed like a control room. There were lines of seats all facing a huge screen. The screen sat blank. Each wall had multiple doors, including two under the screen.

"Ok, so what is it?"

"How do you feel about getting out of here and heading to paradise?"

James and Ariel looked at each other.

"What do you mean?"

"I mean, you guys wanna go to Acadia?"

"Acadia?" they said, almost in unison

"James, you know you've seen it."

He had no clue and continued to look at Dillon with a blank stare.

"Oh, come on. Planet 80121579 ring a bell?"

"How...how do you know that I've seen it? How do you know that number?"

"That doesn't matter. You wanna go or not, simple

question."

Finally, Ariel spoke up. "Not without Earth, you know that."

"Very well."

With Dillon's words, all of the doors opened. Mediators poured in, surrounding them.

"Dillon? What did you do?!"

"My job. I got a deal I couldn't pass up. Seems TK needs my expertise. They need more weapons, but they also needed something else."

He walked up to James and pointed at his head.

"They need coordinates."

"But you were there from the beginning," James began. "You helped Arcturus."

"Arcturus is dead, his ideals died with him. Now I'm helping myself. I'm tired of living in Epcot!" he shouted, holding out his hands. "Give me your weapons."

James exposed the blaster he had under his coat. Ariel did the same and grudgingly handed them to Dillon.

"If you come without a fight, I'm sure we can get you a seat on the Exodus. There's plenty of room," Dillon snickered.

Dillon began walking toward the hangar door while James and Ariel were pushed along by the mediators. Ariel slipped and fell to her knees, James kneeled down to check on her.

"Follow my lead," she whispered.

"Come on Ariel, I know you're not that clumsy.

Don't try to come up with some crazy escape plan."
Dillon scoffed.

He made a motion with his hand and a mediator came
over and handcuffed them. Dillon turned to continue
walking and they followed, pushed along by the mindless
robots. After passing a few ships, they reached a small
vehicle. The door flipped open vertically and Dillon
waved his hands to usher them in. Ariel raised her hands
over her head. James looked at her then at Dillon.

"What are you doing now?"

"I give up."

Dillon began laughing, "Kinda late for that, little
girl."

"Me, too. I give up." James raised his hands above his
head, which caused more laughter from Dillon.

"What is this, Simon says? Well nobody said "Simon
says." Get in the transport."

He waved at the vehicle again. Two blasts came from
across the way and Ariel and James' arms were free. More
shots rained down on them and Dillon jumped on the
top of the vehicle sliding to the other side. The Mediators crumpled around them. Ariel pushed James into the
transport.

"Shut the door!" she yelled, climbing into the front.

James scrambled over to do so then looked all around.
There was no handle. "I don't know how," he screamed as
more mediators arrived and began shooting the transport.

"Just touch the ceiling," Ariel shouted back, she had
disappeared to the front.

James reached up and touched the ceiling, the door closed. He could hear the rounds hitting the outside of the vehicle. He heard a thump behind him, then as he spun around to see what it was, Dillon came flying in the other side, tackling him. The transport began to move. Dillon cocked back a fist and swung. James dodged the first, but the second made contact with his shoulder.

"Ariel, a little help, please!"

Another fist came at him and he threw up an arm to block it. James was on the defensive, doing all he could do, like a boxer on the ropes. Suddenly, Dillon arched back in pain. James dropped his arms enough to see Ariel with a foot in Dillon's back. Dillon twisted to counter, but there wasn't much room to maneuver. James attempted to help and threw a punch of his own. He landed it on Dillon's shoulder blade, but it was hard and James recoiled in pain, his hand stinging. He watched Ariel. She threw a few punches, dodged a couple more from Dillon. She landed a knee to his ribs, he winced in pain. James searched for something to help in the fight. He climbed toward the front, stumbling over seats and looked back to see the fight continuing. His hand slipped as he reached down to the front seat flipping him over the seat back. James tumbled into a heap. Glancing up, he realized he was in the front of the vehicle. He looked out the window. The automobile, as he thought of it, was exiting the hangar onto the street level. People jumped out of the way with surprise as it continued on the pedestrian walkways.

Their speed increased and James realized he needed to do something. He searched, but couldn't find any controls. *Maybe if he used his hands like he had seen Arcturus do in the ship.* He glanced back at the passenger compartment. They were still exchanging blows, but he realized Ariel was becoming fatigued as Dillon was much larger than her. He turned back and ran his hand along various surfaces in the vehicle. His hand hit something causing a hovering, almost transparent screen to appear. He read, quickly trying to decipher what would help him. Looking past it, he saw more people fleeing the pathway as the automobile careened down the road. He refocused, "Manual Override" was written near the bottom and he reached up to push it. He heard a few tones, then "Confirm Manual Override" read on the screen.

"Yes," he stated out loud, pushing it again.

A steering wheel flipped out in front of him. He expected pedals to manifest themselves, but the auto began to slow and he looked down, nothing. He grabbed the steering wheel, his finger hit something and it began to accelerate. He ran his finger up the back of the steering wheel, nothing was there and the auto slowed again. He looked up to see a knee high wall approaching. Quickly, he squeezed the steering wheel as he accelerated and veered around it. Now driving over grass through the middle of a courtyard, he released his grip slightly and slowed down. He had figured it out. He smiled to himself and looked back, proud that he'd figured it out.

Ariel and Dillon were still locked in combat. He had

her pinned to the ground and she struggled to move, kicking at him. He pushed his weight down on her and began to choke her. James heard a loud beeping sound and turned back to the front. He swerved to miss a building he was about to impact. The sound of two bodies hitting a leather couch came from the back seat. James turned to see Dillon and Ariel pinned against the side of the auto. That gave him an idea. Exploring the screen, he found the words "Right Door" and pushed the button. The door next to Dillon opened and he went flying out. The surprise caused him to release Ariel and she fell to the floor. James looked back just as Ariel almost disappeared out the door. Dillon had frantically grabbed her right foot as he exited. She was now partially hanging out. James released the steering wheel, slowing the auto momentarily. Ariel gave a swift kick to Dillon's head, releasing her from his grasp and she climbed in as fast as she could. Then, out of breath, yelled, "Go!'"

James squeezed the steering wheel, and the auto took off. Still in the courtyard, he searched for a road to get back on track. He had no clue where he was going, but he knew he needed to keep moving. Ariel climbed up to sit next to him, and tapped a few buttons. The door closed behind them.

"I'll drive. I think you've had enough fun," she winked.

She climbed over his lap as he released the steering wheel and slid behind her over to the passenger seat. She squeezed, accelerating, moving off the grass and back onto the shiny metal road.

"We need to get somewhere safe, not sure who else he's compromised."

"Okay, but where's safe?"

"I have a spot, somewhere only a couple of us know. If anyone else is on the run, they'll be there, too."

She drove as fast as she could, people zipped by, blurred from the speed.

"What are we going to do?"

"I don't know."

James studied Ariel, she had definitely taken a beating. There were bruises already beginning to form on her neck and she had a bloody lip. He could tell she was in a lot of pain, but was managing it well. All of a sudden, the auto flipped and they went weightless. James was blinded by a bright light glowing everywhere and the automobile kept spinning. He realized they had been hit by a massive blast as the vehicle continued to tumble through the sky. It felt as though it flipped ten times and ground impact was imminent. The vehicle hit the ground still flipping then slid to a stop on its side leaning against a wall. James felt none of the impact, just the soft cushion of the crash impact system. Balloon like fabric engulfed both of them and was now in the process of deflating. They slipped to the bottom of the vehicle.

"Are you alright?" James asked, still feeling woozy from the spinning.

"Yes, but we need to get out of here," she moaned as she tried to sit up.

150

The auto had been crushed and very little room remained. James looked up to see the door missing. He shimmied up and poked his head out. Ships were inbound and a few mediators were closing in on them.

"Give me your hand!"

She reached up and he pulled her out. Ariel grabbed him and they dove down the side of the incapacitated vehicle. Dragging him by the hand, she bolted for a nearby alley invisible to the pursuit.

"What do we do now?"

"Give me a second, let me think."

He could almost see her thinking as her eyes shifted back and forth. She held up her wrist and pushed a few keys, then saw V pop up on the display.

"Where are you? Someone has compromised us."

"I know. It was Dillon. Are you safe?"

"What?! Dillon? Are you sure? He's been with us since the beginning."

"Yes, no time to explain. Are you safe?"

"Yes, rendezvous point Charlie Tango Foxtrot 16. Stay off the roads, there's a city wide lockdown. TK knows all of our data, there's no more hiding."

"What about Nova?"

"He was compromised, too. You're the first I've had contact with since."

"I'm heading that way."

"God speed."

Ariel searched James' face for any sense of hesitation, but saw nothing but complete trust. "We're going

151

to need to move fast and stay hidden. Best bet is the tunnels. Follow me, stay close."

James shadowed Ariel as she navigated alley after alley, finally coming to a dead end. She knelt down and opened a small panel.

"We have to fit in there?!"

"Yes, no choice. Not claustrophobic are you?" she grinned.

"No, but there's no way I'll be able to move in there."

James frowned at the opening. It was so small he'd barely be able to wedge himself in, let alone be on his hands and knees.

"Follow me and don't stop."

James could hear ships overhead and the sound of footsteps heading their way. He took a deep breath, stretched out his arms in front of him and slipped in. It was pitch black. He could hear Ariel wiggling along in front of him and wished for a little more light so he could see her. Though right now he'd just as soon settle for a little more room as he squirmed his way forward, slow at first, then he got into a rhythm. This was even more difficult than he'd anticipated. He was much larger than Ariel and that proved to be challenging. He heard the sound of sliding as he inched forward then felt an opening under his hands and pushed himself up to it. He felt around, there was nowhere else to go. Reluctantly, he pushed forward. He slid down in the dark, luckily being so big helped him slow the fall. As he continued down, he pressed his body against the side walls controlling his speed. A small opening came into view as light shined back at him. He squinted to try and see more detail and could slightly make out Ariel's face looking back at him. He popped his arms and head out bracing himself with his legs.

"Just drop."

"Are you serious?"

"Yes, just drop. Here, give me your hands."

James reached down and they joined hands. He gazed into her eyes as he hung.

"Now drop," she smiled.

James wiggled down a bit more then dropped. It didn't go as planned and he fell on top of her. Lying there, nose to nose, hands above her head and still joined like he'd pinned her in place, they didn't move a muscle. For a heartbeat, neither said a word. Ariel broke the silence.

"You're freakin' heavy," she smirked, eyes crinkling.

James released her hands, rolled off of her and sat up.

"What did you expect?"

"Not that." She didn't say that she meant it in more ways than one.

She sat up next to him and stumbled to her feet, brushing her hands down her pants, then took a deep breath. "Need to move, they'll be in here in no time."

James looked around. There were wires and tubing lining the walls like the tunnel under the wall and the inside of the harvester back home. Ariel walked up to a door, opened it and stepped out into an office. Hundreds of people were standing with screens floating in front of their faces, tapping a myriad of buttons. Ariel walked by, trying to remain inconspicuous. James followed her and wondered what all of the people were staring at. He peered closer at one of the screens and saw what looked like a map of a large town with hundreds of labeled dots moving around. He looked around again and noticed that all of the workers wore fitted grey clothes and black boots, a stark contrast to what the two of them were wearing. Workers started to notice the difference and began talking to each other in low voices. James and Ariel hot-footed it down a break in the blocked dividers separating each worker and headed out a door at the other end. They found themselves in a hallway and James came to an abrupt halt as a flash of light zipped by him. A mediator staged down the hall had spotted them.

They sprinted in the other direction and found an elevator. Ariel placed her hand on the pad to activate it.

"Denied," a voice replied.

She tried it again.

"Denied."

"Crap, they took us out of the system."

"Lockdown initiated," the voice crackled.

Ariel scowled back at the mediator steadily approaching, firing another shot. She frantically began typing on her arm. It buzzed and she placed her hand on the pad once again. The door opened as she was hit in the shoulder with a blast. She stumbled back and pushed James into the elevator then slipped off her Datacle and tossed it to him. She placed her hand on the plate and was hit again. Falling, James tried to reach for her, but couldn't get to her in time.

"Find V," she stated as the door closed.

What just happened?! Desperate to get Ariel back, he placed his hand on the plate to once again open the door.

"Denied," he tried again, and again. "Denied, Denied, Denied."

He picked up the bracelet and glided his finger over it as he had seen Ariel do countless times. A screen appeared on his arm. There was a list of names. When he saw "Vesalius", he tapped on it. The screen read "connecting". He could feel the elevator shooting up, but had no idea what floor he was going to.

"Ariel, what's happening?" James heard V's voice.

"No, it's me James. Ariel's gone!"

"What do you mean she's gone?"

"She pushed me. She, she was shot and threw this to me."

"Ok, take a deep breath. Where are you?"

"I don't know, in an elevator. What do I do? How do I get back to her?"

V was very calm, as a doctor would be talking to a frightened patient.

"Take the Datacle and swipe up until you see it say "location"."

"What do you mean swipe up?"

"Ok, take your finger, place it at the bottom of the screen, then drag it upwards."

James did as he was told and found the word "location".
"Ok, got it," he said half excited.

"Now press on it and it should say "transmit location."

"It does."

"Now press it again. It will say "send to current call". Press that."

James did as instructed. V seemed to be reading something, then she looked at him quickly. "J, don't—"

The transmission stopped. The screen disappeared. James tapped on the Datacle, he swiped his fingers on it, nothing. The elevator doors opened. Two mediators stood there waiting for him. One grabbed him, he felt a warm tingling sensation throughout his body, then everything went dark.

CHAPTER TWELVE

"Oh look, he's awake."

James opened his eyes to see Dillon sitting across from him.

"You're a terrible driver. This ride's going to be much more enjoyable."

James tried to jump up, but his wrists were fastened to the seat. He looked around; they were in a vehicle identical to the one they'd tried to get away in.

"Where's Ariel?"

"You know where she is. You left her. She's dead."

"No, I didn't...she isn't. She can't be. Where is she? Why would you betray her? She was your friend!"

"I was made an offer I couldn't pass up. No more running, no more hiding, elite status on a new planet, able to feel the warm sun, real air, no synthetic or created nonsense. Even where you call home is artificial."

James just stared at him, infuriated that he betrayed them, and his lack of remorse made it even worse.

"What do you know of Earth?" James spat.

"Much more than you. Did you know that everybody on that planet is genetically engineered? TK created them to do the dirty work while they live here in luxury. Well, except you of course. I'd hate to be in your shoes, you have no idea about any of this. If you get the chance, I'd just forget about this whole mess. Your simple life on Earth is much easier."

James gazed out the window at the city moving by.

Was Ariel really dead? He tried to answer it in his mind, he tried to give hope to the possibility that she could still be alive. *He didn't know what he'd do without her.* He glanced down at his wrist, it was bare.

"Looking for this?" Dillon held up the Datacle. "I've never seen one so customized. It's amazing what she was able to do with this. I think I'll enjoy it."

He placed it on his wrist, called up the menu and a few touches later, V appeared on the screen.

"Hello dear," Dillon leered at V then tapped a couple more times. "Better run," he laughed then switched off the Datacle.

"She was the last one we needed to find, but thanks to you, I now have her coordinates."

James took a deep breath. He wanted to say something, but was in no position to talk. Instead he asked, "What do you mean genetically engineered?"

Dillon studied him. "Ever wonder why nearly everybody dies around 60, 65 years old?"

James tightened his eyebrows.

"It's because they're engineered that way. The code for them is made here. Everything from body type to personality is engineered right here, including your sweetheart, Carol."

James clenched his jaw. There was nothing he could say that was going to get him out of this situation. *But was it true? Were the people of Earth all built here?*

"Ah, we're to the pad."

Dillon reached over and unlocked his wrists from the

158

seat then placed them together.

"No funny business this time," he glared, then grabbed the shackles and dragged him outside.

James squinted as the bright light hit his eyes, then focused. Standing before him was a large ship, similar to the one they had blown up not too long ago. He was dragged aboard and thrown into another seat as the ship closed its door and began an ascent. Dillon sat down next to him and pulled an apple out of his pocket.

"This is what Earthlings are for." He took a bite of the crisp apple, then chewing on it, trumpeted, "My favorite."

James looked about the ship. There were mediators all around providing guard for Dillon. He tried to concoct a plan of escape, but he couldn't even figure out how the shackles worked. Dillon got up, threw the apple core in a trash compartment, then headed to the front of the ship. Sonya appeared from out of the cockpit, sucker and all. She winked at James then turned to follow Dillon. James couldn't believe it, he really didn't know anything about her, but they were both in on it. They betrayed their friends and now he was a captive, his only hope was caught and Ariel might be dead. He felt the ship slow then come to a stop. The door slid open.

Outside stood a full entourage, twenty plus people all dressed in fancy jewel-toned robes, surrounded by mediators waited for the prisoner.

"Time to go see the council."

Dillon grabbed his arm around his triceps, picked him

up, and pushed him toward the crowd. He heard people murmuring as he passed

"That's Arcturus' son," said one.

"We can finally leave this prison," another whispered.

He scanned the crowd that had formed in a horseshoe around him. James noticed one person in the middle in front of the rest and Dillon was taking him to them. On closer examination, it was a woman with brown hair, short like a pageboy, wearing a long dress of purple and dark blue. He continued his walk toward her and she moved to meet him as he exited the ship. She was as tall as him, which was surprising. All of the women he knew on Earth were shorter than the men. She looked familiar, but he couldn't remember where he'd seen her. She placed her right hand under his chin and swung his head side to side, examining him.

"Arcturus' son, hmm? And he has the coordinates?"

"Yes, ma'am," Dillon replied. "I'll take him to have it extracted when you desire, my lady."

She studied him further, tilting her head back, frowning and looking down on him.

"Take him to the council room. I'd like to know a few things before you extract the data."

"Very well."

She turned to leave. Dillon remained there holding James and they watched as everyone left.

"Who was that?" he asked

"That was Lady Cyrellia, head of TK council. My advice, don't piss her off."

James looked over his shoulder to see Dillon grinning as he grabbed James' shackles and dragged him along.

"Better not keep her waiting."

They followed everyone to the door and passed a few of the spectators huddled nearby, watching him and whispering to each other. Inside, the building looked almost exactly like the one he'd seen in his dream. Two stairs adorned the walls with a central door leading to an elevator. They entered the elevator and James watched Dillon press the floor button. It read "TK Round Table".

Thirty-nine floors up, they exited the elevator and entered the council room, it was just like the dream. The table was there just as he remembered it except the room was empty this time, only Cyrellia stood at the far end of the table with her back to them.

"Leave us," she commanded.

"Remember what I said," Dillon whispered as he left.

James stood there, still in shackles, and watched as she walked to a small table off to the side of the room. Pouring a drink she started, "So you're Arcturus' son?"

James had heard this, but was still perplexed. *Was this a case of mistaken identity, or was it true?* "I don't know."

"You don't know?" she laughed. "Who do you think you are?"

He thought about that for a moment and answered, "James Campbell."

"I'm guessing you think you're from Earth, don't you?"

James didn't say a word. He thought that was true,

but with what had happened, he was beginning to doubt it. He'd been trying to suss out the facts and really wanted to believe this was all a dream, an elaborate dream. She waved him over to the window where she stood surveying the city below. James joined her as requested. It was so mesmerizing, he had never seen anything like it, and over the past few days had not been able to stop and really look at it. Even now though, he felt he couldn't enjoy the beauty of the city because his mind kept asking what was going to happen to him.

"Do you see all of this? We built it hundreds of years ago. This is all that's left of humanity." She paused taking a sip, never looking at him. "We have suffered much. This place has been our prison, trapped in a metal sphere for hundreds of years with no end in sight."

She spun around and looked him in the eyes.

"But he found it, our sanctuary, our escape. Acadia." She held her free hand up, palm open, fingers spread facing the sky. She quickly clenched it into a fist and her eyes hardened. "Then he took it away, and for what? To save some drones on Earth. We deserve our salvation. We have struggled all these years."

She turned, staring outside again, her rage temporarily leaving her.

"But now you're here and we will finally be free of this container. The Exodus will take us to our freedom, to our new home."

She looked at James, her face demanding and uncompromising.

"You have our blood flowing through your veins; you aren't a drone from Earth. You are one of us."

James just watched as she continued.

"You have a choice to make. Give us the coordinates and come with us or we will take them and leave you here."

Couldn't they just extract it as V had done? No, they couldn't. The data was taken from him, but did they know that?

She walked beside the large window and around the table, running her hand along its edge.

"So, what do you say? Your father was a brilliant man. I'm sure you have that in you. Actually, I know you have that in you."

James watched and weighed his options. His family was on Earth. Carol and his old friends were on Earth. His gut told him it would be wrong to accept the request. He gathered his courage.

"No, I'm sorry, I can't. I don't have the information, they took it from me."

Cyrellia shook with anger, her empty hand clenching into a fist, she threw the glass toward him. He ducked and it shattered on the wall behind him. She ran over to him.

"Fool! You're a fool just like your father. What are you trying to accomplish? To save your Earth friends? We made them, we engineered them, we control them. They are worker ants, nothing more."

She lifted her arm, she was wearing a Datacle like

Ariel's, but slightly different. Her fingers tapped on it and the door opened. Two large men of Zane's build walked in.

"Take him to Mendelev. Extract the data. If he survives, I'll inform you what to do."

She turned to James.

"Last chance to reconsider."

James watched the two men stomping toward him; all he could do was shake his head.

Cyrellia shook and coldly threatened, "You'll regret this, dear J."

Her tone frightened James to the core. The two men grabbed him, one on each arm, and escorted him out. They took him back to the elevator and tapped in a special code. The elevator read "Mendelev's Lab".

Down they went. The two behemoths stood on either side of him and he looked around, trying to figure out a way to escape, nothing. He was in a sealed box with no hope. After what he thought was the longest elevator ride of his life, they stepped out. Lights covered every surface and it was so bright he couldn't tell what was around him or which way to go. He squinted up at his captors to see that they had put on dark sunglasses. James strained his eyes and tried to look around, but they watered from the effort. He walked blindly. They turned left, right, straight for a bit. He was trying to remember the path, but there were so many switchbacks that he lost track. Finally, they stopped. He was forced into a seat and his wrists were released from the shackles only to be reattached to what felt like the arms of a chair. He attempted to open his eyes, but the intense light kept them shut. He could feel the two guards leave the room, or wherever he was. He sat there for a bit with nothing to do but think. He tried again to search for a way out, but no luck. It was still too bright. He heard someone enter the room.

"Hello?" he said.

"Hello. I'm Doctor Mendelev and you are J, son of Arcturus. Are you not?"

James didn't know how to respond and remained silent.

"Matters not. I will get what she wants then she will be content," he said dispassionately.

James vainly attempted to see what was happening, nothing but overwhelming light. He was aware of something being mounted on his head. It felt like the device used on him earlier by V. There was a sharp prick on his right arm, then the left, and he let out a shriek, not only from the pain but fear and shock as well. His head tingled with electricity for a brief moment.

"They removed it, I see. No matter. It is in there. I will find it."

James began to feel woozy and his head was spinning, a very strange sensation with his eyes closed. He tried to open his eyes and was able to make out the hazy shadow of a figure in front of him. He shut them once again and everything went dark.

He sat up in bed and looked around, stretching. He

was unfamiliar with where he was. The room reminded him of the old Tudor style home that the Mayor lived in. James had visited there once for a lunch when he was awarded the scholarship. He stood up and tried to turn around, but couldn't. He walked forward and into a bathroom and looked in the mirror. If he could have controlled it, his eyes would have expanded to full capacity. It wasn't him staring back, it had to be Arcturus. He cleaned his teeth then headed back into the bedroom. James was along for the ride again, but this time he realized it and tried his best to relax and let it play out like a movie. After getting dressed, he stepped out into a kitchen area where a man stood with pancakes, orange juice and bacon on a platter.

"Breakfast, sir? I understand it's a big day today."

"Thanks, Lee. You say that every day. I'm hoping you'll be right."

He followed Lee into a dining area where the food was placed on a table then sat down at a large wooden table and began to eat. Something seemed off. Everything in this place was so different from the rooms he had become accustomed to in Atlantis. Little to no metal could be seen, it resembled an Earth house. Outside the heavily framed windows was a picturesque mountain view. It looked like a beautiful spring day with birds flying by. He spotted a Robin catching a worm. He completed the meal then went back to finish getting dressed. Afterward, he headed through the house and out the front door. He was definitely on the moon.

The steel city rose around him. Lee was waiting,
standing next to an automobile. It hovered effortlessly on
a cushion of air. James climbed in the back and thanked
Lee, who closed the door behind him. He watched out
the window, admiring the city and how amazing it all
was. He still had not become accustomed to the views.
The drive continued for awhile, but passed quickly as
he was lost in his thoughts. *Where were they heading?*
Ariel would be able to explain exactly what he was seeing.
Was she still alive? Of course she was, she's resourceful and
amazing. Stop thinking like that. The auto stopped and
the door opened. He stepped out into the sun and looked
around. He made his way to the large building in front
of him and was met at the entrance by a smaller man in
glasses holding a glass book. He looked familiar, but
James couldn't quite place him.

"Good morning, Jeffrey."

"Arcturus. Big day, I think we may have a breakthrough."

"So I hear. Is Zane in my office?"

"Yes, he's been there for about 30 minutes. Anything
else I can do before we begin today?"

"Just ensure that all of the systems calibrations have
been run. We only get one shot at this. The next window
will be in 1,014 years."

"Absolutely."

With that, he disappeared down a side hall and
James proceeded to the main elevator and rode it up. He
entered his office to find Zane standing there, patiently
waiting. James turned and closed the door behind him,

punching in a special code to lock the door.

"Good morning sir, how did you sleep?"

"To be honest, not very well. How about you?"

"As well as anyone would sleep when the next day the plan is mutiny."

"You know as well as I that our plan is not mutiny. Earth needs to be saved. Those people deserve a fresh start as much as we do."

"I agree, but when you're going to do what we're planning, we in the military would call it mutiny."

"Very well. So I take it you didn't sleep too well, either. Everything still in place?"

"Yes, I tested the ships. All systems are good. Are you sure you want to use those old spacecraft? I'm not convinced that their systems, especially their shields, will function correctly. They've been known to overload at times."

"You know we can't use anything newer, they can be taken over by TK too easily. Those older ships are not networked to the new system. When they upgraded last, they removed all of the old tech."

"I'm still not comfortable with it, seeing as your son will be riding in one of them."

"It must be done. It's the only way. Are the rest of the plans set?"

"Yes, data wipe is set to go. Should take fifteen seconds once initiated. The longest part will be downloading the data to J."

"Don't worry about that, I'll take care of it. You just

concentrate on your part. Is Dillon prepped?"

"Yes, sir. He's ready to go as well. Once you say the word, we'll execute. No loose ends."

James nodded at Zane and, punching the key code in once more, unlocked the door. They left his office and headed up to the control room. There they found a team of scientists all working on various machines. Jeffrey came running up with the glass book.

"We're all set. The path for the shoot will be open in fifteen minutes."

James nodded then headed to the center of the room and stood facing a large screen. It looked like a window into space, stars everywhere. James had never seen them so clearly before. The sky was full of beautiful colors blending into black, purple-blue, and hazy white swirls. On the top of the screen, a countdown clock was running, while other letters and numbers flashed along various parts of the screen. Circles appeared around various stars with labels on them and the view shifted a few times. The countdown neared five minutes.

"Is everything in place?" James asked.

"Yes, system 1 is a go," said someone.

"System 2 a go," said another.

"System 3 a go," said a third.

This continued until all members spoke their part. The clock hit one minute. A voice began counting down. Very curious to see what would happen, James eagerly awaited the result. The timer hit one, everyone went silent. A planet stared back at him on the large screen, scrolling underneath was a series of numbers. He watched for a few minutes, analyzing the picture.

"Arcturus."

James' head swung to the right. Approaching him again was Jeffrey. He handed the glass book to James. "Those coordinates have been verified four times. I think it's the one."

He observed multiple people smiling and hugging, some jumping for joy.

"Have you notified the Kontrolery yet?"

"No, we were going to let you inform them."

"Very well," James looked back at the screen and everything went dark.

CHAPTER THIRTEEN

James sat up, snapping his back. He was in school. He frowned. *How did he get here? What happened?* He looked down at his desk. Drool ran over his open school book, his pencil lay next to a blank piece of paper.

"Welcome back," his teacher admonished.

Tim and Rex were chuckling.

"Good dream?" Rex asked with a laugh. "How was your travel in space?"

"What?" James replied, startled. *Did they know what he just went through? They couldn't.*

"You were talking in your sleep, sounded like quite the adventure." Rex turned to Tim and made spaceship noises. James scowled back at him.

What was he doing in class? What happened in that room? The bell rang and he stumbled out of the classroom. His head felt fuzzy and he felt vaguely sick. He walked down the hall and ran into Carol.

She placed her hand on his arm and looked up at him, "How are you feeling today, any better?"

"My head feels a little out of sorts. What day is it?"

"It's Monday, are you still having some memory issues, you did take a big hit to the head."

Hit to the head? What was she talking about? He ran through his memory of the events on Atlantis, but he didn't remember any hits to the head.

"What?"

"You don't remember, the doctor said it would affect

the last few days or so, and I might have to repeat myself, so I was expecting this, but I thought you might be feeling better by now."

She took his hand and guided him through the hall.

"Saturday during your game, you took a line drive to the head, you were in a coma for six days, then on bed rest Sunday, the doctor said it would be best for you to get back to your normal routine, so you came back to school today."

James reached up to feel his head. There was a small lump on the right side of his forehead. He excused himself to go to the bathroom. Trying to play it cool, he took his time, though inside he wanted to run. Once in the bathroom, he studied himself in the mirror. It had been some time since he had looked at himself. He appeared haggard, his eyelids were heavy, he had dark circles under his eyes and a big bruise on his forehead. He ran his hand over it. He didn't remember any details of the game. The last one he remembered was the Colton game, which they lost when he grounded out. He recalled all of the events after that, trying to place his timeline. He had no clue how long he'd been on Atlantis, it felt like a few days, but may have been a week. He just didn't know. No more enlightened, he strode out to question Carol.

"What game did I get hit in? What happened?"

"It was the Colton game last Saturday, you were up to bat in the 9th inning and a pitch got away and drilled you in the head, so they ended the game and rushed you to the hospital, you were there for a week recovering and I was so worried about you, but luckily you came out of it," she simpered. "I don't know what I would do without you James."

He looked down. *He'd had that same thought about Ariel not too long ago.*

"What about the meteor shower?"

"Oh, that was the furthest thing from my mind, I assume it happened like my teacher said, why do you ask?"

"So, we didn't watch it together?"

"No silly, how could we, you were out, and I was with you at the hospital."

"Did I get in a fight with Rich?"

"Nothing more than usual, I know you really don't like him."

He tried to recall more details leading up to his time on the moon, but nothing came to him.

"Let's get you home."

James nodded in agreement. *Maybe he could find something there that would explain all of this.* They walked out the front doors.

"Hey James! How you feeling? Gonna be ready for Wednesday?" Jason asked, walking up next to them.

"What's Wednesday?" James asked.

"It's our next ball game, pretty big deal. It's against Johnstown. They have a good squad this year, really hoping you'll be ready."

"I don't know, my head is spinning. I'm trying to

remember what exactly happened."

"I imagine Carol filled you in, right?"

"She did. I guess I was hit in the head during our game Saturday."

He felt the lump on his head and gently massaged it.

"Yep, you went down like a sack of potatoes. I thought you were dead!"

"Don't say that, what if it were true, I can't even imagine," Carol chided.

"Anyway, you need a ride? I'm sure Rich could take you home."

James rolled his eyes. Rich. Part of him had completely forgotten about that loudmouth.

"No, I'll drive," James replied

"Actually, his father is picking us up."

James' eyes narrowed, "What?"

"He dropped you off today and said he would pick us up, doctor said no driving or farm work for a week, he wants you to get your head straight before you get back to normal work activities."

James looked over to see his father pull up in his truck, so he said goodbye to Jason, grabbed Carol's hand and headed over. Carol slid into the middle and James grudgingly jumped in next to her.

"How are you doing?" James' father asked, accelerating forward.

"Good, I guess. Don't remember most of it."

"The doctor said that might be the case. Give it some time. He said getting back to a routine sooner rather than later would help expedite the healing process."

"Were you able to fix the bailing system on the harvester?"

"No, I was leaving that up to you? We have some time and I thought it might be good for you to get back to work. In a few days, no rush."

James started telling himself it was all a dream, it must have been a dream. A really vivid dream starring a dynamic, take-charge, spitfire of a girl with brilliant blue eyes. This was reality.

He tried to embrace it. "Can Carol come over for dinner?"

"Sure, I don't see why not. Better call her parents though when we get in."

"What do you say, come over for dinner?" He reached over and grabbed Carol's hand, her face lit up.

"Sure, I would love to, I've missed spending time with you."

At dinner, James continued to ask questions about his time away, or as they would say, while he was in the coma. School had gone on as normal and the ball team had continued playing games, losing three of them. James wanted to tell his story of flying to the moon, meeting Ariel, Dillon, Zane, V, the mediators, all of it. But the more he thought about it, the more he worried they would think he was crazy.

After wrapping up dinner with his parents, he and Carol sat out on the porch swing together, watching the sun set over the wall. It was still there, with the drop-off hidden behind it.

"The Earth falls off just outside the wall," James said in a straight voice.

He couldn't give in. It couldn't have been just a dream.

Carol snickered, "You're very silly, of course it does, you sound like you made a new discovery."

"Have you seen it?"

The vision of the sheer drop off flashed in his mind, his body shivered.

"No, but I've been in all the same history classes as you, did you forget that, too?"

"Why was it built?"

Carol twisted her body and put her hand on his thigh, her face was soft and glowed. He'd almost forgotten.

"Is this a test, you know why."

"Why?"

"To keep us safe of course, don't want to fall off, why this fascination all of a sudden?"

James looked at the wall, then back at her and leaned in close. "Let me show you something, come on."

He hopped up from the swing and extended his hand. She reached up and he pulled her out of the seat and hurriedly took her to the truck. His head was feeling better now and he had a driving need to show her.

"What are you doing James, you heard what the doctor said, you're not supposed to drive."

"There's something I need to show you," he hesitated. "My head is feeling much better, the haze is gone. Come

176

with me."

He opened the door for her and sat her in the passenger seat. He started the truck and smiled at Carol, "It will be amazing."

He began driving toward the wheat fields. James was going to show her the tunnel; that would get things started. He needed to prove it, not only to Carol, but also himself. He drove down the paths he'd traveled plenty of times, his mind focused on the crater, the tunnel, the wall, and Flat Earth. They arrived at the edge of the field where he'd found the tunnel entrance and looked out toward the wall. The ground was undisturbed; he got out and ran to the edge of the property. *What happened? Did someone level the dirt, where was the mound?*

Carol walked up behind him as he frantically searched for the hole. She wrapped her arms around him and nuzzled his back.

"What were you going to show me?"

James hesitated, he promised her something amazing, but nothing was there.

"There was..." he began, but stopped, thinking better of it. Maybe he just couldn't see it from here, maybe he needed to get closer.

He slipped from Carol and grabbed her hand.

"Follow me," he began walking toward the wall.

"James, I don't want to get any closer to the wall, can we stop?"

James looked back at her. "No, I need to show you something."

177

He tugged her along. He could feel the hesitation in her hand. They reached the edge of the property line and he stopped for a moment then turned to Carol.

"Only about twenty more feet or so."

"Are you sure, this is scary, you know what they say will happen if we get too close to the wall."

His mind flashed back to school. The teachers made them rehearse a verse to remember the hazard of going to close to the wall.

"Too close to the wall, you'll take a fall," James recited to Carol. She had fear in her eyes. "Trust me. I've been out there, nothing will happen."

James took hold of her again and marched toward the wall. He felt her hand go limp and heard something heavy hit the ground. Carol lie on the ground behind him. He started to panic. She was still breathing, but nonresponsive, like a ragdoll. He picked her up and carried her toward the truck. She woke up on the way.

"What happened?" her voice was weak.

"You passed out. I'm going to put you in the truck."

After placing her in the truck he ran back to the property line and out toward the wall. Nothing. He found nothing. No sign that the ground had been disturbed in any way. *What was going on?* He ran up and down the property line. Could he have remembered incorrectly? He looked back at the truck and past it to the large boulder he and Carol had laid on to watch the meteor shower. The meteor shower, the device, he remembered the device. He put it in the barn, it had to still be there. He ran back to the truck. Carol was sitting there dazed. He put the truck in reverse and headed back to the barn.

"Come on, this way." He opened the passenger door and helped Carol out. She was still acting a bit woozy, but was able to follow him.

They went into the barn and he looked down. The floor was undisturbed. He dropped to his knees examining it.

"This should be burnt," he said under his breath. "This is where I dropped the torch."

He stood up, ran over to the cabinet and frantically opened it, empty. James let out a frustrated growl, then ran over to the harvester.

"What's going on James?"

"It should have been there. I need to prove that I wasn't in a coma. That I was on the moon."

"The moon, you were on the moon?"

"Yes, the moon, in a city called New Atlantis. It's the home of TK and people like us."

James let it all flow out. He couldn't keep it inside anymore, the details of the city embedded inside the moon.

"James, you're scaring me, this is all a joke right, or a dream, is this what you dreamed about when you were in your coma?"

"Yes. I mean, no. I mean, I don't know. It was all real. It happened. The people I met, the mediators that chased us, Ariel."

"Mediators?"

"Yes, robot humanoid machines that act as peace-keepers."

"James, I think maybe we should head back so your father can take me home, I think you need some rest."

James looked at Carol. She had trouble getting those words out and she was shaking. His protective instincts took over, attempting to put her at ease. "You're right, Carol. I'm sorry, let's get you home. It probably was all a dream, but it felt all too real."

They headed back to the house and asked his father to take them to Carol's. When they arrived, he escorted her to the door.

"I'm sorry for frightening you tonight. I'm just trying to figure things out."

She smiled and gave him a kiss on the cheek, "We'll get through this James, I love you."

She headed inside. James paused. *Love? If the night of the meteor shower had never happened, this would be the first time either of them had said it. She'd claimed that him saying it first had scared her. What changed? What was going on?* He turned and walked back to the truck.

"Everything go okay?" his father asked as James stepped up into the truck, staring out the window into the distance.

"Yep. I've just had a rough stretch and I'm trying to figure things out."

"You two were awfully quiet on the drive over here," his father started forward.

"Yeah, just working through a few things. This coma

has really messed up my head." Again he went back to his thoughts. *Was it a dream?*

"How so?" his father's tone was that of someone who'd been in his shoes and was trying to help.

"I've just had a lot of questions and a few experiences which I thought were real, but now I'm thinking could have been an elaborate dream."

"I see, what was this dream?"

"I'd rather not talk about it. It's confusing, especially to me."

"Alright then. You let me know if you ever feel ready to talk about it."

They reached home. James walked to his room and promptly fell asleep.

The next morning, he woke up feeling much better. His head fog was completely gone and he was ready to get back to his life. He was in denial that he was in a coma, but uncertain how to proceed. *Was TK about to launch the Exodus to fly to their new planet?* James was deep in thought throughout his morning routine. He missed a few things and was more clumsy than normal, dropping a few eggs as he transferred them. At breakfast, he didn't say a word, just ate with a thousand yard stare.

"You doing okay this morning, hon?"

His mom stopped washing the dishes when he didn't answer and turned to look at him, "James?"

He set his fork down on the edge of his plate and refocused his eyes on her. "Yes, yes Mom. I just have a lot on my mind, trying to figure things out."

"Maybe if you work on that harvester for me this afternoon it'll help. The bailing system is still malfunctioning," his father injected.

"Sure, I can get to that. If not today, maybe tomorrow."

"Okay, try and get it done by this weekend though. I want to do a test run on it to make sure we're set for the harvest."

James finished breakfast then his father drove him to school. On the way, he looked up to see the moon shining back at him as if to taunt him. *Was it hollow? Did Atlantis exist?* They arrived at school and Carol was outside waiting for him.

"You feeling better today, you look better," she leaned over and gave him a kiss. James hesitated for a second, she had never been quite so affectionate, at least in public, but he was going to go with it. Maybe the coma had scared her, maybe they would be closer now.

"Are you going to try and go to practice after school today?"

"I was thinking about it. I'm feeling pretty good now."

"Can we go to Sam's tonight after, I'd like things to get back to normal."

James thought about it. Maybe that would be a good thing, for more than one reason.

"Sure, I'll pick you up around six."

"Okay, see you later," she waved as she ran off to class.

He watched her, books in her arms, skirt flowing about her calves. *Was this home? It was simple and he liked it. Or was he just trying to tell himself he liked it?*

"Coming to practice today?" Jason walked up from behind him.

"Yep, I'm feeling better."

Physically that was true but his head was a mess.

"Great, we have some big games this week! See you at practice." He walked off.

James started toward his class, staring down at the ground, running through his evening plans. During class, his mind wandered as he went through the motions of answering questions and fixing recurring malfunctions on the equipment. How simple life on Earth was, much less stressful than what he had just experienced, real or not. James finished up, said goodbye to his instructor and headed to practice.

"How's that head doing? Knock some sense into you?" Rich quipped, sliding on his ball pants.

James acted as if he didn't hear him.

"That hit damage your hearing?"

"No, I'm doing fine," he said, looking down at his laces and pausing.

"Well, I hope so. Our scholarship boy better show up this week, it's a big game."

"So I hear." He finished tying his shoe with a tight tug at the end.

Jason walked up. "Give him a break, he's been in a coma for a week."

Rich rolled his eyes. James had been getting all of the attention and he wasn't enjoying any of it.

"So, seriously. How are you doing?" Jason leaned down near James as he finished putting his cleats on.

"Yeah, just fine. Why do you ask?" There was frustration in his voice.

"Well, you were just in a coma. I've never known anyone to be out for that long of a time. I didn't know how it would affect you. Coach gave us a talk to give you space to figure things out, but I think it'd be better to talk."

"Talk? Since when are you the touchy feely sort?"

"Hey man. I'm just looking out for you. Don't get all weird."

James had responded rather harshly to him, which was a bit out of character, and even he realized it. His temper seemed shorter than normal. He felt as if everyone was trying to be overly nice. Everyone seemed a little off, but maybe it was him. With each passing hour, he felt as if his travels were just a dream, but he had one more chance to find out.

After practice, his father picked him up and he convinced him to let him drive home. He wanted to get the truck for that night. He was way too old to have a chaperone or to be driven around by his father. During the drive, his father relented. At home, he changed then headed to pick up Carol. They chatted on the way over to the diner, mostly about school gossip, who was dating who, who failed a math test, the mundane things teenagers on Earth talk about.

On the way through town, James asked about the

recent power outages and fires. She told him they were still ongoing and even mentioned that her father said they weren't sure what was actually causing them. They pulled up to Sam's Diner and James had a momentary flashback to Atlantis and another girl he'd gone to Sam's with. Then he looked around, scanning the parking lot and the front door. He hopped out and opened Carol's door, his head was on a swivel, searching.

"What are you looking for?" Carol asked, eyebrows slanted.

"Nothing, I was just expecting to see Will outside smoking like usual."

"Who?"

"Will, the older gentleman, always offers me a smoke."

"Are you sure you're doing alright, there has never been a man like that here at the diner, maybe it was part of your head injury, maybe you should see the doctor tomorrow to make sure everything's progressing good."

James wanted to argue, but knew it wouldn't go anywhere so they headed inside. Rich and Jason were in the booth along with Margo. Barbara was at the jukebox picking a few songs, she waved to them as they passed.

"Didn't do too bad with that bump on your head," Rich greeted him.

James rubbed his forehead, it was still sore to the touch. They sat down and were joined shortly by Barbara, she had picked a new Hop song, and the girls were bopping along to it.

"Do you guys remember Will?"

"Will?" all of them said in unison.

"Will who?" Jason added.

They were all intently looking at James.

"He used to hang around outside? Offered smokes to us?"

How could they forget Will? He'd been outside every time they met at the diner.

But everyone looked puzzled.

"You guys seriously don't remember him?"

"We have never seen anyone like that outside," Barbara replied as she chomped on her gum.

"Yeah, maybe it's the head injury," Rich added. "Making you see things." He started laughing.

James couldn't hold it in any longer and it all came pouring out like Mount Vesuvius.

"Do you guys know what's outside the wall?"

"No more than you," Jason piped up.

Carol pleaded, "Don't James."

He continued, "What do you think is out there?"

"A cliff into space, everyone knows that! Did you forget kindergarten?" Rich continued. "Did that hit make you stupid?"

James held back, but really wanted to clock him again.

"Why are you asking?" Jason slightly turned his head as if to listen with one ear.

"I've seen it. The world is flat, but not." He played with his hands in the air moving them about.

"What do you mean, not? And how could you have seen it, it's impossible to get near the wall. You'd be killed."

"Not true. You might get switched off, but it didn't happen to me," his hands continuing the air show.

Carol grabbed his arm. "Let's go," she insisted.

James was too far into the conversation.

"I went past the line and found a path under the wall."

"Let's go!" Carol grabbed him tighter and tried to pull him out of the booth, he resisted.

Jason and the girls looked at him like he'd lost his mind. Rich was still laughing. "No, Carol. Let him go. I want to hear this," his laughter trailed off into a self-satisfied smirk.

"The other side is maybe 100 yards then drops off sharply, but over—"

"I believe you," Carol whispered in his ear.

James stopped and stared at her.

"Let's go," she insisted again.

CHAPTER FOURTEEN

The truck door shut.

"You believe me?"

"Yes."

"What changed?"

James pulled out of the parking spot and headed down the road. His hands gripped the steering wheel while he rubbed his teeth on his bottom lip.

"This," she said as she grabbed his right hand and placed it on the back of her neck.

He felt a small bump that was very warm to the touch.

"It started after I switched off in the field, it tingled all night and has felt warm all day long, I didn't know if it meant anything at all."

James pulled over to the side of the road, dirt kicking up as the truck drifted to a halt.

"What do you think it is, do you think it has something to do with me being switched off?"

He had her turn her head and lift up her hair, but it was too dark.

"We should look at it in better light. Let's head to my house. We can try the barn, plenty of light there in the workshop."

James pulled back onto the road accelerating quickly. "So it tingled?"

"Yes."

"Have you told your parents or anyone else?"

"No, but I have these strange memories, not whole

188

stories but fragments, I thought they were maybe dreams but some of the questions you asked me..."

His hands massaged the steering wheel listening to her answers.

"Go on."

"I remember watching a meteor shower, in your field, I was scared of the wall."

Carol wasn't talking quick enough for James, he wanted more, he wanted it all, he wanted validation.

"What else?"

"Just bits of other things, but nothing substantial, I've also been thinking about a lot today, questions I never really asked before, questions like what you talked about tonight."

"Outside the wall?"

He continued his quick short questions, coaxing her along.

"Yes, I'm very curious if what they have taught us in school is true."

James hesitated, thinking of how to respond. It blew his mind when he flew to the moon and he didn't want to overload Carol. He didn't know how she'd handle it.

"I've been outside the wall," he finally admitted.

Carol perked up and looked at him with wonder in her eyes, like a child learning about Santa for the first time.

"I heard you say that earlier, is it true, what's out there?"

"Just like they say. There's a flat drop off."

Carol sunk back into the seat.

"I see, I thought maybe there was more."

"There is. I just don't know how to explain it."

"Can you try, I'm dying to know, I have this feeling something happened to you out there, what was it, how did you get there?"

James started with Saturday night and the meteor shower then detailed the events leading up to finding the tunnel. She hung on every word, occasionally mentioning that she remembered pieces of the story, including Will. They arrived at the barn and headed inside. James switched on the lights and brought over a portable light to get a closer look at Carol's neck.

"You say it tingled, then felt warm?"

"Yes, what do you think it is?"

James had her hold her hair out of the way then he ran his hand over it. It was still hot.

"Does this hurt?"

He put a little more pressure on it to feel it better.

"No, it's just warm, no pain."

James pushed a little harder and thought he felt something, a small square bump on the bone. He looked closer and tried pushing it to one side, it moved. Whatever it was, it was loose. James wiggled it back and forth a few times with his fingers. Carol winced a bit, but assured James it wasn't painful, it just felt weird, for lack of a better description. James thought for a moment, his mind calculating. *What if it had something to do with her being switched off? Maybe it was a literal switch?*

190

"Carol," James started in a slow, reassuring tone. "I think we should cut it out."

Carol pulled back. "What?"

"I think it has something to do with you switching off. Maybe it's mind control or something. I don't know, but I don't think it's natural."

"Maybe we can go to a doctor and have them check it out, I don't want you to use a knife on me."

"Trust me, I don't want to use a knife on you either. But after what I've seen, I think it could be hurting you. We need to get it out."

Carol felt the back of her neck then stared hard at James. "What have you seen, tell me and maybe I'll let you cut it out."

James looked away. *How was he going to do this? Should he even tell her?*

"I flew to the moon. It's hollow and there's a huge city inside."

He blurted it out as though he had no inner monologue. Carol stood there staring, her jaw dropped. James tried to figure out what he had just said and realized he had laid it all out there. Well, a brief summary.

"Okay, let's take it out."

James was not expecting that.

"Oh...Okay."

The Carol he had known would have probably fought him on it. Her personality had slightly changed since she was switched off.

"Sit over there. I'll get a razor."

191

He pointed to a chair near the wall of the barn, then left to grab a shaving razor from the house. He returned to see Carol sitting in the chair, still rubbing her neck.

"You really think it's mind control?"

James shrugged his shoulders as he approached.

"I heard mention of it and, after what I've seen, it's possible."

She looked down at her feet and pulled her hair to the side. James took the razor between his thumb and index finger and held it next to her neck. His hands trembled; he had never used a knife on a person before, let alone his girlfriend.

"Go on," she said steadily. "I'm ready."

James placed his empty hand on her neck and stretched the skin, prepping for the incision. He took a deep breath and made a gentle cut. Carol pulled away, but didn't make a sound. She slowly moved back as if to say, "Go ahead". He made a deeper cut and blood began to stream down her neck. James realized that he hadn't grabbed any bandages or rags, so he quickly took off his shirt and pressed it to her neck, minimizing the blood flow.

"I'm going to release the bandage and see if I can grab it."

Grab it with my fingers? He realized he would have to make a larger cut to get in there with his fingers, then, "Pliers," he snapped his fingers. "Hold pressure on it."

Carol replaced his hand with hers and held pressure

on the incision while he ran and grabbed a set of small pliers.

"Ok, here goes nothing."

What a stupid thing to say when you've just cut somebody open and are operating on them. Carol released the pressure and James quickly opened the wound then clamped on the pliers. James tugged; Carol winced and let out a whimper.

"I'm sorry," James soothed. "I'll stop"

"No, just get it out,"

He pulled again and it released.

Carol felt his hand leave and pressed the shirt down. James looked intensely at the pliers. Between the jaws was a small square metallic object, and dangling from it was a mass of hair-like wires. Carol turned to look.

"What is it?"

James shook his head, just stared at it. Carol peered closer and tightened her eyes to see it better in the light. James looked back at Carol.

"Bandages."

He handed her the pliers and ran to the house to get medical supplies. He returned to find Carol sitting at the work bench, staring at the tiny object and clutching her neck. James maneuvered behind her and cleaned then wrapped her wound.

"Sorry, not going to win any beauty pageants today."

Carol slapped his arm. "Meany."

They both looked at the table.

"What is it?" Carol asked.

193

"Beats me, but I have an idea."

He grabbed the object, slipped it into his pocket and escorted Carol to his truck.

"Where are we going?"

"You'll see. I have an idea."

"You said that, but what is it?"

James didn't say a word; he just started the truck and headed toward the fields. He followed the roads until he was back at the rock then zipped by it heading straight for the wall.

"What are you doing, James? Stop!"

He didn't, he kept driving.

"Stop. You're going to go past the border!"

James remained silent, the border approached quicker.

"Stop, Stop! STOP!" Carol pleaded, but James drove on.

He glanced out the driver's door to see that they were past it then he slammed on the brakes, skidding over the ground, dirt flying everywhere. Carol was still screaming. The truck stopped. Carol stopped and looked at James. He grinned at her as if he just discovered something, but was awaiting approval. He looked back at the rock, Carol followed suit.

"Where..."

"Yep."

"But I'm..."

"Yep."

She stared at the wall towering in front of them.

"I never realized how big it was."

James hopped out and walked toward the wall. Carol stayed inside with her mouth open. He glanced back and headed to the truck then grabbed her by the hand.

"Come on, nothing's going to happen."

She hesitated, but he pulled her onward. They walked hand in hand to the base of the wall and James reached out and touched it. It was cold and smooth as he remembered in the tunnel, pitch black and had no rust on it, but the seams felt crude compared to all he had seen in Atlantis. Carol hugged James. It took him a second to realize what just happened, then he hugged her back.

"Thank you, James. I feel free, that's the best way to describe it."

They held the embrace for a few moments.

"Can you take me home? I'm tired."

He was, too. All of the excitement had really taken it out of him, and it was getting late, but he still had one more thing to do.

"Sure," he said softly.

They drove back to her house and after dropping off Carol, he turned the truck toward Sam's. By now it was nearing midnight, but he had to see. As he approached, he slowed the truck to a crawl. *Where was Will? Where had he gone?* Nothing, nobody was around. He saw a lone employee cleaning tables and locking up for the night. James headed home himself. Feeling worn down, he crashed as soon as his head hit the pillow.

The next morning, James got back to his routine. He wanted everything to seem normal, even though things were far from it. After breakfast, he convinced his father that he was okay to drive the truck and called Carol. They arrived at school and headed their separate ways to class as though nothing had happened. Carol had been able to replace his shoddy field bandage with a much smaller one which she hid under her hair. At lunch, they ate silently. They hung out with their friends, but engaged in minimal conversation. As soon as the final school bell rang, they met up at James' truck.

"I don't know how long I can do this," Carol slid into the seat as James opened the door.

"What do you think we should do? Tell someone? I was about to and you stopped me."

"That's because of Teresa."

"Teresa?"

"She started asking questions then just disappeared. Nobody even seemed to care. I didn't care. It was like I couldn't care, even if I wanted to, but now it's in the front of my mind. You don't remember her, do you? Most people don't."

"No, but you and I weren't really friends when we were younger so maybe I didn't know here. And after all of this, I can understand how others wouldn't remember."

James shut the door, paused a moment, then began driving.

"Well, we need to do something," he said, tightening his face as he measured the road in front of him.

Carol was staring out the window then she turned to him. "Yes, but I don't know what. You said there was a tunnel to the outside. What happened when you were there?"

His mind went to the clouds swirling about, the underside of the table.

"I saw what Earth really looks like. And in a dream, well I think it was a dream, maybe a memory I'm not sure, I saw the Earth from space."

"Space?"

"It's a long story, but it looked like a series of floating plates with a skeletal structure holding it all together. Umm... like a soccer ball with some of the patches missing."

Carol's eyebrows narrowed, "A soccer ball?"

"Yes, that's the best way to describe it. A soccer ball. Anyway, I stumbled across a spaceship which took me to the moon and there's a city there with an organization called TK who runs everything and wants to fly away to another planet and leave Earth behind to self-destruct."

Carol didn't know how to respond, she just sat there listening. James continued the story, telling nearly everything he remembered, the fighting, the mediators, the machines, everything. Carol just took it all in, asking a few questions as he continued the story, plenty about Ariel. She seemed really interested in her.

"So how did you end up back here? And why doesn't anyone remember you being gone?"

"I don't know. I don't even know why I'm still alive. I think they got what they wanted from me, but I'm not sure."

"What do we do now James? I feel like my mind has been freed, but I don't have any direction. Do we just live out our lives here?"

"I don't know. There has to be a way to get to New Atlantis."

By this time, they'd reached Carol's house. James pulled in and parked.

"Tomorrow, I'll pick you up. Then after school, I'll skip ball practice and we'll go to the diner. Let's figure out what we should do. I haven't got the slightest idea how, but I think you're right to keep it a secret for now."

They both agreed, said their goodbyes, then James headed home. *Huh. She didn't try to kiss him or tell him that she loved him.*

The next day, James headed to the library. His mission was to research the history of their town and try to gain clues as to what was really going on. He had convinced Carol to skip school with him. They split up, both digging through old newspapers and history books. All of the research said the same thing, no clues. *Maybe Carol had found something.* She'd always been a faster reader than him. His skill was in fixing machines, not in the arts and literature.

After fruitlessly searching for hours, James and Carol called it quits and headed to the diner for an early supper. They decided to take a booth on the far end from their usual spot, not that anyone would notice them. All of their friends were still in school, but it made them feel better.

"Did you find anything?" James asked almost in a whisper, leaning forward over the table.

Carol mirrored him. "Not really. Most of it was just the stuff we were taught in school. Very vague info, not many details."

James let his head fall down.

"I'm guessing you didn't find anything, either?"

"Nope, nothing. I don't know what to make of it."

Then James thought of something, something his teacher said about the power supply. He looked at the wall, studying it, then picked up his hand and bounced a finger in the air, as if counting. "Maybe, but how would we?"

"What, James? What?"

Carol sensed he was on to something. He reached his hands across the table and locked eyes with Carol. She returned the gesture. "They won't let us work on the power supply to our harvesters."

"So..."

"So, they have to ship it somewhere. Where does it go? It must be made off-planet. If not on the moon, then somewhere else on Earth where they work on advanced technology, maybe even spaceships!"

James was smiling at his revelation and almost wanted to pat himself on the back.

"But, wouldn't any of us have heard of it before?"

James quirked his mouth to the side, thinking.

"I think they're suppressing our thoughts and questions somehow."

"How?"

"Maybe that thing we removed from your neck."

She reached up and rubbed her neck, looking into his eyes.

"Did you have one?"

"No," James started to doubt himself. She was right. He had never felt one on his neck, but then again, he never really had any reason to question anything. Most things came easy to him and he'd been content with his life, but something had reignited his curiosity.

"I don't know why, but when I asked about fixing the power supply, Mr. MacDunna became very defensive, like he was hiding something. Tomorrow, I'm going to figure out where they send the power supplies. Maybe we'll find a clue there."

The bell rang like it always did when there were new customers arriving. Carol and James didn't pay much attention and continued their conversation. The waiter came over and handed them their food. James was really excited; it felt like he hadn't had a burger and fries in a long time, not to mention a chocolate shake. The door opened again and the little bell rang. Carol and James continued eating their food.

"Have you seen a boy named James? I was told I might find him here. I have information I need to pass on to him."

James swiveled in his seat at the sound of his name to see a man wearing a police uniform talking to the cashier. Carol leaned in close.

"Do you think he's talking about you?"

James turned back around, nervous. Cops always made him nervous.

"I hope not," he continued eating.

"James, there you are, James. Is that you?"

He glanced up to see the cop standing over him.

"Yes," he said his voice trembling slightly. "That's me. What can I do you for Mr. Officer, sir?"

"I have information I need to give to you. Would you mind coming with me down to the precinct?"

James looked at Carol. His eyes said, "What do I do?" Carol just shrugged her shoulders; she was probably more scared than he was.

"Can I get the information here? I'd like to finish my meal with my girlfriend, if that's alright with you?"

The cop looked over at Carol, then back at James.

"No, I'm sorry but I must take you to the precinct. If you would like to finish your meal, I'll let you, but then we must go. I'll give you 15 minutes."

James nodded in agreement; it seemed he really didn't have a choice. Suddenly, there was a loud "pop!" James and Carol jumped; they both felt warm fluid hit their bodies. James looked up. The cop's head was half gone, but there were wires and sparks flailing about. He dropped to the ground. Carol began to scream and tucked herself as far away into the booth as she could, knees in her chest, shivering in fear. He froze, trying to figure out what just happened.

"We have to go," a familiar voice called from

behind him.

He turned around. There stood a small blonde girl wearing a similar outfit to Carol's, a light green skirt with an off-white sweater on top. She was moving quickly toward them. He looked at Carol, still in a ball, holding her knees. The blonde girl slid to a stop next to him and grabbed his hand. "We have to go, J!"

He looked into intense icy blue eyes.

"Ariel?"

CHAPTER FIFTEEN

"No time, we gotta go!"

"What about Carol?"

"If you wanna take her, that's your call, but we need to go now and I only care about you."

James looked back at Carol. He couldn't just leave her, not with what she knew.

"She's coming, too."

"Fine. Let's go," Ariel huffed.

James flipped across the table and grabbed Carol. "It's okay, this is the friend I told you about. If she says we need to go, we need to go."

Ariel headed out the side entrance followed by James and Carol. Almost immediately after exiting, they were thrown into the air as the diner exploded. James flew into a parked car, but Carol and Ariel managed to miss it and tumbled to a stop in the parking lot. He looked up at the diner, now engulfed in flames, and felt a hand on his shoulder. Ariel stood there with Carol behind her, not saying a word. Her eyes filled him with a sense of urgency. James stumbled to his feet and followed the girls as they ran to a nearby alley.

"What's going on? How are you alive? What was that thing?"

"Settle down. I'm obviously not dead, I'm here. No time for the rest right now. We need to keep moving."

Ariel was scanning the streets.

"I'm so glad you're alive," James inhaled as he pulled

her in for a hug. *Burnt air and sunflowers.*

Ariel closed her eyes, momentarily relishing his nearness, then shrugged him off and said, "Come on."

She took off running across the street. James grabbed Carol's hand and they trailed after her. She had ducked into a light blue Studebaker and the engine started as they reached the rear driver's side door.

"Did you have a key?"

"No, I hot-wired it. Pretty simple with these old thi—get down!"

All three of them ducked as multiple police cars flew by, sirens blaring, followed by fire engines. Ariel peeked over the dash.

"Okay, we're good."

She floored it, squealing the tires.

"What's going on? Can you talk now?" James reached over, grabbing her shoulder, his heart was racing and not only because of the near death experience.

"The police officer that was after you was a replicant. Not an original title, but still..."

"A replicant?"

"Yep, basically a robot designed to look like humans. TK only uses them here on Earth, they were replaced with the mediators on Atlantis. Seems everyone was kinda freaked out by how human they appeared."

Carol looked over at James in the backseat and asked, "What was he going to do?"

"I don't know, ask Ariel."

Her voice became aggressive, "So, Ariel is it? What

was the rep—"

"Replicant," Ariel mimicked the tone.

"Yes, replicant? Well, what did he want with us?" Her tone was very cold, James had never seen her act like this before. He recoiled in his seat.

"He actually didn't want anything with you, he wanted J. Which would lead them to me."

She swerved the car to the right down a side street. Carol and James tumbled in the backseat, not expecting the turn.

"Hey! A little notice would be nice," Carol shouted.

Ariel looked back at them in the rearview mirror. "Oops, my bad," she sported a mischievous grin.

"So, where are we headed?" James asked.

"To Atlantis. We need to get back to the others. We have a plan to stop the launch of the Exodus."

She took the next left, heading down a dirt road into the countryside, a dust trail following them. Ariel slowed the car down and headed toward a barn in the distance.

"How are we going to get to the moon? Where's your ship?"

"Destroyed. We're going to have to figure out another way, but tonight we need to lay low. They'll be looking for this car once they figure out it was stolen."

At the barn, Ariel stopped in front of two large doors. "Get out and help me, J."

"On it."

He hopped out and followed her instructions.

"Grab that barn door. I'll get the other one."

Ariel looked back at the car. Carol was still sitting in the back seat.

"Can't she drive?"

They both looked at Carol. She jutted out her chin in disapproval.

James turned to Ariel, "Women can't drive here."

Ariel gave him a death stare, "Are you serious?"

James slowly nodded his head, wincing as if he was about to get hit with something.

"Uggh, Earthlings are ridiculous. Girl, come hold the door."

"I have a name," Carol grumbled.

The barn was old and rundown, like it hadn't been used in years and the doors wouldn't stay open due to the building's lean. James and Carol held the doors while Ariel drove through. Once inside, they buttoned up the barn.

"We'll sleep here tonight. J, what do you know about the wheat shipments?"

"Wheat shipments? Where's your spaceship?"

Ariel took a deep breath.

"I told you. It was destroyed. What do you know about the wheat shipments?"

"What does that have to do with getting to the moon?"

Ariel rolled her eyes, "Where do you think Atlantis gets its food?"

"They make it?"

"Yes, but where do you think all the supplies come

from?"

James wanted to say the moon, but based on the tone he was getting from Ariel, who seemed rather aggravated, he instead answered, "I haven't got the slightest."

"Here! It all comes from here. Each sector harvests different materials for Atlantis. This sector, Sector 11, harvests wheat," she snapped.

"What about all of the other food we eat?" Carol asked.

Ariel glared at her, "I don't have time to give you a history lesson. I need to know what your boyfriend knows about the wheat shipments." She scrubbed her hands over her face and stared intently at J.

"Okay, they load up our wheat with large trucks straight from our harvesters, then they head east."

Ariel walked up to James, stopping mere inches away. Her eyes softened a bit. "What else?"

"That's all I know. It just leaves from there on trucks and heads east."

Ariel pulled out a piece of paper from her blouse. Carol gasped, appalled.

"Calm down, sweetheart, this ridiculous outfit doesn't have pockets."

She unfolded the parchment. On it was an old map of the town.

"Now, thanks to the EM pulse that took out my ship, I've lost all my tech. So we have to do this the old-fashioned way." She pointed at an open spot on the map. "We are here. You say the shipments head east? Which road?"

She pointed at three different lines on the map.

"Why does it matter? Do we need wheat? There won't be another shipment for at least a month, maybe longer."

Ariel tightened her hand into a fist, slightly shaking it, letting out a growl. She took a deep breath. "We. Don't. Need. Wheat! We need the depot where they take the wheat. But without my tech, I don't know how to get us there."

James' mind finally clicked, it had taken him a bit to figure it out.

"So wherever they take the wheat, to this depot, it then goes to Atlantis. I'm guessing on a ship. You want to hijack a ship."

"Bingo, Einstein. You *can* reason. I was beginning to think they'd chipped you."

"Chipped me?"

"Yeah, after Earthlings are born, TK has them all chipped. Well, they put a brain monitoring device on their spine. It can sort of control people. Not completely, but it reduces their free thought."

James looked at Carol who had begun rubbing the back of her neck.

Ariel watched the exchange. "Did you take hers out?"

James hesitated, "Yeah, it had all these hair-like things on it."

"That's what attaches to the brain. Glad you got it out without her head exploding."

James' jaw dropped.

"You could have killed me?!" Carol punched him in the arm.

"I didn't know!"

"Okay, stop with the lover's quarrel. Which road, J?"

"I'm pretty sure it's this one." He pointed to the northernmost road.

When he was first learning to drive he would ride alongside the shipping trucks, but stopped when they turned down the far northeast road. The townsfolk weren't allowed to go further than marker 17 or they'd be switched off. James had always wondered where the trucks went, now maybe he would see it. Outside, the sun was setting. Ariel wanted to wait until the cover of darkness to continue.

Their conversations continued. She wouldn't say what happened after James had seen her last, but told him that she was able to hijack a TK fighter and made it down to Earth to find James. They needed him, or what he had in his head.

"I thought you guys extracted what you needed?"

"We did, but V said she found fragments that she didn't quite understand in the first download."

James wondered if it was something from his dream that they were looking for.

Ariel got up and headed to the door.

"So that's Ariel? I've thought it was a strange name since you told me about her and now I see that it fits."

James was quick to respond. "She's saved me more

times than I can remember and you, too, I might add."

"Still, she is strange. I'm not sure I want to keep going. Seeing...what did she call the cop again?" Carol turned her shoulder away from him.

"Replicant."

"Seeing the replicant explode like that really frightened me. I'm not sure I can handle anything else like that."

"You'll be fine. She'll keep us safe, always has."

"Do you like her?"

Without hesitation his eyes lit up, "Sure, she saved my life."

He immediately realized his emotions were transparent and sunk back into himself. Carol looked daggers at him, then turned away. James reached for her hand but she pulled it away.

"What? We went through a lot together. She was the only person I could rely on when I was on the moon. She's a good friend."

Carol dropped her heated glare and leaned into him. They were back in the backseat of the car. The barn was dilapidated and had boards and junk lying all over. They hadn't found anywhere to sit but inside the car. Ariel came back and slid into the driver's seat.

"I feel like a taxi driver. Can one of you sit up here? I don't care which," her words were tense.

James raised his eyebrows questioningly at Carol then, at her reluctance, moved to the front seat. She tightened her jaw.

"What's the plan?" he asked, falsely chipper.

It was becoming hard to breath amongst the tension.

"We're going to the shipping station. The sun's set so we need to get going. You and the girl grab the doors."

"Once again, my name is Carol. Not girl."

"Right, whatever."

James grabbed Carol; they opened up the doors and were immediately blinded by lights. He placed his hand in front of his face to shield his eyes. The light was so bright he couldn't see anything.

"Halt, stay where you are. Place your hands in the air."

James realized it was the cops. *Or was it another replicant?* He didn't know. He heard the sound of a revving engine behind them and the Studebaker came flying out of the barn. It rammed into the cruiser. James hesitated for a minute, then grabbed Carol.

"We gotta go!"

James ran to the car, Carol in tow, and threw her into the backseat then he followed.

"Go!" he shouted

Ariel didn't hesitate. She smashed the gas pedal, pushing the cruiser backward, the light still shining in their faces. The sound of breaking glass echoed over the rev of the engine as shots were being fired from the cruiser.

"Keep your heads down!" Ariel yelled while slumping down below the steering wheel.

She kept driving forward, shots coming in then threw the shifter into reverse and peeled out backwards. The bumper popped off of the Studebaker, the screech of tearing metal sounded as the two cars disengaged. She threw it into drive and spun the tires, trying to make a quick getaway. The cruiser was too quick and rammed into the side, throwing the two in the back sideways. The Studebaker rocked to one side, but had enough grip to continue. Now in front of the pursuit, Ariel peered back over the rear seat. More shots rang out and she slouched down again. The car kept accelerating, but so did the cruiser.

Ariel headed for the road, dirt flew everywhere. Looking back, James saw the cops' lights flashing red. The distance between them remained steady, the Studebaker wasn't fast enough. She power slid onto the road, the cruiser in trail. James and Carol braced for the shift in G-forces, but to no avail. They lurched across the seat and James grabbed the front headrest to stop himself from crushing Carol. Ariel checked the rearview; her pursuit was closing in on them. She slammed the brakes and swerved; the replicant wasn't quick enough and flew right by. As the cruiser's rear reached the front of the Studebaker, Ariel made an aggressive turn to engage. The car spun out and she slammed on the brakes and threw it in park.

"What are you doing?" James yelled.

Ariel exited the car and headed for the cruiser. James watched as she opened the door. Shots flew at her through the side window, she ducked then disappeared inside. James saw the headlights of the car rocking, a few more shots were heard, and the car stopped rocking. Ariel appeared.

"Stay here," he said to Carol, hopping out to see if Ariel needed help.

He ran up to the cruiser. The replicant was sprawled across the front seat, sparks igniting from various parts of his body. Ariel was around back opening the trunk. As he rounded the corner, a rifle nearly hit him in the face, but he instinctively caught it. Ariel was digging around for supplies. She grabbed a shotgun and tossed it to him.

"Take that back to the car, there'll be more."

Before she could finish the sentence, James heard sirens. He searched the horizon and saw two more cars inbound.

"What are you doing? Go!" Ariel yelled, pointing at the car.

He took off running to the Studebaker. Upon reaching it, he looked back to see Ariel with armloads of ammo.

"Go grab more."

He didn't hesitate and ran back to the cruiser. The trunk was full of ammo and a few pistols. He grabbed what he could and dumped it into their car, Ariel did the same. He started to run back for more, but felt a hand grab his shoulder.

"That's enough, we don't have time."

He looked over. The two new cruisers were closing in fast. James hopped into the backseat again.

"No, you drive!"

213

James rolled over the front seat. Ariel had swung around and was now in the backseat loading ammo into the weapons.

"Sweetie, I need you to load the guns. Can you do that?" Her tone was more pleasant than it had initially been.

"J, drive!"

He stopped watching their interaction and put the car in drive. He was thrown back into the seat as they took off. Ariel quickly showed Carol how to load the ammo then, using the rifle, broke out the last of the rear window glass and aimed at the cruisers.

"Slow down."

"What?"

"Slow down so I can get a better shot."

James decelerated at her command, the cruisers rapidly approached. They were less than 100 yards away. James continued to slow.

"Now punch it!"

James smashed the accelerator, the engine revved and the car took off. Ariel began firing rounds at the pursuit, her shots skipping off parts of the car. Shots rang back at them with no effect. Dust was spewing from under the tires, obscuring her shots. The darkness made it even more difficult to see what she was aiming at, but she fired more shots then passed the rifle to Carol. James continued down the road at breakneck speed. Suddenly, the car pulled to the right. James tried to counter, but lost control. The Studebaker slid off the road sideways then dug into the ground, causing it to flip sideways. The car barrel-rolled, the three of them flailing as they tumbled around. The loose ammo became projectiles, striking and damaging skin as they continued to be tossed around.

The car came to rest on all four wheels, but the left rear tire was blown and the roof was slightly crushed. James ended up under the passenger dash, while Carol and Ariel lay sprawled on each other in the backseat. He could hear groans from the girls as he pulled himself off of the floor. Pain wracked his body, he felt like someone had taken a ball bat to him and didn't miss anywhere. He pulled himself above the seat. The two cruisers had come to a stop surrounding them, their lights shining in on them. James ducked.

"Are you two alright?"

His body throbbed as he struggled to move.

"I don't know if you would say alright, but we're alive," he heard Ariel say.

"What do we do now?"

"Just follow my lead."

Ariel raised her arms. James hesitated then mimicked her. *Same move, different planet.* He glanced out the window to see two cops approaching, pistols drawn.

"Don't make any sudden moves," one of them directed.

James stayed there with his hands up. One of the cops tried to open the driver's door, but it was pinned shut. The impact had crushed its hinges.

"Alright, climb out of there, all of you."

James complied.

"I need to help my friend, she's injured."

James looked back. Ariel was talking about Carol, who was unconscious. Fear swelled inside of him and he tried to get a better look.

"Stay where you are, don't move!" the cop shouted.

James turned back to see a gun in his face. The cop grabbed one of his arms and cuffed him. The other helped Ariel drag out Carol's limp body from the back-seat. James watched in horror, expecting the worst.

"She needs medical attention," Ariel pleaded.

"Officer Pearson, you take the girl to the hospital in town. I'll take the other two in for questioning."

"You help load her in the back of the squad car," he said to Ariel.

Ariel helped take Carol over and placed her in the back of the car, then was cuffed herself.

"I'll see you back at the precinct to debrief after you drop her off."

The other officer nodded and ducked into his car.

"Now, the two of you, over to the car."

He escorted them to his cruiser and tucked them into the back.

"James and Ariel, you will be detained until we can arrange transportation to Atlantis."

James looked at Ariel, his eyes wide, attempting to understand what was happening. Ariel kept her mouth shut and watched the rearview mirror.

"What do you want from us?" James asked.

"That's not something I know."

"You didn't ask?"

Ariel laughed, "He's a replicant. He only follows orders."

The car kicked up sand and dirt as it started forward. The ride was silent as they headed back into town. All James could do was think about Carol. *Was she alright?* He didn't notice the deuce and a half truck they were about to pass. It was the same type of truck that James would load with the wheat for delivery after each harvest. He felt a sharp stab in his ribcage and frowned over at Ariel who was nodding over to the window. As they passed the truck, he saw an individual working on a flat tire. He looked back at Ariel. She was working her arms under her butt and she gave him a wink. He sat back, wondering what she was about to do. Her arms were almost under her knees when the cop looked in the rear-view mirror. James realized she needed a distraction.

"Where are you taking us?"

The cop's eyes shifted over to him. "Quiet back there, you don't need to know."

"But, I do. You know who I am."

"You're just a boy, nothing more. A package to be delivered."

Ariel had freed her cuffed hands from behind her back. Though they were still cuffed, they were now in front of her. She lunged forward, whipping her arms over the cop's head and he let out a garbled scream as she began to choke him. He swerved and James went flying into Ariel. She was slammed into the car door, which opened from the tremendous force. The cop's hands were pulled off of the steering wheel, but his foot was still on the gas. The cruiser accelerated as he struggled to work his way back to the wheel.

James' top half hung out the door for a moment then the door hit the stop and boomeranged back into him. It drilled him on the head, knocking him back inside. Ariel had been pulled back in prior from the cop's struggles. The two wrestled, Ariel's grip got tighter.

"Little help!"

James felt useless. There was no way he was flexible enough to free his hands as she did; they were still behind his back. He shimmied over then lifted a leg and began kicking the cop in the head. Ariel flew over the front seat as the car came to a screeching halt. James' butt hit the rear of the front seat and he fell back. He could hear the two struggling, but was unable to sit up. He looked over the seat and she was still locked onto the cop's neck with her cuffs, sparks were popping out of his neck.

"He's a replicant too?!" James was shocked even though Ariel had pointed it out. From their interaction, he'd believed it was an actual human. *How many of them were there?* James positioned himself to grab the door handle behind his back and gave it a tug. He fell out, landing on his back with a thud. Groaning, he rolled over and gathered himself to his feet. He rushed over and grabbed the driver's door and opened it behind his back then spun around to see what he could do to help, but it was too late. Ariel was lying there with the replicant on top of her, neither of them moving. He climbed in but slipped and ended up on top of both of them.

"Oof! I already know how heavy you are, get off of me."

James was taken back to another time he'd fallen on top of Ariel, but was snapped back by, "It's bad enough I have this fake human on me."

"Sorry," James replied, trying to wiggle his way off of them.

She pushed the replicant to the floor and grabbed the keys off his belt.

"Thanks for the distraction."

James had a small smile, "Anytime."

She un-cuffed him, then popped the trunk, rifling through another assortment of weapons. James stood there a moment just watching.

"How many of them are there?"

"Replicants? Um, not sure, but they're typically all of the police officers in town."

"So, they've been here the whole time?"

"Yep, kinda freaky right? That's why TK did away with them. Too difficult to tell who was real and who wasn't. You going to help?"

"What do we do now?"

"Did you see the truck back there?"

"Yep."

"That's our ticket to the spaceport."

"Spaceport? I thought you said we were going to a

depot?"

"How do you think they transport all that food to Atlantis, teleportation?" she chuckled.

"Teleportation? Oh my gosh, what about Carol?"

James started to pace back and forth. *How could he have forgotten about her? Was she alright?*

"There's no time to get her. We need to get you to Atlantis."

"But she might die!"

"Possible, but we don't have time and it's not worth the risk."

James was torn. Something about Ariel settled him and buoyed him at the same time and he was glad she was with him again, even if they were constantly on the run. But, he thought he might love Carol. They had been through so much together and he may never see her again.

"We need to go get Carol," James said firmly.

Ariel approached him, more livid than he'd ever seen her. "No, we don't! You shouldn't have brought her in the first place!" she yelled, toe to toe with him now. "This is too dangerous, even for me, let alone a country schoolgirl. She's going to get medical attention. If she's destined to live, then she will." Her eyes glistened as they looked up and locked with his, "I can't lose you, now." A slight pause and she seemed to recover herself. She shook her head as she stepped back and said, "I have to get you to Atlantis."

James understood there was more to what she was

saying. She was adamant they continue on without Carol. Part of him knew she was right. Carol was a liability and he didn't want to put her in harm's way.

"What if they..."

"They won't," she softly reassured him. "She's an Earthling and she doesn't know anything. If she makes it, they'll release her."

James grimaced at the word "if". Ariel headed to the truck and started rummaging through the supplies. He followed her as he always did.

"Here, take these," she handed him two revolvers in holsters. "Grab as much ammo as you can carry."

James hesitated, "But, I don't know how to use these."

"Seriously?" Ariel looked at the sky, rolling her eyes. "Just take 'em and the ammo. We need to hurry. Our ticket might vanish."

James stuffed rounds into any pocket he could find while Ariel took full ammo pouches and the shotgun, tossing the rifle to him. They headed back toward the disabled truck.

"Stay behind me and follow my lead. We'll only get one shot at this."

James continued behind her, he could see the headlights in the distance. About 100 yards out she gave him a hand signal to stop then waved him to give her the rifle. He could see a person working on the right front tire, then disappeared as a shot deafened his ear.

"Come on, we need to hurry."

They ran up to see the man lying dead on the ground.

James took a closer look and saw that it was a replicant.

"Is anyone human?"

"You are," she said checking the tire. "We're in luck, looks like he'd almost finished. Tighten the last of the lug nuts."

James ran over, this was something he could do without thought. Ariel checked on the replicant to make sure it was no threat and then hopped into the passenger seat.

"Take his clothes."

"What?"

"Take his clothes. You have to drive, remember? Women can't drive here," she said in a sarcastic tone.

"But..."

"Just do it. Take his clothes and put them on."

James worked on taking the replicant's clothes off then his own. The thing was heavy and took a bit to get it undressed. He glanced up to see Ariel smiling at him as he changed.

"Enjoying the show, are we?"

"Yep."

For some reason, he felt strangely comfortable being around her in his underwear. After all, it wasn't the first time. Plus, he didn't have much time to think about it, they needed to get going. He ran to the truck.

"Don't forget the pistols and ammo."

James ran back and grabbed the stuff out of his pockets. He heard a loud engine coming and looked up to see lights on the horizon.

"Hurry up, J!"

He ran and climbed into the driver's seat.

"Turn this thing around. We need to get out of here."

James pulled a 180 and they headed down the road.

"At the end of this road, there should be a gate with a security guard. You need to do exactly what I tell you or you'll compromise us."

James listened intently.

"Luckily they don't have any procedures for a situation like this, so all you have to do is drive through the gate when they open it. Don't say a word and don't look at the guard."

"That's it?"

"Yep, that's it."

"What do we do once we get past security?"

"There should be an unloading dock. We obviously don't have anything to unload so we'll have to figure something out."

"Is there a maintenance depot? We could say the truck needs repairs and park it there."

"Clever. I guess you do add something to the team," she winked.

"Once we get there, we'll need to make our way to the spaceport and find a way to board one of the freight ships."

James could see something coming into view. There was a small building with a gate and chain link fence running as far as he could see on both sides of it. He slowed the truck and Ariel ducked down.

"Remember what I said."

James didn't say a word and kept his eyes front. The gate opened as he approached and he drove through with no problems.

"Okay, we're though."

Ariel popped up. In front of them was the wall, still miles out, but getting bigger.

"Where's the spaceport? There's nothing out here."

"They aren't going to keep it visible for Earthlings to see. Think about it, have you ever seen a spaceship?"

"Yep," James thought he was being clever.

The look Ariel gave him said that he wasn't. "The ones you've seen over the past two weeks don't count."

She was right, he had never seen one. You would think if they were launching nearly every day, somebody would have seen one by now. As he continued, the wall grew. They were probably less than a mile from it now. James heard the screeching of metal and at nearly the same time, the ground seemed to rise up around them. He was driving down into a tunnel.

"Is it automated?"

"Must be," Ariel shrugged.

As they continued, the ramp stopped. They were enclosed in a tunnel, the sides of which resembled the one he had first walked through, only larger. Light was emanating from in front of them and they were approaching quickly. They popped out into a huge hangar with four large ships on the bay floors. Trucks were loading supplies onto each of them.

"Over there," Ariel pointed at a group of trucks in

various states of repair. "Park over there."

James headed toward what looked like a maintenance depot. After parking, Ariel spotted a ship that was nearly loaded. They headed over, ensuring they weren't spotted. As the final truck pulled away, the ship's cargo doors began to close. They slipped into it, but something went wrong; the doors began to open again. James spotted four mediators making their way toward the ship.

"Crap, stay here and hold 'em off. I'm heading to the cockpit."

James turned around to ask her how he was supposed to do that, but she was nearly out of sight running to the front of the craft. James aimed the rifle as Dillon had taught him. This wasn't a blaster, but he hoped it worked the same way. He fired two shots, one of them hitting its mark, and a mediator went down. The others began to quicken the pace at which they were closing in. He set his sights on the next one, two more shots rang out, and another dropped. He moved to the next, same result. Then to the next. Click. He scowled at the weapon and tried again. Click. He was out of ammo.

He fumbled with it for a moment trying to figure out how to load it, then looked up. The mediators were almost there, maybe a dozen yards off. He felt the ship begin to move. It started up vertically, two mediators jumped on board, then the doors began to close. James dropped the rifle and reached his pistol. He drew it and fired, missed. He fired again, another miss. Turning to run, he felt pressure on his shoulder and was yanked to

the ground. A mediator stared down at him. He raised
the pistol and fired, this one didn't miss, the machine
toppled down toward him. He raised his arms, closing
his eyes for impact, nothing came. He opened his eyes to
see that Ariel had rammed the robot out of the way and
was working on the other one.

"Pistol!"

James threw it to her. She caught it and put a round
into the mediator's head. James let out a sigh of relief.

"Not out of the woods yet."

He followed her up to the cockpit, but there were no
seats or controls. He saw a panel that had been broken
open with wires hanging out.

"Where are the seats?"

"This is a freight hauler, they don't have any. They
operate on a continuous loop, on a program."

"How did you get it to go?"

"I did a manual override. Something must have spotted us and stopped the launch sequence, I simply reiniti-
ated it."

"Can you fly this thing?"

"Nope, and they know we're coming, so it's going to
get hairy."

"How long?"

"About twenty minutes then we'll be docking. Think
you can learn to reload those ancient weapons in twenty
minutes?"

James looked down at the pistol. "Show me."

CHAPTER SIXTEEN

The ship approached the docking bay on the moon in darkness; the sun was hidden on the other side. The bay doors opened to reveal an army of mediators on the hangar floor. As the ship moved in, touching down in the middle of the machines, the ship's cargo doors opened and the mediators flooded in searching for the stowaways. Soon, the whole ship was overflowing with them.

"Search the cargo," one of them announced.

The containers full of goods were meticulously searched, one by one. Ariel peered out from the right landing gear then waved to James that it was clear and flipped down onto the floor below. All of the mediators were busy combing the interior of the ship. James and Ariel had managed to gain access to the landing gear during flight and were now slipping away. They made their way to one of the personnel doors and Ariel placed her hand on the panel. The door opened.

"I thought you were compromised?"

"I was, but Jolt was able to hack it for me."

"Jolt?"

"I mentioned him before. He's the one who got your DNA codes switched so they couldn't find us last time you were here. He's a computer expert, every team needs one right?" she winked at him, but he had no idea what she was talking about. She could tell. "Let's go, I think we're on the far side of the moon and we need to make it to the team."

"What team?"

"The A-team," she silently laughed and knew the humor would be lost on him, but felt compelled to say it anyway. She regained her composure. "We don't have a name, but it's a group of underground people who don't agree with what TK is doing."

"What exactly are they doing now?"

"They're leaving Earth to die. They're leaving on the Exodus."

"I know that, but I thought you didn't care about Earthlings?"

"I do. I just needed you to follow me without baggage. It's better this way."

James scowled. "So, what now?"

"First we need to get out of these clothes. They'll be a dead giveaway that we're not supposed to be here."

James followed Ariel through a maze of tunnels, doors and corridors until they reached a door that finally exited out to the street. Across the road were a myriad of shops, including a clothing store. They quickly headed over. Inside, the owner, an older woman wearing flowing grey robes that matched her hair, gave them a strange look then smiled, "Retro party?"

"Yeah, it was a great party, but now we'd like to get out of these itchy homemade costumes."

James didn't say a word. He was used to the clothes and didn't find them itchy at all, but he knew to follow along. The owner showed them several of her new arrivals and they chose a few outfits to try on, then she showed them to the dressing room. Apparently modesty wasn't a thing on Atlantis as there was only one large dressing room.

"I'll just face this wall so you can change," said James after the owner had left them.

"I thought you weren't going to be shy around me anymore," Ariel teased.

"It's not me that I'm concerned about," James said as he turned away from her and began to change out of his old clothes. "I'm just trying to be respectful of you."

James had gotten his shirt off and was pulling on the new pants when he heard, "J, turn around."

She was sliding her shirt down over her torso and he caught a glimpse of bare midriff before she tucked it into her skintight pants.

"Didn't want your mind running rampant over there, though I was enjoying watching you act all noble."

James blushed, chagrined. He had listened to every slip and slide of clothing and imagined all sorts of scenarios. *But, she had watched him.*

He slipped on his shirt and they both gathered their old clothes then walked out to the owner's desk where Ariel paid for the new clothes. Jolt hacked the system to not only allow unlimited access for Ariel, but to add plenty of funds to her account. Soon they were back on the street and headed for the nearest train. They hopped on a couple of different trains, once again at varying levels, and made their way to a small building. It was unlike most he'd seen on Atlantis. Instead of the rounded corners James had become accustomed to seeing, the whole building was square and black, which made it stand out against the chrome backdrop.

"What's this?"

"It's the memory bank, where all the data is collected and stored for the city. There are three buildings like this. Two are backups should this one, the main bank, be compromised."

James didn't quite understand what she was talking about, but nodded as if he understood.

"So, where is this team of yours?"

"In here."

She grabbed his hand, which always did something funny to his insides, and led him down through a series of elevators until reaching the final floor. James realized they must be close to the moon's surface, it had been what seemed like 100 floors before they stopped. Ariel led them into a room with six doors, above which, each had a unique emblem lit up. Ariel took the second one on the left and opened it. Inside, a man stood facing multiple holograms that were floating in from of him.

"Hi, Ariel, sorry I couldn't help you in the hangar bay."

He talked so fast James almost didn't understand what he said.

"That's okay, you did enough and we're here. J this is Jolt, Jolt this is J."

"Pleasure to meet the son of the great Dr. Arcturus."

He reached out and shook James' hand. James didn't

say anything, he was so mesmerized by the graphics behind him.

"Oh, you like my system. Pretty crazy, right? Built it from scratch, or should I say, hacked it from scratch. Zeb actually built, it, the physical system I mean."

Jolt had a tendency to keep talking, and with the speed of his words, James felt overwhelmed.

"Let me introduce you to the rest of the team," Ariel turned and headed out the door, then grabbed his hand again. He had a moment to reflect on the fact that her hand was soft and small in his rather large, calloused one, which surprised him because of all of the gun play she seemed to do. She took him into another room where Zane sat next to a guy that James didn't recognize, watching a reality show. V was playing with what looked like a kid's chemistry set.

"Zane, V. Nice to see you guys."

"Hey, J," they both said, almost in unison.

"And this is Gatlin, our new weapons expert."

James looked over to see the mountain of a man next to Zane stand up. He was a foot taller than Zane and heavier set.

"What's up, J?"

James looked up at the ceiling and Ariel began laughing, then snorted.

"It's just a saying, J. Like hello."

James felt foolish.

"Don't worry about it," Ariel said, slowly controlling her laughter. "You'll start to get the lingo. Anyway, this is the crew."

James took it all in. He felt like he was in a locker room surrounded by a new team, only he didn't understand what role he would play on the team, or even what the goal was.

"So, how do I fit into this?"

"Well..." Ariel began. "To start, we just need to keep you out of the hands of TK. We're trying to figure out the rest."

"I thought you had a plan."

"Kinda," Ariel said with hesitation. "But, we're not sure how to do it. We start by stopping TK from leaving. Jolt, have you finished analyzing their system?"

"Yep, did that hours ago. They'll be ready to launch in two days. They have to finish loading everybody. Supplies are nearly complete; the ship you came in on was one of the last ones."

"Is there a way to stop it?"

"Not from here. The ship's controls are physically self-contained, not connected to our system. You'd have to go there and manipulate the software on site."

"If we get you in, could you do it?"

"Yep."

"What will that solve though?" James asked. "TK will still be here and they'll still rule. What are you actually trying to accomplish?"

"Your father wanted to wait and build another ship to evacuate Earth. All we need to do is delay the ship one more year. We could cripple its propulsion system; that would buy us some time."

"I'll scan the systems and figure out if it can be done," Jolt added. "Should only take a few hours to complete a solution."

"Hungry?" Ariel asked James.

He nodded, he was starving and his stomach grumbled at the mention of food.

"How's pizza sound?"

"Amazing."

Ariel left the room, so James walked over and sat down on the other side of Zane.

"How are you feeling, Zane? The last time I saw you, you were heading out of the ship on a stretcher."

"I'm good, technology's great. Got some enhancements, too. V was able to strengthen my skin. Normal blasters don't damage me at all."

"Wow, that's incredible. Ariel and I could have used that. It even hurts to breathe right now." Staring in the direction Ariel had just gone, he asked, "Hey, Zane? Speaking of blasters, what do you call the smell of blaster fire?"

"Ozone. Why?"

"No reason. Just something I was wondering about," he trailed off, musing.

V interrupted his thoughts. "J, come over here. Let's see what we're working with."

She had stopping playing with her concoctions and was standing behind him.

"You look pretty rough, but I think Ariel got it worse.

I'm surprised she's still standing. Must have been highly motivated," she commented with a sly wink.

"She's never anything but motivated, that I've seen." James stood up and followed V to a makeshift medical bay where she scanned him.

"Ohh, looks like you have a few broken ribs amongst all those bruises. Lay back and I'll fix you up."

She slowly waived a wand over his ribs, it felt warm, but the pain began to ease.

"How did you get free? I thought all of you had been caught."

"Long story. In short, Jolt was able to hack the security system to release us."

James ran his hands along his ribs, no pain.

"So what do you think of the plan? Seems risky."

"Yeah, but it's the only shot we've got. The Earthlings deserve to live, and not as worker bees anymore."

"They have no idea about any of this and most are happy the way they are," James stated from experience.

"But the systems that are keeping Earth alive will malfunction and fail when TK depart for the new planet," V replied.

James looked around at the makeshift medical room V had built. He was astounded by how resourceful she was, how resourceful they all were.

"How did you get mixed up in all of this?"

"My parents. They always disagreed with the stance TK took on Earth."

"Why didn't they do anything?" James was still

admiring this new world he was in. His feelings of being a stranger were beginning to fade the longer he was there.

"They did. They helped your father hide the coordinates."

James remembered everything he'd seen when he'd been inside his father's mind. He still couldn't believe his parents on Earth weren't blood. He gazed at the wall, unfocused, reached up and rubbed his neck then his head.

"So, is it possible to put memories in someone's head?"

"You're talking about your dream aren't you?"

James nodded. He wasn't sure if it was a dream or a flashback, but it felt so real.

"I suppose so, but I've never seen technology that good. The brain is so complex, it's hard to manipulate. Even the Earthlings revolt sometimes. That's why they're monitored by replicants and are programmed to switch off if they leave a prescribed area or create conflict."

James remembered his fight with Rich and the time he tried to drag Carol across the border to the wall.

"Pizza should be here any minute," Ariel said, peeking her head in.

"Good, that gives me time to examine you. Get over here before you drop," the feisty little doctor said.

"But, I..." At a look from V, Ariel relented, "Fine. Make it fast."

James was eager for the food to arrive; pizza was something he'd always loved but never got to eat very often. Carol constantly wanted to go to the diner. He ambled out to the main room. After V declared her fit, Ariel scanned her Datacle then headed to the door. Zane was still watching his show and getting really into it. James had never seen live shows and he was caught up in the drama of it all.

An explosion came from the other room and the whole place shook. He searched for Ariel and saw her slide in through the doorway on one knee. Zane flew out of his seat grabbing a rifle near him and Gatlin ran in from another room, pistol in hand.

"They found us!" Ariel shouted.

She ran over to James, taking his hand as she ran past. They fled as blasts rang out from behind them.

"This way." Ariel dragged him through multiple rooms, sounds of explosions and fighting right on their tail.

"In the elevator."

Ariel jerked his arm past her through the open elevator doors. Leaping in after him, she pressed the control panel.

"Emergency override initiated," cried the elevator.

Ariel frantically tapped buttons.

"Denied," the elevator shouted back.

She tapped more buttons to the same end. James looked down the hall as the sounds closed in on them. The door down the hallway blew open.

"Hurry!" James shouted.

"I'm trying!"

She tapped and tapped.

"Denied. Denied."

James peeked out and a shot buzzed over his head. He dodged it. Narrowing his eyes, he saw a man running at them, blaster drawn. He shot again and James ducked back into the elevator.

"Someone's coming and he doesn't look friendly."

Ariel stopped and peeked out, then jerked back into the elevator.

"Crap, an E-Rat."

James cocked his head, confused.

"Stay out of the way."

James slid to the back of the elevator and leaned against the back wall. An arm with a blaster peeked around and fired a shot, missing James by mere inches. Ariel grabbed it and cocked it up as another shot rang out, separating the panels above. The man came around after her with a left hook. Ariel bobbed then landed an uppercut to his jaw, he barely moved. The man grabbed Ariel, but she slipped out then landed a knee to his chest followed by a spinning kick to his head. The man stumbled back. She threw a series of punches, all blocked, then attempted a roundhouse kick. The man caught her foot and spun her back into the wall next to James. She dropped something resembling a can of pomade. James dove down and picked it up. Looking up, he saw the man grab Ariel's foot and drag her to him. She looked at him.

"Swing away, Bambino!" She spun around, kicking her assailant in the jaw, his face barely moved. The man grabbed her other leg, she struggled to get free, swinging at him with both arms. James looked at the can, and flipping it over, saw the letters "MLB" engraved on one side. He ran his finger over it and heard a loud "pop".

The sound startled him so much, that he dropped the can, which morphed into a full size baseball bat. Instinctively, he grabbed it and ran after the man. With a great swing, he hit the man in the side of the head, stunning him. Ariel slipped free and aggressively attacked, calling for the bat. James tossed it to her; she wielded it like an expert swordswoman. Body blows, head shots, the man attempted to block them, but was outmatched by her speed. She threw the bat to James and dropped down to her knees. The man lunged at her, but James flew in with all his strength, severing the man's head. James watched as it rolled down the hall. No blood, only wires spewing everywhere.

"What was that?" James stood, still gripping the bat tightly with both hands. It was much more resilient than any of the replicants they'd faced.

Ariel flipped up and grabbed the bat from him, shrinking it into a can again.

"An E-Rat. We're out of time, let's go." She pointed up into the elevator. "We're going to have to climb."

James looked up. The shaft went on for what seemed like forever. The walls were lined with rope lighting and the ceiling was nonexistent.

"Up there? How far?" James was actually afraid of heights.

"Until I say. You first."

James hesitated.

"Go."

He stood there staring up.

"Don't tell me you're afraid of heights?"

James nodded.

"Well get over it."

She pushed him toward the ladder. He gripped it with both hands then took a deep breath and began the climb. He heard two shots below him.

"Faster!"

He peered down. Ariel was taking out mediators as they came into view underneath them. He began climbing as fast as he could, hand over hand. He felt Ariel grab his foot a few times by mistake. James tried to go faster, but the endless ladder above made it seem like an impossible task. Shots continued below, a few passing behind him up the elevator shaft. He felt a hand clutch his ankle then Ariel shot multiple rounds into the wall. The metal crumpled and splintered open.

"In there."

James looked at Ariel, then the hole, then Ariel again.

"But—"

"Just jump."

Ariel began firing down at the mediators who were only a dozen feet from them. James grimaced at the saw-edged opening across the shaft. *Here goes nothing.* His ingrained fight response kicked in and his fear of heights momentarily disappeared. He launched himself at the hole and tumbled through, rolling as he landed.

He looked back over his shoulder. Ariel jumped, but her leg was grabbed in mid air. James lunged over to the gaping hole and reached out for her. Their hands met and clasped together. Her weight dragged him to the brink of falling down the shaft until he clutched onto a piece of the jagged entrance with his hand. Ariel dangled precariously below. James looked down to see that she was trying to kick free with no luck. The sharp edges of the destroyed metal dug into his hand. He held strong through the pain, but blood began flowing out of the wound, causing his hand to slip. Ariel aimed and took a shot. James watched as the malfunctioning heap that once was a mediator dropped free.

"Can you pull me up, J?"

"No, I'm slipping."

"Just hold on."

Ariel holstered her weapon and began to climb up James. He continued to slip and the pain was starting to creep up his arm, he didn't know how long he could keep it up. Closing his eyes, he concentrated on his grip as he felt Ariel steadily making progress to his shoulders. He had to hold on, it was his turn to save her. He felt a tug on his back and looked over to see Ariel dragging him away from the edge.

"Let me see that."

She inspected his hand. The cut was deep, the pulling and tugging during the event had created a bloody mess. She took a little metal pouch off of her belt and grabbed a bandage then wrapped it around his damaged hand.

"This should take about 15 minutes. We need to shut down the propulsion system."

"By ourselves?" James looked at his hand as she finished wrapping it then continued, "I guess the others must have been killed. How else could that E-Rat, or whatever you called him, get to us?"

Ariel was visibly upset, but James could tell she was trying to put on a brave face for him. *He shouldn't have said it that way, those were their friends.* He tried to change the subject. "What is this?" James massaged the bandage. It tingled, but the pain was subsiding.

"It's an M2089 bandage. Used to be standard issue for combat soldiers. It'll heal you up quickly. Works well on superficial wounds but nothing more. Lucky you didn't cut any ligaments."

James tried to form a fist. *Lucky?*

"I still don't understand what we're doing."

"You don't have to. Just do what I tell you. For now, we need to keep moving."

"But—"

She looked at him with stern eyes, then simply turned to head toward the door. He understood, there was no time to argue, and he would probably lose the fight anyway. Ariel opened the door leading outside.

"We need to make it to the store across the way," she pointed to a building, in which the first floor was a clothing store.

"Nice time to go shopping," James sarcastically commented.

Ariel laughed. "Actually it is. There's a sale. Everything left on the shelves is free."

James didn't understand, but as they were running across the street he realized how quiet it was. There was nobody around, not a soul. Even the trains had stopped moving. It was eerie, like a ghost town. Ariel broke the silence, shooting a hole in the storefront. As he stepped into the store, something hit him in the chest. He fumbled around with the items Ariel had thrown at him. He was holding a pair of boots.

"What are these for?" He had boots on. As far as he could tell, the only difference between the two pairs was the color and these had a metal buckle across the front of the ankle.

"To wear."

James gave her a look.

"They're grav-bootz. Help you walk on walls like Spiderman."

"Spiderman?"

"You're impossible," Ariel shook her head, chuckling. "Just put them on."

James plopped down on the ground, staring back at the elevator shaft they had escaped from while he changed his boots. Suddenly, a squad of mediators emerged with two men alongside them.

"Umm....Ariel?"

She looked up.

"Put those bootz on quick!"

She yanked him up as soon as the boots were on and

dragged him outside.

"We're going to have to climb again."

"Climb? Where? How?"

She pointed up toward the outside surface of the building then tapped on the outsides of his heels. He heard a high-pitched hum. Ariel was already walking up the exterior of the tower and waived him on. He checked on their pursuers, they were almost on them.

"Here goes nothing," he said under his breath, then put one foot on the vertical surface.

He followed with the other, his abs straining, but couldn't hold himself up for very long. Seeing this, Ariel slid down the building.

"Grab my hand, hold on tight. We gotta run."

Shots hit the glass next to them. James didn't hesitate and took off running, Ariel dragging him upwards. He looked back to see the E-Rat grab at his boot. Ariel vaulted down, spinning James over her back. She let a kick fly and knocked the E-Rat back, stunned. Continuing the spin without stopping, she ended up facing the sky and again took off running with James in tow. They were about twenty stories high and still climbing. James was beginning to slow. His stamina, built for baseball and farm work, wasn't strong enough for distance running in the high atmosphere of the moon. The E-Rat was soon hot on their tail. Ariel spun around again, face to face with the assailant, her arms locked with James'. She exposed two blasters and let round after round fly. The E-Rat tried to dodge, but was hit multiple times as volley after volley rained down on him. The blasts were enough to peel him off the exterior and he plummeted to the ground.

James was helpless, staring at the sky. He felt his boot detach as Ariel flipped him over her head toward the wall. She put a few shots into the exterior, creating a hole for him to slip through, then followed. After hitting the building floor, he crawled to the yawning hole and looked down. The E-Rat had gained his feet.

"He's still coming?!" James yelled, incredulous, glancing back at Ariel.

She was standing inside looking at a large door. Hands on her hips, she grinned over her shoulder. "Here's our way out."

CHAPTER SEVENTEEN

The door opened, what seemed like an endless hallway lay beyond. Ariel took off running and James followed, struggling to keep up. James was still amazed as to how fluid her movements were with no sign of fatigue. She rattled off a few shots down the hallway, the light glowed as it zipped along, blasting the door into nothing. Ariel jumped through it in stride and James followed suit. Inside was a large room with chairs and sofas arranged on a hand-woven rug and a staircase to a balcony on one side. James assessed the room. He saw no point of escape, no door other than the one they had come through. On the opposite end, grand windows rose four stories tall and banners hung from large metal rafters.

"I thought this was our way out?" James said in a slight panic.

Ariel ignored him, studying the space as if she was trying to find something. She ran over to the far wall next to the windows where bookshelves stood from floor to ceiling. She started fingering each, reading titles as she went. James realized she was searching for a specific title.

"What book are you looking for?"

"Pride and Prejudice."

"Pride and Prejudice?"

"It was my mothers' favorite book."

"This is your parent's place? But I thought your mother was..."

"Yes, and no, it was confiscated after the coup. Luckily

the new owners kept most of it intact. Very rare to find books these days, I'm actually surprised they're going to leave them."

James didn't ask any more questions as he sensed Ariel didn't really want to talk about it and there were more pressing matters at the moment. He began going through the books. "Treasure Island", "Journey to the Center of the Earth", all of the classics were there. Then the titles became unfamiliar, strange names he had never heard of.

"What's "Catch..." he was about to ask, but remembered there wasn't time; TK's minions could be on them at any moment. James heard a sound and turned to see the E-Rat standing in the doorway, pistol aimed, ready to fire. The E-Rat stumbled back, hit by a blast. Ariel had been ready for him. He turned and fired back. As they continued exchanging fire, Ariel went running up the stairs for cover. James frantically began searching again, "Harry Potter", no, "Ready Player One", no, then...finally.

"Here it is! "Pride and Prejudice"," he raised the book triumphantly.

The book exploded in his hand. The E-Rat fired another shot, barely missing his head and James dropped to the floor and rolled behind a couch. The couch burst into a pile of charred floating feathers, then the chair with the same result. He looked up to see the blaster pointed right at him. Ariel dropped down on the E-Rat from the balcony. She disarmed him and the two engaged in hand to hand combat, exchanging blow after blow. James got to his feet and went over to examine the remains of the book. There was nothing, just burnt papers everywhere.

Then out of the corner of his eye, he caught something. As he moved, he saw a flash coming from under the scorched chair. He ran over sliding toward it. By this time, four mediators had entered the room and were on their way to detain him. He reached under the chair and felt something rectangular and metal, polished, but on one end jagged. James grabbed it and pulled his head back just in time to see a mediator a few feet away. He whipped out his blaster and fired multiple shots, dropping the robot almost on top of him. He looked over at Ariel. She was equal to, if not more skilled, but the E-Rat was stronger and it was beginning to show. James aimed his pistol and fired. The first shot skipped off the E-Rat's back; the second landed between his shoulder blades providing enough distraction for Ariel to slip loose. She landed a few blows before running toward James. The other three mediators had almost reached her. James fired several more shots, narrowly missing her, but managed to slow down the bots.

"Flip it here!" she yelled as she drew near.

He tossed her the newly discovered object, she caught it in stride and ran past him. He continued to fire his pistol back at the mediators, dropping one more. Behind him, he heard the sound of metal grinding on metal.

"J, get over here, now!"

He turned to see Ariel standing near two separate, newly opened doors that hadn't been there before. He took off running.

"Toss the blaster!"

James threw it like a fastball. She caught it, flipping it into position in her hand, and fired over his head. He heard the mediators being hit behind him, the twisted metal crashing to the ground.

"In there." Ariel was pointing to one of the open doors. James ran into the door, it closed behind him and everything went silent and dark. Suddenly, lights hummed on and a seat popped up from the ground, more or less forcing him to sit. He obliged, he didn't really have a choice. A four point strap system buckled him in then a door in front of him opened. The chair motored forward into position. He was in another spacecraft, facing out elongated windows in front of him; displays filled the air around him.

"Welcome. Defense protocol, Samson, initiated. Unlocking all systems, weapons active. Ship ERK122 fully operational, ready to launch."

James looked around, he realized the ship was talking to him. Above him in the air, he saw the word "Launch". He pressed it and the wall in front of him split open to the city outside. The craft launched out. James was pinned into his seat momentarily, then the pressure released. Intuitively, he grabbed the controls. He remembered how it felt to fly the ship. He had done it before, or watched and felt it as Arcturus flew. He gazed out the cockpit windows and noticed movement to his left, another craft was flying parallel to him.

"J, can you hear me?"

It was Ariel's voice. James tried to figure out where it was coming from.

"If you can hear me, speak up."

"I hear you."

"Good, now listen to me. They'll be sending ships right on our tail, so we need to get moving. There are two holes to put your hands in. Do that, then grab the rods like an old Atari joystick."

James realized what she was doing and interrupted, "I know how to fly this thing."

"Okay then, Maverick. Let's see if you can keep up, no hard deck here."

James still couldn't understand half of the things she said to him, but it seemed to delight her to confuse him, so he just let it go. Ariel banked hard and James turned to follow. The controls were coming to him; he made a few inputs, testing them out. He heard the sound of a bass drum, the whole ship momentarily glowed a deep blue like a shell had wrapped around it.

"Rear shield hit, shields at 99%."

James remembered his dream. He looked back. Four ships were in the chase and not holding back. A few more blasts came inbound.

"You're right, we didn't have much time. They're right behind me."

"Copy that, switch to combat mode."

"Combat mode, what are you talking about?"

James didn't recall a combat mode. He remembered changing shields in his dream and making lots of fancy turns, but nothing about combat mode.

"I thought you knew how to fly that rig?"

"Yeah, but I don't know anything but the bare bones. I can steer it, but that's about it."

"Touch the air in front of you."

"Okay."

Without hesitation, James reached up and a glowing list of words dropped down.

"Now, do you see where it says "system"?"

"Yep."

"Touch that."

James touched it and a new list appeared. *How long was this going to take?*

"There's a new list I—"

The ship glowed again, and then again. The enemy ships had closed in and he was taking direct fire.

"They're right here."

"Shields 90%," the ship screamed out.

"J, see where it says "audio controls enable"? Press it."

James quickly read through the floating screen and reached up, pressing the words.

"Audio controls initiated."

A few more shots hit the shields, the percentage dropped again.

"Now what? My shields are going down."

"Say "enable combat mode, auto target auto rifles"."

James started, "Enable combat mode, auto rifles."

"Combat mode initiated, unknown second command."

He relayed the error to Ariel. The ship automatically switched to full rear shields, the blasts continued, but the shield held up better.

"Enable auto target auto rifles."

She fed the words to him and as he finished, two small screens appeared, each with round and square gun sights. He watched them move around, locking onto the trailing targets. They started firing a stream of blasts. He looked past the screens at Ariel. She dove down toward the city, he followed, both of them spinning, attempting to avoid the trailing gun fire. His auto turrets kept firing throughout the maneuver then he dove between two buildings.

"We're going to take the long way, but it might help us lose them."

James could see the ground rapidly approaching. Her ship was about to impact, but just as in his dream, the ground opened up. They were taking the tunnel to space. As he entered, he glanced back. The doors began closing, but two of the pursuit ships made it in with them. They emerged into space. Everything seemed to slow down, his sense of speed diminished. Just as before, there were no references to gauge his movement. He looked back at the moon, they were steadily moving away at a rapid pace. Ariel banked right and he watched as one of the two ships turned to chase her.

"Try and shake that ship. I'll take this one," she said spinning away.

James began maneuvering. He spun, flipped, and

rolled, but his pursuer stayed on his tail. The auto rifles did no good, they were missing nearly every shot. He saw Ariel having difficulty with hers as well.

"Is there a way to fire forward?"

Ariel talked him through the menus. He could hear her breathing heavily as she spun and jinked in an attempt the shake the TK craft. James pulled up the targeting system, aiming toward Ariel. He was inbound and attempting to shoot down her bandit.

"Ariel, turn around," he ordered over the comm.

"J, I'm not certain that now is the time..." she teased.

"Turn toward me," he blushed, not that she could see it.

She banked almost immediately and headed straight for him. His shields were beginning to dwindle, he hoped his plan worked. The two ships, nearing collision, swerved to miss. James had a clean shot on the enemy and fired away. The craft burst into pieces in a huge explosion! The sight was surreal with no sound.

His ship shuddered. "Shields 80%."

He looked back. Ariel had somehow missed. The TK ship broke off from James and was now chasing Ariel. He flipped the ship around, getting in a position to help. Ariel started to spin, the shots from the enemy ship glancing off the exterior of her craft. James continued his course, mimicking the maneuvers of the two craft in front of him. In the distance, something moved, causing James to tear his eyes away from the aerial ballet in front of him. He couldn't believe his eyes, it looked like a whole armada of ships headed their way.

"Ariel—"

"I know."

"But—"

"Just get this guy off my tail," she gritted out.

She maneuvered toward him, then away again. The enemy craft persisted, almost attached. James closed in. He tried to focus on the ship, the armada like a swarm of bees continued to distract him. In position, he fired, missing the target, but it was enough to distract the ship which peeled off and engaged him. His auto rifles started firing, but no luck, the ship was too quick and nimble. Then he saw it erupt into a ball of flame, now nothing but floating debris. Ariel had turned her ship and dispatched it. She called him on the radio, telling him to follow her toward Earth. James trailed, increasingly checking back to see the swarm's position.

"Where are we going?"

"To Earth, Sector 3. We need some help from an old friend."

She explained how to direct the rest of the shield energy to the propulsion system, which drastically increased their speed. He looked back as they separated from the swarm. Approaching Earth, Ariel had them chart a course in between the plates. This was the first time he had seen the framework of the planet up close. It was magnificent; he couldn't believe that anyone could build such a large structure. The wall had been quite the sight growing up, but this was on another level.

Large, intertwined metal columns sprayed out of the central hub like a spider's web. The hub itself was round and glowed with a soft orange pulse. But he never got a full glimpse of any of it because the swirling clouds filled the whole interior. Weaving through the structure, they made their way to the far side of the planet. James tried his best to stay focused, but he was still astounded that all of this had been underneath him his whole life.

Upon reaching the other side, a large tunnel appeared near the edge of one of the plates. James configured the craft as instructed by Ariel.

"Configured for landing," the ship confirmed.

They landed inside the tunnel. The area looked like a huge parking lot and they each positioned their craft in a different space, automatically touching down with precision. The canopy opened and James climbed out. Ariel was already outside of hers, waiting for him.

"Who are we meeting?"

"A friend, Professor Thompson."

They began walking down a long hallway leading away from the ships.

"How can he help?"

At this point, nothing would surprise him, or so he thought. Maybe he had a magic key to make this all go away, but deep down, he knew that wouldn't be the case.

"He designed a lot of the systems on the Exodus."

James thought that strange. *Why wouldn't he be on the Exodus with all of the others?*

"What's he doing on Earth?"

"He always loved sharing his knowledge and teaches mechanical classes."

After a short walk, they reached a large room with rack upon rack of clothing.

"What is all this?"

Ariel was already pushing through multiple hangars. She threw him a pair of pants and continued on.

"This is a dressing room. Each sector has a couple for incoming visits. It's filled with Earth clothes to blend in. That's where I got the outfit I was wearing last time."

James looked down at the clothes he was given; jeans, a white t-shirt and a black leather jacket.

"Really?"

"Yep, it will work the best in this sector."

James began putting the clothes on, but he felt uncomfortable. He was used to more formal attire or overalls. He felt like a greaser, but at this point figured it would have to do.

"Don't like it?"

"Well..."

"You look good, Danny."

"Who?"

"Never mind," she grinned. "We shouldn't be here long."

That was a relief. He was anxious about being in a new part of Earth. He had never been farther away than the four small towns near his. In the past two weeks, he had been not only out of town, but to the moon, twice, and now another plate. He glanced over, Ariel was still changing. He tried to be modest and avert his gaze, but he was drawn to her. She looked up at him with a secret smile as she slipped on a dress.

"Can you help me?"

She turned to expose her back to him, pulling her hair to the side. He just stood there, staring.

"Can you get the zipper?"

"Uhh, sure."

He made his way over and gently held the dress and the zipper. He was nervous and his hands trembled slightly. She noticed and tucked her chin, her lips quirked up. He fought through the unnerving feeling and finished. He had never done anything like that, even with Carol.

"Thanks," she said, spinning around as he finished, her dress flowing out. She fixed her hair then took his hand and led him into a room labeled "Tubes". Inside, there was a large tube where a cylinder with an open door sat.

"What are these?" James asked, having never seen anything like it before.

"They're travel tubes. It's an old vacuum system, quite fast, but pretty old tech. I'm actually surprised they never upgraded them. Still, they do the job."

They climbed into the cylinder, Ariel pressed a button and a door closed around them. The travel cylinder was big enough for six passengers, three across with two benches facing each other.

"Destination?" a voice asked.

"Brentwood," Ariel replied.

"Brentwood, time en-route, five minutes."

He felt the travel pod move, slow at first then it picked up speed, nothing like being in the spacecraft as it initially accelerated. Almost as quickly as they hit top speed, they began to slow, then came to a stop.

"Brentwood. Please watch your step exiting and have a pleasant day."

James and Ariel stepped out into another room exactly the same as the one they had just left. James thought for a second it may even be the same one. They entered an elevator and rode up to the surface where it exited into an alleyway. James turned around as the doors closed, then disappeared. All he could see was the brick wall of a two story building, no proof of a door whatsoever.

"This way."

Ariel grabbed his hand and guided him through the alleyway. Her hands were still surprisingly soft for the combat they'd seen, he loved the feel of them in his. His mind went back to Carol a moment. *What was she doing, was she okay?*

Sounds of motor cars filled the air and the smell of freshly baked bread hit his nose. They were in a market. It was laid out similar to his hometown, but felt very different. The buildings were almost all made of stone and they were built extremely close together. There were shops all around; the bakery he smelled, a tailor, a few clothing stores, and what might be a bank. As he surveyed the town, he noticed that none of the signs were in English. The writing was completely foreign and he couldn't read anything.

"Where are we?"

"Sector 3, like I said."

"But why can't I read anything? What are these words?"

She chuckled a bit, "It's German."

"German?"

"Each sector has a different culture, this one is German. You have a lot to learn, J."

James had learned about it from the stand point of a country but had never actually seen the language before. He found the accent fascinating, and the words appeared so unique. James listened, trying to pick up something in conversation, but he couldn't understand anything people were saying. So he just followed Ariel as they passed through the marketplace. He got caught up in the spectacle, trying to take it all in then felt her give him a gentle tug. After a maze of streets, they found themselves on the outskirts of town. Ariel found a truck parked behind a small building.

"Hop in." She jumped into the driver's seat. "Come on, get in."

James looked at her with a slight scowl.

"Don't worry, we'll bring it back."

His moral compass hesitated, Ariel started the truck.

"We can't walk. It's too far from here, just get in."

James took a seat next to her. "We're bringing it back."

"Of course," she replied emphatically. "They won't even know it was gone."

They started down a cobblestone road that exited the city. It became a dirt road at the city limits.

"So, this Professor Thompson, how do you know him?"

"He's a family friend. After designing the Exodus, he moved here, said he loved the old way of life. Not enough tech for me, not sure how he does it. My uncle, who raised me, would send me here for schooling from time to time."

They chatted about life on Earth, how different it was to Ariel. It was like living in the past for her. In some ways, she understood the professor. It was simpler, there were fewer things to worry about, the air was different, it had actual weather, and less people. Still, she'd grown up around the technology and hustle and was used to it all. It was fun visiting Earth for a bit at a time, but she was always ready to go back.

After a while, they approached a small fairytale cottage in the middle of several fields. Ariel pulled up and parked the truck.

"He's a bit...odd," she said, pausing, thinking of how to explain. "Sometimes he can be a little difficult to understand and for some weird reason, he loves cats."

James just took it in, not asking another question. He figured seeing it would make him understand. Ariel knocked on the door. It opened, then with a strong accent James had never heard before, the gentleman behind the door spouted, "Ariel! I am so glad to see you. What brings you here? I have not seen you in a year or so."

James watched the exchange as they hugged and she received a kiss on each cheek.

"Here for more lessons?"

At this point, a small black cat darted out from behind his legs and sat down, looking up at them. "Meow!"

James bent down to pet it.

The professor laughed. "Careful now, Tiki is a biter."

James pulled back his hand as the cat bit his finger, more from the surprise than the pain. It was just a nibble, nothing to really injure him. The professor laughed. He had a deep voice and a very jovial laugh.

"Where are my manners? I am Professor Thompson. Who is your friend?" He reached out his hand.

"This is J."

James reached out and shook the professor's hand.

"Just J? Not a very common name," the professor held his hand, continuing to shake it as he scrutinized him.

"It's James, sir."

The professor released his hand abruptly, "That is alright then. Come in, we are supposed to get a storm tonight."

James glanced at the sky. He hadn't noticed it before, but dark clouds were beginning to cover the sky. They found themselves in the professor's sitting room. All means of trinkets sat on every surface, from teacups to statues, to ornate knives. Scattered throughout must have been a dozen or so cats in various shapes and colors; some with long hair, some short, some with flat faces, some with folded ears. The black cat stayed near James' legs the whole time and, as he took a seat on the sofa, jumped into his lap, purring.

"He likes you. That is good, it means I can trust you. Not that I had any concern since Ariel brought you."

He glanced over at Ariel with a grandfatherly smile.

"What can I help you with today, my dear? Oh tea, would you like tea?"

"Yes, please. Some of your Earl Grey would be nice. Haven't had that since the last time I was here."

The professor exited the room followed by two of the cats, meowing at his feet.

He designed a spaceship? James thought the professor was quite peculiar. He looked older than anyone he had ever met, his face was wrinkled, and he seemed a bit off, like he was somewhere else when he was talking to them. He reappeared carrying a kettle with two cups and handed one to each of them.

"Sugar or cream?"

James didn't drink tea, but felt obligated in this instance. "Sugar, I suppose."

"You suppose? You do not like tea?"

"Not particularly."

"Well, you will like this tea. It is a special batch imported from Sector 22. You cannot find it anywhere else in this sector, or your sector either. Sector 11, correct? The town of Eggerton."

James was surprised. *How did he know that?*

"How..."

"Your accent. It is most definitely from Eggerton."

Accent? James didn't feel he had an accent, not one that distinguished himself. Ariel sounded different, but he hadn't really paid attention before. The professor placed two lumps of sugar in the tea.

"Stir it. Make sure the sugar is evenly distributed."

James did as instructed then took a sip. He was pleasantly surprised. It tasted much better than any tea he'd tried, not that he'd had much. Milk and water were his go-to drinks, or the occasional soda.

"Now what can I do...Oh, sandwiches. Let me make you some sandwiches."

He left the room again. James quirked his eyebrow at Ariel.

"Told you. Just roll with it," she sipped the tea.

James shrugged and did the same. He took a closer look at the eclectic room they found themselves in. There were blueprints from all sorts of machines, some framed and hung, others laid out or rolled up, tossed in a pile. He recognized one of the machines. It was a harvester, just like the ones he had back home. Next to it was a breakdown blueprint of the power supply. He stood up to go examine it and as he did, the professor entered the room to see James studying it.

"That is a Uridium 695 power supply. My design, you probably recognize it."

"Yes, it—"

"Powers your harvester back in Sector 11. It is an older design but works well enough for harvesters. I tried to use it on another project, but it did not work out so well."

"Where are they repaired?"

"They are not repaired, simply replaced. By my calculations, there are enough in stock for 1,000 years at the rate they currently break down."

"Where are they stored?"

James was fascinated with the familiar and was trying to ask more questions, but Ariel interrupted. "We need the Exodus blueprints and a way to shut down the propulsion system."

"Straight to the point, you always have been. Let us eat first then I will see what I can find."

He offered her the plate of sandwiches, then James.

"How is Sector 11 doing these days? It has been years since I visited."

"You've been there?"

James still couldn't bring himself to call it Sector 11. In his mind it was just Earth, plain old Earth. Something about calling it a sector seemed to make it feel less like home and more like a prison. He was beginning to realize that it *was* more like a prison than an actual home.

"It's good, though we've had lots of fires and electrical failures recently."

"Yes, that is because they have not updated the systems. All of the resources went to the Exodus. I told them it would happen, but TK are stubborn."

"Are you staying here? Why haven't you boarded? The ship leaves in less than two days," James asked.

"I prefer here, life is simpler. No TK nonsense forcing their will on everything."

They finished up their meal.

"Now, the data you requested."

He waved for them to accompany him and they headed down a set of wooden stairs into the basement, followed by multiple cats. The basement was lined with stone walls and miscellaneous items were strewn about; several metal scraps, car parts, and plenty of items James didn't recognize. Professor Thompson reached up and touched a stone near the bottom of the staircase; a door opened exposing an elevator. They stepped in, the professor last with two furry friends at his feet. Tiki was at James' feet, he was constantly pinned to him. The elevator descended. When the doors opened, James felt like he was back on the moon. The room was all metal and display screens littered the walls. The professor walked up to one and started tapping buttons. A three-dimensional ship appeared in the middle of the room.

"Is that..."

"Yes, that is the Exodus. The pride and joy of TK."

The professor tapped more buttons in rapid succession, changing the ship's size and zooming in on the heart of it.

"Here is the propulsion system. You say you want to disable it?"

"Yes."

"Well, you will need an override key and a backdoor into the system to shut it down. Are you attempting to cripple it or destroy it?"

The professor spoke as if he hadn't a care in the world, like it didn't matter to him if they were going to blow up a spaceship large enough to transport everyone on the moon, or not.

"Cripple it. We just need to delay it a few more years to build larger cargo holds to evacuate Earth."

"You plan to leave me behind, do you?"

Ariel knitted her brows, "No, of course not. You can come with us to the new planet, start over."

He shook his head, time had taken its toll on him. He looked at his hands then around the room and took a deep breath. "It is okay. I will stay here. I am not in any condition to be traveling to a new planet to start over."

"But—"

"Do not worry about me."

He pressed a button and a small card slid out of a slot in the wall. This will get you into the system and will install a malware program, disabling the propulsion system. Only this card will be able to unlock it without rewriting the firmware. TK has no one who can do that, I created it."

Ariel took the card and studied it. "How do we get into the Exodus?"

"Tiki will guide you."

Both Ariel and James looked at the cat circling

James' feet.

"Tiki?"

The professor picked up the black cat and scratched under his chin, Tiki purred with delight. "Tiki, English mode."

They watched him to see what was going to happen next.

"Tiki, you know James and Ariel. Say hello."

The cat stopped purring and turned his face toward the two of them, "Hello."

James' jaw dropped. "It talks?"

"Yes, it is a robotic cat. They were all the rage about a century ago, but fell out of favor. I prefer the real ones."

Tiki looked at the professor with a noticeable scowl, "And I prefer Earthlings."

The professor laughed and set Tiki on the ground. A slot opened on the cat's back and the professor bent down and slid the card into it.

"This will be your key and the cat, your guide."

Ariel nodded, but James was still trying to wrap his head around it. The cat wasn't real, it'd felt pretty real in his lap.

"Why program it to bite?" James burst out.

The professor laughed again. "That is a glitch, it is not supposed to happen. They have been said to develop their own personality and Tiki is no different, you will see."

Tiki padded over to the elevator and sat down, watching them.

"You should get some rest before your task. I have a spare room upstairs, you may use it for the evening."

"No, we haven't the time for that. The ship is going to depart in a little over a day."

"It is not going to do much good if you cannot think straight. They say that lack of sleep is like being drunk, you know. You will need your wits about you," he tapped on his temple.

Ariel and James knew that he was right, and it had been awhile since they'd slept. They headed up to the main house again and discussed the plan. The professor handed them a small tablet which they used to display the ship. He gave them the entry points, some small details that only he knew and an escape plan once they were onboard. The sun was setting and the professor showed them to their room. He opened the door to reveal a quaint little room on the second story with one bed in the center and a chair off to one side. James and Ariel looked at each other.

"You can have the bed, I'll take the floor," James began.

The professor laughed and headed down the stairs.

"I will leave you to it," he said, disappearing out of sight.

"You'll need your sleep, too. No need to be modest, besides, it looks big enough for both of us."

James felt weird about the sleeping arrangements. He'd never shared a bed before, let alone with a girl.

"I'll tell you what, we'll sleep in shifts. I need to go

over the plans again anyway. You go first," she suggested.

James walked over to the window and gazed out at the fields below. He missed his room, the farm, his parents, even the chickens. Sleep was creeping up on him. He was used to waking up early, his eyes were heavy. He turned to Ariel, "Ok, I'll try and get some sleep."

He still felt strange, but could tell he wasn't going to win and the wood plank floor didn't look very inviting. He slipped off his boots and crawled into bed. Ariel sat in the chair examining the tablet, tomorrow would be a challenging day to say the least.

CHAPTER EIGHTEEN

James awoke with an arm around his chest; Ariel had fallen asleep on him. His initial reaction was to jump up out of bed, but he resisted the urge. He didn't want to wake her and something about it made him feel at ease, calming him. His uncomfortable feelings soon washed away and he lay there enjoying the embrace.

He watched the sun rise through the window, changing the fields to a beautiful glowing orange. Ariel's body felt as if it had melted into his. Her hair smelled of sunflowers, taking him back to simpler times. She tightened her grip on him, which startled him a bit, enough to make him flinch. Ariel raised her head, opening one eye, then shut it and plopped back down. James slipped out of bed, doing his best not to wake her.

"I told you it was big enough for both of us."

James looked back. Ariel had one eye slightly open, watching him. He didn't know how to respond, so he went over to the window. A crash came from downstairs, then another. Ariel jumped up and James almost lost his balance; she wasn't wearing much. He shook his head, trying to regroup, and glanced at the door. Ariel flew through it and down the stairs. He followed as quickly as he could, hearing choking coming from downstairs. As he rounded the corner at the base of the stairs, Ariel was standing there, fists clenched, staring intently into the living room. James looked past her. Two men were standing there, one holding the professor in the air by the throat, the other staring back at them.

"Dillon!" Ariel angrily started. "Have your Rat put him down."

"Certainly."

He motioned to the man holding the professor. James heard a snap then watched the professor's body fall lifelessly to the ground. James could see Ariel's whole body clench. She took a step forward.

"Nah, don't do that," Dillon aimed a large blaster at her.

"Bastard!" Ariel yelled. James could see the tears welling up in her eyes as she shakily spoke, "You Bastard."

Dillon started laughing, "Did you have a good night?" He leered at her state of undress. "By the looks of it you did."

Ariel stared back at him, teeth clenched, a single tear gliding down her face. James stepped forward.

"You too lover boy, not another step. I warned you not to fall for her. Now you're in way over your head. You two are coming with me. Let's make this easy for all of us, no funny business."

Ariel put her hands over her head then glanced back at James, "Go on, J."

She turned, giving him her signature wink, still fighting the tears as her lips quivered. James wanted nothing more than to comfort her and make Dillon pay for putting that look on her face, but he shook off those thoughts and raised his hands over his head. The E-Rat next to Dillon began to walk over to James while Dillon approached Ariel.

"You always were a beauty." His lascivious gaze ran over her barely clothed body. "So much fire inside. Too bad you were bred for the wrong thing."

He slithered his hand over her neck then, using his thumb, wiped the tear from her eye. "He was past his prime, no more usefulness. You on the other hand..." He moved his hand down toward her chest. As he did, she grabbed his wrist with both hands and twisted his arm behind his back. She tripped him, falling on top of him. The E-Rat looked over at the two, distracted. James let a punch fly, landing it on the back of his head then took off running upstairs, shaking his hand. He dashed into the bedroom. Finding his blaster next to his jacket, he spun around; the E-Rat was right there. James fired a shot, hitting him in the chest, but felt the sting of a punch before he could get a second shot off. His pistol winged away, hitting the wall. The two locked eyes. James frantically tried to figure out his next move. He scuttled over to the gun, but was yanked back by his ankle. Rolling over he saw the monster cocking back a fist, but out of nowhere, he heard the scream of a cat. Tiki came flying in and landed on the E-Rat's face, locking on with all four claws. James' foot was released and he slipped over to the blaster, turning to aim. Tiki was thrown from the E-Rat, leaving sparks popping out from the damage inflicted by the cat.

James fired volley after volley, striking him multiple times in the chest. The E-Rat fell over in a heap. Tiki was on all fours shaking off the blow he'd taken from being slung against the wall. James took a moment to catch his breath, then heard the commotion downstairs.

"Ariel," he said under his breath. He ran downstairs.

She was pinned up against Dillon's back and had his arms pinned behind him. He flailed about trying to get released, but she was locked on and not letting go. He started to ram her into the wall then stopped as he noticed James standing there, holding a blaster aimed at his head.

"Tell your little princess to get off of me."

"Maybe, if you ask her nicely," James replied. *That sounded like something Ariel would say. She must be rubbing off on him.*

Dillon gritted his teeth, "Please get off of me."

Ariel released Dillon and stepped away from him. Dillon grabbed his shoulder, massaging and rolling it around.

"Why are you after us?"

"Seriously? Is that a serious question?"

James frowned at him, then looked around, then back at him. "I thought so..."

"You realize I work for TK and you're trying to stop them from leaving."

James nodded his head. Dillon began to speak, but was cut short by a shovel to the back of the head. His body toppled forward to the ground. Ariel dropped the shovel and ran over to the professor. She picked up his head and checked his pulse; James knew the answer as tears finally slipped free and ran down her face. He didn't know what to say, he had never dealt with death before, not on a personal level. He stood there a moment then realized they needed to get moving. If previous encounters were anything to go by, more would be coming. He ran upstairs and grabbed the rest of his clothes, then Ariel's. He handed them to her as he returned.

"We need to go," he said softly. She nodded and took the clothes from him.

"Start the truck. I'll be out in a moment," she said quietly.

James didn't waste any time. He rushed out and got the truck started. Ariel appeared shortly, hopping into the truck. They headed back toward the town as fast as they could on the old dirt road. A few miles down, James slammed on the brakes.

"The cat!" he shouted at the same time as they heard a thud come from behind them. They looked in the bed of the truck. Tiki was shaking off the impact of the stop.

"Maybe I could ride up there with you?" he said in a condescending tone.

James and Ariel looked at each other.

"Sure," James finally said, reaching through the rear window to pick up the cat. It was very strange to hear an animal talk, but things were beginning to be less shocking to him. James started the truck, and put it into gear.

"Thanks," James said hesitantly.

"Of course, no problem. It looked like you needed a bit of help back there."

Ariel cocked her head toward James.

"He distracted the E-Rat for me."

"Distracted? I nearly ripped off his face," Tiki responded indignantly.

James smiled, thinking of the cat's little body flying through the air to come to his rescue.

"When you get to the next road crossing, take a right."

"A right? But that's away from town," James questioned the cat's directions. "Besides how do you know where we are? You're a cat."

"Not just any cat. I'm a cyber-genetically engineered cat and the town is crawling with replicants searching for you two. You can't take the tube; you'll have to drive to the west wall."

"How far is that?"

"An hour and eight minutes at this speed."

"Better step on it, J."

He looked over at her. He could see she was still troubled.

"You okay?"

"I'll be fine. Let's keep our minds on the mission."

Mission. James had never thought about it as a mission. But they did have a goal and they needed to accomplish it. He took the right, following Tiki's instructions. James asked a few questions, but most of the ride was quiet. In what seemed like no time at all, they arrived at the wall. James stopped at the imaginary border before no man's land. It was just as imposing as the one he grew up in the shadow of.

"Where to now?" he looked down at Tiki.

"100 meters to the north."

"Meters?"

"Yes, meters. That's right, American. Approximately 109 yards."

James looked around, trying to figure out which way was north.

"Go to the wall and take a right," Tiki shook his head at James.

"By the way, why the biting?"

"There is an issue with my teeth. The biting sooths them."

"You feel pain? Why didn't the professor fix it? He seemed handy."

"He didn't design me and the only repair stations are in Atlantis. He never took me there, not a big deal."

They approached the wall on foot, alongside Tiki who happily pranced along in the grass. He stopped and sat down.

"Pick me up."

James reached down and picked up the cat.

"Hold me up to the wall there."

He pointed with his paw and James couldn't help but laugh. It was kind of funny to see a cat acting like a little person. Tiki twisted his head around, unamused. James did as he was told and Tiki touched a few locations on the wall, exposing a door. The three of them walked inside.

"You can't use the ships you rode in on. They are being guarded."

"How do you know all this?"

Ariel didn't ask too many questions; she understood, but James had no clue.

"I'm connected to the network. I have access to all of the systems, cameras, sensors, etcetera."

"Network?"

Tiki glared at Ariel who had a big Cheshire cat grin on her face, "Have you not taught him anything?"

She just shrugged her shoulders and winked at James, "It's more fun this way."

Tiki took off down the hall and began to explain the network, how everything was interwoven and how each system talked to the others through code. Plenty was lost on him, but he was able to grasp the overall concept. Tiki led them to an emergency bay.

Ariel stopped when she saw the escape pods, "No. There has to be something else?!"

Tiki turned, "This is the only way you can get close to the Exodus without TK noticing. They'll think you're just an escape pod from Earth. A last minute passenger who missed the main transport shuttles."

James was puzzled, "What's wrong with them?"

"They suck. That's the gist of it," she sighed. "Okay, this tech is very old. It's only operated by voice and the onboard ship navigator is really annoying."

"Annoying and old? That sounds familiar. Is anything around here new and properly functioning?"

James queried.

"You'll see. Tiki, what are the chances they will malfunction?"

"They have a proven 65% success rate."

Ariel rolled her eyes. "Is this really the best option? Scan again, please."

Tiki paused a moment. "Yes, this is the only option."

"Okay, J, you get the cat."

"My name is Tiki." He resented being called a cat, especially when someone knew his name.

"Let's get this over with," she said, scrubbing her hands over her face. "I'll take this one."

She pointed to the pod on the right, walked over to the table next to it and laid down. The table slid into the wall. James headed to the other pod and did the same. He was lying down in a small tube, Tiki between his feet. A strap went over his torso and shoulders then lights flickered on, but the right side immediately turned back off.

"Hey, hey, hey you cool cat! Welcome to the Mark5 escape pod. Please select your destination by telling me where you would like to go, then we'll be off," a very chipper voice asked.

James could tell why Ariel didn't appreciate the pods. The digitized voice sounded like a radio game show host, way over the top. Who designed this thing?

"Exodus."

"The Exodus, the gateway to the stars, your getaway retreat to another planet."

James felt like he was in a living commercial.

"Hold on tight and we'll be on our way."

James heard metal sliding, then he was falling out of the small porthole in front of him. The walls moved from his feet to his head, the dropping sensation increased and then he saw sky. He felt and heard a rocket boost, then watched as he climbed into the clouds, exiting into space. The inside went dark.

"Lighting malfunction. Attempting to restore, please wait, please wait..."

James didn't mind the lighting failure. He could see outside the ship better and the stars were remarkable. *I'll never get used to that view.*

"Oxygen system malfunction. Attempting to restore, please wait, please wait..."

Now this was a little more concerning. "Tiki, how long until we get there?"

"Another ten minutes."

"Umm, Mr. Escape Pod, how much air is left?"

"Why you have eight minutes of air left. Attempting to restore systems, please wait, please wait..."

James was starting to understand Ariel's concern. He hoped he could hold his breath for two minutes. The pod continued on, the stars appeared almost stationary.

"Initiating approach, please wait..."

James lay there, trying to control his breathing, then the Exodus came into view. It was on the dark side of the moon, protruding from the surface, and it was enormous. James was impressed; it was even larger than he could have imagined. From his vantage point, all he could see was the exterior structure pass by as the pod slid into a tube. James was starting to feel short of breath. The oxygen was depleted and he was having a hard time keeping his eyes open.

"Hold your breath," he heard Tiki say.

James tried, but was drifting off. He felt the impact as the pod came to a stop then closed his eyes.

"Wake up sleepy head."

He opened his eyes. He was lying in a field surrounded by lush grass. He looked over at Ariel, who was lying next to him.

"What happened?"

"You fell asleep."

"But where am I? I don't recognize this. What happened to the ship?"

"What ship? You're home, on Earth."

James took in his surroundings. He was lying on a small hill, the sun was setting in the distance. There was no wall. The Earth just dropped off and he could see sky above the grass. He dropped his head back to the grass, oddly he felt at peace. Ariel climbed on top of him, her hands supporting her chin on his chest as she gazed up into his eyes. He looked at her, really looked at her. She was so beautiful. Not just in her sundress, but inside as well. She rose up and gave him a long sweet kiss, pleasure surged through his body.

Suddenly, he was lying on the cold pod table. Ariel released her kiss. He coughed as he came back to life, his eyes opening wide.

"That's why I hate those stupid pods. Always malfunctioning."

She climbed off of him.

He subconsciously rubbed his aching chest. "What happened?"

"You were out, no pulse. I didn't have time to find a med kit, so I brought you back old school."

James coughed some more. As he rolled over, he looked down at the floor to see Tiki sitting there, watching.

"Ready to go?" he asked.

James sat up. "I think so."

Ariel helped him to his feet, he was a bit woozy.

"They're still loading the sleep chambers. I'm charting a path to circumnavigate the security protocols," Tiki said while standing up. "This way."

He headed out of the escape pod receiving bay. They followed the little black cat through a maze of corridors; he made sure to disable all security systems in each location as they went. Soon they found themselves nearing the powerplant section. One door remained between the control room and where they stood.

"There are 14 mediators in the control room and four technicians prepping for the launch. Countdown reads 22 hours."

Ariel and James drew their blasters and looked at each other.

"Guns blazing?"

James looked at her, "Any other options?"

She shook her head then nodded to Tiki, "Okay."

The door opened, the mediators all turned toward them, but James and Ariel weren't looking at them.

"Bless it!" Ariel ducked to the side and James did the same, each going to a separate side for cover. "You said there were four technicians!"

Tiki was standing over by James who was kneeling, watching her for instructions. "That's what the system told me."

James peered around the corner again to confirm what he thought he saw.

"James and Ariel," Dillon began. "My head still aches."

James ducked back behind the wall. They definitely weren't technicians. Dillon and three E-Rats stood there waiting for them. Back to the wall, he turned his head to look at Ariel and mouthed the words "what now?" Ariel chewed her lip, trying to think of a plan.

"If it were up to me, I would have killed you by now. But I'm to take both of you alive. Not sure why, we have everything we need to get off this Godforsaken rock."

"Close the door," James told Tiki. The door shut then opened again.

"Shut the door."

"I'm trying. You realize there are two sets of controls." He shut the door again only for it to be opened immediately.

"Stop playing around. Drop your weapons and come

281

on out," Dillon demanded.

Ariel leapt, rolling toward James, gun blasts followed her. She frantically shot as she rolled, skidding to a stop next to James.

"We're going to need more weapons. Tiki, where is the armory on this ship?"

"On the other side. It will be nearly impossible to get to."

"Don't think we have a choice."

"Last chance, then we'll be forced to take you down the hard way," Dillon continued.

James stood up and blasted the manual door controls. The door shut.

"Well, where to?"

"This way."

Tiki ran off, James and Ariel in tow. The corridors twisted and turned. He worked to disable the security systems, but suddenly, a red light began flashing and a loud buzzing horn blasted.

"They're locking everything down!"

They looked around. At one end of the hall, the doors began to close; at the other was a T junction.

"Tiki, what's underneath us?"

"The maintenance bay."

"Do they have cutting tools?"

"Yes."

"Can you—"

"Already on it."

James looked at Ariel, brow raised, then realized what

she was planning.

"Check the corridor, J."

He ran up to the T and looked right. A door was closing to the hallway beyond. He then checked behind him, the door was still open, but he was greeted by half a dozen mediators. He turned, ducking to avoid the incoming blaster rounds, and ran toward Ariel, screaming, "They're coming!"

Ariel tucked herself against the wall. James skated across the hallway mimicking her position. They waited for the enemy to appear.

Like clockwork, the mediators began to pour from the opening, firing as they came. Blasts skipped off of the walls and floor, James took out a few while Ariel was managing more.

"How's the cutting coming, Tiki?"

"Almost in position. It took me a bit to hack into the system again."

James was hit in the shoulder. He spun back onto his back, looking up as a beam of light popped through the floor a few feet in front of him. James rolled over, the beam moved toward him at a steady pace.

"Tiki! Where's this going?"

"Straight at you. I had no choice. It will stop one foot in front of you."

Ariel yelled for him to get behind her. She took a glancing blow off her thigh and fired back, wincing in pain. The light moved in a rectangular pattern as the mediators continued to pour in, firing shot after shot at them. James was hit again in the side as he switched positions behind Ariel. The light was rounding the final corner. He watched the floor drop out and Tiki hopped right on in. James crawled over and peered down. Tiki was looking up from the piece of floor that was now floating on something. Around it he could see the maintenance bay. The actual floor was a good fifty feet below them, but something was holding up the recently cut flooring. It must be the cutting machine. *Wish I had one of those working on the farm.* James glanced over at Ariel; she had been hit again and was struggling to continue the fight. James got to his feet and grabbed her hand, pulling her over to the hole. Without looking, they jumped to the awaiting Tiki. Above, they could see the laser blasts trailing off as the platform descended. James looked around. There were a number of what he thought were heavy machines, some resembled equipment he had on the farm, only brand new.

"There a med station in here somewhere?"

Tiki looked at him a moment, "Aft wall, near the entrance."

"Aft? Can you just get us there?"

Tiki hovered the platform over to the wall, coming to a rest above the floor. James scooped up Ariel behind the knees and carried her off the platform to the med station, though he was struggling through his own pain. Tiki hopped down and followed.

"I'm perfectly capable of making it there under my own steam," she gritted out.

"You probably are. You're the toughest person I know. But right now, I need to take care of you."

She just looked at him, as if she was mulling over something that she'd never thought of before.

He reached the station and gently set her down on the table, then opened the case and grabbed the medical gun.

"How do you work this?"

"Press the power button, then select "exterior wound"."

Ariel guided him through the steps. He ran the kit over her shoulder and thigh then gave her a painkiller shot. She took the medical gun and began treating the wound on his side, but it was blasted from her hand. They looked up; mediators were jumping into the bay. Tiki was busy attempting to open the locked door behind them and Ariel raised her blaster to fire back.

"Fuel cell depleted," the weapon chirped.

James passed her his.

"How's the door coming?" she yelled over the loud blasts.

"I think I've got it."

The door sprang open. James yanked Ariel to her feet and they fled through it as Tiki closed it behind them.

"Now where?" Ariel asked.

"Down the hallway to the right, through the dining hall, then down the elevator to the ammo dump."

James was glad Tiki was there, he would have gotten completely lost. They headed to the dining hall, Tiki opening doors as they went. They were one step ahead of the mediators, but were never able to gain ground. They ran through the dining hall where people were eating. As they passed, people scattered, screaming and panicking. A few were hit by stray rounds as the mediators were not very accurate, a flaw that TK had never been able to work out. The three darted into the adjacent elevator.

"What floor please?" the elevator asked.

"What floor, Tiki?"

"B-4, Ammo Dump."

The elevator repeated "B-4 Ammo Dump" then didn't move.

"What's going on, Tiki?!"

The door remained open, the mediators were approaching. The first couple reached them and Ariel attempted to fire point blank, but her attempt was met with a "Fuel cell depleted". She grabbed the first robot and spun it around firing amongst its own.

"Got it," she heard Tiki yell out. She threw the metal monstrosity away and dove into the elevator, the doors closed.

CHAPTER NINETEEN

The elevator started down.

"You know there will be a welcoming entourage at the depot," Tiki counseled amongst the heavy breathing of the two humans.

"Yeah...But we don't have any choice...we need those weapons if we even hope to stand a chance."

"What are you reading down there?"

"Can't tell. The system's locked, not responding."

The elevator came to a stop, the doors slid open, and James stepped back, surprised.

"Welcome to the party." Zane was standing there with a big grin on his face. Behind him, James saw a pile of damaged robots.

"How..."

"Long story for another time. Looks like you'll be needing these."

He tossed rifles to Ariel and James.

"You have your pick, but I thought these'd be best."

"Thanks. Any detonators?"

"Yeah, there's a whole crate, but I don't know if you want to use any in here."

Ariel gave him a look that said, "How well do you know me?" then headed off to grab some.

Zane turned and looked at James. "You guys doin' alright? Jolt got me in when we heard the intrusion alarms going off. Figured Ariel would try something." Tiki chose that moment to wrap between James' legs.

"What's with the cat?"

"That's Tiki. Like you said, long story. He's been helping us hack the systems." Ariel was back. She handed the guys a few small can shaped devices. Zane looked at her disapprovingly.

"What?" James asked. "What are these?"

"Think of dynamite, but with a much bigger boom," Ariel volunteered excitedly.

He gingerly put a couple in his pockets.

"Now what?" Ariel looked at Zane. "Jolt hacking for you?"

"Yep."

"Explains why Tiki couldn't get into this room. Tell him to let Tiki help. We need to get to the propulsion room. There's got to be a back way."

Zane opened his Datacle to give Jolt the information, Tiki interrupted the discussion. "I hate to be rude, but there are multiple enemies inbound."

"Right. How did you get here?" Ariel looked at Zane for an answer.

"Same way as you, but I was a ninja and didn't trip any alarms."

Ariel tightened her eyebrows.

"In the elevator. We'll figure it out on the way up."

The now four of them piled back into the elevator. Tiki mentioned a possible route on the top floor. They would have to use one of the docking bays and exit the ship, but it would be the quickest way. Between Tiki and Jolt, they were able to clear a path. James, Ariel, and

Zane donned exterior walking suits. They were relatively tight fitting and the oxygen system on their back was quite small.

When he put on the helmet, the system automatically powered up. James could read the system status, oxygen time remaining and a few other things like suit pressure. He started touching his visor, the helmet, his arms, chest, he looked like he was swatting at bees. Zane tapped on Ariel's shoulder as she finished with her helmet and pointed at James.

Ariel doubled over laughing, "What are you doing?"

"Isn't there a button or something to turn off the words? I can't see a thing."

"Just say "suit, hide menu"."

James stopped his flailing and did as instructed, the menu went away and he could see again.

"Decompressing the bay then opening the doors," Tiki informed them.

He also told them there were multiple mediators outside the door trying to get into the docking bay and that he couldn't hold the interior door locks much longer, they were overriding his commands. The exterior docking bay doors opened. Ariel went out first, reaching for the ladder just outside the bay doors. James and Zane exited soon after. They followed the instructions fed to them by Tiki and Jolt, both informing them of the potential threats on their tail. James saw a bright light out of the corner of his eye. The mediators had gained access to the bay and were now outside shooting at them. They came to a junction in the ladders and their pace quickened, up they went.

"Once we get to the top, we're going to have to make a run for it. Those med heads are gaining on us." Zane was taking up the rear, firing back at the pursuers, dropping a few but then he'd have to strap on his weapon to move.

They reached the top and Ariel took off running. There was another docking bay near the middle of the ship and as she approached, the doors began opening. More mediators with jet packs appeared. Ariel and James didn't waste any time. They fired their rifles as they continued their run. James looked behind him; Zane had just crested the top and was shooting back down the ladder. He looked back at Ariel, there must have been over twenty mediators littering the sky. He watched her slide to a stop then throw something into the sky. She turned and dove at him. The device ignited into a large blue globe. James watched the light as he was hit in the chest by Ariel's shoulder and thrown to the ground. Remembering how they'd met, he thought this might be her signature move. He smiled faintly and heard a fizzling sound then a "pop", like a firework. Lying flat on his back with Ariel on top of him, he saw sparkles falling from the sky, not an enemy in sight. Ariel scanned the area.

"Up."

She jumped to her feet and took off running, James trailed. Tiki was by his feet and almost tripped him as he started. Ariel made it to the door first and jumped in,

James blindly followed. He looked down. *This is going to hurt.* He was thirty feet above the ground, but the gravity was acting strange, he didn't fall as fast as expected. He watched Ariel land below as if falling on a pillow in slow motion. His landing a few seconds later was the same. He heard a deep scream and looked up. Zane was descending right on top of him. He scrambled to get out of the way but was pummeled by Zane's huge body. James lay there a moment watching the bay doors closing while Zane pushed himself up.

"You okay?"

He helped James to his feet.

"Yeah."

He looked back up as the doors collapsed together.

"Where to now?" James asked.

"Tiki says that way," Ariel pointed toward a door. "Only a few hundred yards, but plenty of mediators in between."

James heaved a heavy sigh. Challenge after challenge seemed to be placed in their path and it never got easier. Ariel grinned as she continued her labored breathing. James did the same, it was infectious.

"Okay, knock it off. We need to get moving," Zane chided as he took off his helmet. The bay had been re-pressurized and oxygen filled the room.

The other two popped off their helmets. James was glad to be out of it, he felt claustrophobic.

Zane started toward the door.

"I don't know if we can do this," James said, leaning

with his hands on his knees.

"Don't give up on me now," Ariel responded. "We've come too far to not finish this."

James was worn out, he was still in pain from his injuries as they hadn't had a chance to heal him yet, and the path to victory seemed nearly impossible. Ariel stretched out her hand.

"Think of Earth."

James thought about Earth and his family, his friends, and Carol. Life was so much easier before any of this happened. He was beginning to wish he could just go back to the way it was when Ariel pulled him close and locked eyes with him. "We will stop them."

Her icy blue eyes were powerful. She believed what she was saying and it carried over to James. In that moment, even if he didn't care about Earth, he would have done it for her. He nodded his head in agreement. James looked over. Zane was almost at the door, Tiki wasn't far behind. The door slid open and gun fire poured out, cutting down Zane. He fell in a heap. Tiki bolted under a small cargo vessel. Ariel and James tumbled behind another one that was further away and James peeked around the corner. Dillon stood in the doorway cradling a high-yield ordinance cannon sporting six separate barrels in a circular pattern. He sauntered toward them, overconfident, with no fear of retaliation.

"You had your chance. Now I'll close your eyes for good."

James leaned back, looking wild-eyed at Ariel.

"Now what? We need Tiki, he has the card. I don't know about Zane..."

Ariel searched for an answer, analyzing her surroundings.

"I'm sure Zane will be fine, he always bounces back, you'll see. He can't die. You get Tiki and get to the control room."

Before he could respond, she took off running from under the vessel, away from Dillon. James watched as Dillon let a full automatic burst of fire spray toward Ariel. She tumbled and slipped behind another ship. She looked at James and pointed to the door. James mouthed the word "no". Ariel gave the same command, but James didn't want to leave her. She popped out enough so that Dillon could see her. He laid down more fire, but she was too quick. James focused on what was around them, there had to be a way to help her. The bay held multiple cargo ships. Ariel was behind one, Tiki behind another and himself another.

There were four more aircraft ranged throughout the hangar. He peeked around; Dillon was still walking out, but had changed course direct to Ariel. She opened herself up again, more rounds fired, skipping off the ground and the cargo ship. He got up and started running to Tiki and slid behind the ship, his baseball coach would have been proud.

"Tiki, can you control those ships? Can you fly them?"

Tiki closed his eyes as if to think.

"Yes, but I don't know for how long. TK is overriding all of my access, they're locking down the systems. If you want to get to the control room, we have to go now."

"What about Jolt, can he do it?"

"Yes."

"Okay, tell him to create a distraction for Ariel and you come with me."

Almost on cue, one of the cargo ships came to life as he and Tiki scrambled to the door. He stopped at the door and looked back, Dillon was almost right on top of Ariel.

"Ariel!" he yelled.

Dillon turned and began firing, the door closed before the blasts could get to him. James hoped he made the right decision. He and Tiki began the trek to the control room, he followed Tiki closely, weapon drawn. Door after door, they found nothing. James, even with his almost non-existent amount of combat experience, was getting anxious.

"Where is everyone?"

"I can't tell. The only systems I have access to now are about half of the doors and lighting controls."

The lights went out.

"Now just the doors."

"How much further?"

"After the next room, there is a long corridor, then we'll be there."

James couldn't see anything, it was pitch black like a cave without an ounce of sunlight.

"How are we going to even find it? I can't see my, well, anything."

A beam of light appeared next to him. He looked down, Tiki's eyes glowed like a flashlight.

"That works. You lead."

Tiki headed to the door. They made it down the corridor to the control room. James stopped just outside and readied his rifle, then nodded to Tiki. Tiki looked at James blinding him with his glowing eyes. James winced, throwing up his arm to shield his own.

"I'm ready."

The door opened. James glanced in. The room was pitch black. He nodded to Tiki then quickly recalled that the nod was a stupid tactic.

"You first."

Tiki padded in, he peered in after, nothing. The room was empty except for the large table-like structure in the middle of the room. He cautiously entered, rifle leading the way. He panned around looking for anything, nothing. He called Tiki over to him.

"The card."

Tiki popped the card out of his back and James grabbed it.

"Where does this go?"

He searched the table, but Tiki had already found it.

"Here," he put a paw down on a small panel, a slot opened up in the shape of the card and James slid it in.

"Now what?"

"Hold on, I have to run a program."

He waited as he watched Tiki sit, staring at the card slot. James fell to the ground, pain shooting through his body. He was unable to move. He lay there a moment as he shook involuntarily, then, as suddenly as it hit him, it stopped. He was staring at the ceiling, his body wouldn't respond and he heard heavy footsteps approach. It was a mediator. The machine reached down and picked him up by the shoulders. James' only choice was to hang there, unable to move, his head slumped down. Tiki was lying motionless on the table. He tried to speak, but his tongue was incapacitated as well. He watched the room move away as he was hauled out into the corridor. The lights flickered on. The mediator took him through corridor after corridor, room after room, until finally coming to a stop.

They had entered a room, but James could only see the floor, his head still uncontrollable.

"Release him," he heard a familiar voice command. His body fell into a heap onto the ground. He wiggled his fingers, then his hands; his body control was slowly coming back. He heard murmuring, talking between multiple people. He raised his head trying to get to his feet, no luck.

"Ugh. Pick him up," she commanded.

James felt the mediator grab him once again and lift him to his feet. He tried to look around. The room held a large round table as he had seen before, but was much smaller than the one on the moon. He looked across the table. The woman he had met before stood there holding the card, Cyrellia.

"You and your band of misfits thought you would stop our launch? Why? What are you trying to accomplish?"

James didn't even know if he could answer her, he remained silent. The room was filled with many other individuals, they were talking amongst themselves. He noticed Tiki lying on the table in this room as well. Cyrellia grabbed the card with both hands and flexed it; the card snapped. She tossed it on the floor and moved around the table toward him.

"Why do you want to stop progress? Why do you want to stop us from going to our new home? One which will be better than the last. I gave you a chance to come with us to the new world. I will only offer it one more time."

At this, a gentleman entered the room.

"What is it?" Cyrellia snapped.

"We will have the ship repaired in 6 hours then we'll be ready to launch."

She waived him away then turned to the room.

"You have somewhere else to be."

The room began twittering again and headed out behind James, leaving him with Cyrellia. She walked around him, he was still held by the mediator. His body control was coming back to him, he could move a bit more now. She stopped in front of him, examining him.

"You believe what you are doing is noble. Trying to save the humans on Earth. Let me ask you something.

Do you know where they came from?"

James was confused by the question and his face showed it.

"Let me explain it a little better for you. Hundreds of years ago, the Earth was overpopulated. The climate changed with the influx of people, the planet was eating itself up from the inside out. Earthquakes were prevalent, volcanoes began popping up, there were pandemics, the human race looked for a way out. The initial group, which I'm sure you have become acquainted with, was the Kontrolery. Those members began the move to the moon, colonizing it, but there was an issue. The sustainment of food. Knowing that the Earth was a ticking time bomb, they strategically dismantled it and created the structure you called home. They arranged it in sectors. Each focused on farming, raising cattle, or a multitude of other renewable resources needed to sustain life in New Atlantis. But who would work on Earth while we lived here and built this great ship to take us to a new home? Humans were the best option. They didn't need materials that were set for the Exodus. Our bioengineers created humans to fulfill the workforce requirement, freeing up precious materials. They are our creation, like a hybrid plant would be. We use them. Then, when they are no longer of any use, we discard them. Ever wonder why no one has lived past the age of 65 in your town? They outlived their usefulness."

Dillon had said the same thing. James ran through his memories, but he still couldn't think of anybody who had lived that long. *Carol, Carol couldn't be just a drone. She was as human as him. Was she going to die at 65? Was it predestined or something enforced by TK?*

"Now that brings us back to you. You are not like them. You, by birth, are a member of the Kontrolery, whether you believe it or not. Your father had delusions that Earthlings were more than worker drones, but he was wrong."

She clenched her fist at chest level. "His plan would never have worked. It was the plan of a dreamer, not based in reality. Moving an entire planet, impossible. But a select few..."

"I'm guessing you're the select few?" James finally spoke up.

She looked at him like a mother at a questioning child. "You are too. Don't you understand? Your line needs to continue on. You are destined for greatness."

"What makes me better than the Earthlings? I lived there, I was raised there!" *What am I saying?* But he couldn't stop himself, "I am an Earthling!"

"You. Are. Not!" Cyrellia yelled back, fire in her eyes, fist still clenched and shaking. "You are my son and you're coming with us."

CHAPTER TWENTY

James was dragged out of the room. So many questions flooded his mind. His world had already been turned upside down, now it had exploded. *Was this all a lie? Was he in a dream? Or was his life on Earth a lie?* James contemplated what all of this meant; for a few moments, he convinced himself it was a dream. His feet dragged on the ground as the mediator steadily marched down yet another maze of corridors. James stared at the ground. After a short elevator ride, the doors opened. James looked up to see a large group of people moving down the hallway in front of him. He recognized a few of them from earlier in the room with Cyrellia. The mediator waited for all of them to pass, then fell in behind. They entered a room where all of the people who had passed by were climbing onto beds inside of what looked like large cans. After lying down, the can closed and was moved down a conveyor disappearing into a shadowed receptacle. Soon it was his turn; the mediator stepped up and forced him to lie down. The capsule began to close. James struggled to break free, but his efforts were fruitless. The mediator shocked him, his body went limp again.

He watched as the mediator stepped back and the can closed around him. It was dark; there were no windows to see anything. Had he been able to move, he would have been flailing about, panicking, but only his mind had the freedom to do so. He looked around, nothing.

It was pitch black, not a speck of light. The sound of gas filling the chamber echoed in his ears. He felt his eyes becoming heavy.

James opened his eyes and looked across the dining room table at his father reading the newspaper.

"There's something your mom and I would like to discuss with you."

James looked over at the sink; his mom had her head down, doing dishes. She turned and had a seat at the table. His father folded the paper and put it down then looked at his mother.

"Son, you see, well..."

"What your father is trying to say is that you're adopted."

James didn't know how to react. Incredulous, he looked from his mom to his father; his rocks, the steady constants in his life. And he lost it.

"You're telling me this now! I'm about to graduate, I have a scholarship, and now you're telling me this? Why didn't you tell me sooner? Or wait until after graduation? Or just not tell me at all?"

"We didn't want you to stress over it," his mom said sweetly. "We're just drones, we just farm. You're royalty. A true rags to riches story. You'll have everything you want."

"What I want?!"

James grabbed his head with both hands, squeezing. His entire life was a lie. *Where did he come from? What was he going to do? Who was he?*

"Ahgggg."

He ran out of the house.

"Carol. I need to find Carol."

He ran to his truck and hopped in, turning to look behind him. He jumped. Carol was sitting next to him.

"Where did you come from?" he said in a panic.

"I've been here, I'll always be here, I'm your girl James, until I'm 65."

James felt frozen. *What was going on?* He looked out at the fields, a harvester moved along on its own cutting down the wheat. James looked back at Carol.

"Take me with you, please, I would love to be your queen," she latched onto his arm and sidled closer as she smiled up at him.

"What are you talking about?"

"You're royalty, part of the Kontrolery, your mother is the person in charge, you can have anything you want, so why not me?"

James began to sense that something was off, none of this made sense. *How did he get on Earth?* He couldn't remember where he was last. He felt an arm snake around his neck and looked down to see Carol leaning in. She kissed him. His emotions subsided momentarily as he closed his eyes and kissed her back, but something didn't feel right, a thought was burning in his mind. He pulled back. He stood on the edge of the Earth gazing down at the structure below.

"Magnificent isn't it?"

His head snapped over to Cyrellia.

"Imagine what it will be like on our new planet with all of this technology. We can make a new world, a better world."

"Why can't we make this one work?"

She walked over to him and placed a hand on his shoulder.

"Because, I said so."

She pushed him off the plate; he fell backward staring up at her as she looked down at him. He began to tumble through the air as he continued his fall. Spinning around, he watched the central ball of the structure get closer. His momentum slowed. He stopped short. He was suspended in the air, floating.

"It's so beautiful."

James turned to see Ariel hovering next to him. She was wearing a red dress, a sparking necklace and metal shoes.

"I'll help you all I can, but we'll need what's in your head."

"In my head? You already extracted what you could and TK still got it."

With a mischievous twinkle in her eyes, she grinned. "Silly rabbit, there's another way to save the Earthlings."

James didn't understand. She clasped her hand in his then pulled him close.

"Wake up sleeping beauty."

Her eyes glowed electric blue as she leaned in to kiss him. His whole body tingled with pleasure; he wrapped his arms around her and felt complete. Their lips unlocked and he opened his eyes.

"I thought I'd lost you!" J stared up at Ariel, the glow in her eyes had faded.

"Wish I had a video of that. New age sleeping beauty."

J recognized that voice. He looked past Ariel.

"Hey, kid. You doin' ok?" asked Sonya.

"Where am I?"

"On my ship, the Eleftheria."

J's eyes flitted around. He was in a cargo bay, across from him the pod in which he was imprisoned sat empty.

"What happened?"

Ariel was still straddling him. "We busted you out."

"I realize that, but last I saw you, Dillon was about to..."

"Your last minute distraction helped. Stupid, but helpful. He took off after you, seems you were the important one." She poked him on the forehead. "Then I was able to get out with the help of Sonya. But we need to know, did you get the card installed?"

"No, Cyrellia destroyed it when she captured me."

Ariel stood up, hands clenching the hair on either side of her head. "That's what we thought, but couldn't confirm it."

J sat up. "What now?" he asked, massaging his temples. He was starting to get a headache. He looked at Ariel, her eyes were welling up, but she didn't let the tears flow. J got to his feet and reached for her hand, she jumped onto him, latching on with both arms.

"We failed."

J held her tightly against him. He was caught off guard; he hadn't seen this much raw emotion from her before.

"No, we can't give up. Who's here?"

J heard Ariel sniffle then she leaned back, "The five of us. Gatlin, Sonya, Jolt. You and me."

"Zane?"

Her bottom lip quivered, "I don't think he made it."

"V?"

"No contact."

"Where are the others?"

"On the bridge, I'll take you," Sonya answered. He hesitated, taking it all in. For all that it was a quick exchange, it was a lot to process. Ariel released J and he followed Sonya to the ship's bridge. Suddenly, he remembered. *Sonya was there with Dillon. She had betrayed them! What was she doing here?*

"Is there a bathroom?" he asked.

"Back in the cargo bay."

He turned and headed back, trying to act casual. Ariel was on a bench messing with a blaster, her eyes still red. J sat down next to her.

"Ariel, I know this won't help, but...."

Ariel stopped fiddling with the pistol and looked at him, "What?"

He leaned in and wrapped his arms around her. Anyone looking at them would think he was consoling her. He placed his lips next to her ear and spoke so that only she could hear. "I think we may be in trouble. Sonya was there the day Dillon first captured me. Where are we going?"

Ariel hopped to her feet and took off running toward the bridge, J followed. *There went his attempt at working this out quietly. He should have known she'd go charging in.*

Ariel pressed the door to the bridge and stepped inside, raising her blaster. Sonya was in a seat looking out the cockpit windows. Jolt and Gatlin were seated on the sides of the bridge, each playing with an electronic device. Ariel walked up, grabbed Sonya by the shirt and threw her aside. Sonya hit a control deck a few feet away. Ariel aimed the pistol at her.

"Where are we going?"

Sonya raised her hands slowly while she stood up.

"Where do you wanna go?" She looked surprised at the whole event.

Ariel studied her for a moment. "Were you with Dillon?"

Sonya looked at J, then looked back at Ariel as if she didn't understand the question.

Ariel walked up to her, pressing the barrel to her head.

"Were you with Dillon when J was first captured?"

"Relax, Ariel." She looked over at J. "I was hoping they would have erased that from your memory."

Ariel pressed the blaster harder. "So you were there! Tell me why I shouldn't splatter you all over this ship?"

Sonya gestured to be able to move her hand. Ariel

306

nodded, wanting to see what she had to offer. Sonya pulled out a small black square from her pocket and tossed it on the ground, stepping backward.

Not wanting to take her eyes off of Sonya, Ariel said, "J, come grab it." Then to Sonya, "What is it?"

"It's a peace offering."

J approached and picked up the object and showed it to Ariel. "Do you know what it is?"

Ariel glanced over. "It's a message plate. Press the center."

J pressed it, a hologram appeared, a series of numbers floating in the air. Ariel looked at them then back at Sonya.

"What are those codes for?"

"A launch." She stood there with a smug look.

"Of what?" Ariel pressed sternly, aiming the blaster at Sonya once again.

"The Exodus."

"How did you get them?" She was still in an aggressive stance, her voice strong. She began to move closer.

"Let's just say I have my sources," Sonya smirked.

"Are these the only codes?"

"No, but with them, Jolt can enter the system and disable the countdown."

"All of this still doesn't answer why you did it." Ariel was almost on top of Sonya.

"My own ship and more money than I could ever dream of."

"Then why are you helping us now?"

"I was always helping," she pulled a sucker out of her pocket and popped it in her mouth.

"Don't lie. How did handing J over to TK help us out?"

Sonya sighed, pulling the sucker from her lips, "That part I had no choice in. Had I not complied, Cyrellia would have had me executed."

Ariel released the pistol from her forehead and walked back.

"How can we trust you now?"

"See for yourself," she pointed out the window. The ship was on a course for the Exodus. "I hate Cyrellia as much as you. I'll do what I can."

J handed the plate over to Jolt he examined it then passed it to Ariel.

"We're going to have to be plugged in to use this, and you're going the wrong way."

Ariel spun around, eyebrows raised questioningly.

"We have to go to the launch controls, off ship. They're located in Atlantis."

Jolt explained that the launch system would be initiated from a control room where the ship attached to the moon. It was designed as a failsafe so no one person could launch the ship. The downside was that one person would be left behind, but it was for the greater good. Sonya turned the ship. Ariel still had her eye on her and wouldn't be so quick to trust her anymore. J felt the same way, but his disdain was stronger since he had no past history with her and she'd helped take him to his captors.

The clock was ticking, they only had two hours remaining until the Exodus would be ready for launch. J walked back to the cargo bay and sat down, rubbing his forehead, his temples still pounded.

"It's the sleep agent they use. Still hasn't been perfected."

Ariel sat down beside him.

"How you holding up?" J asked.

She stared down at her boots, hands clasped between her knees, "I'll be fine, we can still do this."

J looked at Ariel; he had his doubts, but didn't say a word. Maybe they could pull it off, but the possibility was looking dismal. J sat there, mired in his thoughts. He had almost forgotten what they were doing, and why. He thought about his family back on Earth, or what was actually his adopted family. It still seemed strange. They'd been moving and running and so completely inundated and overwhelmed that this was the first chance he had to decompress and let his mind try to make sense of it all.

"Do you go to school?"

Ariel looked over at him. "Not in the sense that you did on Earth. All our learning is done through simulations and from our parents or guardians. Also, we don't typically study every subject. We learn our parents' trade. Take V for example. Her parents were doctors, so she learned medicine. She's brilliant, but ask her anything related to finance or growing crops and she'd just stare at you."

"Where is V by the way? You said she was missing. Do you know where she was last seen?"

"She's with Zane."

"Zane? I thought he didn't make it? Is V..."

"No, she's alive, last I saw her. After Dillon left to chase you, Sonya docked and we loaded Zane in the Eleftheria. V said that she didn't know if she could save him, but if he was going to have a chance, she needed her facilities, so we dropped the two of them at her lab then came looking for you. That's the last I saw of her."

J studied her for a moment. "What's the plan then? Go in guns blazing?"

Ariel smiled and bumped shoulders with him, "I think you've been hanging around me too long. No, we need a better plan. Jolt is analyzing the control room's weaknesses. With our ship cloaked, we have a bit of time."

"Thought we only had two hours?"

Ariel checked her Datacle, "An hour and forty minutes now." She changed topics. "What made you think about school?"

"I'm just trying to figure things out. My life was just put in a mason jar and shaken up. What happened to my father, Arcturus?"

She shrugged her shoulders. "Nobody knows. Most think he died, some say he was Nova, others think he flew away in his own ship."

"What do you think?"

Ariel looked J in the eyes, "I think he's out there

somewhere and you'll get to meet him one day."

"If I do, I hope the intro is better than mother's," J groaned.

"Mother's? Who's your mother?"

"Cyrellia."

Ariel slapped him in the chest. "Get out, seriously?"

J tightened his face, "You sound surprised."

"Yeah, I'm surprised. Nobody knew she had a child or that Arcturus and her were a thing. Are you sure?"

"No, but that's what she told me."

"She told you? Herself?!"

"Yes, before I was thrown into that tin can over there."

J watched Ariel deciding what to say next, even opening her mouth only to close it again.

"How do you hide a pregnancy?" she said under her breath.

"I think I have a solution." Jolt charged in and pulled up a map of the launch complex on a three dimensional screen.

"If you look here and here, these doors are the only way in, but..."

He zoomed in.

"There's a maintenance hatch, here."

He pointed to a small tunnel which entered the complex and led to the ceiling of the control room.

"That's your best chance of getting in."

Ariel studied it for a moment. To her is seemed a bit too small, but based on the blueprints, it led to where they needed to be. "And you have access to that?"

Jolt looked up with a crooked, cracked smile. "You betcha."

J looked closer. He leaned in trying to get a good reference point for the size of the entry point.

"How big is that?"

"Three feet by three feet."

J's head snapped over to the bridge where Gatlin still sat, then to Ariel.

"I guess it's just us."

Ariel nodded.

"Can you give us a diversion?"

"I'll do better than that, we'll put on a show out here," Sonya answered.

Ariel watched the rising intensity on J's face, "Okay, let's do this."

Jolt finished detailing how to use the codes to shut down the launch sequence and what they would have to do to disable it for the long term. It seemed simple enough, but the trick was going to be getting to the console to do it. Sonya worked to position the ship over the entrance while J and Ariel prepped themselves with the external suits needed to exit the craft.

"We gonna fit with these suits on?"

"Hope so. If not, I'll have Sonya ram us in," Ariel laughed.

She was trying to deflect the pressure, J laughed back. The bay door opened. Ariel dropped out first and floated about two feet before touching the top of the structure. He looked past her as he went. A panel popped open,

Ariel headed over to it. Behind him, the ship disappeared as the cargo door closed. Ariel shimmied into the tunnel; it seemed a bit larger than three feet. J was relieved to see that. He hated tight spaces. Over the past few weeks, he'd been crammed into enough to last a life time. As soon as Ariel disappeared, J went in after her. The tunnel was dark, but he could see a little light ahead of Ariel.

"Lights," he stated.

The suit lit up the tunnel in front of him. He moved his elbows underneath his body and began shimmying down. He followed Ariel through a series of shafts, then she stopped. Due to the heightened security, they couldn't risk comms, so they'd scheduled a time for the diversion. J waited, it seemed like it was taking forever. Finally, Ariel jumped down into a small room; he followed, dropping in behind her. The room had multiple pieces of equipment and wires running along the walls. There were airlocks on two of the walls and Ariel opened one into a compression chamber. She waved him in and shut the door. The sounds of hissing rang through his ears then he saw a large green light illuminate over the entrance. Ariel grabbed her helmet and slid it off, J followed suit. They'd been carrying rifles, which made their assessment of the size of the tunnel seem even further off, and J rested it into his shoulder. He was beginning to feel comfortable with the weapon.

Ariel opened the door and they strode down a hall and into another room. It was large, the size of J's shop classroom in high school. The entire front wall was made of glass and he could see the Exodus resting outside, steam floating around the exhaust ports. Above the glass read "5 minutes" and it was counting down. J looked down at his arm; he had been given a Datacle that showed the countdown clock, but his said "25 minutes". Ariel took off running to the controls, realizing at the same moment that their time was off. J was about to follow, but a man hopped up from behind a desk.

"You're not supposed to be here. What are you doing?" He reached for a button, "Intruders!"

Buzzers started going off, the door behind him closed. Ariel pushed the man aside and he ran off. The clock read under 4 minutes and counting. J heard a noise behind him and turned to see the door open back up; he spun around and began firing. An E-Rat came flying out and tackled J. Ariel was trying to find the location for the code deck with no luck. J wrestled with the E-Rat. Finally breaking free, he stumbled over to Ariel and fired a couple of shots at his attacker. Ariel continued to search, "3 minutes." The E-Rat, seemingly unphased, got up and ran toward J, tackling him again and knocking down Ariel. J's rifle flew from his hand during the collision, he scrambled to grab it. Ariel stumbled to her feet and gave a swift kick to the E-Rat's head, stunning him enough for J to get away. She began searching again then stopped abruptly. Pulling the card out of her suit, she triumphantly exclaimed, "A-ha!"

She pushed a panel and a slot slid open. She placed the card in the slot, two minutes and counting. J grabbed

the rifle and began firing; round after round hit the
E-Rat who was attempting to jump back onto him. J kept
firing until the enemy fell into a heap. His eyes bounced
between Ariel and the clock. "1 minute". Ariel was frantically flying through menus and J couldn't do anything
but watch. "30 seconds." He wanted to say something
but his baseball instincts kicked in. *Stay quiet for the
pitcher; let her do her thing.* "10 seconds." She looked
up at the clock, then back to the screen. "5 seconds."
"3,2,1..." A bright blue light filled the room, J covered his
eyes.

CHAPTER TWENTY ONE

Ariel stood looking out into the vastness of space. Any other day, the view would have been staggering as galaxy swirls filled the sky. Her bottom lip quivered, a single tear slipped down each cheek. J looked over, then out to the stars. They were both silent. So many stars, such an immense universe, but they were on an empty wasteland waiting for time to take over. J reached his hand over to Ariel's, she grabbed it tightly, he still didn't say a word. Footsteps echoed behind him, but he didn't look.

"J, Ariel, you guys okay?"

The footsteps got closer. Ariel closed her eyes, doing her best to hold back her sobs. J turned his head. *It couldn't be.* The hall light surrounded a shadow in the doorway. The flashing red light had gone out with the countdown. He couldn't quite tell who it was for a second, then his eyes adjusted.

"Zane?"

J forgot what had just happened for a moment.

"Zane. You're alive?!"

Ariel whipped around, and seeing him, fell to her knees, tears of joy mixed with guilt and failure overwhelmed her. J reached down and helped her up, supporting her with an arm around her waist, hugging her to his side.

"Hey there kiddo, it's alright," Zane took a step forward.

"But how..." J started as V stepped out from behind

Zane, a hand on his arm holding him back. She looked like a child next to him.

She gave a slight smile and a small wave, "It was pretty touch and go there for awhile, but I was able to bring him back."

Everyone stood there for a moment. Even with the joyous news about Zane, it wasn't the time.

"You guys are a mess," V broke the silence in her upfront way. "You need to get some sleep."

V was always looking out for everyone, her doctor genes showed through, though they were very direct at times. J looked at Ariel. He could tell that she hadn't slept in awhile and could only imagine what he looked like. Zane and V turned and headed out the door, expecting them to tag along since there wasn't any more to be done in the control room. J gave a slight tug and Ariel followed, stepping over the malfunctioning E-Rat. They made their way to the Eleftheria. Sonya had returned to a docking bay located near the control room. As they entered, Sonya and the others were exiting the ship.

"Guess we're the proud new owners of the moon," Sonya quipped, trying to lighten the mood.

Everyone remained quiet.

"What happened?" Jolt interrupted the silence.

"Ran out of time," J responded. "What now?"

That was the question. The Exodus had launched, the Earth was on life support and nearly all of the supplies were taken from Atlantis.

"Can we sleep on it?" Ariel finally spoke up.

J felt it, too. Their bodies were depleted, running on empty. Sleep sounded wonderful.

"There's a resort near the trading block that I've always wanted to try. Let's go there," Ariel suggested, trying to liven the dead room.

J was learning that Ariel was quick to move on from tragedy. He knew it was still there, she might even feel it more than they did given her reactions the few times he'd seen her fail, but she did her best not to show it. The others nodded in silence. A resort sounded nice, and it was free.

They loaded into the Eleftheria and in no time, they were entering the trading block, so called because of the multitude of stores located there. You could find all of the goods and services you could ever dream of, a sort of playground for TK. Sonya hovered down onto on the resort's landing pad, reserved only for special TK ships. But today was different; they had the run of the place. This would have been better under different circumstances. Still, it felt like they were getting away with something, like having a party when your parents are away. Jolt unlocked the whole resort. They found some food and made their way to the most luxurious rooms they could find. All of them were furnished with contouring beds that made it feel like you were floating, sleep was never going to feel so good. J picked a room and headed for the shower. Laying his clothes aside, he hopped in.

It seemed like years since he'd had a proper shower, and with twelve heads blasting him with warm water, his whole body relaxed. He stepped out and dried himself off, then picked up his clothes. They were filthy. He hadn't noticed before, but now his nose was screaming at him. He wrapped the towel around his waist and looked around the room, searching for a robe or a clothes delivery system. Nothing would surprise him, and if he could imagine it, he was sure it existed in this crazy futuristic world. He found a closet and opened the door. Inside, there was a strange sort of chute and a black screen. He touched it.

"Hello," a voice announced. "Please let me know what you would like to wear."

J thought about it, "Pajamas."

"DNA recognized. Delivering pajamas to Mr. J."

The chute opened up and out popped a set of pajamas, underwear, a shirt and pants. J turned to the door, someone was knocking. He walked over and asked the door to open. Ariel was standing there in her own set of pajamas.

"Can I join you?"

She looked incredible, the short bottoms showing off her toned legs. J stuttered, "Sure."

She reached up and placed her soft hand on his chest, over his heart. It was pounding.

He was still in his towel and just then realized it. "Crap, let me go change."

He scurried off to the bathroom and threw on the pajamas. When he reappeared, Ariel was lying on the bed.

"That shower felt awesome," he said as he walked toward the bed. "I'll bet you enjoyed your shower, too."

What was he saying? He was over-thinking things, he was distracted by her beauty, and she was in his bed. She didn't say a word, just smiled at him sleepily. He climbed in next to her and lay on his back, fingers laced behind his head. She snuggled up beside him and put her head on his shoulder, her arm over his chest.

"What do you think we should do?" he asked, trying to act nonchalant when he was anything but.

No response.

He lifted his head and looked down. She was out, her breathing soft and slow. She twitched a bit then stopped. He double-checked to make sure she was still breathing then wrapped his arms around her, tucked her head under his chin, closed his eyes and took a deep breath. *Sunflowers.*

A blue light flashed in front of him and then it was gone, only stars remained. He was back in the control room, staring out at the stars. He looked around for Ariel, but she wasn't there. All he saw behind him was the surface of the moon. In front of him were the panel that Ariel had so frantically used and the frame of the large window and control screen. He stepped back. The man made materials sank into the rock face, he was standing there exposed. He felt the wind move across his face and dust sweep over his legs, then he turned and began walking. He had no idea where he was going, just had the urge to walk.

The moon face was quiet, serene. He felt contented, safe, relaxed. His footsteps were light as he looked up at the stars. He tilted his head back down and was met with a face. Startled, he stopped.

Before him stood a man, a man he recognized. Arcturus.

"J," he started then pointed to his head. "You just need to get it out."

J reached up with one hand and touched his forehead.

"What do you mean? Get what out? How?"

The man crumbled into moon dust, the wind taking him away. J turned around to follow it. He was in a wheat field, wind gently blowing the stalks. It appeared to be harvest time. The wheat was mature and ready for the harvesters. J always loved this time, the hard work of the year seemed to pay off and he knew he would get a few days to recuperate afterwards. The ground began to shake under his feet, a crack opened up between them. He stumbled to one side and the crack expanded into a crevasse. J lost his balance and pitched forward. The ground still shaking, he clung to the edge. He looked up. V's mother stood over him and bent down to give him a hand.

J opened his eyes. Ariel was still asleep, curled up next to him. *How long had he been asleep?* He inched his way out of her hold and looked around for the first time. He opened the door, the smell of freshly cooked bacon filled his nostrils. He followed the scent to a large kitchen. The sight before him had him rubbing his eyes to see if he was still dreaming. Zane had on a frilly white apron and a chef's hat and was flipping eggs, hips swaying to a beat only he could hear. J looked around at the stovetop; there were pancakes on the griddle, scrambled eggs, bacon, sausage.

"I'm in heaven," he blurted out without even knowing it.

Zane's booming laugh filled the air. "I'll take that as a compliment. Good morning, or should I say, afternoon."

"What time is it?"

"1300 Atlantis time. You were asleep for 14 hours. Have you seen Ariel?"

Without thinking, J replied, "Yeah, she's in my bed."

Zane grinned widely and winked, "You sly dog, you."

J, realizing what he'd said, began waving his arms in front of him, his voice was rushed and cracked a little, "No, no, it's not like that."

"Sure it's not," he slid a plate over to J. He couldn't stop smiling.

"No, seriously, it's not," he continued to plead.

"What are we talking about?" Sonya came in, grabbing a piece of bacon off the griddle.

"Hey, that one's not done yet," Zane retorted, scrunching his nose, revolted.

"I don't like them crunchy and burnt," she took a big bite of it and sat down next to J. "So, whatcha guys talkin' about?"

"Ariel's in J's bed," Zane snickered, holding in his laughter.

J just scowled at him.

"So, you two a thing?"

"A thing? What's that mean, a thing? We just slept together," J realized what he said again, his inner voice screaming, *not helping!*

Sonya just nodded and swiped another piece of bacon. Zane handed her a plate.

"Here you go, floppy bacon and all."

"Where's V?" J asked, desperately trying to change the subject.

Sonya came back with, "Did you have a good night last night?"

"Yes, I mean no, I mean, where's V? or Jolt? Gatlin?" he looked over at Zane whose shoulders were jumping from his laughter as he flipped more pancakes.

Sonya was completely enjoying harassing J.

"V had breakfast a few hours ago. Said she wanted to work on something at her lab. The other two are off doing whatever it is that they do," Zane finally said as he sat down with a heaping plate of food.

"Where's V's lab?"

"Actually only a few blocks away. I can take you if you like. Or you can wait for your girlfriend to wake up."

"She's not my girlfriend, gosh..."

J stopped. He felt somebody behind him.

"Does she know that?" Zane was grinning from ear to ear.

He turned around. Ariel was standing there with a slight scowl.

"How...how long have you been standing there?"

"Since you told them you slept with me."

"I didn't...I mean...I did...but, not like that!"

She started to laugh. She couldn't hold it in anymore, he was just so cute when he was flustered.

Sonya and Zane couldn't hold it in either, they all burst out laughing. J's face turned a deep shade of red, his embarrassment flushed through his body. He was hoping it was a dream. Ariel helped herself to the food then sat down next to him.

"So, you want to go see V. What for?"

"I had this strange dream and I feel like she can help me. How? I haven't the slightest."

Ariel nodded then asked what the dream was about. J tried to do his best to describe it, but a lot of it had already slipped away. The four of them finished up their brunch and, having nothing better to do, all went with J to see V.

"You once said something about your mother working on a device that had something to do with dreams?"

"Yes, my mother worked on, for lack of a better term, a dream extractor. But really it was a memory extractor. She could never get the dream files, if that's what you want to call them."

"Does she still have it?"

"Probably. We could check her lab."

"If she has it, could you maybe try it on me?"

"I have to ask. Why the fascination with it? Did you dream something?"

"Yeah, but I'm starting to forget most of it. The bits
I do remember had your mother in it, she was helping
me out of a pit and she told me something that I can't
remember."

"It was my mother? How do you know? You've never
met her."

"I know, but she resembled you, only older, and I
saw her in my dream the first time you put me under to
extract the information. Could it be coincidence?"

"Maybe, I'll take you to her lab and we'll see what I
can do."

Her mother's lab was on the other side of the moon.
The trains were shut down and the systems were operating on minimal power, so they elected to fly. Sonya
fired up the Eleftheria and they made it there in no time.
Having the skies to herself kept a smile on her face, she
felt most at home in her ship and elected to stay.

Once inside, V started rummaging through a few
rooms full of miscellaneous objects and test equipment.
J felt helpless. He and Ariel had no idea what they were
searching for, so they wandered around trying to look
useful. They weren't fooling V, but she appreciated the
sentiment. Zane realized there was nothing for him to do
either, so he left to scout the area for supplies.

"Aha!"

V had found a piece of the machine shoved in a
corner covered by a pile of random equipment.

"How long since your mother was here?"

J didn't realize she had passed a little less than a year

ago. V explained that one of their tests had gone wrong and she lost both of her parents. J wished he hadn't asked the question, but V took it in stride. She wheeled out a pure white table, the back was slightly raised and it was as high as J's knees. She brushed off the things that were on it and asked J to lie down. He did as asked and watched her scrounge around to find more items that seemed to fit; hoses, electrical cords, and a helmet, which she placed on his head. Out of the helmet hung a bunch of metal electrodes. She attached each of them to his head then searched for more pieces.

Ariel laughed, "You look ridiculous."

J made a funny face, getting even more laughs.

V came over and attached an electrode to his finger, she smiled briefly. "You do look pretty absurd. Give me a second to switch on power to this room," she said, walking away.

Ariel looked at J. She didn't say anything, but it was enough. He'd been thinking of V's parents blowing up. He could be the next to go, but just Ariel's presence put him at ease. The bed came alive; he could feel a soft vibration go through his body.

V popped back in. "I think we're almost ready, just a few more details. The devil is in the details."

She plugged several cords into a control panel at the far end of the room.

"You might... you might want to come over here," she waved Ariel over to her.

J looked distressed. "You're not going to kill me,

are you?"

V shrugged her shoulders and hit a button.

J stood at the top of the wall observing the Earth below, nothing moved. It almost looked frozen. His vantage point presented him with a view of the farmland and the town beyond it. It was his hometown of Eggerton and the farm closest to him was his house. He looked to his left. Jeffrey, the man with the glass book, stood there looking down at the same picture.

"That's the planned family?" he asked.

"Yes, they will be the best fit," Jeffrey replied.

He looked back down at the house in the field, his house.

"J, you will be well cared for."

He turned to the other man and nodded to him. Jeffrey turned and walked away down the wall.

"J, if you are seeing this, then a few things have happened. One, they have found you and extracted the implanted coordinates to Acadia, and two, you failed at delaying the launch of the Exodus. This technology has never been properly tested or perfected, but Dr. Mallow has been working on a prototype I hope will soon be perfected. With TK leaving for Acadia, they will have left Flat Earth to crumble and fail over time, with no management. The streets of Atlantis will be clear and you will have access to a large amount of technology not seen on Earth for hundreds of years. You can use this to help the people there. But first, you must stop the planet from its own destruction.

The first indication will be power failures then spontaneous fires caused by a number of failing systems. Then the earthquakes will begin. You must stop this from happening or else the Earth will rip itself apart. I engineered the Earth to fail to drive TK to Acadia. They want the world for themselves and have gone to extreme measures to ensure each class remained where they stood.

After the launch, several things should have been set in motion, but even one not working will still cause the Earth to crumble. The path you take will not be easy, and there will be challenges along the way.

First, go to Sector 21 and seek out Dr. Craig. He will help you accomplish the initial step..."

His father's voice trailed off. J opened his eyes, Ariel was holding his hand. A large hum started to come from the table.

"Ariel, get him out of there!" V cried, frantically tapping buttons.

Ariel wasted no time in yanking J off the table and over to where V stood. The table threw sparks and a crackle then a loud "pop!" It caught on fire. The three of them were huddled near the wall. The room began to glow red, sirens went off then foam sprayed out of holes in the ceiling and walls. Soon the fire was out, the sirens ceased and the room looked like it had been used for a giant-sized bubble bath.

"What happened?" J asked.

"Not sure, the system overloaded."

"Can you fix it?"

"I don't know, I'd have to find the data files with all my mother's notes. I don't even know if she kept any. Her mind was a vault and she was in the habit of not writing things down."

Ariel turned to J and snickered, "You look like a fluffy yeti." She brushed some of the foam out of his hair. "Did it work? You were muttering a few things, but we couldn't make out what it was."

"Yeti?" He shook his head. She was always saying things that made no sense to him, but as long as she smiled at him like that, she could say whatever she wanted. Determined now, he looked from V to Ariel, "Yes, we need to go to Sector 21. We need to stop the Earth from destroying itself."

CHAPTER TWENTY TWO

"We'd better use the underground tunnels, don't want to freak out the Earthlings. They'll probably think we're aliens."

Sonya was right. If he had seen a ship arriving from the heavens, he would have freaked out, too.

"So, you said your father told you to seek out Dr. Craig and that's it, no town name?"

"No , right after he said his name, the table malfunctioned."

Ariel frowned at him, "Great. Do you know how big Sector 21 is? That's on the North Pole, it's freaking cold there. I still don't know why TK even put people up there."

"Fur, that sector is for fur. TK loved their fur," Zane said smiling as he continued to load the ship.

"We talking cute little chinchillas or big scary bears?"

"Bears." Zane picked up three more boxes.

Ariel looked inside one of them. "Knives? What, are we going old school?"

"Blasters don't work in Sector 21 or in 15, 18, 9 or 2. It's protocol."

"Can't Jolt just hack it?"

Zane laughed. "He's been trying all morning. It's been pretty entertaining watching him struggle, don't get to see that much."

Ariel picked up one of the smaller boxes. "Fur, huh?" The box she held had an outfit made of polar bear fur.

"They couldn't synthesize it? How much do you really need?"

"You've been in some of TK's estates; they are crazy for the exotic. Took them years to build up the amount of bears in Sector 21." Zane loaded a couple more boxes.

J was just listening, trying to figure out what they were getting themselves into.

"So they raise polar bears there? How?"

"I don't know the particulars. I just know that they do. And the people are nomads, they move around a lot, which is going to make finding your doctor that much harder. Now can you help with the supplies?"

J picked up a box of rations and loaded it into the ship.

"I think that's all of it," J stepped inside the cargo door and it closed behind him.

Zane just grumbled something about "one box" and rolled his eyes as he walked to his seat.

"Any ideas where to start?" J asked.

The ship shook as it left the ground.

"There's a scientific outpost at marker 19. We'll start there. Hopefully someone will know him."

J though it was funny that they had traded metal mediators for large, man-eating bears. Still, everyone seemed more upbeat at the news that they had a chance to save Earth. Gatlin was the only one left behind. He stayed on Atlantis to monitor the systems and try to find the guy from the control room. None of the others had even hesitated to go on the hunt for Dr. Craig. J fell asleep on the way, the vibrations and rocking of the ship lulled him to a deep slumber. He woke up to see Zane and Ariel donning their cold weather gear.

"Come on, J. Once we get this stuff on, we're going to want to get outside before we sweat."

J hopped up and slid on the pants and jacket then Zane tossed him a belt with a large knife attached.

"So, no guns?"

"Told you, they don't work."

"But you said Jolt was working on it. What if he gets it fixed?"

"Ha! He won't. Besides, you have enough to carry."

Zane threw a large bag at him, almost knocking him over. J strapped it on his back then threw a hat on his head.

"Have fun boys and girls," Sonya waved to them as they de-boarded.

"You're not comin'?"

"Nope. Gotta stay here with the ship; still needs a few repairs from the last excursion."

He turned and followed the others to the elevator. The doors opened, a cold blast of wind hit his face. It was like nothing he had ever felt before; it almost sucked the breath right out of his lungs, it was so cold.

"Temp's showing -30. Need to keep moving," Ariel checked the map on her Datacle. "This way."

J followed Ariel while Zane took up the rear position. He glanced back. Bundled up in their jackets, not a piece of skin showing, they had exited out of a small mountain.

The wind howled and blowing snow zipped around their legs. J looked up at the sky, crystal clear blue as far as he could see in all directions. Everything below 50 feet was nothing but white, the blowing snow obscured everything. They marched on. He was getting tired, the deep snow was taking its toll on his legs and they had been walking for hours.

"Can...We...Take...A break," J managed to squeak out.

Ariel stopped and looked back at him, she plopped down on her butt. "Sure."

Zane did the same, so J followed suit, flopping down.

"How much further?"

"Map says about two miles, but that was based on the last update 12 hours ago, hopefully they didn't move."

J hoped. He'd never been in such extreme conditions before, and frankly, it sucked. His whole body was cold.

"My hands are freezing."

"Turn your gloves on," Zane said.

"What?"

"Your gloves, turn them on."

"How do I do that?"

J could see Zane roll his head. He was pretty sure he just got an extreme version of the eye roll. Zane walked over to him and grabbed his wrist, he tapped on the Datacle scrolling thru menus.

"Your feet cold too?"

"Yes."

Zane finished and closed the menu.

"It feels like I'm taking care of a five year old," he

333

heard Zane laugh.

Warmth began circulating around his hands and feet.
"This is amazing."

Zane continued to laugh, then tucked his chin down, looking at J like a parent over a pair of reading glasses. "Just like a five year old."

Ariel began laughing, too.

J went to make a face at her, then she disappeared in the snow.

"Crap, Zane!"

A polar bear had found them. Zane drew his knife and threw it at the beast. It reared back in pain then charged. J dropped out of the way while Zane used its momentum against it and threw it behind him.

"Run!"

J ran over to Ariel, her gear was ripped and she was bleeding.

"Take my hand."

She grabbed his hand and they started to run. He heard the bear roaring behind them. He looked back. Zane wasn't too far behind, but the bear was about to pounce.

"Zane, behind you!"

Zane flipped on his back and crossed his arms in defense, the bear jumped on him dagger still protruding from its back. J stopped, pulled out his knife and ran toward the bear, yelling. He hoped it would distract the bear. It did, but maybe too well. The bear changed directions and charged. He tried to backpedal, but tripped, falling back first into the deep snow. The bear reared up over him letting out a great loud growl, he closed his eyes.

He heard a whimper from the bear, then a growl. He opened his eyes, a spear stuck out of its chest. The bear stumbled back, then broke off the spear and charged away. J rolled over onto his stomach, watching the bear run away, or that's what he thought. On closer inspection, it was running after someone standing a great distance off. The bear reared up again, he heard a roar, then it toppled over onto its side.

"Ariel," he said to himself, then hopped to his feet, running over to grab her.

She was standing there, scrutinizing the bear laying in the snow and the man behind.

"You alright?" he asked.

"Yeah, how's Zane?"

They both looked over, he was climbing out of the snow and began walking toward them.

"Zane!" J yelled over the wind. "You okay?"

He could see him nod his head. Once he was closer, J could see that his face was scratched and bloody, but it didn't look too serious. They headed to meet their rescuer. They passed the bear, it was obviously dead, and the man approached them.

"Whar you tree com from?" he spoke with a very strange accent.

Ariel chimed in. "From Kirkstad." She knew it was on the far side of Sector 21. It should be a good cover story.

"Do you know Dr. Craig?"

"Craig?" he stepped past them and studied the bear a moment.

"Yes, Craig."

He bent down, examining the bear closer and, pulling the knife from its body, slid it into a sheath. The man then pulled the broken spearhead out and glanced up at the three of them.

"Charley?"

He continued putting away his weapons and attempted to roll the bear over.

"No, Dr. Craig," Ariel snapped back, her lips chattering in the cold.

"Ya, Charley. E'rybody call him Charley."

Ariel looked at J who just shook his head and put his hands up. She turned back to the man who was still working on the bear.

"Do you know where he is?"

"Ya, he go to station noomber 5 two days ago, he travel a lot."

"Can you take us there?"

He tried again to roll the bear over, then stopped and studied Zane.

"Sure, if you help me wit da buur."

They agreed and, after strapping several ropes around the large mammal, began tugging. They pulled the bear for a couple of hours before reaching the town of Bearsport. It was a small village where all of the buildings were made of wood. J wondered where it all came from, but he was assured there were trees further to the south. They sat by a fire and warmed up, piles of bear fur stacked outside, bear rugs adorned the walls and floors.

"You said he travels a lot? How often do you see him?"

"E'ry mont or so, he stops by fer a drink er tuo."

"How far is... station number 5, you said?"

"Fer hour walk, but we can make it tuo wit da dogs."

With the help of another man, they loaded up two large dog sleds with eight dogs each. After seeing Zane's size, they added one more to his sled. Once they were packed up, they headed out. J was taught how to drive and he and Ariel took turns. They stopped halfway for a break to let the dogs rest then continued on. The wind had died down and the sun was warming things up.

"What's the temp?"

"-20. Heat wave," Ariel groused.

They reached their destination, station number 5. It was comprised of one small building with smoke billowing out of the top. They hoped they were in luck. Opening the door, they found three men sitting around a table.

"Dr. Craig?" Ariel queried.

One of the men answered. "Yes?"

Zane shut the door behind them.

"You're from Atlantis."

The two other men looked at him, brows knit.

"Have a seat. I'm guessing you want to discuss some very important things."

J, Ariel and Zane sat down at the table, it was large enough for about eight people. Around the room were multiple bunk beds of various heights against the walls, J counted 12 in all. The man who spoke to them looked to be no older than 40, the other two men must have been in their 50s, while their guide was much younger.

"The Exodus launched," he said, placing a spoonful of soup into his mouth.

"Yes," Ariel responded. "But how do you know all this?"

"Arcturus was a very wise man. He had a contingency for nearly every scenario. This one I get to play a part in."

The three of them leaned in to listen. Outside, the wind had picked up again.

"I never enjoyed Atlantis, even though I grew up there. When I was younger, I would take short excursions to Earth and found it much more enjoyable. Many Atlanteans would take vacations on Earth, most called it a slum-cation, but I felt more at home. I believe it was for this reason that Arcturus approached me. He asked me if I would like to stay on Earth and I agreed, made Sector 21 my home."

J didn't understand why anyone would actually choose such a place. His body was still cold, even in the warmth of the building. Dr. Craig pulled a square data plate from his pocket and slid it over to Ariel.

"This is what you came for."

Ariel picked it up and examined it. "What's on it?"

"Coding to reboot the system. There are three of

them in total."

"Three?!" J dropped his forehead to the table.

Ariel looked back at the doctor, "Where are the other two?"

"Based on the look of your friend, you won't like the answer."

Ariel waited.

"I was only given the name of one of the remaining two; Arcturus really didn't want TK to have them."

"What do we do with them?" J asked, forehead still down, talking into the table.

"Once you acquire all three, go to the mainframe located in the central hub."

"So, where do we go for the second data plate?" Ariel asked.

"Find Will in Sector 11."

J's head popped up. "Will, did you say Will?"

"Yes?" The man looked surprised at his reaction. "Do you know who I'm talking about?"

"Yeah, or I think I do. But last time I was back home, he wasn't where he normally is."

J remembered after TK had erased his friends' minds, Will was nowhere to be seen and how strange it was, going to the diner, not being asked if he wanted a cigarette. Zane was now sitting by a fire on the other side of the room with his own soup.

"We good now? I'd like to get somewhere warmer than this," he took another sip of his soup.

"Yeah, we can get going." Ariel began to put her gear

back on. "Can you take us all the way to marker 15?" she added.

Their guide stood up. "How fer is dat from whar I foond ya?"

"Not far."

The three and their guide said farewell to Dr. Craig and headed out into the snow. J hoped they could avoid any more bear encounters. After a few hours, they made it back to the ship. Sonya was laying on the open cargo ramp, she sat up when she heard them come.

"That was quick."

Then she noticed the dried blood on Ariel and Zane.

"What happened?"

"Bear attack, or should I say Buur attack?" J injected.

Zane and Ariel laughed at J's comment, they had found the guide's accent quite humorous.

"Did Jolt have any luck with taking down the weapons restrictions?"

"No, he gave up about an hour ago. Said he might try later if you were still out there."

Zane nudged J and gave him a wink. J had thought Jolt would figure it out and had almost bet Zane on it, but all he lost were bragging rights.

"Where we headin'?" Sonya asked.

"Sector 11. J gets to go home," Ariel replied.

CHAPTER TWENTY THREE

J felt weird about going back. All those years he had
lived there, his family was there, his friends, his girlfriend? *Carol, he had almost forgotten about her.* He'd
been swept up into the new world he'd discovered and
now felt torn between the two worlds. In the short time
he had spent with Ariel, Zane and the others, he felt like
he belonged, more than he ever did back home. Ariel
slipped her hand into his, he retracted it a moment. His
mind was on Carol.

"You sure you're alright?" she asked.

"Yeah, just have a lot on my mind."

She boarded the craft and J followed. The engines
spun up and the door closed, Sonya lifted off. Next stop,
Sector 11.

J slipped off the winter gear, they had a couple of
layers on. He was still fascinated by the heated gloves and
stopped to examine them.

"Pretty great stuff huh?" Ariel asked.

"Yeah, amazing. I'm still astounded by all these
gadgets..."

He looked over at Ariel, she was down to her bottom
layer, tossing the heavy fur overcoats into a box. Her
outfit clung tightly to her body, distracting J. He tried to
regain his thoughts.

"You can just wear that, I mean, can you just wear that
outfit without the overcoat?"

"You could, the whole suit is heated and designed for

extreme temperatures, both hot and cold, but we needed to keep up appearances."

J finished with the top layer, and looking up, saw Ariel working on her final layer. He quickly snapped his gaze away, concentrating on his own suit.

"You said you know this Will?"

"Yes, well sort of."

J finished stripping the final layer off and was quickly trying to get his regular clothes on. He missed the pant leg hole and slipped forward, falling on his face. Ariel laughed, she tried to stop laughing, but it had still come out.

"You okay?"

J tried to play it off. "Yeah, my pants moved," he said with a slight groan.

"So, how do you know Will?"

"I think he's the guy who gave me the key to get beyond the wall?"

"Key?"

"I guess it was a key, it allowed me to unlock a panel. Anyway, it's a long story, but it led me to the ship and finally Atlantis."

J sat down and began putting his boots on, Ariel sat next to him doing the same.

"So where do we find him?"

"At the diner, the one you picked me and Carol up at. That's where he always seemed to be."

J explained the mind wipe that all his close friends appeared to have gotten. Ariel understood, there were protocols when extraordinary events occurred that might lead people to the real world outside of Earth. TK would erase anything that people might question, the whole diner incident in the minds of the staff never occurred.

"So, after the last mind wipe, you didn't see him again?"

"Nope. I don't know anything about him except he smoked like a chimney."

Ariel stared off, pausing for a moment. "Well that's a start."

Zane walked out from the bridge.

"Sonya says we're five minutes out, but the closest docking bay to J's town isn't responding, she says she has to go to an alternate."

Ariel laughed, "If it's not one thing it's another."

She stood up and headed to the bridge, passing Zane along the way.

"You okay?" Zane asked.

"Yes, why is everybody asking that? Don't I look okay?" J stood up and began to pace.

"Well...you did just have your world turned upside down and now you're heading back to the place that you thought was home, but maybe it's not. Not sure how that would feel for me."

J stopped and studied Zane. He'd just pictured him as a jovial, gun-toting workout junkie, but he was actually quite insightful. J would have to think about that.

"Have you ever fallen in..." he stopped. He wasn't used to opening himself up to anyone, let alone someone he had only known for a short time.

Zane smiled, commiserating. "Into a pit? Sure, it sucks. Hard to get out, but you can just lay there and give up, or you can find a way to climb out. And there is more than one way to climb out." He turned and headed to the bridge.

"What was he talking about?" J said to himself out loud, staring down at the boxes of gear.

On the bridge, Sonya piloted the ship. She loved to hand fly it, even though the systems made the ship autonomous. As J stepped up, he heard Ariel and Jolt discussing something, they seemed heated. Ariel was yelling and Jolt fired back. Zane was leaning against the wall, gazing out at the sky, not paying much attention.

"What's with them?" J asked.

"Not sure. They were going at it when I got up here."

Ariel cocked her hand back in a fist, Gatlin grabbed it before she could swing. She yanked her hand out of his grip, dropped it, and clenching her jaw, stomped away. Jolt remained in his seat a moment then spun around looking back at his screen. Ariel breezed by him, she was steaming.

"Might want to figure that out," Zane said, walking further onto the bridge.

J walked over to Sonya, she had been the closest to the conversation.

"What happened?"

Sonya looked up. "I didn't catch most of it, something about the systems malfunctioning? I don't know."

J turned and headed back to the cargo hold. Ariel was pacing, talking to herself. He couldn't understand any of it. She saw him and stopped.

"What's going on?" he asked.

"Nothing."

"That sure didn't sound like nothing."

She sighed, trying to calm down. "Really, it was nothing."

J didn't want to prod any further, maybe he could get it out of Jolt later.

"One minute out," Zane yelled from the deck.

Ariel turned and grabbed a blaster from the rack, "Take this. They should work here."

"Should?"

She looked at him, eyes narrowing.

J didn't have to say a word he just looked back.

"I'll explain later."

J took the blaster and holstered it, Ariel did the same with another one. The ship landed, and Ariel and J exited.

"Are the others coming?" he asked.

"No, it will be easier if it's just the two of us."

"Why?"

She tilted her head slightly as she tensed her face. J read the body language, no more questions.

They exited the craft and headed to the dressing room. J found it funny that he got to go through outfits like he was in a department store and use whatever he wanted for free. Ariel threw on a sweater similar to what she had worn the last time, but it was red and she added a black skirt. J put on his normal clothes. They felt like home, he actually missed the working jeans and shirt. They exited out of an ally just like the one in Sector 3, Ariel pointed at a car on a nearby street. They ran over to it, being careful not to raise any suspicion.

"What town are we in?"

"Lynchburg, I think." She checked her Datacle. "Yep, Lynchburg."

She hopped into the driver's seat, J stood behind her on the same side. She looked up at him for a second, then rolled her eyes in the back of her head.

"Stupid history."

J laughed, "You said we needed to keep a low profile."

She stared at him intensely, eyebrows lowered, before sliding over to the passenger side.

"How did you get this started?" J said, searching for a key.

Ariel bent over to reach under the steering wheel while J sat there, hands at 10 and 2. She bumped him, he winced and groaned a bit, then Ariel popped up. J looked out the window, shaking it off. Two teenage girls walked by giggling. He watched them, trying to figure out what they were laughing at, he glanced over at Ariel. Her hair was a mess and she flipped it back trying to fix it. He realized what it looked like and his face went red. Ariel grabbed the ignition and started the car then looked up at him.

"What?" she asked, noticing him blushing.

346

"Nothing," J slipped it into gear and took off.

"So what was with you and Jolt back there?" he was desperate to change the conversation before Ariel figured out his thoughts.

Staring out the window, she said "He could have shut down the protocol on Sector 21."

"Wait, what? What makes you think that?"

"When I walked on the bridge he still had his hacking app up. The code was simple enough that I could have done it."

"Why would he do that?"

Ariel looked at J. "I don't know, but when I pressed him about it, he closed the program and I would have sworn he was working on something else, but I couldn't tell what it was. That's when you walked in. He wouldn't explain what he was doing."

J looked back at the road, "Am I going the right way?"

He had never been to Lynchburg before. It was in a completely different county.

"Yeah, it'll take us four hours to drive there."

J had never driven that long in one stretch before. He had ridden on the harvesters longer, but never on the roads. Ariel looked back out the window, J could tell she was deep in thought and he didn't really know what to say. He reached over and switched on the radio, then started to laugh. Ariel peered at him over her shoulder.

"What's so funny?"

J didn't say a word he just turned up the volume, Frank Sinatra was mid-song. "Fill my heart with song and let me sing forever more..." J sang along for a minute.

"What's so funny, I don't get it?"

J laughed harder, he was enjoying knowing something Ariel didn't for a change.

"What?" she turned to him fully and punched him in the shoulder.

"Ow! The name of the song is "Fly Me to the Moon"."

It took Ariel a second, then she understood. She smiled lazily and watched him finish singing. He continually belted out tunes as big bands played. He had missed music since being on Atlantis. That was the one thing he felt was missing. Ariel enjoyed watching him sing, she didn't know any of the songs, but enjoyed them anyway. The two continued down the road happily.

After an hour or so, Ariel looked over at J, his eyes were tense as he stared at the rearview mirror.

"What?" she asked.

She looked behind them, a black car was following them, a red light flashing on top of it. "Crap! I was hoping to avoid this."

"Should I stop?" J asked.

"You know it's a replicant."

"But if we make a scene, he'll call for backup."

Ariel scanned for options. "Okay, pull over. This is what we'll do."

J slowed the car down and pulled over. Ariel jumped out of the passenger side screaming.

"You jerk, I hate you!"

J got out, attempting to walk around to her, she

was still screaming like mad. She took her shoe off and threw it at him, he ducked. The replicant approached cautiously.

"Ma'am, I need you to calm down."

"I will not calm down." she screamed, throwing the other shoe at him.

He dodged it and headed straight for her

"Ma'am calm down," he stated again, almost reaching her.

J had rounded the car to the passenger side, he approached the open door. Ariel slipped and fell to the ground. J kicked the door closed. He raised a blaster at the replicant. Click. He tried again. Click. The replicant drew his pistol, J dove back in front of the car. Ariel reached up, grabbing the gun; it went off into the air. She sent an uppercut to his chin with her other hand, it ricochet off. J came running around the car and knocked the police officer down, Ariel grabbed J and pulled him off the replicant.

"Get in the car!"

He wasted no time dashing back to the driver's seat. Ariel performed a roundhouse to the replicant's face then tumbled off the road.

"Hit him!"

J threw the shifter in reverse and floored it, dirt flew everywhere. The rear bumper smashed into the replicant's head as he was getting to his feet. A ball of flame came from where the replicant used to be, the car flipping forward into the sky from the explosion. J held tight to the steering wheel as the car landed upside down, rocking a few times. Ariel kneeled on one leg, watching as fuel spilled out of the car. She could see J lying on the ceiling of the car.

"J!"

She forced herself up and ran, the fire from the explosion was slinking toward the pooling fuel as if on a mission. She worked her way into the flipped car and grabbed him, he was unconscious. She was able to get him free, but struggled to move him. She glanced over at the fire, it was almost there. The road fell off into a ditch and she finally managed to pull him from the wreckage and push him down into it then slid down with him. The fuel ignited, lighting up the sky like the sun. She looked down at J and slapped his face. He began to come to.

"Wha?" he looked up at Ariel. "Did we get him?"

Ariel smiled back at him; that was all she needed to do.

"Come on, we gotta get moving. I'm guessing that explosion will have drawn a bit of attention."

They gathered themselves and headed for the cruiser.

"I'm driving," Ariel stated.

J didn't object. He plunked down in the passenger seat. Ariel put the car in drive, then staring straight ahead, she stopped and put it back into park.

"Get the weapons."

"What?"

"In the trunk, get the weapons."

J hopped out and opened up the trunk, it was a treasure trove of firearms. He grabbed a bunch and threw them in the backseat. Ariel sat in the driver's seat listening to the police scanner. He finished collecting the armament and hopped back into the passenger seat. Ariel took off.

"They know one of their officers hasn't checked in, only a matter of time before they find us. Get in the back and load the guns."

He didn't waste any time. He hopped over the seat and started loading. Ariel began to drive, ripping down the road. The radio crackled constantly with unanswered calls, the police station was trying to reach their car.

"Should we answer it? Maybe we could play it off, pretend we're the replicant."

J flopped into the front seat.

"Okay, give it a try," Ariel handed him the radio mic.

He waited for the next transmission.

"Car 54, where are you?"

J hesitated, then talked.

"This is Car 54," he looked over at Ariel guiltily.

"This is Car 54, come in," he tried again as Ariel watched him.

"You have to push the button when you talk."

"What?"

"The little black piece, squeeze it when you talk," she was smiling, shaking her head.

He depressed the button.

"This is Car 54. Like that?"

Ariel swatted the mic out of his hand. "Release the

button when you're done talking."

The station came back.

"Car 54, state your location and status."

"What do I say, where are we?"

Ariel consulted her Datacle, she had the map up.

"County road 26."

"We're good, on county road 26."

There was a pause after the transmission.

"Car 54, who's with you? Please verify your badge ID."

"Badge ID? Where are we going to find that?"

Ariel grabbed the mic and slipped it back on the holder. "That's enough of that."

The station called a few more times and they heard them calling for more cars to head to county road 26. Ariel drove, her head on a swivel, searching for a road to pull off on. They were surrounded by trees, there was nowhere for them to go. She kept the throttle pegged, only slowing for the occasional bend. In the distance, they could see something blocking the road. As they approached, they saw two police cars blocking their path. Ariel grimaced, J looked over.

"Are you planning on—"

"Yep."

"But what if—"

"Get the guns."

J reached back, placing two revolvers on the seat between them, then grabbed the rifles and shotguns, all loaded and ready for action. Ariel placed the revolvers in her belt. J tried to fit them in his pockets, no luck. He shoved them in his waistline. Ariel kept her speed up.

"You're gonna want to hold onto something."

He grabbed the door handle and the back of the seat, then placed his foot firmly on the ground. The blockade was rapidly approaching. Ariel had picked her target, the trunk of the far right car. J braced for impact as he watched the replicants outside the cars scatter, realizing they were not stopping. Crushing metal sounded out as they impacted the cruiser's rear end. The car spun out in front of them. Ariel kept her foot on the gas, their car plowed through, only momentarily slowing before accelerating again. Ariel checked the rearview, the cars turned to follow them. She thought for a minute, J was looking around and monitoring the cruisers behind them. The car began to pull to the side and Ariel struggled to keep it straight.

"What's going on?" J yelled, his senses heightened from the impact.

"Flat tire, must have damaged it in the collision."

She pulled the car off of the road and they piled out the passenger side, away from the oncoming replicants. Hunkered down and leaning with their backs against the car, they waited.

"Wait for them to come around so we can get a clear shot."

J nodded, he checked the rifle one more time. It was ready for action. They could hear the cars skidding to a stop on the other side, gravel tumbling along the road

353

top. Ariel gave a peek under the car and watched four replicants exit their cars. She looked at J and raised four fingers, he nodded.

"Come out with your hands up!"

They remained still.

"Come out, we are authorized to use deadly force if you do not comply."

Nothing. J closed his eyes for a moment as they waited. It was a quiet day, the sound of the replicant's boots crushing the sand underneath echoed around them. They threatened again. Ariel took another peek under the car, they were right up on them. J's finger rubbed along the trigger gently, anticipating the next event. He slowly raised the weapon, aiming past the rear end of the car. Ariel did the same at the front. The replicant stepped around the front of the car, Ariel let two shots go. The replicant stumbled back. J held his ground. *Where were the others?* He looked under the car, one of them was staring back at him and began to aim a pistol.

"Freeze," he shouted.

J grabbed Ariel and pulled her away from the car. They ran into the tree line just off the road as shots started flying past them. One drilled J in the thigh, he instantly grabbed it in pain. Ariel threw him behind a tree then took up a defensive position and began firing back.

"You alright?"

"I got hit in the leg."

"How bad is it?"

He looked down, blood was beginning to flow out, pain ran up his body.

"It's bleeding a lot," he panicked.

Ariel continued firing at their pursuers.

"Put pressure on it."

He placed a hand on the top of his thigh, then realized blood was flowing out of the back of his leg as well.

"My whole leg's bleeding, it's coming out both sides!"

Ariel firmed her lips and, with a nod as the only signal, tactically advanced on the officers, laying down fire then skipping to the next spot of cover and repeating. She utilized every shrubbery, fallen log and standing tree she could. She went through all of the rifle rounds then pulled out the revolvers. J sat there holding his leg, there was a lot of blood. He bent back, watching the battle. Ariel had put down another replicant, there were two left. She quickly went through six rounds and tossed the first pistol away. She spun around another tree. The remaining two replicants had taken up positions behind a couple of trees. One of them exposed himself, hunting for a shot. Ariel put two rounds in his head, dropping him instantly. She spun to another tree, looked at the revolver. Four shots left. She took a deep breath then slipped out from her cover and ran straight toward the remaining replicant, he was only about twenty yards from her.

She slid as a ball player would into second base. J was impressed, watching it all unfold, the display was keeping his mind off of his leg. She fired the final four rounds, all of them finding their mark in the replicant's chest.

He fired back missing every shot. He was empty as well, but still standing. Ariel, now only a few feet away, spun a kick to the replicant's face, he stumbled back, sparks flying from his chest wounds. She spun around with another roundhouse kick, then closed in with a volley of furious punches, elbows jabs and knee thrusts.

The replicant was in a defensive posture, unable to counter any of her attacks, but he anticipated her next move and grabbed her arm, throwing her away from him. She stumbled back, but went after him again. The break had allowed the replicant to recoup and land his own punches. Ariel winced in pain; she had a bloody lip and possibly a couple of broken ribs. She wiped the blood from her face and adjusted her fighting stance. The replicant charged, she spun sideways, the way a matador would to a bull. As he passed she grabbed his head, snapped his neck severing his spinal cord, and the replicant fell down in a heap. Ariel didn't have time to revel in her victory, she sprinted back to J who was laying on his side holding his leg.

"Let me see."

He didn't offer any resistance, he was beginning to lose consciousness. She wasted no time ripping her sleeve off and tightening a tourniquet around his thigh.

"You've lost a lot of blood. We need to get you to a hospital, quickly." She helped him up and they stumbled to one of the police cruisers. J felt light-headed and was beginning to resemble dead weight. Ariel struggled, but got him seated in the passenger side. She started the car.

"You'll be okay," she reassured him, then he closed his
eyes.

CHAPTER TWENTY FOUR

Sunlight shone on his face. He was in a hospital, a nurse attended to his IV. He turned his head. Ariel was sitting next to him.

She breathed a sigh of relief then spoke to the nurse. "Thank you, I owe you and the doctor so much for patching up my love."

J scrunched his eyebrows up into a question mark. *What was she talking about?*

She turned to J, "Sweetie, I'm so thankful you're alive!"

She was acting very bubbly which made him a little worried. He began to say something, but was cut short by a finger to the mouth.

"Shhhh, you need your rest, don't exert yourself."

Okay, something was off. Ariel was still smiling at him. He couldn't help but smile back, but quickly returned to his puzzled look.

"Thanks again," she said as the nurse left the room.

"Let me know if y'all need anything," the nurse said before stepping out.

J glanced back at Ariel, her face grew serious. She stood up and grabbed his legs, sliding them off the bed. J started to scream in pain but she covered his mouth with her whole hand.

"We need to get out of here, now."

"Wha—"

"Come on."

She tugged at his arm and pulled him onto his feet. The pressure sent a shot of pain from his leg. He winced, but managed to keep in the scream. She tugged at him holding his hand, he gritted his teeth.

"We gotta move faster."

He attempted to move faster, but his leg felt very stiff. Then he looked down, he was in a gown. He reached behind him, he was exposed.

"Where are my clothes?!"

"Shhh, quiet. We need to get you out of here. We've already been here a couple hours." She yanked out the IV from his hand.

"The fire escape." She led him through the large recovery room, past a couple of patients who were sleeping soundly.

"What's going on? What was that back there?"

"Nothing, had to tell them you were my fiancé to be able to see you. When we got here, I told them you were shot by a hunter."

They continued to the fire exit at the far end.

"So what's going on?" J stopped Ariel, grabbing her wrist.

She turned and stated quickly, "Don't you remember being chased by the replicants?"

J was hesitant at first, but the thoughts of being shot, and seeing Ariel eliminate the replicants with surgical precision, jumped into his mind.

"Yeah."

"Well, it's only a matter of time before they come

looking for a fugitive."

Ariel opened the door, he released her wrist.

"You first."

"But, my clothes!"

She looked back at him, then tilted her head, nodding outside. Her eyebrows jumped, "Just go, no time for modesty. We'll get ya some soon, promise."

J struggled down the ladder, placing most of his weight on his good leg. He felt so exposed, the gown was blowing all over the place, his butt hanging out. Reaching the bottom, he grabbed the gown, holding it tight behind him. Ariel hopped down just after and was searching for a car to borrow.

"There."

She pointed to a car across the road. It was late afternoon and people were beginning to close up their stores. They received a couple of strange looks, a few stares, and one five year old yelled, "A butt, a butt! I see his butt!"

J attempted to spin around to hide it, but there were people everywhere. They made it to the car and Ariel had him climb into the back so he could stretch out and stay out of site.

"Stay down. We don't want anyone else to see you."

She checked in the rearview mirror, he was hidden well.

"Too late. Everyone's seen my butt!" he laughed at himself as a defense mechanism.

Ariel joined in as she pulled away from the curb.

"That's my car!" she heard a man yell.

Glancing in the mirror, she saw him running after them. She sped up, maneuvering through an intersection. They made it out of town without any other issues.

"Sooo...when do I get clothes?"

"When I've had enough of staring at your butt," she said with a wink to the rearview mirror.

"Ariel..." J warned.

"You're so easy. We'll get you clothes when we find a shop."

J raised up his gown. His leg was bandaged and there were no signs of blood. It ached, but he was surprised at how little pain he felt now that he was lying down.

"How long 'til the next town?"

"About twenty miles. How are you feeling?"

"Pretty good, actually."

"Enjoy it while you can, the crash isn't going to be much fun."

"Crash?"

"They gave you morphine for the pain. Once you come down from the high, it won't be much fun. Such an archaic place."

J sat up and watched the countryside fly by. His mind was wandering and he couldn't quite keep one thought in his head. The tree line opened to fields. He recognized the fields, they were corn.

"Where are we?"

"Passing through County 7, town up ahead is Colton."

"Colton?"

"Yep."

J clenched his jaw. Colton, their arch rivals. Memories of countless defeats on the ball field flooded back. He thought about how important those games had felt, how they had shaped his life. None of that meant anything now. He gave a light chuckle, if only they all knew what the real world was like, and he didn't just mean after high school, but what was above him in that tiny round glowing ball. His eyes drifted to the road ahead, buildings were coming into view.

"Think we can find some clothes?"

"I'll find some bloody clothes. You're staying in the car."

J agreed that was probably best, nobody else needed to see his bare bottom. Ariel pulled up to a department store.

"I'll be back," she said in a deep voice, then laughed at her own joke as she got out of the car and headed inside.

He didn't realize why that would be funny and sat there watching a few kids play across the street. A couple holding hands walked past and there was another group of kids playing marbles about a block away.

"Eggerton," he heard a voice say. "You're the star from Eggerton, aren't you?"

He turned. Outside the car window were three boys his age. At first he didn't recognize them, but then like a kick to the head, it hit him.

"I remember you, from the last time we whooped your butt," said the meathead.

It was the same three Colton players that he had met at the diner, which seemed like a lifetime ago. The smarmy, pretty-boy approached the car door.

"Nice dress!"

The others laughed.

"What are you doing out here? Playing dress up? Where's your mommy?"

More laughs.

J gritted his teeth and tried to remain calm, he kept his mouth shut.

"Is that dress part of your scholarship?"

The two others were almost rolling with laughter. J couldn't contain himself. His easy-going demeanor normally helped him maintain a thick skin, but maybe the morphine, or his recent brushes with death, had changed that. He'd had enough. He opened the door and stood up. His gaze was locked on the jokester. Standing upright, the wind blew his gown open. J just stood there.

"Ha!" the smarmy jokester pointed.

J clocked him upside the head; he crumpled and fell limp to the ground. The meathead charged him, but J slid to the side, watching him switch off and land face first on the concrete behind the car. The third tried to run off, but was met with a kick to the face. Ariel placed her leg back on the ground and threw a pile of clothes to J. She gave him a devious grin.

"Nice butt."

J's face went beet red, he grabbed the gown and tried to cover himself. Ariel shut the car door and looked back.

363

"Coming?"

He gave her a look, then hopped in the back.

"What was that all about?"

"Just some jerks from Colton's baseball team."

J realized that he was about 45 minutes from Eggerton.

He dug through the clothes. "No underwear?"

"Based on what I just saw, thought you might like to
go commando," she laughed a little.

He didn't see the humor in it, but began to dress.

"You want to start at the diner?"

"Probably the best place, what time is it?"

"Almost five."

Hopefully his friends weren't going to be there. He
had no clue how long he'd been gone and it would be
quite the story to try and explain everything. He finished
dressing and gazed out the window.

"Am I your taxi driver?"

"What?"

"Hop up here. You don't need to stay back there."

He gingerly climbed over the seat.

"What do we do if he's not there?"

"Then we play detective."

J wondered who Will really was. It had always
puzzled him, nobody knew anything about him. In such
a small town, you'd have figured somebody knew something.

Ariel pulled into the diner parking lot. J was actively
searching, no sign of him anywhere.

"Should we go in?"

J looked around again, this time searching for Rich's car, it wasn't there. "Yeah, but let's make it quick."

Ariel searched his face for the reason behind his attitude change. She didn't know the history between J and his friends, if that's what you'd call Rich. "Okay," she said drawn out.

They entered the diner, it was relatively empty.

"Hello," the manager greeted them. "Take your pick, any seat that's open."

J walked up to the counter leaning forward on it his elbows planted on the horizontal surface.

"Have you seen Will?"

"Will?" the manager said with an eyebrow raised, polishing a dish.

"Yeah, Will. He used to stand outside everyday..."

The manager shook his head slowly, looking like he had no clue as to what J was talking about.

J went on, "Smoked a bunch..."

The manager continued his shake his head. J turned around, the door opened.

"Hey! James!"

It was Jason. He'd hoped to avoid anyone he knew until they'd gotten things straightened out. He was a fugitive after all. Word would travel much slower on Earth, but still, he was worried about involving his friends. They weren't ready for any of this. Or maybe he wasn't ready for his two worlds to collide.

"James, where have you been?!"

365

The name felt foreign to him, James. He'd become accustomed to J and it seemed to fit who he'd become. James sounded so formal.

"Been out of town."

"Out of town, without telling anybody? What were you doing?"

They were innocent questions, but J felt like he was being interrogated. The door opened again, J looked up at the ceiling and sighed heavily. Rich.

"Well, look what the cat dragged in. Where have you been?"

J gave him a look.

"What?" Rich said, not really caring what was said earlier.

Barbara popped in after him. J held his breath. Carol was next. A big smile appeared on her face and she ran over to him, jumping on him with a big hug. He hesitantly hugged her back, but she didn't notice his lack of response.

"James. Where have you been?"

She leaned back staring into his eyes. Ariel was watching intently behind them.

"Out of town."

James wanted to sink in the ground or become invisible, better yet maybe just disappear altogether.

"Doing what, you never leave town, I was worried you went off to college early, on your scholarship."

His mind raced. *Think of a story, something believable.*

"No, just a parts run for Father."

She leaned forward and kissed him, full on kissed him, on the mouth. He was slow to react and stumbled back.

"Missed you, next time let me know you're leaving, I was pretty upset at first, but somehow I knew you wouldn't just leave me."

J searched for words.

"James," Ariel started. The name sounded weird coming from her mouth. "Can we talk outside?"

Carol turned around.

"Who's that?" she asked as her smile dimmed.

J looked at Ariel, who was trying her best to hold back the fact that she was displeased with the display that just occurred. His eyes moved between the two girls. She'd met Ariel before... they must have wiped her memory again. He focused back on the story.

"Uhh, she's a parts supplier, yeah for the harvester company. Remember how I was telling you our power supply was going out in harvester #2? She's here to take a gander, that's why I left, to pick her up."

Carol studied him, she was trying to figure out if he was telling the truth. He'd never lied to her before, so her hard look softened. She was a little jealous, Ariel was one of the most beautiful girls she'd seen. J gently unlocked himself from her arms and made his way to the door, Ariel was already there waiting.

"Is she single?" Jason asked as he walked by.

He didn't bother to answer, just shook his head. Ariel

stepped outside with J. At first she was reading him, then began, "So any ideas?"

"About what?"

His head was going through a bunch of things, seeing his friends, and Carol, his mind felt like scrambled eggs.

"The ball game...seriously? Will. Any ideas about where to find Will?"

J snapped back to their task. "No," he said. Then thinking about it a moment longer, remembered their last meeting. "The last time I saw him, he ducked down that alley over there," he pointed.

Ariel took a few steps away from the building to get a closer look. The door to the diner opened.

"James, aren't you coming in, everyone missed you so much, we really want to hang out, get back to normal, you want that, too, right?" Carol asked.

Ariel scowled, J turned around.

"No, I have to take her...back to the barn, yep, gotta go to the barn, check on the harvester, parts and all."

He was a terrible liar, but it seemed he was getting away with it.

"Be careful, there are a couple fugitives on the loose, it's terrible, I guess they shot up some cops."

"Replicants," Ariel said under her breath.

He looked back, she was standing there with her arms crossed.

"I'll be careful."

Carol stepped out and gave him a big hug, then a quick kiss. She smiled possessively at J, then turned to

Ariel with a look that said, "He's mine." J watched her walk back into the diner.

"Ready to go now...James?" Ariel's voice was dripping with sarcasm at his name.

"Relax. Yeah, I'm ready. You?"

She didn't respond, just hopped in the car, J jumped in the passenger seat. They headed toward the alley.

"Can we park around the block?" he requested.

Ariel didn't say a word, but passed the alley then turned down a side street. She found an empty place to park and they walked toward the alley.

"This one?" she asked.

"Yep, he ducked into this alley after giving me the cigarette. When I got here, he was gone."

"Must be an elevator to the tunnels. You search over there. I'll start over here."

"What am I looking for?"

"There will be cracks around the mortar in a pattern outlining a door. Very hard to see unless you're close and know that it's there."

The sun was setting. It would be hard enough to find in the daytime, nearly impossible at night.

J ran his hands along the different edges of the bricks, nothing. Ariel didn't fare much better. She scanned, but with the failing light it was very hard. J sat down.

"This is impossible. We need some light."

"I'll just summon Ra. That help ya?"

J could tell she was testy. He was getting that way as well.

369

"Actually, yeah. Summon him with one of your fancy gadgets, maybe that Datacle thing you're always using."

"This?" She took it off and threw it at him, hitting him in the chest. "Here, you try it. Are you going to help or not?"

"Hey, you're not the one with a hole in your leg, give me a minute."

"Well cry me a river."

J was getting frustrated and angry at this point, but he could tell Ariel was, too. He wanted to get to the bottom of it.

"What's going on with you?" he raised his voice and stood up holding the Datacle in his hand.

"Nothing. Let's just find the stupid door."

"Something's up. You don't want to talk about it, that's fine, but we need to stop sniping at each other and find the danged door," he said determined. He took a deep breath, then asked, "What if it's not here?"

"You're the one who said it is."

"No, I said the last time I saw him, he turned down this alley."

He looked back toward the street, a flash of movement caught his eye. He began walking back down the alley to where it met the main street. Ariel began searching again, but saw him walking away out of the corner of her eye.

"Walking away huh? Typical."

He just ignored her. She obviously needed to cool off and he was fixated on something that didn't look quite right. Where the final layer of bricks met the cobblestone, he saw a piece of cloth blowing up and down as the cars drove by. He couldn't place it, but something didn't make sense. He reached the cloth and bent down for closer examination, it was trapped between the cobblestone and the brick wall.

"Ariel, I think I found something."

"What?" she yelled bitterly.

"You need to come see this."

"Fine."

She stopped searching and stomped over to him. He was pointing at the cloth and as she got closer, she hurried her pace.

"Yes, that could be it. Press your hands on the bricks. See if you feel anything unusual."

J started on his side and Ariel on hers. They moved from brick to brick looking for something, anything that could be a switch to open the wall.

"Ha!" he heard Ariel cry out.

"What did you find?"

Ariel pressed a brick a couple of rows up from the ground level. The brick slid out and on top was a glass panel.

"Crap."

She stood up and walked away, pacing back and forth, hand on her chin.

"What?" he asked, seeing she was disturbed with the finding.

She threw her hands in the air and huffed as she

continued to pace. "It's a DNA scanner. I can't hack this."

"Why not?"

"I don't have the right equipment."

She began pacing again and rubbed her temples with her hands, stopping to look toward the street. She dropped her hands and turned her head to look at him.

"We'll have to get back to the ship. You need medical attention anyway."

J, who'd been kneeling, shot up straight, his leg pain ignored.

"Back to the ship? The same way we came? I don't know if you forgot, but that wasn't easy and now they're after us," his arms spread out as he spoke.

"Well do you have any ideas? What? Maybe we can just blow it up, or knock it down? These systems don't work like that. You could tear down the whole building, but this shaft would still remain, they were built bullet-proof, indestructible."

He could tell she was discouraged and still angry over something, anyone would have noticed that. He looked at the glass, Ariel was still ranting. J wanted to know what her deal was, but it had to wait. He placed his hand on the glass as he had seen her do plenty of times before. The brick pulled back into the building, then the rest of the bricks reorganized themselves silently and quickly into a doorway. J thought it was actually pretty eerie.

"But, how?" Ariel exclaimed.

He looked at her and naively shrugged his shoulders.

She grabbed him and they went into the opening. The door shut as quickly as it had emerged.

"Welcome, J. Which floor?" the elevator greeted him in a sensuous female voice.

Ariel's jaw dropped open. He was as surprised as she was, not only that it opened, it knew his name.

"Will's floor?" he replied.

"You would like to see Will, I take it?"

Ariel and J looked at each other. J thought the question was strange, maybe Ariel would find it normal. She didn't.

"Yes, are you an AI?" Ariel asked.

"Yes, my name is Sarah. Are you looking for Will?"

They stood there a moment then Ariel jumped in, "Yes, can you take us there?"

"I can take J, but must get authorization for you. Who are you?"

"Ariel, J's Girl....friend?"

"You don't sound too sure of that. I need to hear it from J."

"She's my girlfriend?"

"And you authorize her to come along with you?"

"Yes."

"I'm sorry, I need to hear you say, "I authorize Ariel, my girlfriend, to accompany me."

J looked over at Ariel, she smiled at him as if to say "please" and "sorry" at the same time.

"I authorize Ariel, my girlfriend, to accompany me."

"Very well, we will arrive in 7 minutes."

They looked at each other, puzzled. That seemed like a long time for an elevator ride. J felt the room begin to descend. The walls became transparent, and they watched the dirt and stone fly past them, then felt the descent slow as they popped out underneath the Earth. Their eyes filled with amazement, they could see the underbelly of Sector 11, along with the support structure. Clouds rolled by, obscuring most of it. The sight was awe-inspiring. The elevator made a turn and rode along, picking up speed. They could see the rails above them as the room hung underneath. They zipped by column after column and J imagined they went to other plates, all holding it together. Once again, the elevator slowed. They ascended and began to slow again. The walls became opaque, J felt the room stop and the doors slid open. They stepped out into a large room. On the left, floor-to-ceiling glass windows stood, they must have been right on the edge of the plate. Outside, clouds swirled by and small glimpses of the gigantic metal posts could be seen.

"I'll let Will know you're here with a guest," Sarah said. "Please have a seat. Would you care for any refreshments?"

"Just a water, please."

"Me too," Ariel added.

They were both parched from the long day. J noticed a couple of sofas facing out over the center of the Earth. He winced as he hobbled over, holding his leg, and took a seat; Ariel followed. It felt good to sit, pain was radi-

374

ating from his wound and the intensity was starting to grow from all of the movement. Glasses of ice water rose up from the floor in front of each of them. J reached out taking his and Ariel did the same, the table they sat on descended, disappearing into the floor.

"Beautiful isn't it?" a voice came from behind them.

Both turned to look. Will was standing there drinking an amber liquid in a short glass.

"I designed some of that, you know."

J looked closer. *Was it Arcturus?* He couldn't tell, but the possibility spun in his mind.

"Do you two have something for me?"

Ariel nodded her head.

"Sarah tells me, J, that you have a pretty nasty wound in your right leg. Would you like me to take care of that?"

"Yes, please, sir," he gritted out, trying to push through the pain.

"Sarah, can you bring out the med kit?"

"Of course."

The floor in front of J rose up again, this time with the gun device familiar to him on it. He had seen Ariel use one several times on Atlantis.

"I'll do it," Ariel said as she reached for the device, then looked at him with a devious grin. "Take your pants off."

"I'd expect nothing less from his girlfriend," Will commented.

J kept his mouth shut. He didn't know how he felt

about that. *His girlfriend was topside, right? Or was she right here, taking care of him, like she always did?* J covered himself as he worked his pants down, his face flushed, he was still commando. Ariel attended to his leg and he was quick to replace his pants after the procedure was done. Ariel pulled the square chip from a pocket and held it in the air. Will walked over and gently grabbed it.

"Funny that this is how Arcturus wanted to protect Earth. By making it destroy itself, only to be saved by teenagers," he chuckled. "But teenagers are very resilient and resourceful," he said, walking up next to the sofa. "So you know what's next, don't you?"

"You give us the next key and we find the third?" Ariel questioned.

Will chuckled again. "Well sort of."

"What do you mean?" J asked as Will took a sip of his whisky.

"Don't make it like this anymore. Macallan, vintage 2020, over 2,000 years old."

J looked up at him, "Wait. What? What year is it?"

"It ain't 1956, like you think it is."

He was astounded, "What do you mean?"

"It's 4040. They picked the year 1956 because much of the world was at peace and most of the technology that would propel the human race along was in its infancy. Yet machines were readily available like your harvester for example...with some upgrades. TK found humans would be easier to control that way. Life was simpler back then, there was a definite order to things, and TK loves order.

"So who are you, exactly?" J asked.

Will walked over to a small table and set down his glass, then took a seat in a chair next to them. The floor rose up with a lighter, cigar and cutter on it. He picked up the cigar, cut and lit it, and took a big draw. He blew it out steadily, forming little rings with the smoke.

"Just a caretaker. That's what I am now. Kind of a retirement gig for me, never liked Atlantis. Before that, I was one of the architects tasked with redesigning Earth. Those were the days."

He stared off into the dimly lit clouds as they floated by, puffing on his cigar.

"So you said "sort of". What does that mean? Is there no other key?"

"Arcturus was the lead engineer on the project. A real Leonardo da Vinci. He had all the insight of a genius if you ask me, had his hands on everything. Even before we began the project he had this plan in place. It wasn't until later that he picked his team, his inner circle. There were many design flaws intentionally built into the system, which could only be reversed by three things. Hence the three keys. You actually have two, but the third one is going to be the toughest to acquire."

"Two? But we only have one, the chip we handed to you."

Will laughed, "You have two, one just isn't obvious. How did you get down here? Luck, chance, force? No, you used a plan and a key."

J squinted his eyes, thinking.

Ariel's eyes lit up, "J's DNA."

Will smiled and nodded.

"So, if we have two of the keys, where do we find the third?"

Both of them leaned toward Will twisting their heads exposing their ears to listen.

"It's not necessarily a key. It's actually a device, a powerplant to be precise."

J looked at Ariel; she was still leaning in, focused on Will. Her blonde hair flowed over her neck, his eyes were lost in it a moment.

"Where is it?" she asked

"Atlantis."

That snapped J back to the conversation, he turned to Will. "Well that should be easy to get. TK's gone."

"Yes, but I've been monitoring their systems. Seems someone is still working for TK."

"That little rat. I knew it!" Ariel stood up, clenching her fists as she paced. She mouthed more words, J couldn't pick up any of them. He thought about it a moment, it must be someone he knew, the way she reacted.

"Jolt?" J asked, already knowing the answer.

Ariel nodded, "I knew he was up to something."

J stood up, still watching Ariel. He began to raise his arms as if to hug her, but let them fall back down. He wanted to comfort her betrayal yet again, but was still torn about his feelings toward two different girls. Instead he said, "What about the rest of the crew?"

She was still pacing, one hand clenched to her side the other raised up, her fingers on the lip she was chewing on. She dropped her hand, letting it hover and stared out the window.

"Zane would never do that, the others I'm not so sure. Sonya's betrayed us once before. Where's the powerplant exactly?"

She spun around to look at Will.

"It's in Arcturus' secret lab. I have the location. I'll upload it to your Datacle."

Ariel looked expectantly at J, he glanced at his hands. "Crap, I left it outside."

Ariel scolded him with her eyes.

"I have a spare you can have. I'll get one for you, too, J."

Ariel's eyes softened, but she remained fixated on J.

"How big is the powerplant?" she asked.

"It's a prototype MDD550, about twenty feet by twenty feet."

Ariel turned and began pacing again, tapping her index finger on her lips.

"We'll need a Power Loader, and most ships would be too small, so... a KracKen cargo carrier. We'll have to find one."

"You should be able to find both of those at the loading dock on the outskirts of Sector 11. Pretty sure they left a few behind in their hasty exit."

" Okay, now about the crew?"

"We at least need to get Zane out of there," J spoke up.

"Where does the MDD550 need to go?"

"The central hub. You'll switch it out with the old one. There'll be a temporary complete shutdown that will begin when you install the new chip, triggering a self-destruct sequence. If you don't swap the power supplies quick enough, the planet will detonate."

"Who would design it like that?!"

"Your father. It would stop me from doing it, unless I was sure."

J looked offended for a moment.

"So, what do we do about Zane?" he asked, turning to Ariel after a brief pause, soaking in the task at hand.

"We'll figure that out in a moment. First, we need to know how to give Flat Earth a heart transplant."

CHAPTER TWENTY FIVE

Will opened the door. On the far wall displayed nearly every weapon imaginable, from low to high tech blasters and everything in between. Will seemed prepared for any eventuality and, based on his speech about Arcturus, they understood why. Leave nothing to chance.

Ariel scanned her choices. They couldn't take it all, so the right ones would be key. She began to pick, carefully choosing each one. She wanted to go small, it seemed like they were always on the run, and anything large and cumbersome would just slow them down. J was standing next to her, a few of the weapons he recognized, but plenty he did not. He took what was handed to him and tried to find places to put it all. They had changed outfits again, they were forever changing outfits, and J had more holsters and pockets than he knew what to do with. Luckily, everything he was given was relatively light for its size, except one. The item was the size of a bible and nearly the same shape. It was red with four straps and had an indented symbol of a bull stamped on it. Ariel helped him strap it on like a backpack. A bar of gold might have been lighter. He questioned Ariel about it, but she just smiled at him impishly. He took the hint, they moved on to the next item. In an attempt to avoid the terrifying click J had heard earlier on the road, they packed older gunpowder weapons as well. Ariel had a feeling that Jolt would find a way to restrict their use of blasters again.

"All packed?" Will asked, rubbing his hands together like they were about to play a card game, a big grin on his face.

"Are you coming with?" Ariel asked. She'd had the impression he was going, but he hadn't grabbed anything.

"No, I'm a caretaker, not a warrior. There are two ways this ends. You perform the transplant and I have a job, or you don't and we all die. Try and keep me employed."

He walked off and disappeared down a hallway.

"Will would like me to show you to your transport, if you are ready now," Sarah announced.

Ariel turned and looked at J. He mirrored her movements. Her hair was pulled back into a ponytail, pistols under her arms, weapons strapped to her back, loaded holsters on her thighs, knives near her ankles, and he was sure she had a few more surprises he didn't yet know about. She looked like a tricked out space Viking warrior, he liked it.

"Ariel—" he began.

"You ready for this Mr. J?" she interrupted in a higher tone voice than he was accustomed to then quirked her lips up. She seemed to know he was getting maudlin and was trying to lighten the mood to keep him on task.

J wasn't really sure how to answer that. He was as ready as he could be under the circumstances, but felt ill-prepared. Still, they'd made it this far, and together, their chances of survival were greatly improved. He simply nodded.

Sarah lit up blue arrows on the floor, leading them to the small twin cruiser. It had two wings, rounded slick-looking cans for engines and a V-tail. It seated two, and with all of their gear on, the seats were a bit small. Ariel insisted they keep everything on, and while it was uncomfortably tight, his luck seemed to call for it as well. Neither said anything after Ariel had questioned him. They'd gone over the plan multiple times, both were running it through their heads. Ariel picked up the ship and headed out the bay. Next stop, the Eleftheria.

"Eleftheria come in."

"Yeah, we hear you. Where ya been?"

"Out. Found out where the second key is. Now we get to go home for a bit."

"Atlantis?"

"Yep. You follow us, we have the coordinates."

"Roger that. We'll be out there in a snap."

Ariel took a deep breath. J was sitting behind her, he could tell she was concentrating on the game plan.

"You think they suspect anything?" he asked.

"I don't know, it's hard to tell. I hope not."

J thought the transmission from the Eleftheria sounded normal. Sonya sounded like her devil-may-care self, but she had lied to them...twice. The larger ship emerged from the hangar bay, nose to nose with theirs.

"Lead the way princess."

J couldn't see it, but he felt Ariel clench her jaw. She turned the craft and hit it. J was pinned back in the seat. This time he expected it and it was kind of exciting. The sensation of the G-forces was still new to him and he was beginning to enjoy it. They broke in between two of the plates. J looked back at the sectors below, quickly shrinking, each with their own perimeter wall so large that even at this altitude, he could distinctly see them. He looked back up. The moon was growing in the windscreen, the fun was about to begin. He hoped he'd be able to play his part. Ariel began the docking sequence, Sonya and the Eleftería followed along as planned. They both had the feeling that they were made, the way a scheming child feels after telling a lie.

After entering the tunnel, Ariel began the landing sequence and touched down along one of the back walls, leaving space for the much larger Eleftería. The cockpit top slid open, Ariel straddled the side and paused, scrutinizing the Hangar.

"What?" J tried to see what she was looking at. All he could see was a sign at the other end that read HANGAR 18.

Ariel remained silent for a minute.

"Nothing."

She climbed down, he followed. They began the walk to the Eleftería. Sonya was the first to step out as the cargo door opened.

"Looking like you're goin' to war young lady. What's the occasion?"

Ariel didn't answer, just stared straight ahead and continued her walk.

J was only a few steps behind. "Ariel, come on, I

didn't mean it!"

Ariel quickened her pace, blowing right by Sonya.

"Come on, don't be mad," J pleaded with Ariel, beginning to jog.

She disappeared into the ship, J had fallen behind. He passed Sonya who was now leaning on the side of the ship, lollipop in her mouth.

"Wow, you really pissed her off. What'd you do?"

J just stared at his feet and shook his head, then continued in. When he entered, Zane was sitting down across the way. He gave J the look you get when someone wouldn't want to be in your shoes. J walked over and sat down next to him. He watched Sonya walk out. She was performing the post-flight on the ship, it was her usual ritual, training that was ingrained in her being.

"So what'd you do?"

J worked his shoulders to loosen the heavy plate on his back.

"Lover's quarrel."

Zane laughed, "No, really. What'd you do?"

"You don't believe me?"

Zane gave another half laugh, "Must've been something pretty rough, she really digs you. Whatcha got there?"

He handed Zane the heavy block.

Zane took a look at it, his eyebrows raised toward J. "So you really did that?" he said a little louder.

Sonya walked back in. "So what'd you do? Or is Zane going to have to rat you out?"

Zane slipped the device on his back.

"Tell her...you should get a woman's perspective." He stood up and waved Sonya over to take a seat.

J was still sitting, gaze intent on the floor, elbows on his knees, hands together, rocking slightly. Sonya approached and bent down. She tried to look in his eyes, but he turned his head. She tried another tactic and sat down next to him, she was dying to know.

"So what'd you do?"

"Well..." he looked up into her eyes. "I didn't betray her."

Zane clocked her on the back of the head, she toppled down to the ground. Blasters started firing. J and Zane whipped around, it sounded like it was coming from the cockpit. Ariel came running out, laser blasts following her.

"Let's go!" she yelled, passing them like they were traffic cones.

J took off after her, Zane didn't waste any time either. Gatlin appeared from the bridge door and let loose with a barrage of fire. Ariel had already made it out, J and Zane ducked and dodged while they made their way to the door as fast as they could. Emerging outside, Ariel was running backwards, she had two blasters drawn.

"What happened?" J yelled.

She didn't respond, just began firing, shots whipping by them. Zane hopped over the smaller ship, J followed him. Ariel continued her cover fire while Gatlin was taking potshots, hiding in the door of the Eleftería. Then she spun over the front of the ship, joining the others.

"What happened?" J asked again.

"I got punched in the mouth, after leaving a surprise in their system."

He examined her face, it sure didn't look like she'd been punched.

Ariel saw the inquisitive look he gave her. "Let's just say plans changed. Get to the hangar door."

J looked at Zane.

"Go!"

He took off running to the door, Zane following close behind.

"I hope you guys are right, otherwise Sonya's gonna be pretty pissed at me."

J didn't answer. All of his energy was focused on the door. He placed his hand on the wall, the door sprung open.

"In," he pointed to Zane, then waved to Ariel. She was already on her way. He pulled out one of his pistols and fired back at the ship. Gatlin was still inside, but getting more bold by the minute. Ariel ran through the door, J closed it behind them.

"Going up."

"Can someone please fill me in? Did they really betray us?" Zane was puzzled. Luckily the note on the device had gotten his attention.

Ariel leaned back against the wall. She looked at J then Zane. She was breathing heavily, they all were.

"Glad you believed us."

"Well, not for lack of convincing. His acting sucks," Zane mocked.

"Sonya fell for it," J defended himself.

"Ha, I'm not sure if she did or it was just so bad she felt sorry for you."

"You're telling me you didn't believe me?"

"I believed her, she sold it. It was like you were cheating on her," Zane said, pointing at Ariel.

That comment triggered J's memory. He remembered the awkward scene with Carol and changed the subject.

"Sonya was there when they grabbed me the first time."

Zane looked at Ariel, her face was hard.

"What about Jolt?"

"He's the reason you got mauled by the bear."

"You mean Buur," J tried to lighten the conversation, but they both just looked at him deadpan.

"He could have hacked the system; I saw the code on the computer. Then he almost got us killed in Sector 11. J tried to use a M2K Blaster on a replicant and it was locked. I know J sucks at weapons, but a five year old could have used it."

J scrunched his eyebrows together.

"No offense, J."

He lightened them a bit, still not happy at being called a five year old.

"So , Gatlin?"

"He's the wild card, I don't know much about him. You were the only one we trusted, we had to get you out."

"So, what's next?"

"Well... they were supposed to all be knocked out. I got Jolt, but something tipped off Gatlin. You guys got Sonya, but I'm sure Gatlin's getting the others up now. We have to make it to building 492, section 6, room 4. We have a code to get into Arcturus' storage facility, then we get the new power supply."

Ariel continued to fill him in. They reached their floor and proceeded on the route. Ariel was worried that they would get locked out if they traveled on the ground, Jolt could hack nearly everything in Atlantis, but their destination was off the grid. Getting there would be the trick.

Her plan began at the top. They reached the balcony. J walked to the edge and peered down. It was one, if not the tallest building on that side of the city. Ariel approached him from behind.

"It's that one," she pointed. "You remember how to use your boots?"

J nodded then looked at Zane. "How's he going to get there?"

Zane pointed at Ariel. "Don't think I'm going to ride with one of you. I'll fall like a rock. You know I've tried those boots myself, they can't handle my weight, let alone with someone else."

Ariel snickered then walked up to Zane and slipped her arm around him as if she was giving him a hug. He winked at J who didn't look too pleased at the sight. She pressed a sequence on the block, stepping back. Zane stumbled, catching his balance as two large wings unfolded.

"Red Bull gives you wings," she chuckled. "Those could hold three of you. You coming?"

He glanced at the wings. "You got directions for these or is mama bird going to just kick baby bird from the nest?"

Ariel smiled mischievously, "I got directions. Come here, I'll explain."

He waddled over and she stepped aside so he could look out over the city.

"You take this..." She reached up to take something off one of the straps and stuck it on his temple, it was about the size of a dime. "...and you just think of how to fly."

She ducked under one of his wings and pushed him off.

"Think happy thoughts!" she yelled as he plummeted down off the building.

"Did you just do that?" J asked in disbelief. "What if it doesn't work?"

He looked down, Zane was still falling. "You know if it does work he's going to be pissed."

Ariel laughed, she'd been laughing since she shoved him. "He'll be fine. Seeing his face was worth it."

"You're evil. You know that, right?"

She grabbed his hand and jumped. J's stomach was in his throat for a second.

"Like Dorothy, remember?" he heard her calmly say.

She spun to face him and clasped his other hand. He clicked his heels together and his boots came alive. He searched the sky below them, half expecting to see a flattened Zane underneath. He was glad to not only see himself slowing up, but Zane was gliding around in circles, even doing loops. They looked at each other then down at Zane, Ariel laughed again. J really liked her laugh, it was hearty and he could tell it was genuine. Zane looked like he was doing great and enjoying it as well, until a blue fireball hit one of his wings. Their heads swiveled toward the direction it came from.

"Buzzardz. Jolt must be awake."

Four tiny ships were aimed straight at them. The closest had fired on Zane and was acquiring him for another shot. Zane started maneuvering, he was almost to the landing location, about a mile from the building they'd entered. Ariel rotated them to head downward, she positioned J, still holding his hands, fingers intertwined. They rocketed down, the Buzzardz engaged, firing shot after shot. She took charge of their aerial dance, spinning, swaying, flipping, they were almost to the ground. She turned in time to come to a rest at the landing spot and they hit the ground, running over to Zane who had taken cover near a building.

"Could have given me a gun," he shouted.

Ariel reached for her left leg holster, pulled out a blaster and chucked it at him as they passed. He caught it then started returning fire, J and Ariel just ran. They reached the wall of the building next to a door.

"This is you," Ariel said, pulling a blaster from her right leg.

She let a couple of shots fly. J placed his hand on the entry pad, the door opened, and the three of them piled in, the door closing behind them.

"Thanks for the bite mama bird."

It took J a minute to realize Zane was talking about the blaster.

Ariel smiled then consulted her Datacle. She looked back up and, without a word, headed for another door. J thought that was strange and looked at Zane questioningly. He just shrugged then got up to follow. After traveling through a reception area they were at another door.

"What's—"

Ariel shook her head, putting her index finger over her mouth, he took the hint. They made their way down a series of hallways and doors into a briefing room. After a moment of searching, J found the hidden door panel and they were in Arcturus' secret facility.

Ariel looked at J, "Almost there."

"What was with the silent sneaking around?"

"I didn't want Jolt to possibly hear where we're going. The rest of the building is still connected to the main systems, plenty of mics out there."

J and Zane understood, now to find the power supply. Just inside the hidden door was another elevator shaft.

"Down we go," J said, pushing the button.

They descended very quickly, the enclosed box making a few squeals along the way. J thought it must

392

have been a very old system, the finishes were not nearly as polished as everything else in the city. The ride screeched to a halt, then the doors opened with a grind. An enormous room lay out in front of them, various objects lay scattered among ships and vehicles. J spotted a large container that looked different from the others that met the description given to them by Will. Ariel hurried to approach the container, on the way she noticed a KracKen ship sitting next to it.

"J, you open the box. Zane, we need a Power Loader. I'll fire up the KracKen."

They split up. J ran to the container. He walked around it twice before noticing a small panel hidden in a grove of panels. As he touched it, a smaller glass panel exposed itself. It was like the one in Will's alley-way entrance. He placed his hand on it and a large horn sounded, there was a hissing noise and steam billowed out from the side of the container. He backed away, waiting for the powerplant to be exposed. The side panels slowly lowered, the steam was so thick it obscured what was contained inside. The doors came to a stop, he waited with anticipation.

CHAPTER TWENTY SIX

J walked into the enormous cargo bay of the KracKen. It was an incredibly large ship, he thought his home baseball field could have fit into it. He made his way up to the bridge. Ariel was there, face full of screens, going through system after system, ensuring everything was operating properly. They would only get one shot at this. He walked up and stood beside her, still pecking away at items.

"You get access?"

J held something out in his hands, no words. Ariel paused at the silence and looked at J's face then the item. It was a small card about the size of a playing card, but much sturdier.

"What's this?"

"I was hoping you could tell me."

J had no idea what it was and thought she might have a clue.

She took it and held it up in front of the screen, "I've never seen one of these before." She flipped it around in her hand, spinning it from side to side, "Where did you find this?"

"In the crate."

"With the powerplant? Was it in it or laying next to it?"

J pinched his lips together, not saying anything.

Ariel stopped playing with it and studied him. "It's in there right?"

J's forehead crinkled and he looked away. "Well... no."

Ariel visibly paled. "What do you mean, no?"

"That card was sitting on a table in the middle of the crate."

Ariel closed her eyes and took a deep breath, behind them they heard the rumbling of heavy machinery.

J turned toward the noise. "Sounds like Zane found the Loader."

No sooner than he said that Zane walked in. "Loader's ready, is the package ready?"

They both looked back at him, he stopped mid-stride. "What?"

Ariel tossed the card at him.

Zane caught it, "What's this?"

"Hoped you would know, looks old."

"It's a secure message disk, encoded. Where'd you find it?"

"In the crate, where the power supply is supposed to be."

"Supposed to be, as in not there?" Zane asked, very surprised.

"No, it was empty except for that," J replied.

Zane studied it a moment.

J watched him intently. Then it hit him. "You were there! You were part of this."

Zane studied him, one eyebrow raised. "What are you talking about?"

"You were there the day my father found Acadia."

Calling Arcturus his father felt weird for J, he didn't

think he'd ever get used to it. Zane tightened his eyes, his mouth hung open slightly. J continued, "You were there. He gave you a task, you completed it."

Zane was still watching him; J could tell he was shocked in disbelief.

"What was the task?"

Zane straightened up. "It was encoding the coordinates and destroying all other copies, to include releasing a virus which would destroy all the code used to find Acadia."

Ariel looked at J, then Zane. "You were there?"

Zane nodded, then turned to J.

"But... how did you know all that?"

"I've had a few pretty weird dreams lately. Why didn't you tell Ariel about all this? Do you know where the power supply is?"

"I was just instructed to care for you as your father sent you to Earth. I don't think anyone knew about this plan, even I didn't."

"Will did."

"Who's Will?"

J was feeling uneasy. *Dillon was there and he had betrayed them. Was Zane a traitor too?*

Ariel began to sense the tension. "How do we read what's on that?" She nodded at the card.

Zane felt J staring at him. He stepped up to the controls and slipped the card into a slot then waved J over.

"If I knew your father well enough, I'm guessing it's

your blood that we'll need."

"Blood?" J asked.

"Yes, this was old technology even back then. It'll unlock the programming with the right blood sample. Don't worry it's just a prick."

J approached, Zane showed him where to place his hand, and a needle shot out, withdrawing a sample of blood. J didn't feel it until it was over, it stung. Zane tapped a few commands in the onboard computer, code streamed across the screen then an image of Arcturus appeared.

"Nice to see you, Zane, old friend."

Ariel and J looked over at him, Zane was staring at the image.

"J, it's amazing to see you all grown up. And who is this with you?"

J swallowed hard, "Ariel."

"Ah yes, the daughter of Natia and Dougald. I'm sorry for the loss of your parents, dear."

The three of them were silent. *Was this a transmission from somewhere on Atlantis? Was it coming from a bunker on Earth?*

"You may be wondering if this is a transmission. Sadly it is not. I'm a program created in Arcturus' image, with all of his traits, a copy of his consciousness. You undoubtedly know why you are here and that what you seek is not where it once was. I apologize for the move, but I uncovered information that led me to believe there were a few spies who had access to this location and could have interfered with the plan. Now that you are here, and have begun the preparation, I will provide you with the location of the powerplant. Before I give you the information, I must know that all three of you can be trusted, including you Zane."

Ariel looked at J, he nodded back. They turned their attention to Zane. J had always thought the best of people, but recently he'd been burned. He would let Ariel make the decision. He'd never doubted her intentions, not once during this entire crazy life-altering journey. "You've known him longer than me. Can we trust him?"

Ariel studied Zane a moment, he was like an uncle to her. "Yes, he can be trusted."

Zane grumbled, "Glad to see I pass muster, kid."

"I'm sorry, but I must hear it from J."

J looked down, took a deep breath and went with his gut. "Yes, we can all be trusted."

"Very well, I will release the coordinates."

A separate screen slid into view with the location of the object.

"It was hidden on an old satellite orbiting Earth. Included are docking procedures and speeds needed to safely load the powerplant without damage. I am compelled to give you fair warning, the cargo class cruiser you will be using can only make the trip there. You must utilize another way to depart after installing the new powerplant."

J nodded, acknowledging, then his attention fixated

back on the image.

"I have uploaded installation procedures for the transplant; you will only get one attempt."

They had heard that before and it wasn't making it any easier, no pressure. J was thinking about what was at stake, Earth. Not just his hometown, or his friends, but all of Earth. It was almost too much to fathom.

"I will now answer any questions you have and will be with you during the operation, provided you utilize this ship."

Wow, he had so many questions, he didn't know where to start. He knew the mission to save Earth was important and very pressing, but maybe he could get some answers.

"Where are you?" J's first question spewed out.

"I'm in the ship's data system, but I know you are not asking about me. You are asking where the real Arcturus is. I'm sorry, but I cannot answer that. I was created well before you were sent to Earth."

J shrunk down. "Is Cyrellia my mother?"

"Yes, the details are long and, due to the tight timeline required to accomplish the current mission, I will postpone that answer to a later date. Time is of the essence and you must perform the transplant quickly."

J struggled with his emotions, but his rational side was able to win the battle.

He looked at Ariel, "What are we waiting for then?"

Ariel smiled at him.

"Zane, is the Loader ready?"

"Yes, I'll have it secured by the time you break out

from the moon's gravity."

"Thank you, Arcturus, please help us in any way you can."

"It will be my pleasure."

The screen with the image of J's father dissolved and Ariel began the start sequence.

After maneuvering through the bay doors and the launch corridor, the KracKen was free of Atlantis and outside the grip of the moon. Ariel programmed the docking sequence as detailed, they would be there in less than fifteen minutes. She finally sat down at the controls, she'd been running or standing since they landed the two-seater.

Zane returned from the cargo bay and sat down next to J.

"What was Arcturus like?"

"He was a very good man, very smart. I had only known him for a year when I was transferred to his section, but he treated me well and we had the same belief."

"What was that?"

"That all humans should have a chance to live. Just because we had so much more in Atlantis, we shouldn't be playing God."

As they continued their discussion, J learned a few tidbits about his father. Most were generic things, Zane had really only spent time with him during his projects. J wondered what he was like in a social sense. *How could he have been in love with Cyrellia? She seemed the polar oppo-*

site of him. And how would you be able to keep a pregnancy secret?

"Approaching Satellite 2087, docking sequence initiated," the ship announced.

Ariel was busy monitoring everything, she didn't have to make any inputs, the ship knew what to do. J wanted to ask how everything was going, but figured the lack of ship announcements meant it was all fine.

"Incoming." the ship announced.

"Crap, figured it was only a matter of time."

"The Elefthería?" J asked.

"Yep, at their current speed they'll be here in ten minutes."

Zane stood up, "How long's the docking sequence?"

"Twenty."

"Anyway to speed it up?"

Ariel started rummaging through menus, reading as fast as she could. Mumbling under her breath, "No, no.... no, umm, no."

J could tell she wasn't getting anywhere.

"How big is the satellite thing?"

Ariel slowly shook her head, biting her bottom lip, "About the size of a large house, why?"

J looked toward the cargo area, then back at Ariel, "Would it fit in there?" he pointed to the cargo hold.

Ariel was confused, "Yes, of course it will. That's why we chose this ship."

J started playing with his hands, trying to figure out how to best explain his question. He snapped his fingers, as his face lit up. "Could we eat it like a big fish eats a little fish?"

Ariel realized what he was getting at, the plan had been to dock, then grab the power plant with the Loader, then undock leaving the satellite in space. J's idea, on the other hand, was to catch the whole satellite in the cargo bay.

"That just might work J!" Ariel exclaimed. "Zane, can you unload the device from the satellite in the hangar?"

"Sure, wasn't that the plan?"

"But if the whole satellite is in the bay?"

Zane caught on. "Yep, you know you'll only get one shot at this."

"That's all I'll need," she said with shear confidence.

Ariel pushed a few buttons, switching the ship to manual mode.

"Incoming craft engagement in five minutes," the ship bellowed.

She adjusted the ship's speed to overtake the orbiting satellite and moved into position. A screen popped up with video of the incoming craft. It looked so close, J didn't know if they would have time.

"Three minutes until engagement."

Ariel dropped in front of the satellite's path. With a few taps, J heard the bridge lock down, then the pressure was released from the cargo bay.

"Cargo bay doors opening," the ship stated.

Another screen popped up next to the one showing

the view out the cargo bay. The satellite was trailing them, and just behind it was the Eleftería, closing quickly. Ariel reduced speed, watching the screens and data flowing in. The satellite entered the cargo bay, she closed the cargo doors, then returned pressure and gravity to the KracKen.

The whole ship shook as the large piece of space debris came to rest on the steel grating.

"Engagement, Engagement." A siren pulsed, red flashed on the screen.

Ariel tapped a few more menus. "Buckle up boys."

A set of physical controls emerged from the panel in front of her, she grasped them, ready for combat.

"This thing have any weapons?" J asked.

"No," Ariel responded as she adjusted the controls.

J watched the screen as they spun down toward Earth. The screen showed incoming blasts from the trailing ship, the hull rattled as they hit.

"Shields?

Zane looked over at J. "It's a cargo ship. No weapons, no shields. Better start praying."

J held onto his seat as more shots hit the hull. Ariel was spinning, jinking and doing whatever she could to stay out of the line of fire, but the ship was far from nimble and it proved difficult, if not impossible.

"Hull breach. Hull breach. Hull breach," the ship shouted.

Ariel tapped a button and the ship went mute.

"How far out are we?" J asked.

"Another ten minutes."

"Ten minutes?! I don't think we're going to last another five."

"What do you suggest we do? Say please?"

"*Can* we talk to them?"

Ariel twisted around and glared at him, studying his face.

"Well...yes, they've been calling for the past twenty minutes. Why?"

J had an idea to delay their inevitable boarding.

"Trust me, let me talk to them."

"What?!" Ariel retorted.

"I'm going to say, please," J quipped.

"You're joking right?"

"No, just trust me."

Ariel realized their current strategy wasn't working, they had nothing to lose.

"Okay, I'll patch you through."

Ariel toggled through menus and pulled up another screen. A video appeared with Jolt's smug face.

"Give up?" he stated first thing, as if there was no other choice.

"Jolt," J began. "Hold your fire, the powerplant has become unstable. If we take any more damage it could ignite"

Ariel caught on. "Jolt, if the powerplant ignites, its blast radius will destroy you as well."

Jolts eyes hardened. "So, I suppose you just want me to let you go on your way?"

J fought the urge to say "yes". He realized that wouldn't go over so well so instead he replied, "No, but we do need you to hold your fire."

"Then what?"

"You escort us down to Earth."

"How about we just dock you, or better yet, you return to Atlantis and you give over the power supply."

Ariel spoke up. "Our fuel cells are nearly depleted and our cargo bay has been breached thanks to you, so our only option is Earth."

Jolt studied her for a moment. "Very well. Sector 19, northwest corner, inside the wall."

Ariel nodded then turned off the comm-link.

"Guess you bought us some time. What's your plan?"

"That's all I had. Figured you guys were better with the shooting and fighting stuff."

Ariel sat back in her seat. J could tell she was in deep thought.

Zane began to scratch his chin. "Sector 19, that's in Southeast Asia isn't it?"

Ariel looked over to Zane. "Petty sure, let me check." She scrolled through a few menus then pulled up a map of the Earth. "Yep."

She zoomed in to the northwest corner.

"Why would he want us there?" she said under her breath.

"What's that?" J was pointing to a small structure maybe 100 yards from the landing location.

"Looks like just a building."

"Can you make the picture bigger?" J walked closer to the screen.

Ariel spun a few imaginary dials and the building increased in size.

"Is that..." Ariel said out loud.

"Sure is," Zane replied emphatically, a bit disturbed.

"What?" J didn't see anything except the small building.

Zane walked over to him, straightened his arm over his shoulder and pointed, "See those?"

J's eyes followed the big arm of Zane to the screen, zeroing in. The building appeared to be a small hut with clay tiles lining the roof. None of that seemed out of the ordinary, but as he looked closer, he noticed a small round metallic object protruding from a part of the roof line. The object sparked every 30 seconds or so, J had no idea what it was.

"What am I looking at?"

Zane dropped his arm. "It's an EMP cannon. Seems like we aren't the only ones with a plan."

"EMP?"

"Electromagnetic pulse. Each sector has a couple. It'll shut down all our systems, figure they don't want us trying to run. I'm sure they've already gained access to it and will fire it if we try anything funny."

"How long will it shut us down for?"

Zane was rubbing his chin again. "Maybe twenty minutes. What do you say, Ariel?"

"Yeah, about that. Could completely short circuit the

whole ship, like last time," Ariel responded automatically. She had other things on her mind.

"What are you thinking, Ariel?"

She didn't respond initially, just stared at the screen.

"Ariel?"

She looked over at him almost surprised.

"What's on your mind?"

"What are they trying to accomplish?" she answered.

"What do you mean?" asked Zane.

"Well, do they want to use the power supply or destroy it?"

"I think they would have backed off and shot us down had they wanted it destroyed."

"That's what I figure too, but why try and take it from us now? Why not let us install it, then attempt the coup if that's their ultimate goal?"

Zane just shook his head without an answer.

"So what are we going to do?" J asked.

Ariel began rummaging through more menus, she pulled up a page. "We run."

She stood there, regarding J. Behind her, the title of the page read, "Escape pods online".

CHAPTER TWENTY SEVEN

J closed his eyes. The last two times he had attempted this were not pleasant experiences. He felt the table slide, he opened his eyes. This time was going to be different he told himself, and it already was different. He could see out. He looked up, Ariel kissed her fingers then placed them on the glass above him. He gave a half-hearted smile back, it was all his nerves would allow. She walked back to the bridge.

"You still with us in there?"

It was Ariel checking up on him.

"Yep," was all he managed to get out.

What was he doing in an escape pod again? His mind flashed back to the sensation of suffocation, but Ariel and Zane had assured him that this model was different. And now, being in it, he could see it was very different. The simple fact was, it was more comfortable. It was slightly larger, the table contoured to his body, and the whole front face was a large window. It almost seemed nonexistent, claustrophobia wasn't attacking him today.

"We have about two minutes before we jettison you."

Jettison, like the garbage? He really didn't like the sound of that, but he had agreed to it. Partially because... completely because, Ariel had asked him to do it.

He lifted his right hand to his chest and felt his left breast pocket. It was still there, the chip that could save them.

"We're on final approach, J. You know what to do.

Godspeed."

J hoped that wouldn't be the last time he heard her
voice. Pressure surged through him down to his legs,
the lights above him moved faster and faster. He briefly
closed his eyes and said a short prayer. When he opened
them back up, he stared into a beautiful blue sky, not a
cloud in it. He felt strange though; there was no sensation of movement, no visual cues. It was as if he was just
floating in the sky.

He placed his hands on his hips. Good they were still
there, the pistols Ariel had given him. She had called
them Desert Eagles, taught him how to load them. He
felt his thighs, the spare magazines were still there. He
hoped he wouldn't have to use them, but knew it was all
but inevitable. J slid his left arm up to his right shoulder,
the knife was still there. He double-checked everything.
He had a habit of being paranoid ever since that time in
little league when he forgot his mitt at home. The peaceful floating was interrupted by rumbling, shaking and
the impact of the ground. Dirt flew all over the glass, he
squinted in anticipation of the glass shattering. He even
raised his arms up in defense. The noise and movement
finally stopped, the last bit of dirt and water splashed on
the pod and slid off. The glass moved away from him and
the pod began to fill with water. J released the restraints
and stood up, he was quick enough to only get his feet
wet. He stood for a moment, looking out over the rice
paddy he had come to rest in. Two workers with large
straw hats stared at him. They dropped their baskets and

ran away, speaking fast in a language he'd never heard before. He raised his left arm, the Datacle came to life. He scrolled through a few screens.

"Crap," he said to himself.

He still had trouble with the thing, it didn't come naturally to him. Finally, the map came up. His position displayed as a red arrow, then a trail of blue dots dropped one after another showing his path to the objective. He gazed out over the fields.

"Better stay on these berms and hurry," he said to himself.

He knew he didn't have much time and it looked like he had been dropped further than anticipated. He began to jog. While he wasn't enjoying the run, he was glad Zane hadn't talked him into the scout rifle, it would have been a bear running in the mushy rice paddies. After departing from his entry vehicle and running for a few minutes, he could see his objective. His pace quickened, the building grew closer. He saw the KracKen landing in the distance, past the hut, followed closely by the Elefthería. He hoped that the diversion had worked or else his attempt at accessing the building would be short-lived.

J stopped at the door. He drew out one of the two pistols and clicked off the safety. Ariel had made it a point to remember the safety, so much so that he would never forget it. He gently opened the door then stood back. The room was about two feet by two feet, but from the outside, he could tell that it was much larger than that. No doors, dread zipped through his body. He stepped in, his eyes searching. He frantically ran his hands all over the walls. Zane and Ariel had not mentioned this, and he knew they were running out of time. No luck, no sign of a door panel, no grooves like Will's hidden door, nothing. Out of frustration, he kicked the wall then fell down in pain. He grabbed his foot.

"Bless it!"

He typically controlled his anger, but his emotions were all over the place lately. Then he remembered. Ariel had done it multiple times and he hadn't paid much attention to it. He opened his Datacle and scanned through menus, then stopped. The screen read, "scan". J pressed the final execute button and watched as it went through a series of sounds and graphics showing the layout of the room, then suddenly the sound of stone sliding on stone grated in J's ears. To his right, a control panel opened. He turned and stared down at it. The words read, "enter code". He panicked then checked the Datacle, sure enough there was an eight digit code on it. He quickly punched it in. A door swung open behind him, he was in.

A large cannon-like device stood before him. It was smaller than he had envisioned, but that didn't matter. If it did what it was supposed to do all would be fine. He hoped he wasn't too late. In his mind, they would have boarded the KracKen by now. He had to act fast. He approached the control panel and snagged the chip from his pocket, placing it into the slot.

"Welcome to the Freeze Ray, remote use override."

Someone must have had a sense of humor when they programmed it. J tried to ignore it and began his task. He was able to find the correct menus as Ariel had described them and switched it to voice commands.

"Say command," the machine instructed.

"Scan for targets."

He watched on the large display screen as it pulled up overhead images. He could see both the KracKen and the Eleftería.

"Choose target."

"Target the northern ship."

J had expected that to be the Eleftería, but he was turned around. The weapon displayed cross hairs on the KracKen.

"No, No," J protested.

"Confirm target."

"No."

He looked around, waiving his hands, frantically thinking of what to say.

"Target the other ship."

"Switching targets," the system boomed back.

The cross hairs appeared on the Eleftería.

"Confirm target."

"Target confirmed," J said emphatically.

"Waiting for command," the cannon responded.

"Fire."

J waited, sinking back into himself, expecting a loud

burst, but instead there was a soft hum.

He watched the screen, nothing noticeable occurred. *Had it malfunctioned?* He continued staring at the screen, everything looked as it was.

"Target neutralized," the computer bellowed.

J didn't know if he should cheer or what, the whole thing seemed anticlimactic. At that moment, he saw two people exit the Eleftería and rapidly approach the KracKen. J turned and headed out the door, he had to get there fast. Outside, he ran toward the ships along the central berm, rice paddies on both sides of him. As he approached the Eleftería, he heard shouting coming from near the KracKen. J looked over, but he couldn't see anyone there. *Two people had left the Eleftería. That meant there was one still in there, the question was, who?*

J stopped just outside the ship and rested his back against one of the four large metal landing gear struts. He was breathing heavily, though not as heavily as he might have been; all that running on the moon had probably helped his stamina. He slowed his breath down and gained his composure. His whole body trembled slightly with anticipation, there was going to be a fight. He stayed close to the body of the craft and scanned around as he approached the cargo bay. He drew one the Desert Eagles, it felt comfortable in his large hands. Scanning back and forth holding the weapon with two hands he climbed in. The bay was empty. He checked at the ceiling then spun around to look out the bay door, still nothing. *Must be on the bridge.*

He cautiously made his way to the open bridge door, the ship was silent, nothing but the sound of a slight breeze coming from outside. He slowly stepped in. His face was met with a boot having no time to duck. His head snapped to the side, body twisting, he fell down onto his chest. He tried to gain his feet but felt a fist to the kidney, he winced in pain. He spun around firing the pistol at nothing. His aim was thrown off as his assailant chopped his arm away, the pistol went flying out of his hand. He looked up and his vision met with a fist, his head snapped back. He tasted blood in his mouth and it felt like his nose was broken.

Sonya was now straddling him one hand on his chest the other cocked back ready to fire. J raised his empty hands in submission, he turned his head and spit out some of the pooling blood.

"That was pretty tricky," Sonya started. "Didn't realize you could do that."

Ariel had secretly hacked the Eleftería after she had suspected Jolt. She was able to trick the cameras and sensors to mask J's escape pod departure, but it would only work for a small amount of time before Jolt's programs would have recognized it.

"What other tricks do you guys have planned?"

She took the other Desert Eagle from his holster and placed in on his chest. J didn't say a word, he just glared at her as he clenched his jaw. She raised herself up, now standing above him and took a step back.

"Up on your feet, lover boy, and put your hands on

your head."

He rolled onto his side, moving his face around. It hurt like the dickens.

"Now let's get you somewhere you're not going to cause any more trouble."

Her tone was that of a seasoned headmistress determining the punishment.

"Turn around. Let's take you to the cargo bay."

J did as commanded, he felt her nudge him in the back.

"Start walking."

He began to walk, just off to the side he noticed his pistol. *If only he could get a hold of it.* He ran through a few scenarios in his head, he had one shot. He fell down onto his hands and knees coughing up blood, he spat a couple times trying to clear his mouth.

"Okay, enough of that, back on your feet, kid," Sonya commanded.

J stayed on the ground, he raised his hand to feel his nose.

"I think you broke my nose."

Sonya approached placing the barrel in his back.

"Get up. I don't care about your nose."

J hesitated a second then spun as fast as he could, sliding a blade into Sonya's right shoulder. Her arm went limp, she screamed in pain and the pistol fell lifeless to the ground. J released his grip on the knife, scrambling for the downed pistol. Sonya stumbled back a few steps then lunged for the Eagle as well. J was quicker and secured it. Sonya gave him a left hook to the head, he handled this one better. He'd have to be dead before he lost his weapon again. He sent an elbow back at her, clipping the knife; it twisted, backing her off. J tumbled away, grasping for the other pistol. As he turned, Sonya was midair, the knife in her left hand. She had pulled it from her body, blood was streaming down her uniform. J fired from the seated position, left, right, left, right, a couple at the same time. Eleven rounds in all, though he wasn't counting. Sonya landed on him, lifeless, the knife hand empty and limp. J sat there, his arms still extended holding the Desert Eagles, trembling, his breath short and quick.

Ariel! His mind snapped to Ariel motivating him to get up. He pushed Sonya's limp body off of him. Trying to gain his composure, he holstered one of the pistols. J exited the Eleftería running, he needed to get to Ariel and fast, he didn't know what to expect. As he neared the ship, he saw Gatlin and Jolt pacing back and forth. J slowed to a stop and ducked down, hoping not to be spotted. It was too late, they must have heard the shots. He saw Jolt point at him and mouth something, Gatlin headed toward him. J aimed the pistol, he raised himself to one knee noticing Gatlin was unarmed. The EMP blast must have taken out all their weapons. He held still, Gatlin would soon be in range. *How close was too close?*

J was about to fire when Gatlin disappeared into the flooded rice paddy. He held the pistol fixated on his last position. He waited, nothing. He looked over at

Jolt, but he was gone, as well. J freaked out inside, but held his ground. He needed to find Gatlin. He heard a buzzing sound, then the KracKen's cargo bay door hissed as the pistons moved, lowering the ramp. J straightened up to get a better look then walked forward. For a brief moment, he forgot about Gatlin. He stopped, remembering the enemy. He began again, at a crawl with his weapon outstretched. The water of the rice paddy rippled, he must be in there. He stopped at the edge, scanning the surface and below, nothing. His Datacle vibrated, he looked at it. The name Ariel appeared and below it read "incoming transmission."

He released one of his hands from the pistol to accept the call. He felt something grab his foot, his body was yanked under the water. Unprepared, he swallowed some of the tepid muck and struggled to free himself but couldn't. He kicked then randomly aimed the pistol, shooting frantically toward his feet, the hand released. J swam to the surface breathing in deeply and pulling himself ashore. His lower body still in the paddy, he coughed trying to clear his lungs. Water splashed on his back as he heard something behind him. He rolled over and Gatlin sprang forward, pinning J's pistol to the ground with one hand, the other formed a fist.

J moved his head to the side, dodging the attack. He reached for his other pistol, but it was on the opposite side and impossible to grab. Another fist came at him, this one at his chest, there was nowhere for him to go, his ribs cracked, he winced in pain. He looked up, another fist was about to come crashing down, but a blast hit Gatlin's chest, then another. J turned his head to the ship. Ariel lay prone inside the cargo hold with a sniper rifle, her first two rounds meeting their mark. Gatlin fell into the paddy, sinking to the murky bottom. J laid his head back down, staring at the sky, his body flushed with pain.

"J? J!"

He heard a melodious voice calling his name.

"J," Ariel breathed a sigh of relief upon finding him still alive. She slung the rifle onto her back and knelt down. "Up you go," she said, lifting him to his feet.

He struggled, his chest was throbbing and he coughed up more blood.

"You're a mess. Why'd you do that to yourself?" Ariel cajoled.

J returned her smile the best he could, but his face was swollen and it faded back into the tension of pain. She supported him as he leaned on her shoulder and hobbled through the rice paddies.

"Where's Jolt?" he asked.

"Not sure, he disappeared. Sonya?"

J hesitated, his mind went back to her limp body laying on him. He'd never killed someone before.

"Gone," was all he could manage.

Ariel sensed his distress and didn't push any further.

"We'll get you fixed up once we're on board."

They entered the ship. Zane was standing guard with a large auto rifle, he looked at home with his best friend by his side.

"Close it up Zane," Ariel said as the two hobbled past him.

"You bet, any luck with Jolt?" He hit the switch and the door began to close.

"No, Gatlin's taken care of."

"Sonya?"

She turned to J who nodded, then looked down at the ground.

"Yep."

Ariel set J down in a seat.

"I'll get the med kit."

She walked away, he leaned back and closed his eyes. He was glad to be back with her.

"Good job, kid."

J nodded, eyes still closed. It lifted his spirits a bit, but didn't help with the pain. Ariel showed up with the med kit.

"You look like you went nine rounds with Mike Tyson."

He opened his eyes, "Who?"

She laughed, it never got old. One day, she would have to get him up to speed on human history, especially the 20th century, which was her favorite era. But then again, it might not be as much fun.

"Ship still working?"

She stared at him a moment, seeming to translate his question. His mouth was swollen and his speech was impaired.

"Yep, you did good. Took you a bit. I was worried, but when I saw the Eleftería go offline, I knew our plan was going to work."

She scanned him with the medical wand, the pain began to subside and the metallic taste of blood gradually lifted.

"Let's get this baby to the center of the Earth."

J's mind flashed to the Jules Vern novel. No dinosaurs or underground lakes where they were going. Ariel headed to the bridge, he was right behind her. He felt the ship shake slightly as it lifted off the ground. When they entered the bridge, Zane was at the controls. He had set the course. Next stop, the central hub.

CHAPTER TWENTY EIGHT

The Loader rumbled to life. J asked Zane if he could give it a go and Zane reluctantly agreed since they had some time and no enemy hot on their tail. Zane talked him through the controls, he was tempted to use the auto-load feature, but where was the fun in that? J worked the controls, he was a bit jerky at first, but soon smoothed out his movements succinctly.

"Drive the Loader over there."

Zane was pointing in front of the satellite. As big as the Loader was, it was still smaller than the large object in the center of the cargo bay. J repositioned, approaching the metal and glass structure, the solar panels had seen better days. He came to a stop and stood up to let Zane take over.

"Nope, it's all you, kid."

J felt unsure and hesitantly responded, "No, I think you should do it."

"Nonsense. You picked it up so quick, you got this."

Zane was smiling at him, he seemed sincere.

J sat down. "What now?"

"Let me see if I can get the satellite to open up."

Zane walked over and climbed up to the top. It had to have been six stories tall with ladders positioned all around going in every possible direction. If J didn't feel the artificial gravity, he wouldn't have known which way was up. Zane disappeared into a hatch, he waited there to see what would happen. He leaned back in his chair and looked around, what an incredible view. Here he was, in the middle of space, inside a ship nearly the size of a small town, working to transplant a new heart for Earth. It hit him all at once, he took a deep breath then exhaled. Zane sprang into view.

"Well, it's in there, but it's not going to be easy getting it out."

His words were slow and stretched at he climbed down to meet J.

"Gonna take three of us. How about you go get Ariel? I'll figure out the best way to do this."

J didn't argue, he wanted to see Ariel. He'd only seen her briefly after they took off, she was busy managing the ship, and Zane had pulled him away to help with the extraction. He made his way up to the command center. Unlike the other ships he'd been in, this one had an elevator and multiple rooms including sleeping quarters, a dining hall, and workout room. It was designed for extensive time in space to collect old space junk to be recycled into the Exodus. He reached the command room; Ariel was standing analyzing a structural layout of the heart of the Earth. He walked up next to her and remained silent for a second. Before he could speak a word, he felt her hand slip into his, he looked over at her.

"Can you believe this was your father's plan and we're only a few hours away from saving millions of lives?"

J looked back at the screen. A single central hub pulsed as the panels and skeletal structure slowly spun.

"You get it out yet?" Ariel asked suddenly.

"No, well it's there, but it's complicated."

"Complicated?"

"Zane says we need your help."

~~She turned to the screen and tapped a few buttons,~~ the word "autopilot" appeared in the bottom corner.

"Well, let's see what we need to do. You're looking better, by the way." She tugged on his hand playfully and they walked, arms swinging between them, toward the bay.

Zane was nowhere to be seen when they arrived.

"Zane?" Ariel called.

"Maybe he went to the bathroom?" J said.

Ariel pulled up her Datacle, and after a few taps, Zane appeared as a 3D image.

"Where are you?"

"Look up!"

J and Ariel looked straight up at a large glass bubble protruding from the ceiling, in the center a claw-like device hung from hundreds of cables.

"Here's what we're going to do," Zane started.

They listened to his instructions. Ariel would climb into the satellite and, once Zane had it in the air hanging by the claw, she would open the cargo doors. J would be waiting to use the large arms of the Loader to grab it and pull it free. Each of them got into position. Zane lifted the large metal remnant and Ariel took her position inside. J drove the Loader to the side where the cargo doors would open. Ariel held her breath and hit the switch, the doors creaked open. J sat there waiting, he could see the new heart coming into view. The doors stopped half way, Ariel tried the switch again, no dice.

She climbed down to investigate. It looked like the doors had been damaged by a meteor or space debris colliding with it.

"J, you're going to have to use the Loader to open the doors the rest of the way."

J nodded, then realized she couldn't see him. "Got it," he said.

He positioned his machine and began to pry the doors open, the metal creaked and screeched, it was working. J stopped, there appeared to be enough room to reach in, but the arms of the Loader were too short.

"Release the straps," Zane instructed Ariel. "Then I'll tip it for J to catch."

"I don't know about that," J replied.

"It'll be just like playing catch."

J knew it wasn't going to be anything like catch, not the way he would describe it anyway. He had no other ideas, so it would have to do.

"Okay."

Ariel hit the switch, three of the four straps released and the powerplant began to slide. J braced himself then realized that would do no good. He gripped the controls harder in an attempt to be better prepared. The heart stopped, it was caught. The final strap had never released and it was stopping the whole thing from falling the final ten feet. Ariel tried the switch again then, realizing it wasn't working, slipped down the ladder from the bay's control section to the final strap. She found the manual release and prepared to activate, but before she could, the strap snapped throwing her off balance. She tumbled down with the power supply unable to grab onto anything, the floor was smooth and featureless.

J stood up in the control seat, his eyes wide, mouth speechless, the package continued to plummet toward him. Ariel had tumbled in front of the falling power supply. He continued to stand, desperately trying to see her, but he lost sight, the package was on top of her. He regained his composure and manipulated the controls, the powerplant slammed into the Loader. J clamped it tight. As it pushed the Loader back, sparks flew, a sound like a car crash echoed throughout the ship, then it went silent.

He wasted no time hopping out of the Loader and ran to find Ariel. As his feet hit the ground, he saw her lying in a heap under the Loader, not moving. He sprinted.

"Please be okay," he implored more than once as he ran.

Coming to a stop on his knees next to her, he picked up her limp body. He didn't know what to do, he had no medical training. He looked her over, there was no blood. *Was she alright? Why wasn't she moving?* He pulled her in tight and hugged her, he had no other ideas.

"Chose the machine over me," he heard her weakly say. He loosened his grasp, Ariel's beautiful icy blue eyes gazed back at him, slightly dazed.

"No, I..."

She smiled at him then grabbed her head.

"I feel like I was out all night and had one too many."

J didn't know what to say, he just stared. She was alright and that's all that mattered.

"Okay, enough of that. We need to get this thing to Earth. I'll be on the bridge taking a bunch of meds. You and Zane get this baby ready for the procedure."

He helped her to her feet and other than initially being a bit wobbly, she seemed no worse for wear. He pulled her in for an embrace, not quite ready to let go. Closing his eyes, he breathed in her unique smell of ozone and sunflowers. *One of these days he'd figure that combination out.* Grateful that she was alive and unable to explain his feelings, he kissed her then quickly released her and turned to go to Zane.

"Well, that was..." Ariel muttered to herself as she stumbled to the bridge.

J and Zane repositioned the powerplant, moving it into place for the swap, then headed to the bridge to check on Ariel and wait for the arrival at the hub.

"That was exciting," Zane said in a peppy tone as the two of them walked onto the bridge.

"How're you feeling?"

Ariel turned around, she still looked a little out of it.

"Like I fell from a satellite and knocked my head, I'll be fine. You two get everything prepped?"

Zane plopped down in one of the leather seats and kicked his legs up onto a control panel.

"Yep, it's in between innings, show's all yours for now."

J appreciated the comment, finally something he could understand. He was ready for a break and sat down across from Zane, who had promptly fallen asleep. He studied Ariel, he was worried about her.

"You sure you're alright?"

She just waved him off, then went back to work. He leaned back and closed his eyes.

"How long until we're there?"

"About twenty minutes," she responded.

He had mixed feeling about following Zane's lead. A nap sounded mighty fine, but he also wanted to get this thing over with. He dozed off for a second. Snapping his head back upright, he stood up and thought it best to keep moving. He moved to a control panel near Ariel and watched as the Earth fell away in the screen, the plates drifted away above.

"Looks so peaceful from in here," J said. "Hard to believe all of the people up there are essentially slaves."

"Were."

J looked at Ariel, not following. She turned to him and grabbed his hand.

"Were slaves. That's about to change."

As they slipped between the plates into the underlying clouds, all visuals disappeared, though the occasional metal rod would flash into view as the ship's outer lights pulsed. The KracKen slowed down.

"Initiating docking sequence," it announced.

J could see the central hub. Compared to what he'd seen since flying to Atlantis, it seemed small, but he didn't know if that was because of the clouds. He never got a good glimpse of it in its entirety. Still, it didn't contain a hangar bay like everywhere else. The KracKen hovered in, attaching an umbilical cord to transfer the precious cargo. The two of them watched the ship systematically and precisely finalize the whole procedure, the words "docked" read across the screen.

"Let's do what we came for." Ariel turned to leave the bridge.

J woke up Zane and in no time he was in the Loader waiting. J was standing with Ariel as she commanded the cargo bay doors to open. They opened slowly at first, then gained speed. Moving at a brisk pace, the power-plant, the heart of the Earth, the motherboard of the entire eco system controlling everything from rotation, to weather, to gravity, began its trek to its new home. Ariel wasn't far behind, followed closely by J. Zane and the Loader took up the rear, he carefully entered the room. It was like being inside a ball about the size of a football stadium, wires went everywhere, looping along the walls, draped from one side to the other. The lines ran through the floor in what looked like a tangled mess of spaghetti. This surprised J, everything else he'd seen from his new world was neat, tidy, precise.

"Wow. This place is old," Ariel spouted.

J could tell she'd had the same surprise as he had. They continued to walk further into the room and up a ramp to another. Ariel found the controls and opened the doors. There it was, the old powerplant. It sat there

humming, supplying the lifeblood to run the essential
systems. It was worn and rundown, like everything in
there, its life had not been kind. Ariel waved Zane in
with the Loader, it was going to be a tight fit, but it
would work. She reached into her jacket pocket and
exposed the data card. J smiled and nodded. They had
all the keys, the power plant, the data card, and him.
They walked up to the panel, physical buttons protruded
from a large table-like structure.

"I know I've said this before, but this thing is a relic."

J gave a small laugh then helped her search for a slot
for the card. He found a button that was labeled "data
disk". He pushed it and a plate slid out with a slot the
size of the data card. Ariel placed the data card then
attempted to push it in. It wouldn't budge. J examined
it then pushed the data disk button again, the card slid
away. He looked at her, grinning.

"Not a word," she replied quickly.

It was back to work. Ariel pulled up the list on her
Datacle, they had to push a series of buttons, and the two
began searching. There seemed to be over one-hundred
buttons, all labeled with symbols, English and other
languages even Ariel didn't recognize. She pressed the
final button, a video screen rose from the dash and sprung
to life. It was Arcturus.

"J, you are the only one who can begin and finish this
procedure. Once you begin, you will have two minutes
to finish. During those two minutes, all systems will be
offline. You will have to utilize what you brought to swap

out the power supplies. Your DNA will begin and end the procedure utilizing this pad."

A plate slid from the table with an indent of a human hand.

"Ensure you understand the procedure before beginning. Good luck, my son."

The video faded out.

"Two minutes. Can we hook up all those lines in two minutes?" he asked.

They had both looked over the procedures with Will. There were 12 large cords, it seemed pretty straightforward.

Ariel nodded, "Yep, we got this. Ready?"

J nodded back, it was now or never. He placed his hand on the plate, the screen spoke.

"DNA confirmed. Initiating replacement sequence, system shutting down."

Zane had already set down the new power supply and was in position to grab the old one. The lights went out. Zane switched on the Loader's lights, multiple beams shot out around the machine. J and Ariel began pulling the old cables as described, the first seven came loose, then something started to happen. J felt light on his feet. He pulled two more while Ariel managed to pull the final three. Zane picked up the old powerplant, the Loader nearly flipped over, he had given it too much input. He set it aside then grabbed the new one. No countdown, power was completely out. Ariel started a timer on her Datacle, hopefully she was close, setting it for one minute.

Zane had a little trouble getting the Loader in and struggled to get the unit in position. J continued to feel lighter, he looked at Ariel and together they spoke.

"Gravity."

They were losing gravity! Zane placed the power-plant down hard, locking it into place. He grabbed onto the side of the Loader and headed to help. Ariel and J were now floating a few feet above the ground, the gravity beginning to fade faster and faster. She looked down, 30 seconds. Holding onto the unit, the two scrambled to place the wires.

"J, you need to turn it back on. We'll finish this!"

Zane had made it to the cables and shoved J toward the exposed hand plate. He nearly missed as he floated over, but managed to grab it. He looked back. Ariel had two left, Zane was working on one more. She looked down at her wrist, 5 seconds! She placed one more cable then began the last one. The timer went off, Zane quickly locked his last one into position, Ariel did the same.

"Now!" they both yelled.

J placed his hand on the plate. He expected something amazing, but nothing happened. He looked over at the other two, both floating, holding onto the cables. J tried again, nothing. *Had they failed? Had it been over two minutes?* Without an accurate timer he didn't know. Out of frustration he punched the console, lights flickered, the screen raised again, his father standing there.

"Congratulations. I'm proud of you, son. The Earth

is now yours, treat her well."

The image faded, he felt gravity beginning to be restored. He placed his feet on the ground and grinned from ear to ear. Ariel tackled him, her signature move. He stumbled back, but kept his feet this time.

"We did it!" she exclaimed with the most ecstatic expression on her face J had ever seen.

She leaned in and they kissed.

"You'll have time for that later lovebirds, need to get going."

Zane was standing behind them.

"What do you mean? We just saved the Earth. Can't we have a minute to celebrate?" Ariel glowered.

Zane pointed at the old power supply, "That's a nuclear reactor. One that is about to ignite. Why do you think we had to replace it? We need to get rid of it."

Ariel and J released each other. J didn't quite understand about the nuclear part, but the word "ignite" stood up the hairs on his neck. Ariel ran to the KracKen.

"You need help?" J asked Zane.

"No, you help her. I'll get this on the ship."

J took off after Ariel and found her on the bridge, working overtime to get all of the systems up and running.

"What can I help you with?"

"Get back down to the cargo doors and shut them as soon as Zane gets on board with that thing."

He made a beeline to the doors, Zane was entering with the powerplant as he arrived. He punched the door switch, they closed, then secured the Loader and power-plant.

"What are we going to do with it?" J asked.

"I assume we drop it off in space somewhere. Thought you guys had a plan," Zane replied, staring at the powerplant.

"Nobody told us we were picking up a bomb!"

They turned to head to the bridge.

"So what are we doing with it?" Ariel asked as they entered.

"I was going to ask you that."

"You guys didn't know you were swapping out a nuclear reactor?"

"No," they said in unison.

"How come you didn't tell us?" Ariel shouted at Zane.

"I assumed you had a plan!"

J butted in, "Enough! Shouting at each other isn't going to get rid of the bomb. Does anyone have any ideas?"

Ariel focused her attention on flying the ship. She set a course for Earth orbit, they would need to make a decision, but it would be best to start there. As the ship ascended, they began to throw ideas at one another. Zane said to set a course for a distant star, then use the remaining escape pods to evacuate to Earth. Ariel wanted to do the reverse of the satellite pickup and toss it out into orbit. Both ideas had their flaws.

"What about attaching it to the other ship?"

Zane and Ariel looked at him for a moment.

"What other ship?" they both said.

"The one in the cargo hold."

Ariel and Zane's jaws opened slightly, their arms raised into the air very slowly. J didn't understand. *Were they making fun of him?*

"'I'm serious guys, there's another ship in the cargo bay."

J pointed at the cargo bay turning to follow his arm. "It's mine."

Jolt stood there holding a blaster and behind him stood five replicants holding various weapons.

"Now this ship's mine, too."

The door shut behind them. They were in the dining hall, not as dinner guests, but as prisoners. Two replicants stood guard at the door, motionless. J studied them. Ariel was pacing around a table, one hand up to the lip she was chewing, the other under her elbow. It was her thinking pose. What she was thinking, J hadn't a clue, but knowing her, she had something brewing. Zane sat in a chair, legs and arms crossed, with a thousand-yard stare, his eyes half closed. J seemed to be the only one searching the room for any means of escape. The main door was covered by the aforementioned replicants. There was a door leading to a galley, but the only thing in there was a freezer. The final door led to a hall and onto the bridge, it was locked.

"Any ideas?"

He threw the question out to his cellmates, neither of them replied. He continued to scan for anything, a vent, possible distraction, nothing came to mind. The doors to the bridge hissed open, Jolt stepped into the room followed closely by his guards. His demeanor had changed, he seemed more sure of himself.

"First, I'd like to say thank you for saving my world."

His speech was much slower and more elegant than J remembered it, as well.

Ariel dropped her hand. "Your world?"

"Yes, well TK is gone, the Earth isn't going to

destruct, and it needs a ruler."

He walked around the perimeter of the room with a smug look on his face as he approached Ariel. "Would you like to join me? I could use someone with your particular skills."

Ariel gave him no answer, just glowered at him.

He turned to Zane. "You? You're handy with a gun."

He too didn't partake in the conversation.

He walked over to J and adjusted his bottom lip as he tilted his head back slightly, analyzing him. "And how about you? The savior. Arcturus' son. You care to join me? You could leave all the pain and suffering of Earth behind."

J followed their lead and bit his tongue.

"Nobody's talkative today, I see."

He waved to one of the replicants behind him, then took a step back. J was suddenly restrained from behind, his arms contorted backwards. He let out a groan, it felt as if his shoulders were about to pop out of socket. The replicant kicked the back of his knees, J went down, his upper body being held up by his arms.

"Why? What do you want?" J asked through groans of pain.

"Now the son speaks."

He motioned to the replicant, more pressure was put on J's arms. He tried to wiggle free, but the pain became worse.

"You see, one of you still has something I need, and I know which one. But I don't think you'll give it to me freely, so we're going to play a game."

He walked around J, looked at Zane then Ariel, both stood silent, watching the torture.

"Every time I ask for what I want, little J here will enjoy the pleasure of more pain. First let's see..."

He paused and looked directly at Ariel.

"Pick him up."

He waved his hand upward, the replicant lifted J up by his hands, arms still behind him. He tried not to move, every twitch made the pain worse. Ariel's face trembled in pain as if she was feeling it also. Jolt pulled a knife from under his shirt, he flicked the tip of the blade with his finger.

"Let's see how well you bleed." He raised his hand to strike J.

"Noooo!" Ariel screamed. "It's on the bridge"

She hung her head as if she had just betrayed a friend. Jolt turned toward her with a smirk.

"What's on the bridge?" he motioned to drop J, who fell into a heap.

"Your data disk with the Atlantis codes."

He began to walk toward Ariel. "Thought it was you. Tell me, how did you get it?"

She smirked back at him. "Very carefully."

His eyebrows pinched together. "Very well."

He turned to one of the replicants.

"Kill them."

Ariel lunged at Jolt, spinning around him as she relieved him of his weapon. During the physical display, she pinned him to the ground, the knife at his throat.

"Call off your drones. Stick with hacking, you're better at it."

Jolt told the replicants to back off and open the door. Ariel motioned to J and Zane to head out, she was going to follow. They headed for the cargo bay.

"What's the plan?" he asked Zane.

"We'll improvise."

They ran past the powerplant. Zane stopped a moment near it, J turned to see what he was doing. He looked back at the doorway and Ariel appeared, running toward them, blasts soon followed. She waved for them to go. Zane took off, J followed. They headed for the small personnel transport ship that Jolt had arrived in. Zane reached the craft first, lowering the rear hatch. J was only a couple steps behind, he looked back. Ariel was still running full speed toward them.

"Hurry!"

Zane was already firing up the engines. Ariel turned, no longer heading toward them but running for the bay doors. *What was she doing?*

"You better get in if you wanna ride!" Zane yelled.

"Ariel's not here yet!"

"Get in, we'll pick her up."

J tumbled onto the ramp backwards, the ship picked up off the ground. Zane hovered it along the ground. J could hear the hull being hit by a multitude of enemy shots. The ramp remained open, the ship continuing at about a foot off the deck. J could see Ariel now behind them. Zane was using the craft as a shield to help her escape. J stayed on the ramp, his plan was to help Ariel. She looked back but kept running away. Zane kept the ship in position, hovering backward now just behind Ariel. She was about five feet behind them, still running away.

"What are you doing?" J yelled.

"Door."

"What? What door?"

J could tell she was out of breath, she just pointed. He looked past her, the large hangar doors stood shut. He nodded to her then ran up to Zane.

"She's going to open the hangar doors."

"Yep."

"Wait, you knew?"

"No, just figured. Can't open them from the ship."

J stared out the cockpit window, large blue blasts were flying at them, plenty hitting their target. The craft was screaming about shields decaying.

"This ship have any weapons?"

"There's a turret up top."

J turned around and saw a hatch.

"How do I get in?"

Zane pressed a couple of menu options, a ladder dropped down in front of J. He wasted no time climbing up and found a seat, quickly plopping into it. The controls were similar to some of the ships he had flown in. He slipped his arms into the two cups and grabbed the interior controls. The turret came to life, the screen flicked on. On the right side, a menu of weapons appeared, on the left, the shield status showed; it was down to 68% already. He manipulated the controls, flipping it around a few times, spinning. He finally figured it out and pointed it toward the oncoming replicants, he depressed the fire button, nothing happened. He looked down at the controls, then back out the screen. He felt the controls with his fingers, each hand had four buttons.

"Here goes nothing."

He toggled through each one, as he depressed his middle finger, the guns came alive. He aimed at the targets and fired, one by one they went down, then he ceased fire. Ariel had reached the cargo bay doors. J spun the turret to find her. She had reached a station with space suits and was pulling one on.

The craft shook, the shield instantly went from 60% to 40%, the turret swiveled around. In the distance, he could see someone with a large weapon on their shoulder. A flash came, the ship rocked again, 30%.

"Tell your girl to hurry!"

J let off a barrage of rounds, the ship rocked again, 20%.

"Okay, go!" a familiar voice shouted.

Ariel was on the ship. J turned the turret, the doors were opening. Zane maneuvered the ship to exit, it rocked again, a large bellowing sound echoed throughout the small ship as he read the shield display, 5%. Once again he spun the weapon around, the doors now fully open. Zane hit the accelerator and they sped out into the black ocean of space. J was disoriented, working to find his bearings, he climbed out of the seat and slid down the ladder, met by Ariel. She was clicking the helmet snaps and pulling it off.

"That was close," she said working on the rest of her suit.

"Not over yet, Jolt still has that time bomb."

Ariel looked at him, scrunching her lip to the side. She finished with her over-boots and tossed them aside.

"We'll deal with that soon enough."

She stood up and headed to the cockpit.

"Zane, what's the status on the ship?"

"Not good, shield is down below 5%, can't take another hit."

She looked at the screens, the shield flashed at 4.5%, the rest of the systems were still good.

"What's Jolt doing?"

Zane pulled up an image of both ships on a map, the KracKen was chasing after them.

"We're much faster, what do you think he's doing?"

J looked out the window.

"Where are we heading?"

"Out to space, why?"

"What's that?"

J pointed out the cockpit window, lights like distant stars appeared.

Punching the wall, Ariel shouted, "Bless it! I was hoping he couldn't hack that system, he's a clever devil. How many are there?"

Zane panned the screen over toward the lights. They were tiny ships, or that's what they looked like to J.

"What are those?" he said.

Zane touched the screen then flicked his fingers apart, the image zoomed in. The picture became clear, each one was a battle craft with multiple weapons hanging off both sides.

"Those would be Vipers," Zane said. "They're a defensive Earth system. Last I knew, there were maybe twenty satellites orbiting the Earth, each with twenty plus ships on board."

J placed his hand on his forehead, this didn't sound good. He watched Ariel who was deep in thought, analyzing the screen. She stood erect, full of energy.

"Zane, turn us around. Head for the KracKen."

"What?" J exclaimed.

Ariel didn't skip a beat.

"J, you grab blasters for all of us. This is a personnel transport troop carrier. There should be a weapons locker in the back."

"What are you going to do?" Zane asked.

"Start dressing."

J didn't ask another question, he knew Ariel had something planned and she had gotten them this far. The locker was where she said it would be, he began loading up. Two blasters apiece and one rifle should suffice. He turned around, Ariel was putting the suit back on.

"Should have left it on huh?" he said.

"Yep."

She opened a locker next to her.

"Here's yours," she tossed a package over to him. "You're coming with me."

"What about Zane? This ship is almost crippled."

"He's coming, too, just not right away."

Their tiny ship sped toward the KracKen. J didn't like it, but the cargo ship didn't have weapons. The Vipers, on the other hand, would make easy work of them. J stood by the rear cargo bay door, Ariel was with him.

"You ready?"

He nodded to her. She'd told him the plan, but his body was flowing with anticipation, she could tell. She smiled at him then winked, the cargo doors opened and they exited the bay. J looked back. Their newfound ship, still piloted by Zane, continued toward the KracKen on a head-on collision course. The smaller ship would be annihilated by the KracKen's huge mass. J knew that Zane would have mere seconds to bail out himself. Both watched the ship continue, impact was nearly imminent.

"Come on, get out, Zane," J said under his breath.

The ship erupted into a tiny flame. J didn't see Zane get out, he squinted his eyes, but the ship was so tiny it was pointless. The KracKen grew larger. It had run through their ship like a bug on a windshield and was continuing to head toward them. Ariel grabbed J's hand tightly.

"Now."

He pushed a button inside his glove as she had

instructed him. Their boots came alive. They'd have to match the speed of the KracKen or they would be lost in space, they had one shot at this, only ever one shot. Ariel pushed and pulled J, as if they were dancing, to place them in position to grab Jolt's ship. The ship was almost on them, they were matching speed quite well.

J saw an external ladder. "There!"

"Got it," Ariel answered back. She adjusted their trajectory.

J let go with one hand, reaching for the ladder. Ariel switched and grabbed his waist. He made contact and latched on, wrapping his arm around it. He held his other in a fist, she slipped. Her hands ran down his torso toward his feet. She scrambled to get a grip, her boots were running out of power. Her hand slipped off.

"Nooooo!" J cried out, watching Ariel float away.

She hit part of the ship and bounced off, away from the KracKen. He watched her spin away and froze. *What to do? What to do?* He held tight to the ladder, she was gone. There was nothing he could do, he'd never catch up to her. He took a deep breath, he knew their mission. It was now his mission, there would be time to grieve later. Earth needed him.

He began climbing up the ladder, one rung at a time. *He could do this, he had to do this, for Earth, for Ariel.* He crested the top of the ship and opened a hatch, peering down he found it empty. He slipped in and hit the compression button. They would be waiting for him, but he'd be ready. He un-slung the rifle from his back, checking the fuel cell capacity one last time. Click. He flicked the safety off, it was game time.

He took a deep breath and set his shoulders, like he had so many times during a big ball game. The stakes were so much higher, but that didn't enter his mind, he simply focused. The hatch opened, glowing robotic eyes peered back at him. He opened fire, eradicating what stood under him. He dropped down onto the corpse of a replicant. Two more were in the room; he lit them up like a Christmas tree and headed to the door. The metal sheet opened, he let off more rounds dropping yet another one. He ran down the hall, almost there. He rounded the corner, a shot hit his rifle, his hands burned. He dropped the disabled weapon and ducked back around the corner. Back to the wall, he drew one of the blasters, safety off, fully charged, he was about to stand up.

"J, we don't have to do this."

It was Jolt, but J had made up his mind. No amount of pleading, or dealing would alter it. *Jolt had to die.* He lunged from around the corner and opened up. Jolt was standing at the end of a hallway and fired back. Jolt fell to the floor, he was hit in the shoulder. A replicant behind him fired at J, he spun back around the corner.

"We can rule together. Can you imagine all the power? The power to do whatever you please, have anything you want?"

J's mind fired. *Anything he wanted? Ariel was all he wanted and Jolt took her from him.* He stood up and spun out firing then drew the second blaster and began running. The replicant fired back, but missed. His shots, on the other hand, fell true, the replicant dropped to the ground. Jolt lay there, grasping his shoulder. J approached, breathing heavily. He pointed one of the pistols at him.

"Can you bring back Ariel?"

"Ye...yes...yes, we can clone her, like the Earthlings. You'd never know the difference."

He was speaking fast again, like the first time J had met him. J looked at him and took pity on him, he couldn't kill him, not like this, not executioner style. He drew his hand back and pistol whipped him. Jolt, mid-sentence, snapped back, unconscious. J stood over him, staring, the overwhelming rage that pumped through his body was now subsiding. A blast hit his leg, he toppled to the ground spinning. A replicant had snuck up on him. He fired at it, dropping the replicant in its place. J glanced down at his leg, his hamstring was scorched but he could still use it. He grabbed the wall and helped himself up, he needed to get to the control room.

J studied the controls as he stood amongst bodies of replicants. He swiped at the screens, going through menu after menu as Ariel taught him. He found what he was looking for and pressed the button.

"Voice commands enabled, please say command."

J had one command, and he hoped it would end this chaos.

"Set destination...the sun."

"Confirm destination, the sun?"

"Yes."

Ariel had decided the best way to dispose of the nuclear powerplant was to send it into the sun. He had control of the ship and now control of its destination. J watched as the ship corrected course, the bright glow of the sun became centered on the screen. He stood there, marveling at its beauty. *Maybe he would stay, it would be easy. No, he was better than that. He wasn't going to throw his life away, Ariel's, Zane's, their deaths would be meaningless. He had to survive.*

He turned to head out of the control room, his way was blocked. Jolt stood in front of him with a blaster, his left arm hung limp at his side.

"What are you doing?" he cried.

J had holstered his blasters, he looked down at them.

"Uh uh uh, nope. Keep those hands up."

J scanned the room, there had to be a way out of this. For a brief second he wished he had just finished him before, but he didn't think he could live with that. Jolt leaned against the doorway. J could tell he was in plenty of pain.

"Med kit?" he asked.

"No, I'll get one later. First, I need to deal with you. Where are we going?"

J didn't say a word, he bit his lip. Jolt attempted to stand up, but couldn't and fell back into the door jam.

"I said, where are we going?" he demanded, losing his temper. J continued his silence.

Jolt fired. J had anticipated it and had begun a dive

out of the way. He pulled out the blasters, one slipped out of his hand but he still had the other. He scrambled behind a control console.

"Come out and face me!" Jolt shouted. "Where... Are...We...Going?!"

He was getting ever more impatient, if that was at all possible. J looked at the pistol, the energy cell was empty. "Bless it!" He peeked around the corner; Jolt was about 40 feet away. He looked back down at the blaster and popped off the energy cell, it was round and resembled a baseball.

He would have one shot at this, it seemed as if his life revolved around one shot, life-threatening events. He peeked again, Jolt fired at him, the shots skipping off the ground. J took a deep breath and slightly closed his eyes.

"Here we go," he said softly. J threw the blaster, Jolt began firing at it. J popped up as if he had just fielded a ground ball, clutching the cell in his hand. His shoulder and head dropped, his arm came over the top, the cell slipped out of his hand like a fastball at the World Series. Jolt turned to look at him. J watched in slow motion as it sailed along its path, the cell spun and met its mark. Jolt dropped as it crashed into his temple. J watched his body crumple and fall to the floor motionless. He slowly stood up, watching for any signs of life. Nothing.

He made his way over, picking up the blaster that had slipped out of his hand, the cell was less than half full. He knelt down and rolled Jolt over, he didn't think he was going to be getting up this time.

"Ship," J started as he stood back up. "Set a pass code for override."

"Override pass code ready to be set, say pass code."

J took a deep breath

"Ariel."

"Confirm, Ariel?"

"Yes, Ariel."

"Pass code now set."

J walked out and found himself in a familiar position.

"Boy, I do not want to do this," he said to himself. He stared down at the table of an emergency escape pod. He took a deep breath and climbed onto it then watched as the pod closed in around him. He prayed this would be a smooth ride. The pod locked into place, making the sounds of metal rolling on metal. He tapped on the glass, a menu came up. He scrolled through the features. Sleep mode caught his attention, he pressed it. The pod launched and the stars came into view, it was so peaceful. His eyes became heavy and slowly closed.

CHAPTER THIRTY

He twirled the ball in his hand behind his back, the catcher giving him signs. He shook off the first two, then accepted the third. J wound up and slung the ball toward home plate.

"Strike three! Batter's out," the umpire yelled.

The crowd erupted into cheers then stormed the field, they had won. J's first game back from his absence and he threw a full game. His body felt new, but his mind was elsewhere. It'd been a week since he'd returned. No one knew the true story, he felt it best to keep it from them. He didn't want to freak anybody out. He was going to tell them, but for now, he just wanted things to settle down and become normal again, whatever that meant now. The fans continued cheering and celebrating with the team on the field. It was the first playoff game, they were moving on. J tried to enjoy the moment, but it didn't feel the same. After what he'd been through, the thrill of the game had left him.

Carol appeared and threw her arms around him, he hugged her back, giving her a forced smile.

"I'm so glad you're back, I'm going to miss you when you head off to college, you played so well, James!"

It didn't take him long after returning to realize TK had re-embedded the mind chip when she was taken to the hospital. In essence, he was starting from scratch with the old Carol. The past week, he'd been deciding how to play it. On one hand, he could go about his life and turn his back on the truth. That would be the simple answer, but living a lie was never really simple. On the other, he could open her up to the stark reality that she was only a drone, designed to sustain life on Atlantis...and he'd fallen in love with someone else. Either way, he'd have to choose, and soon. In order to buy himself some time to sort through his new struggle, he'd told everyone he'd visited the college that offered him the scholarship. He knew that was a lie, and that there was no such thing as a baseball scholarship to college on Earth. Still, it seemed like the easiest way to explain his absence.

The cheering settled down and the fans began to head out. Carol took his hand and walked him to the truck. They pulled away from the ballpark, but J was silent, just staring at the road in front of him.

"You've been very quiet since you returned from your trip, everything okay, anything I can do?"

Carol sensed something was wrong.

"No, just thinking about the future."

That he was. But more and more he thought about Ariel. He felt like he was in a topsy-turvy world, his thoughts on Carol, now they constantly shifted to Ariel. The future, he mused. Once it had seemed so distant. Now it was here, or rather, in the past. The events had gone so fast that he didn't have much time to soak it in, but now with what seemed like all the time in the world, his thoughts were focused on making sense of everything.

"Carol," he started very softly. "Do you think man will ever walk on the moon?"

"I suppose so, they do in the movies, so maybe they will figure out a way, that would be neato, don't you think?"

J smiled, knowing the truth.

"What made you think of that?" Carol inquired.

J glanced over at her.

"I wanna show you something."

He turned the truck and headed into town. Carol was smiling, anticipating a good surprise. He took the left onto Main Street and headed for the diner. He pulled the truck into a parking spot and placed it into park.

"The diner?" Carol asked puzzled.

"No, not the diner. Something better. The first time I learned about this, it was hard to take in, so I want to warn you that it may be a little overwhelming."

Carol now looked concerned, "What are you talking about James?"

"It's easier if I show you." He opened her door and ushered her out. They passed by the diner, heading down the street.

"Where are you taking me?"

"You'll see."

Carol smiled, she had other ideas about what was going to happen. They came to the alleyway and turned down it. Carol scrunched up her nose and looked around, searching for the answer, "What are we doing here?"

J held up one finger indicating for her to wait. He knelt down and placed his hand on the brick, the panel slid out as before. He looked back at Carol, her jaw was open.

"What is that?"

He didn't say a word, just placed his hand on the plate, the wall opened. Carol grabbed him, hugging his arm tightly. The elevator sat empty. J stepped in, dragging a reluctant Carol with him. Sarah came to life.

"What floor would you like, J?"

"Will's floor."

He looked over at Carol, she was speechless.

"And I authorize my girlfriend to accompany me."

"New girlfriend?" Sarah asked.

He laughed uneasily.

Carol was looking at him, eyebrows knit together.

"What is she talking about and who is she anyway?" Carol asked, her displeasure beginning to show.

The elevator descended. J tried to deflect, pointing out the glass walls. It worked. He watched Carol, her eyes flitting about, trying to make sense of what she was seeing. She stepped up to the glass, staring out into the cloudy abyss, she was mesmerized by it.

"Beautiful, huh?"

Carol didn't respond initially, she just watched as they rode along silently. His thoughts flashed to riding with Ariel. He had grown close to her through their adventures, everything reminded him of her. He loved her, and not the way he loved Carol. It was different, she created a spark in him he had never felt before. He tried to push her out of his mind, out of his heart. She was gone, she wouldn't be a part of his future, he needed to move on. There was nothing he could do about it now. But the heart wants what it wants.

The elevator came to a stop and the doors opened. J stepped into the room, almost having to drag Carol out. She was still gazing at the clouds.

"Where are we?" she asked, looking around and holding onto him. "What is this place?"

"You're underneath the Earth."

"I don't understand, how can we be under the Earth, what's going on, James?"

"I see you brought Carol down."

Carol spun around. Will was walking in from another room.

"Who's he?" she asked shakily.

J remembered that along the way, her memory of him was wiped.

"His name is Will. He helped me accomplish a very important task."

He turned to Will, "Can you help me?"

"Where's..." Will hesitated for a brief second, knowing it might not be the best time to mention Ariel's name. J picked up on what he was going to ask.

"Gone," he said, looking down at the ground, his face anguished.

Will turned to stare out the window.

"Oh," he said somberly. "I'm sorry to hear that. And the task? I'm guessing it was completed."

"Yes."

"So what can I help you with?"

J looked at Carol. "Her implant."

Carol still had a puzzled look on her face, she had no idea what either of them were talking about. Will nodded and asked them to follow him. They worked their way back to a medical room and Will asked Carol to take a seat. He explained to her about the chip and what he was going to do. It took a bit of persuasion on J's part, but she finally agreed.

"How do you feel?" J asked.

Will had finished the procedure, it was pretty quick taking out the chip.

"Different," she replied, rubbing the back of her neck. There was no proof that Will had done anything.

"So, that was controlling my mind?"

"Sort of," Will injected. "More like suppressing certain things and suggesting others."

Carol hopped off the table. The three of them headed to the main room where Will explained the current situation in brief terms, Carol seemed to understand most of it. Between Will and J, they detailed the past events, his adventures, the struggles and triumphs. As he described everything, he mentioned Ariel, nearly in every breath. To him, it came out naturally. She was a big part of his journey in the new world. His face would light up when talking about her, and Carol noticed. She stayed quiet, asking only a few simple questions. J detected that she was already acting a bit differently. Her questions were those she wouldn't have asked in the past. He hoped she'd be able to cope with her newfound knowledge. After all, he was still struggling with it.

"So, what are your plans now, J?" asked Will.

J looked at Carol, then back at him.

"I'm not sure what to do."

"Well you're the surviving line of TK. You technically own everything," Will said.

J stopped a moment and tried to let that sink in. *He owned everything, it seemed impossible.* His life was simple until that meteor shower, one which he had spent with Carol who now couldn't remember it. All of his new friends were gone, the friends he had grown closer to than anyone on Earth, and in such a short time. He missed Ariel and her constant harassment, it really made him feel...loved.

"I'd like to take some time to think, get back to a version of normal."

He turned to Carol.

"Milkshake?"

He knew that would be something Carol would like, and maybe, just maybe it would take his mind off of Ariel. She smiled at him.

"That sounds great."

She was trying to make sense of everything and welcomed the comfort of the diner. They said goodbye to Will and headed back topside.

"Do you really own everything?" Carol asked as they emerged onto the street.

"Supposedly," he answered. It was still hard for him

to fathom.

They walked to Sam's Diner and headed inside, taking their usual seat in the corner. It was late by now, the waiter walked up.

"What will you have?"

"Chocolate milkshake," he replied.

Carol ordered a strawberry one. The bell attached to the door jiggled and Carol looked over J's shoulder. "Wow, she has pretty hair."

J swiveled in his seat, a woman with red hair was approaching the counter, he couldn't see her face. *Could it be?* He continued to stare.

"You know her?" Carol asked.

J turned around, she was looking at him intensely, waiting to see his reaction.

"No, I don't think so," he tried to play it off. It couldn't be her. He saw her float away into space. That picture would forever haunt him.

"Well, she's coming this way."

He leaned back, surprised, then turned. Ariel stood in front of him. He scrambled to his feet, no words were exchanged. He grabbed her, she reciprocated and they embraced. Ariel pushed him back slightly gazing into his eyes then pulled him in for a kiss. Their lips met, a warm sensation flowed through his body. He forgot where he was. Emotions flooded his brain, he was in heaven. She leaned away again.

"You're alive!" He pulled her in. He wasn't going to let her go. Ever.

"But how? I watched you slip away," he continued to hold her tightly, his heart raced, the world around him drifted away. It was just them.

"V."

J's eyebrows went up as he contemplated what she said.

"V picked us up," she said.

"Us? You mean Zane made it, too?"

"Yep, he's back in Atlantis with V. I told you he couldn't die. I came to get you."

Just then, J remembered Carol was with him. He turned, she was sitting there staring at him, a tear ran down her cheek.

"Carol," J started. She stood up and moved over to him, he was still holding Ariel. She leaned over and kissed him on the cheek.

"You were meant for each other. Goodbye, James."

She walked past them and headed out the door. J was saddened, but he wanted Ariel more than ever. He looked back at Ariel, her icy blue eyes glowing. She smiled that impish smile at him.

"I know where your father is."

END OF BOOK ONE